More praise for Corinne Holt Sawyer and HO HO HOMICIDE!

"Sawyer's humorous yet sympathetic look at retirement-home life and her lovable sleuths keep the reader's interest."
—*Publishers Weekly*

"Sawyer has a knack for working wit, wisdom, and humor into her stories."
—*Abilene Reporter-News*

"The Upstate's own Jessica Fletcher."
—*Greenville News*

"Sawyer writes with wit, and her characters are well drawn. . . . Entertaining."
—*The Post and Courier* (Charleston, SC)

D0057550

By Corinne Holt Sawyer
Published by Fawcett Books:

THE J. ALFRED PRUFROCK MURDERS
MURDER IN GRAY AND WHITE
MURDER BY OWL LIGHT
THE PEANUT BUTTER MURDERS
MURDER HAS NO CALORIES
HO-HO HOMICIDE

HO-HO HOMICIDE

Corinne Holt Sawyer

FAWCETT BOOKS • NEW YORK

A Fawcett Crest Book
Published by Ballantine Books
Copyright © 1995 by Corinne Holt Sawyer

http://www.randomhouse.com

Library of Congress Catalog Card Number: 96-96450

ISBN 0-449-22409-0

This edition published by arrangement with Donald I. Fine, Inc.

Manufactured in the United States of America

First Ballantine Books Edition: November 1996

10 9 8 7 6 5 4 3 2

Acknowledgments and Kudos

To William Hunter, M.D., superior physician, excellent writer, and friend—who took time from his busy schedule to act as my guide in some of the medical matters in this book.

To Wayne Stroup and Madeline Holt Campillo, who strained their eyes and their tempers to proof- and copy-read the first draft—and who never failed to offer encouragement along the way.

And to all my friends at Carlsbad-by-the-Sea (the wonderful retirement home which is the original of my Camden-sur-Mer), who have applauded each book as it came out—and who always beg me to write them in as characters. Though I cannot write about real people in these works of fiction, you have been an inspiration to me because, though you grow older, you do not grow old.

Dedicated to the Campillo family
Madeline, Bob, Grace, Fred, and Chris

Chapter 1

DECEMBER HAD arrived in Southern California. Santa, swathed in red and sweating in his phony beard, appeared in front of every supermarket ringing his bell for contributions to the bucket which swung gently in warm breezes beneath drilled rows of royal palms. Thanks to the Chamber of Commerce, the light standards up and down the main street were adorned with outsized red ribbons, flocked to look like velvet and woven round with colored lights. Just as in chillier climates, banks and hardware stores sent out calendars complete with scenes of ice-choked rivers, and sometime in the weeks between Halloween and Thanksgiving, when all right-thinking merchants start the push toward their biggest profits of the year, the display windows of downtown shops in Camden, that sleepy little town just north of San Diego, began to feature plastic evergreen, mounds of artificial snow, and drifts of cotton batting.

And the old luxury hotel, Camden-sur-Mer—now converted to a retirement home—had joined the spirit of the season with cutouts of snowflakes pasted to all the windows facing the main street and a lobby decorated with unrelenting red and green. There were wreaths or swags of fake pine, interlaced with huge bows, hung on every vertical surface. On every horizontal surface except the floor there were Santa's Workshops of plastic and New England villages of china. Set up beyond the grand piano and filling the lobby at the end furthest from the main entryway, there was a giant tree—a real one, for a wonder—laden with ornaments and brilliant with

1

colored lights. And in case the residents with failing short-term memory should still forget what the season was, their ears were filled morning and evening with Christmas carols played over the lobby's ubiquitous intercom speakers.

"The only time off we get for good behavior," Mr. Grogan complained to his fellow residents in one of his sober and lucid moments, "is when they ring the chimes to tell us the dining room is open. And then we have to look at the waitresses dressed like elves!" Drunk, Grogan was unpredictable and unpleasant. Sober, he could be even more unpleasant, though completely predictable in his irascibility.

"It's a toss-up to me whether I'd rather have him around when he's had a couple or when he's on the wagon," Tom Brighton said, shrugging off Grogan's complaint. "I think the waitresses look kind of cute in their little caps and red-striped aprons. And everybody goes around smiling and . . ."

"And hoping for a big tip," Grogan tossed back over his shoulder, heading full speed toward his lunch, now that the Westminster chimes had interrupted the strains of Mendelssohn's "It Came Upon a Midnight Clear," and the double doors of the dining room had swung open.

"Why do we put up with that man?" Trinita Stainsbury muttered, her thin lips drawn even thinner with distaste. "The management ought to ask Grogan to move out. Everybody would be better off!"

"Except Grogan," Tom Brighton said. "Where would the man go? Be charitable, Trinita. Here, let me leave my cane before I go in. Might trip somebody."

The Christmas carols picked up again throughout the lobby and the crowd of residents surged forward into the dining room, streaming eagerly toward the lunch that was their midday highlight.

"Forgive me if I don't walk all the way to your table with you, Tom," Trinita Stainsbury said. Tom Brighton's startled expression seemed to say that her company was really the last thing he'd expected, but she was oblivious. "I've got an announcement to make . . . ," and she peeled off to the left of the doors where there was a microphone on a small desk, feeding into the dining room's independent speaker system and primarily provided so that the visiting pastor or some devout resident could say grace. But since mealtimes were the only moments when it could be assumed that all residents were together in a single place, the Residents' Council had decreed that announcements of general interest could be broadcast using the same mike.

"Unfortunately," Caledonia Wingate muttered to her tiny companion, Angela Benbow, as they sped past the microphone desk on their way to their assigned table by the garden window, "unfortunately that woman has taken their permission to be an order. Has one day gone by this week, for instance, when she hasn't started our lunch off with some announcement?"

The speakers in the dining room crackled to life and a squeal of feedback howled briefly till Trinita got the volume regulated. "Hasn't anybody fixed this thing yet? You'd think our maintenance people . . ." Her plaintive voice, electronically enhanced, sounded from overhead to warn the diners of her impending intrusion into their auditory canals.

"I know you'll want to be in the lobby this afternoon," she began in a voice intended to convey the impression of unparalleled excitement and glee. "I know you'll want to be present when our program for the day begins at three-thirty. That's three-thirty sharp, mind you. No stragglers. The . . . let me see, what is the name of that group . . . the children's choir from the Church of the Golden Light of Rapture in Escondido will be with us for a program of carols."

The groan from several diners was clearly audible, drowning Trinita's electronic voice for one blessed moment.

"You can sing along. I know you'll like that. And we'll have the words on mimeographed sheets . . ."

"Not if the Wart Hog has his way," Caledonia snorted. Wart Hog was one of the nicknames by which residents designated the less-than-admired administrator of their communal home. Fighting to maintain a balanced budget might endear Olav Torgeson to his stockholders, but never to his residents. "It would cost our beloved administrator maybe as much as a dollar fifty to run off two dozen or so sheets of song lyrics, and heaven forbid he'd spend a dime he didn't have to."

"Did you hear about his latest?" Angela said to her gigantic friend. Caledonia and Angela, one nearly six feet tall, the other barely five feet, one dressed habitually in a swath of material shaped into a floor-length caftan that only made her look larger, the other in neat little suits and dresses, were both a bit tubby (to put it kindly). Time tends to do that to women. They were also alike in that they were both well-to-do and both the widows of admirals, but the first thing people noticed was that difference in their respective sizes: Mutt and Jeff, Laurel and Hardy. On the inside, they were vastly different as well. Tiny Angela lived an early-to-bed, early-to-rise schedule while the massive Caledonia watched *The Late, Late Show* and slept till nine each morning. Little Angela darted when she walked, a manifestation of her perpetual eagerness to get the next page of her life turned and get on with it, while the statuesque Caledonia rolled serenely through her days, no less determined and forceful but with a grander, more ponderous rhythm. But differences aside, their friends and fellow residents often regarded them as merely two sides of the same coin: two people in whom the life forces ran as strongly as ever, even in their sunset years.

"Our Mr. Torgeson has decided to cut corners in the kitchen," Angela went on, shaking her head in disapproval. "Mrs. Schmitt's fit to be tied. She says she can't create these gourmet meals if he—"

"What's he done? Surely he isn't going to cut back on the portions," Caledonia said in dismay. "Oh, Chita," she said, handing her menu back to their favorite waitress, who had appeared silently at her side, "I'll have double a helping of the lamb whatchacallit . . ."

"Shepherd's pie, Mrs. Wingate," Chita said, writing the order down.

"Double portion now, don't forget," Caledonia said.

"Ordinary serving for me, Chita," Angela said. "That's a

gracious plenty—although Mrs. Schmitt always does the shepherd's pie so well. I keep thinking I can eat more than . . . but it's really filling. She browns that potato crust just so . . ." Chita, nodding, turned away to take an order from the next table before she relayed the orders to the kitchen. "No use coming in with a half-loaded tray," as she told the approving Mrs. Schmitt.

"You can relax, Cal. Torgeson's not making Mrs. Schmitt cut back on portions. He's insisting on things like . . . well, for instance, in the Jell-O salad we used to have fresh bananas and grapes and canned mandarin oranges, you know? But from now on we'll have either bananas or grapes, not both, and he plans to save the mandarins for when there's no special deal on fresh fruit. And he asked Mrs. Schmitt to cut the number of onions in her meat loaf to half the amount. And we're going to have a choice of either cereal or eggs at breakfast but not both. And—"

"—and something will have to be done," Caledonia said, forking into a small green salad set by her place. "That niggling, bean-counting approach to cooking will drive everybody in the kitchen crazy. I'll go to the next meeting of the Residents' Council and see if we can't . . ."

Conversation languished as the two friends addressed the real business of the mealtime.

"You haven't forgotten," Angela said as lunch ended, "that today's my little tree-trimming party, have you?"

Caledonia groaned. "I had. Mercifully, I had."

"It's the same thing every year, Cal. In the first week of December. I get one of our handymen to bring my storage boxes up from the basement and you untangle and test out the strings of lights while I put up the tree. Then you advise and complain while I hang the ornaments."

And so the friends squabbled till dessert was over and they left the dining room with Angela calling out "Four o'clock now, Cal," as they parted.

Like most of the other residents, neither woman scheduled any activity for immediately after lunch. That was nap time for most of the residents of Camden-sur-Mer, and even those who didn't nap were disinclined to violate what they had come over the years to believe was the natural order of life.

Promptly at 4:00, despite her complaints, Caledonia, trailing a cloud of lavender silk in her wake, her jewelry blazing in the late afternoon light, arrived at Angela's apartment in the south wing of the main building's ground floor. She had dressed up for the get-together, even though she was aware that *get-together* was just a euphemism for an hour or so of helping Angela decorate, but dressing up for Caledonia was no great chore anyway, since it merely meant changing to a fancier edition of her caftan, a garment she'd had replicated in dozens of materials and myriad colors to cover her from Adam's apple to instep. As for her jewelry, the diamonds on her fingers and the magnificent rope of pearls around her neck did not mean "dressed up" to Caledonia; she wore her jewels with denim or knits as readily as with satin.

"Okay, I'm here. Where do I start?"

"Well, I'll get you a glass of sherry . . ."

Faintly through Angela's closed door the sound of juvenile voices came floating in:

We three kings of Orient are.
Bearing gifts we traverse afar.
Field and fountain, moor and mountain . . .

"Oh boy, they're at it—those kids Trinita Stainsbury announced at lunch."

"Shall I open the door, Cal? So you can hear the youngsters singing?"

"Good heavens, no! We get enough of the same carols over and over on the lobby speakers. I don't need to hear the little nippers showing off their nasal tones! Besides, they come every year about this time. The Entertainment Committee really hasn't much imagination when it comes to Christmas programs."

It was true. Starting at Thanksgiving, every church within

twenty miles sooner or later was scheduled by Camden-sur-Mer's Entertainment Committee (headed by Trinita Stainsbury) to bring a little Christmas joy to the retirees. Every other day, the cavernous, marble-floored lobby filled with fat little women in sensible shoes and printed rayon dresses serving raspberry Kool-Aid and sugar cookies in the shape of Christmas trees to throngs of residents (who never missed an opportunity for a free snack between meals). And a piano player perched on the bench of the grand piano and banged out "Deck the Halls" or "Good King Wenceslas" so loudly that the punch-servers had to shriek their little pleasantries like, "How about another cookie, dear? Christmas comes but once a year, as they say!"

On the alternate days, down there between the piano and the big-screen TV at the far end of the lobby, a miscellaneous collection of choristers huddled, singing "The Holly and the Ivy" or "Away in a Manager" or "The First Noel." And most often the singers were children who punctuated their songs by hawking and wiping their noses. Children even in Southern California have colds at Christmas time; it seems to be one of the rules of the Yuletide. On the last day of school before the holiday break, prudent mothers—even on the blessed stretch of shoreline just north of San Diego where the weather seldom varies much from the mean of seventy degrees—crack out the Kleenex. Then they get the kids together to join others with the same afflictions, and they all go over to the retirement home to spread the cold among the elderly residents.

"It's the sort of Christmas tradition one might hope would be honored 'more in the breach than in the observance,' " Angela often said.

"Fat chance," Caledonia would mutter in response.

There were always a few wonderful exceptions to sniffling children and punch-serving ladies. On the serious side, there was the Reverend Mr. Boggs from the Episcopal church down the street. Pastor Boggs came every year on the Wednesday before Christmas to preach a gentle sermon about the nature of love and to bring a supply of woolly bedsocks, hand-knit by his parishioners in token of the fact that the residents of Camden-sur-Mer had most of the material things they might want but because of slower circulation always managed to feel chilly.

On the comic side there was Desmond Peabody, an amateur magician of unbelievable ineptitude who showed up in the second week of December every year to drop the brightly colored half-balls he meant to make multiply between his fingers; to get tangles in the string of silk handkerchiefs he sought to pull from his vest pocket, so that it wouldn't come out at all; and to cheer his whole audience up with his hearty laughter and his refusal to despair. Even the elderly need to be reminded, now and then, of the virtues of perseverance in the face of adversity—not to mention that, as much as the rest of us, they like a good laugh at the expense of their fellow man.

"Bloody fool tricks that never work worth diddly," Mr. Grogan would complain every year.

"Only time I ever agree with Grogan is at Christmas," Caledonia observed.

But every year Grogan and Caledonia both slipped into the audience and howled with the rest of them as Mr. Peabody dropped and broke the "magical never-empty glass," minced the dollar bill he was supposed just to pretend to cut, and nearly sat on his hat, managing to rescue from annihilation the captive rabbit within by throwing himself violently to one side so that he missed not only his hat but the entire chair, finally sliding awkwardly onto the floor with a terrible thump. The rabbit poked its head out to see the cause of the commotion, and the audience roared its appreciation.

Not that most of the residents were ungrateful for the other December diversions offered them by well-meaning town residents and ladies' aid societies. They appreciated the attention. "I just wish they'd spread it out to the rest of the year," Caledonia Wingate complained. "I resent it that they notice we're alive only when they remember that they have to impress Santa Claus with their virtue."

Now, mellowed by her second glass of sherry, Caledonia found herself nodding in time to the faint strains of "Hark! the

Herald Angels Sing" as she laid out the last strand of lights. She hauled herself to her feet with effort and headed toward the hall door.

"The sherry's over here, Cal," Angela called to her.

"Well, I do need another, but that wasn't what . . . I thought maybe, after all, I'd open your door a little crack and listen to those kids . . . This lot isn't half bad, for a change. Most of them are right on key, and they all seem to know the words."

The herald angels squeaked out *Peace on the earth, good-will to men from heaven's all gracious king* for the last time and the accompanist segued into "Angels We Have Heard on High."

"Let's see if they can stay together on the *Glorias* in this one," Caledonia chuckled. "It's a toughie. And now for that refill on the sherry . . . and listen, you might want to put more lights over there on the left. There seems to be a blank over that way, and there's one more string."

"You'd think you could help me hanging these, since you seem to have such a good eye, instead of just criticizing," Angela said as she hoisted the last length of blue, red, green, and yellow lights and began to weave it through the branches.

"I'm so glad you have colored lights, girl," Caledonia said, contentedly settling herself back into her loveseat. "Those modern trees with all white lights give me indigestion. So cold and cheerless. I always wonder if the people who use all white lights had really happy childhoods."

Angela nodded. "It reminds me of the years when it was considered chic to have a tree all done in blue and silver— lights, ornaments, tinsel, the works. It never seemed very Christmassy to me. And remember those awful metal trees? I even saw one made of pink aluminum. They had chartreuse ornaments on that one."

"Oh, listen. They're doing 'Silent Night.' I suppose that means the program is just about over."

Sleep in heavenly peace.
Sleep in heavenly peace.

The voices floated serenely in—on key and in unison.

"The old ones are the best, aren't they?" Angela said dreamily. "I never did like 'I Saw Mama Kissing Santa Claus' or even 'Santa Claus Is Coming to Town.' They seem, you know—irreverent to me. And not very pretty. I mean, this is beautiful and gentle—" And just as the words left her mouth the lobby erupted in a blast of confusion. The carol dissolved into shrieks.

Radiant beams from thy holy face.
With the dawn of redeeming graaaAAAAAAAAGH ...

"In the name of Rudolf, what's going on out there?" Caledonia lumbered to her feet and flung the hall door wide.

"It's a body!" little Mary Moffett gasped. "They've found a body!" Mary, the only Camden resident who was even shorter than Angela, had been sitting on the topmost of the four steps that led to the lobby from just beyond Angela's door. Mary always tried to get to programs early to get a seat in the front rows, but she had overslept on her nap and had to plunk her tiny person down on the steps as the only way she'd be able to see as well as hear. Now she had a bird's-eye view of the crowd in front of the tree, and she was literally bouncing up and down with excitement.

The children, as Mary managed to explain to Angela and Caledonia, had formed up into a semicircle in front of the big lobby tree, three deep.

No one could see the lower branches, let alone the floor beneath, and even if they could, it is doubtful that anyone would have discerned the body crumpled in the shadows among the mounds and folds of white sheeting bunched around the tree's base to simulate riplets of snow. Certainly the eyesight of the majority of Camden-sur-Mer residents would have been too dim, and the children when they arrived were too excited—whispering, giggling, pushing, and shoving. Their chaperones and their flustered director were concentrating with glazed eyes on getting the little singers into rows and lined up in reasonable order, sopranos with sopranos, tenors with tenors, except for Joey Fink. Joey, a premature baritone and the only baritone in the preadolescent chorus, had been asked to stand a little off by himself, not just to keep his choral part from interfering with the others, but to keep Joey from disrupting the program by teasing the girls, which he found a way to do at every possible opportunity.

With Joey safely relegated to the far end of the line, things had been going smoothly, and the choir director was breathing a sigh of relief and pleasure. Could it be that they would get through to the program's end without a hitch? She should have known better. At the close of "Silent Night," she had arranged for what she considered a dramatic finale. The children were to split their semicircle into two wings that would back up, and the children would solemnly point their upstage arms toward the little creche in front of the tree, a Nativity scene that had up to that time been hidden by the forest of little legs in ankle socks.

So as the children sang the last bars of their hymn, they shuffled backward until a gap of perhaps two yards across appeared between the right and left phalanxes. The children's arms moved upward and toward the tree in a graceful arc . . . and Janey Campbell began to scream.

Joey Fink had been unable to resist the target of pudgy, rosy-cheeked little Janey, with her old-fashioned braided hair that dangled halfway down her back. He had dropped to all fours and begun to work his way up the line toward Janey, behind his fellow choristers and unnoticed by them. But from that position, he could clearly see a face looking back at his from under the lowest boughs of the majestic balsam, a face that didn't move, eyes that didn't blink even when the light caught them as the children moved aside.

"Geez!" he gasped. In his moment of shock, he forgot all the profanity he had so carefully cultivated and reverted to his most childish vocabulary. "Wow! Oh, wow! It's just like on *Murder, She Wrote*! Janey, look!" Unconscious of the fact that he was giving away his change of position and revealing his plot, he rose to his feet and tugged at Janey's arm. "Bend over. Look down here . . ."

Janey, still singing, bent low and without pausing moved from song to screech. She was joined quickly by several children, a few of whom had bent over to look as well, but most of whom were just reacting like lemmings. If someone had giggled, they'd have giggled. If someone had turned to walk out, they'd have made an exit right behind. Now someone was screaming, so they shrieked as well, empty noise with neither fear nor pleasure in it. And a pair of women in the front row of the audience joined the chorus as, bending over, they too caught sight of what had jolted Joey—the body tangled in the sheeting.

It was several long minutes before Clara—the retirement home's receptionist, amanuensis, and general factotum—coming all the way from the front desk, could get through the milling crowd of children and residents, figure out the problem, and react by making her way back to the telephone switchboard and summoning the police.

Chapter 2

IN LIFE Beatrice "Birdy" Benton had been a woman of quiet habits—small, usually soft-spoken, though sometimes exceedingly stubborn, somewhat self-centered perhaps, as the elderly can be, but one who in the ordinary run of days might well be ignored by her fellow residents. In death Birdy certainly continued to be small and quiet, but nobody in Camden-sur-Mer could ignore her. Nor did they have any intention of doing so. It isn't every day one finds a corpse in one's living room, so to speak. Beyond their normal reactions of horror and sorrow, most of the residents responded to the unusual situation with chatter and laughter—obviously thrilled right from the crown of their gray heads to the toes of their orthopedic shoes.

They weren't really unfeeling. It was just that days at a retirement home tend to run along in well-oiled repetition. What the residents did this week they will do next week. Unvarying routine is soothing and a great help to those whose memory has begun to turn to Swiss cheese. Furthermore, most activities planned for the elderly are easygoing, out of deference to weak hearts, creaky knees, and bad nerves—not too much action, nor too much excitement. In short, life at Camden-sur-Mer was comfortable, but it could get boring.

Birdy's death, by contrast, was excitement of the highest order. And it was certainly a departure from the cycle of inept and predictable Christmas activities—punch and cookies, carols, recitations, and talent shows. Birdy Benton would have been gratified to realize that she was the center of every conversation, that perhaps for the first time in her life she was an object of total fascination.

"Sweet," Emma Grant was saying loudly. "Sweet, that's what she was. Sweet! No, really. Some didn't care for her, I've heard. But she never had an unkind word to say about anybody, and she fed the birds every day. Did you know that? Now how could someone be so bad if she loved dear little birds? So I say she was really sweet. Sweet!" Emma's voice rattled the chandelier overhead and made folks at the far end of the lobby turn to stare. Her hearing aid was giving her trouble and she was unable to gauge her own decibel level accurately. Tonight her voice rang out like one of those tinny bus station speakers gargling out unintelligible lists of arrivals and destinations.

"Hold it down to a yell, Emma," Caledonia Wingate said. "We may all be a little hard of hearing, it's true, but we're not in the next county!"

"Oh, sorry. Was I too loud again?" Emma Grant moderated her voice to something just short of thunderous. "I was only saying she fed the birds every day. That's how she got her nickname, you know."

"Well, I'm not sure that would make me describe her as sweet. You know how I feel about birds. They're noisy, greedy things with nasty personal habits—really sloppy eaters, and they don't housebreak worth a toot."

"You're indulging in sheer hypocrisy, Cal," Angela scolded. "Everybody knows you adopted that talkative lovebird from the lobby to save him from the animal shelter. And now you keep his cage in your living room even though that clumsy wrought iron clashes with your decor. And you spoil him with so much food that he's absolutely round. He looks like a flying powderpuff!"

"Well." Caledonia shrugged her heavy shoulders. "That lovebird is kind of cute! Pretty blue feathers, you know. And the words he comes out with . . . sometimes he gets me laughing so hard . . . maybe I do spoil him. But that's a far cry from letting him bother the neighbors like those birds that Benton woman fed. I want to tell you . . ."

The residents had gathered in the lobby prior to the dinner hour as they usually did. Ordinarily the lobby filled gradually, starting about fifteen minutes before mealtimes. It was a happy hour devoted to gossip rather than to drink, and the exchange of news was almost as much a high point in the residents' day as was the food. Today, however, on the evening of the discovery of Birdy Benton dead beneath the Christmas tree, there was far too much to talk about for the residents to wait till just before mealtime. Consequently, people began to enter the cavernous space of the lobby a full forty minutes before the dining room doors were due to open.

As she and Angela entered the lobby from Angela's apartment, Caledonia was tall enough to see, above the heads of the residents thronging the area, an unruly thatch of white hair rising like a cockscomb in the middle of a knot of people whispering and nodding to each other in the far corner of the lobby, over near the doors to the garden. It was their friend Tom Brighton at the center of one group of residents. Another group had gathered near the piano, nervously eyeing the yellow plastic tape that still roped off the Christmas tree itself, by police order. Little knots of three or four residents buzzed busily on a couch near the desk, in a pair of chairs by the main entrance, and over in front of the fireplace, where a smallish group was presided over by Trinita Stainsbury, her newly dyed copper hair matching perfectly her rust-colored sweater, the knit studded with bright golden sequins that reflected the light in a dazzling display of twinkle and glitter.

"My latest from the Home Shopping Club," Trinita simpered, when Dora Lee and Donna Dee, the Jackson twins, joined the group and admired her glitter. "Don't you just love their bead-and-sequin things? And those cubic zirconia . . . such sparkle!" Trinita was saying as she twirled to show off her spangles to general admiration.

"She reminds me of that hymn we used to sing as children," Angela whispered to Caledonia as they came down the four steps into the lobby and caught sight of Trinita, glinting and glimmering across the room. "She brightens the corner where she is!"

Caledonia snorted and, lest the object of her mirth discover her laughing, she hastily turned the "Ha!" into a sneeze, bringing forth a huge handkerchief from her sleeve to cover her grin.

"Of course her hair is simply ridiculous," Angela went on. "For heaven's sake, the woman's been gray for years and everybody knows it. Who's she trying to fool? But I *really* object to those clothes. One dresses for dinner, of course. But this isn't some New York disco, after all. And there has been a death among us . . ."

"Blinding display, isn't it?" Caledonia nodded. "But don't pretend to be surprised. If she could, Trinita would stage-manage her own funeral. She'd have the coffin set with rhine-stones and ask the undertaker to dye her hair to match the shroud!"

Steering as wide a course around Trinita and the twins as the expanse of the room would allow, Angela and Caledonia hurried the length of the lobby to join Tom Brighton's group. Time was when Angela would not have been included—at least not voluntarily—by her fellow residents in their activities or their conversations, because they feared her sharp tongue and impatient temper. But the years and her association with Caledonia had mellowed Angela considerably. Now and then she could still let out a blast—as she just had about Trinita Stainsbury—but even that was mild in comparison to what she might have said a few years before. Now Tom Brighton's group of gossips opened ranks and welcomed the two new-comers warmly.

"We're just comparing notes on what we saw of this after-noon's excitement," Tom Brighton said by way of greeting. "And comparing notes on what we know about the late Mrs. Benton."

It was at this point that Emma Grant had roared out her description of Birdy Benton as "sweet," and Caledonia had been sidetracked to discuss her own lovebird. That didn't suit Angela in the least, and she yanked the discussion back on track by main force. "Emma's opinion is all well and good," she said, "but what exactly do we know about Mrs. Benton? Not much, speaking for myself. She was on different committees from the ones I work on, and she was so quiet in public, I don't suppose I spoke with her more than a dozen times in the year she lived here."

"A year and a half! A year and a half!" Tootsie Armstrong corrected her. "Benton was in the cottage apartments for six months before she moved to a studio apartment here in the main building . . ."

"A lot less expensive." Tom Brighton nodded approvingly. "I don't mind the smaller quarters myself in order to save money. The garden apartments are beautiful, of course." He smiled at Caledonia as though to forgive her for being so rich that a garden apartment was easily within her means. "But I have a garden view from my room right here in the main building, and if I stand close to the wall and lean out, I can see the ocean from my window. I don't want to spend the extra for a clearer view, and I don't suppose she did either."

"I don't think she moved to the main building to save money, Tom," Mary Moffett ventured with diffidence. "I mean, I heard her say once . . . well, never mind. You don't want to hear . . ."

"Go ahead, Mary," Caledonia rumbled. "If not to save money, why did she move? She was in the little one-bedroom place almost across the garden from me . . ."

". . . and right next to Grogan," Mary said with a shrug.

"Aha!" A noise signifying understanding rustled through the air from most of the group.

"Yes, Grogan was serenading us again two nights ago," Caledonia said. "Mostly sea chanties, and mostly with double meanings . . . no wonder Benton didn't want to say! Between his singing and the thumping sounds—"

"Thumping sounds? What on earth . . ."

"Oh, Grogan flinging open his door till it bangs against the wall. Grogan stumbling through his living room. Grogan kicking over a chair on his way to the kitchen to pour a drink. Grogan dropping a tray or a teakettle. Grogan falling into bed. Grogan falling out of bed. . . . Sometimes it goes on for an hour before he settles down and gets to sleep." Caledonia shook her head. "Some nights I swear I'm going over there to throttle the man myself. In fact, when he started to sing the other night, I went over and banged on his door and threatened to run a bathtub full of ice-cold water and hold his head under if he didn't shut up. I think he believed me. He certainly quieted down!"

"I would myself! You're a formidable woman," Tom Brighton said, but he was laughing, and it was obvious that Caledonia was no threat to him.

"All of this is not to the point," Angela said impatiently. "What else do we know about Birdy besides that Emma thinks she was sweet and that she moved from the garden apartments to get away from Grogan?" The question was never answered. Instead, the sound of the Westminster chimes rang out over the loudspeakers and for the moment discussion was forgotten. Out of deference to the late Mrs. Benton, the office staff had canceled the broadcasting of Christmas carols for the remainder of the day, but it was their consensus that the meal-announcing chimes would not be disrespectful. So the usual signal announced dinner, the double doors of the dining room swung open, and the residents surged forward, conversation forgotten and priorities back in their accustomed order—meals before all else.

Not that speculation about Mrs. Benton was forgotten. She was the conversational center at every table between the cranberry cocktail and the main dish—braised lamb shanks, on this particular evening.

"We ordinarily see lamb once a month at most. But today it was lamb for lunch, it's lamb for dinner . . . Mrs. Schmitt wouldn't usually repeat herself like that," Angela complained. "Whatever can be the problem?"

"I'll bet some trucker ran off the highway with his load of

lambs on the way to slaughter," Caledonia said sourly, "and I'll bet he decided to cut his losses with a sale on the spot to some wholesaler, and Torgeson got wind of it somehow and took advantage. We'll have curried lamb for tomorrow's lunch, and maybe shishkabob at dinner, and lambburgers the day after."

Happily the meal was up to Mrs. Schmitt's standards—imaginative and delicious—so it occupied Caledonia's attention completely until she sighed, replete, and sat back to wait for dessert.

"Cal," Angela said, "have you seen Lieutenant Martinez around here yet? Surely he'll be in charge of the investigation, and I assumed he'd come to see us or call us in for an interview as soon as he arrived. But . . ."

"You're awfully full of yourself, aren't you, girl? What makes you believe we have anything to say he'd be interested in? You said you didn't know Benton at all well, and I surely didn't. And I don't know anything about her family and friends . . ."

"Oh, he'll want to see us all the same, I'm positive. After all, we're his most useful contacts here at Camden-sur-Mer, aren't we? And I flatter myself he considers us friends as well."

"And so I do, dear lady. Indeed I do." A soft baritone sounded above and behind Angela's shoulder and she turned in delight to see her favorite policeman smiling down at her. So handsome . . . so much the image of the late Gilbert Roland at his best . . .

"Oh, Lieutenant, do sit down," she beamed. "Join us at least for coffee."

"Yes, please do," Caledonia added her invitation.

"I wish I could, Mrs. Benbow . . . Mrs. Wingate . . . but as you can guess, we're in the middle of our investigation."

"We didn't see you in the lobby as we came in."

"We finished there late this afternoon," Martinez said gently. "We've moved on. We were in Mrs. Benton's apartment for a while. In fact, some of my men are still up there. Incidentally, we were sorry you had to be cleared out of the lobby while we worked . . ."

Shortly after the discovery of Birdy's body, the children had been marched off to their bus and sent home. The residents had been asked to return to their rooms, and the staff had been allowed to tidy away the rows of chairs that had formed an audience. Then the staff too had been asked to clear the area, and the police had completed with remarkable dispatch whatever they had to do in the lobby, strung their tape, just in case they needed to re-examine the area under and around the tree, and departed.

Angela and Caledonia, shooed back to Angela's room where they settled in for a last pre-dinner sherry, had been able at least to hear a bit of what was going on—Angela had left her room's door ajar expressly for that purpose. They could see nothing, of course, except for the quick, reflected glare of flashbulbs as a photographer did his work. But they listened closely, trying to make sense out of what little did leak through to them, straining to hear every word, every sound. . . .

"Bring the stretcher over here, but don't move nothing . . ."

"Take one behind the tree, will you? From that angle . . ."

"What's this broken glass? Smashed ornament, I guess. Under the body, but—"

"Not a lot of blood but they ought to clean up anyway here before the old people see . . . I mean, it's still a mess."

"How'd she get so far back under? You really can't see her from out here . . ."

And then the lobby had grown quiet. Angela and Caledonia, leaning as far toward the door as they could without falling out of their respective chairs, finally heard car doors slam and heard cars driving away—some of the police presumably headed home to their own dinners—and they'd heard the metallic sounds of a stretcher being loaded into the ambulance that had parked by the curb just outside of Angela's window. Then the vehicle roared away.

"No siren," Angela commented. "I wonder why."

"A body doesn't need emergency treatment," Caledonia said. "Time for one more sherry before dinner. And I think we need it."

And that had been the last of the afternoon's activities so far as Angela and Caledonia had been concerned. Now Martinez apologized for the disruption of their routine. "We got out of your way as soon as we could, of course, and I've set up shop in the meeting room on the second floor."

"We call it a sewing room, Lieutenant," Angela said. "Of course they do hold meetings there as well. Committees and—"

"The lieutenant doesn't care about that, Angela. He's only trying to tell you where he'll be when he wants us to come up and report to him."

Martinez smiled tolerantly. "That's about it, Mrs. Wingate. I'd be obliged if you could drop in after dinner. I've only just got started asking questions, and so far I've had only one significant comment. From your friend Mr. Grogan. He volunteered that he was about to kill Mrs. Benton himself, and he was chagrined that somebody beat him to it."

"Oh, surely, Lieutenant, you can't believe—"

"No, I can't take that too seriously, knowing your Mr. Grogan. He seemed to have consumed a fair amount of alcohol before he came into the interview. But I considered it indicative of there being more to the lady than at first appeared. I mean, we were told to begin with that she kept to herself and that she was generally so quiet that almost nobody noticed her. And that her nickname indicated her soft heart . . . that she gave lavish gifts to her family and that she spent quite a bit of money on seed so she could feed the wild birds. That she did her part on committees and paid her bills on time . . . in short, not the kind of person to have died by violence. Then Grogan registered such extreme dislike—well, it was enough to make me wonder, at any rate, and I thought you two . . ."

"Well," Caledonia began doubtfully, "we were just saying we really didn't know her—"

"Of course we'll come up," Angela interrupted, with a dig at Caledonia's ankle below the table. "We'll pass on everything we know, and if you like, we'll be happy to ask around . . ."

"No, no, no, not necessary. Certainly not yet. As you're

aware, we don't even know how the lady died yet. And until we know that, we also don't know whether this was a case of murder, of accidental death, or death by natural causes."

"Natural causes! Oh, no! Surely not!" Angela's disappointment was comic enough that Martinez was moved to hide his quick smile behind a sheltering hand with which he pretended to smooth his mustache.

"It's possible," he said gently. "She could have suffered some sort of vascular accident—a stroke or a heart attack, you know. They're responsible for more deaths than murder and mayhem. And if she fell hard enough, her head striking that marble floor might have finished her off."

"I don't believe it," Angela insisted. "How come she was way back under the branches of the Christmas tree? It's obvious to me that someone put her there deliberately to hide her. I mean, if it hadn't been for that little boy crawling along on all fours, she could have been there till the tree was taken down after New Year's."

"Oh, I don't think so, Mrs. Benbow. It's really quite warm in the lobby, and that would be four weeks . . . Forgive me for pointing out the unpleasant obvious, but I think you'd have discovered her rather sooner than New Year's. But be that as it may, it was possible, I suppose, for her to be standing by the tree when she had a stroke or whatever, and for her to stagger and struggle a bit as she was dying, and perhaps to fall against the tree through the branches and to the floor. I don't want to be too graphic about it. I could give you nightmares. But struggling to get her breath, or disoriented and dying, she might have pulled herself in further quite by chance. Without meaning to hide herself."

"What a dreadful notion!" Caledonia said. "Are you suggesting that if we'd been able to find her we might have saved her?"

"No, I didn't mean that. I was just working at an explanation of the spot she was found in. An explanation that didn't involve her being murdered and hidden there. Well, be that as it may, I hope I haven't spoiled your appetite for dessert, dear ladies, and I shall see you in a few minutes—perhaps a half hour? Up in the sewing room." And the lieutenant took his leave.

"Spoil my appetite for dessert?" Caledonia forked into the handsome slice of strawberry-rhubarb pie that was set before her. "Not very likely. Though I'm sure *you* won't be able to decide which is the bigger treat for the evening—this lovely pie . . . mmmm, how delicious . . . or the chance to spend some time with Martinez. You have such a crush on him, Angela!"

Angela blushed pink, the exact shade of the filling in her pie. "Don't be silly, Cal. Crush indeed! Although . . . ," she went on defiantly, ". . . you have to admit he's every bit as good-looking as a piece of pie!"

Caledonia's hearty chuckle didn't interfere in the least with her enjoyment of the rest of her own dessert.

Chapter 3

LIEUTENANT MARTINEZ came into Camden-sur-Mer's sewing room on the second floor of the north wing in a rush. "I need your help, Swanson," he said to his young partner. Officer Swanson was seated at the conference table that filled the center of the room, sorting a collection of looseleaf notebook pages pulled from their binder. A dozen freshly sharpened pencils lay around the carcass of the notebook, ready for use. When Martinez spoke, Swanson jumped to his feet—or rather, he tried to. As usual, Charles "Shorty" Swanson, a thin, tall young fellow with size thirteen feet—the kind of man for whom the word *gangly* was invented—seemed unable to move those feet in a coordinated effort to set them side by side to make standing up possible. Instead, he was rising even as the toe of his right foot caught itself behind the heel of his left, and as a result, he pitched forward, catching himself just in time by grasping the table with both hands, sending his pages of notes flying in all directions.

It took a few seconds for Martinez to help straighten both notes and junior officer and to restore order. Then he apologized. "I never meant to get a response like that, Swanson. I was just talking about Mrs. Wingate and Mrs. Benbow . . ."

"Something wrong with the ladies, sir? They were okay last week."

"No, they're fine, but . . . last week? You saw them last week?"

"Yes, sir. I was over here talking to Chita after work, and I saw them just leaving the dining room. Chita's studying for exams at the college but trying not to cut back too much on her work here—they're shorthanded, what with two girls out with the flu, you see. But she just hasn't got time for everything. Studying, her waitressing, and me . . . so we decided not to date for maybe a couple of weeks. Till the semester exams are over. Seemed like a good idea when we decided on it, but . . ." He shrugged boney shoulders helplessly and Martinez smiled.

"Got lonely for your girl, didn't you? So you just stopped by for a chat. Well, nothing wrong with that. You don't have to account to me for your after-hours time."

"Well, it wasn't exactly after hours, sir. I mean, you remember we had to go to that fellow's place outside of Vista? The guy who shot his mother-in-law? And you told me to drive over to Oceanside and pick up the wife's aunt to stay with her? Well, I just detoured over here for fifteen minutes on the way. I figured that long wouldn't matter. But I felt bad about it all week."

"So you're making a full confession now." Martinez nodded, his face serious but his voice full of amusement. "Okay, I accept your apology. You don't play hooky often, and that once didn't hurt. Now about our friends, Mrs. Benbow and Mrs. Wingate . . ."

"Oh. Oh yes, sir. You said you want my help?"

"To find some kind of assignment for them that will make them feel useful and will keep them out from under foot. Of course we don't even know that we're dealing with a homicide here. We don't know what killed their Mrs. . . . Mrs. What-was-her-name—"

"Mrs. Benton, sir. Beatrice. A.K.A. Birdy. Because she fed the birds." Swanson, who had reseated himself when he discovered that his superior's request for help was not really a matter of urgency, quickly shuffled the looseleaf pages into his small notebook and snapped it shut, ready for action.

"Yes, yes, yes . . . thank you. I knew her name, of course. But it's too easy to forget it . . . there are so many these days . . . so many victims of so many crimes. . . ." Martinez passed a weary hand over his forehead. "You can get shot these days for being a bad driver and cutting somebody off in traffic, or for wearing the wrong colored shirt. I can't keep the victims straight in my mind. They all start to run together for me. They all start to look alike."

"Yes, sir."

Martinez shook his head and roused himself from his musings. "Now. What I started to say was that these ladies like to feel they're helping, and if I don't give them something specific to do, they'll find something on their own. And it may be something we don't want them to mess around with. They've certainly done that before."

"But you're not sure there's a crime . . ."

"The mere fact that we're here is enough to get those two excited and active and nosing into heaven knows what. Besides, it's Christmas."

"Sir?"

"It's Christmas, and I feel charitable. I'd like to give all my friends presents, and I can't think of a better gift for those two than some useful task to help out our investigation. Well, perhaps not really to help, but certainly to *seem* to help."

At last Swanson smiled. "Of course. Great idea!"

"So put on your thinking cap, because if I know the ladies, they'll be up here any minute, raring to go. And I'd like to have the assignment ready when they arrive. Which will be shortly, if I know our friends."

The men set to work sorting through and talking over Shorty's notes, but they had scarcely begun when the door to the sewing room popped open, admitting Angela and Caledonia. Swanson jumped to his feet once more, but with greater success this time than last, to greet them warmly.

"So sorry you won't be able to see your girl tonight, Shorty," Angela said to him. "I guess you know she had a big exam this afternoon and another tomorrow. We miss her not being in the dining room for every meal, of course. But we get to see her once a day or so, anyway, and—"

"That's enough personal gossip, Angela," Caledonia said

impatiently. "Let's sit down here with our favorite policemen and talk seriously about our murder case."

"We don't know whether there is a murder, Mrs. Wingate," Martinez reminded her again, holding a chair for her as Swanson gallantly seated Angela. Then the four old friends faced each other across the corner of the worktable, the women looking hopeful and the men with their heads down, apparently going through Swanson's notes.

"Well?" Caledonia's voice boomed out through the silence. "You asked us up here. Let's get on with it. You say you're not sure it was actually murder?"

"True. But we have to proceed as though it were, of course, until we know better. Get the preliminaries done in case it wasn't death from natural causes."

"Oh, don't worry about that. I'm sure it was murder!" Angela said breathlessly and blushed slightly at the expression of amusement on the faces of both policemen. "I'm sorry. But you know what I mean."

"Of course I do. You speak with the heart of a hunter, Mrs. Benbow. You're thinking of the excitement of the chase, and you're not feeling sorrow for the victim. Not at the moment."

"Something like that, I suppose. But I never thought of the comparison with a hunter."

"Oh, it's no idle comparison, believe me. Otherwise no law officer would be able to put up with the drudgery of real detection. Most of it is not in the least like the movies. On the contrary, it involves hours of sorting through phone records, examining bank accounts and deposit slips, talking to one acquaintance of the deceased after another . . . And yet each page of paperwork, each apparently trivial interview is another step along the trail. You begin to sense that you're getting closer and closer. The shadowy figure of your quarry begins to take shape in your mind, and—"

"Sir!" Swanson seldom interrupted his senior partner, but it had begun to sound as though Martinez was enjoying his own oratory just a little too much. "About this case . . ."

"Ah, yes." Martinez focused his gaze on the two women

across the table. "The first thing we wanted to do, of course, was to talk to the two of you and find out what you know about Mrs. Uh . . . Mrs. Uh . . ."

"Benton, sir," Swanson prompted softly.

"Benton. You can tell us about her. What kind of person she was, what enemies she might have acquired, what special friends she had here, what visitors came and went, what activities she was engaged in."

"That's the trouble." Angela's disappointment was patent. "We want to help, of course. We really do. But we really didn't know her at all well, except for what others have told us. You see," she went on apologetically, "we never really had the chance. She hadn't lived here very long."

"Eighteen months, according to my notes," Swanson said in a puzzled voice.

"Surely that's long enough," Martinez began.

"You don't understand," Caledonia laughed, making her opulent rope of pearls bounce up and down on the silk of her caftan and gleam with subtle little rainbows in the artificial light. As he always did, Martinez admired the display without comment—huge and magnificent, the pearls radiated the understated elegance of a woman who didn't need to advertise her position in life. Now she twisted the pearls this way and that as she tried to explain.

"We have a high rate of turnover here," she said. "It's one reason why when one of us dies, we don't get as upset as maybe you think we should. I mean, we're all nearing the end of our lives, and some of us are already ailing when we arrive. People are dying all the time naturally. I mean, naturally from natural causes, if you follow me. At least, natural death is the expected thing around here. We get quite used to it. But my point is that as soon as they can, the management fills the vacant apartment with a new resident. Can't afford not to. So folks are always coming and going. But there are several of us who—thanks to heredity and relatively good health—have been here for several years . . . a stable, steady little community of residents, kind of like a family, and though we really do welcome the newer residents, it takes a while for them to be fully accepted. Especially if, like Birdy, they're kind of . . . kind of disruptive."

"Disruptive?"

"The birds," Angela said. "I live downstairs from her place and way kitty-corner across the hall, if you see what I mean, so I didn't really notice. But apparently a lot of people complained."

"About the noise. And the dirt," Caledonia said. "I didn't like those birds much myself, though I didn't have the problem some did. But they did wake me up some mornings. Woke everybody in the garden apartments. So I certainly understood the complaints."

"Clara—you know Clara, at the desk?" Angela asked. Martinez nodded and Angela went on, "Clara had to stay late tonight. Our regular night clerk is a student over at the college and he's got exams. Like Chita . . ." She nodded at Swanson, who smiled back in acknowledgment. "Anyhow, Clara was here and we stopped to talk to her a minute after dinner tonight. We thought we might pick up something you could use; she knows everything, you know." Martinez nodded and Shorty grinned, acknowledging the encyclopedic value of Clara in her position at the desk and switchboard, the nerve center of all of CSM, as the residents fondly called their home.

"She was telling us," Angela went on, "that several residents had gone to Torgeson about the birds. She said Torgeson had tried to speak to Birdy about it. But of course Birdy paid no attention to Torgeson and did exactly what she pleased. It annoyed a lot of folks, Clara said." Angela, who had often in the past been similarly headstrong, could not bring herself to sound entirely disapproving.

"So maybe that's what Grogan was talking about when he expressed such anger against her," Martinez said. "What was that he said as he left? 'I'd like to have killed her myself,' or something like that?"

Swanson referred to his notes. " '. . . but somebody beat me to it,' was what he said," Shorty read.

"That sounds like him, all right," Caledonia said. "Grogan can talk really mean, mean as a snake, but it's all just that. Just talk. Well, maybe not all. He might . . . oh, he might sneak over to her table before she arrived for lunch and put salt into her sugar bowl. That was his kind of revenge. But he wouldn't do her any permanent harm."

"He might deliberately wake her up in the middle of the night," Angela took up the story. "You know, phone her number over and over. Or he might order a catalog to be sent her from Frederick's of Hollywood. Then he'd sit back and chortle when she picked it up at the desk and started to leaf through it and—one assumes—register her shock and dismay. Not hurting her, really, but finding something that would annoy or embarrass her. That's Grogan's style."

"Would he grab hold of her?" Martinez asked. "Suppose they were talking one day. Suppose Grogan was complaining about those birds waking everybody up and down the garden apartments. And suppose she brushed him off. Verbally, I mean. And suppose she started to walk away. Would he grab her arm? Pull her back? Or if she laughed at him, would he lose his temper and give her a little shove? Not hit her, you understand. But kind of give her an angry push?"

"Hmmm . . ." Caledonia thought about that awhile. "Sober, of course, he'd never touch her. He'd have better sense. But drunk? . . ."

"No." Angela was firm in her response. "No, he'd never do that, no matter how annoyed he was. He didn't strike at us when we tried to sober him up, Cal, did he?"

"That he didn't," Caledonia grinned. "We were pretty rough with him, Lieutenant. Angela and I once manhandled him into a shower. He was fully clothed at the time, which didn't help his temper. Then we marched him around his apartment while we poured coffee into him, whisked him into his bathroom when the coffee came back up, hosed him down again, and then marched him around some more. We were determined to dry him out so he could start a process of recovery."

"Didn't work, did it?" Swanson grinned widely, then looked

at his partner and tried to put a straight face back on. "Sorry, sir. But he'd certainly been drinking when we talked to him today."

"Oh, we were far from successful in the long run," Angela conceded. "But Cal's point was that rough as we were with him and resentful as he was, he still didn't strike at us. He tried to escape several times by wriggling and twisting out of our grasp, but he never once raised a hand to us."

"Of course he's a small man," Caledonia smiled. "Not a very brave one, either, from what I can see. And it would take a brave man to lift a hand to me!"

Martinez grinned and bowed to his gigantic friend. "Point taken. He's not a violent man. But an accident . . ."

"My guess would be no. If he'd knocked her over by accident, he'd have gone to the front desk and asked for help. Grogan's language is colorful, to say the least. And his temper is certainly short. But under that gruff exterior, he's really got a good heart. If I were you, I'd look elsewhere for a culprit," Caledonia said.

"Well, I'll take your word for it. Can you two ladies suggest anyone we should consider?"

"I'm afraid not, Lieutenant." Angela's voice was crestfallen, and she moved in her chair as though to rise. "I guess we're not going to be of much help at all to you."

"Oh, on the contrary. You can be of great assistance."

Angela's face lit up, and Caledonia, who had also started to rise, sat back in her chair, but the lavender silk of her caftan shimmered in a way that suggested that she was vibrating with eagerness. They waited for Martinez to continue, but he hesitated, and only Swanson could correctly guess that Martinez was frantically racking his brains.

"Yes, Lieutenant?"

"Well . . . what I need is . . ." His eyes fell on a listing of sewing room reservations, tacked to the bulletin board across the room. "What I need is a list. Yes, I really need a list. I want the two of you to put your heads together and to compile a list . . ." He hesitated again, and once more his audience waited. Swanson was perhaps even more curious about what Martinez would say than either of the two women. "A list . . ." Inspiration came at last. "A list of the people on Mrs. Benton's side of the building. And those who had the most contact with her in activities and on committees. Yes, that's it exactly. I want to know the people most likely to be annoyed with her."

"But, Lieutenant," Angela said, with a touch of disappointment. "You could get a list of the residents and their room numbers from the desk. You don't need us to—"

"Ah, but I don't want just a simple list of names. I mean, I want a list and . . . and . . . and a descriptive paragraph about each of them."

"A paragraph? I don't understand . . ." Angela was bewildered.

"You know, a brief explanation of why each one might be angry with the deceased. You see? A note of whether or not they argued and what they argued about. A comment on personality—assuming that opposite personalities might develop antipathies like cat and dog. Include your own opinions, of course, of whether or not each person might be capable of violence. Then summarize your findings in a table or chart. Oh, and draw me a map of this place with each apartment identified by resident's name. Do you understand what I want?"

"Not quite . . ."

"Okay, I'll be more specific." Martinez' voice gained authority as the idea formed more fully in his own head. "I want to know who to concentrate on if it becomes necessary to interview these people about a crime. People living close together as you do here at Camden-sur-Mer develop all kinds of frictions, some important, some trivial. But things an outsider might not catch. You, on the other hand, would be sensitive to all kinds of nuances. And you can point me in the right direction when . . . *if* I have to come back here to conduct interviews. Now do you understand?"

"If she doesn't, I do, Lieutenant," Caledonia said. "I'll go over it again with Angela later if she still doesn't get the idea.

By the way, since you said 'a paragraph,' I take it you want this in writing?"

"Yes, I do. You know my schedule. Oral reports take time to deliver properly. So I want written reports instead—something I can read at my convenience. Oh, perhaps in the car while Swanson is driving me from one place to another. That kind of thing. So I need you to write down whatever you want to tell me. But edit it carefully to emphasize the important things and cut out the side issues. And I hate to ask this, but does either of you type?"

"I do," Angela said quickly. "My handwriting is so awful people can't read it, and I type all my letters, even though my mother would have thought that was a dreadful thing to do— she said a typewritten note looked distant and impersonal. The only letter I write by hand nowadays is a letter of condolence. I mean, I still do that. It does seem kind of false to tell someone you care about their loss, and then not take the time to write it out with a pen. A fountain pen, mind you, not one of those wretched ballpoints." Her little chin went up. "Personally I think part of society's trouble today has to do with ballpoint pens."

"What does that have to do with the notes I asked you to take?" Martinez asked.

"I'm sorry," Angela said blankly. "What were we thinking about?"

"You said you used a typewriter, Mrs. Benbow, so I was going to ask if you'd mind typing up those little biographical notes for my convenience."

"Oh . . . oh, I see. Why of course, Lieutenant. I'd be glad to," Angela said. "I type slowly, mind you, but I'll make our notes really neat for you. Oh, this is so exciting . . . to be of real use!" And after a few more pleasantries, the ladies took their leave.

"That," Martinez said smugly as the door closed behind them, "that should take care of them. They want to be detectives, they'll be detectives. And I might even get something reasonably interesting from this, without their getting in our way. Sometimes I surprise myself, I'm so brilliant."

"Sir . . ." Swanson's voice was diffident. "I remember once a long time ago asking you if letting the ladies mix in police business might not be dangerous for them, and I was wondering—"

"What's dangerous about sitting in their own apartments writing biographical sketches? All they'll do is make a list, talk endlessly to each other, and probably argue about who's writing what part of their report. They may not even get to the typing phase, but if they do, that'll keep them busy as well. Nobody at all will know what they're up to. It's not as if they were going out interviewing suspects. They'll be tucked away, happy and out of harm's way."

At just that moment, the door opened again and a young man in suit and tie came rapidly into the room. "Lieutenant Martinez?"

"Oh. It's Stevens, isn't it? What're you doing here?"

"Got a message from the office. They phoned here, but who-ever's on the desk was so vague taking the message, they got concerned. I was on my way to this area anyway . . . supposed to check on some kids shooting at each other in some teen club. The local uniforms have it under control, but I was supposed to do some investigation . . ."

"Okay, okay," Martinez said. "I know the kind of thing. Question is, what message did the office give you for me?"

"Oh. Oh sure. They radioed me to stop here on my way and deliver the word . . . which is that the medical examiner says it's inconclusive."

Martinez groaned. "Great! All that telephone and radio and personal service and . . . just nothing?"

"He says . . ." Stevens pulled a small notebook out of his pocket. "I took this down to be sure I had it right. He says that it looks like it was a bump on the head did her in, but he'll know more after the autopsy. He says to tell you he's busy, but he'll get on it anyway and make a full report in maybe a couple of days at the latest. As a favor to you." Stevens grinned. "How do you do it? He makes me wait sometimes four, five, six days for a report."

"That's the only advantage I can see to having rank, young man," Martinez said grandly. "When you're a lieutenant, you'll get preliminary reports and fast service on the final reports, too. Well, thanks for playing messenger boy."

Stevens took his leave and Martinez stretched and yawned. "Swanson, I'm not sure we should waste any more of the taxpayers' time here tonight. And maybe we don't need to bother tomorrow either."

"But—"

"I know you were counting on the chance to see Conchita every day while the case is active. But there's probably no case at all, you know, once we've finished writing up a report and talking to the Benton relatives, whenever they get here. Sorry about your not getting to spend time with your girl, Swanson, but we've got so many things waiting for us, we can't really justify staying around here—not unless we were to find out for sure there's something other than an accidental death to deal with." He pulled himself to his feet. "Come on. Let's call it a day."

It was all very well for the two policemen to pack up their papers and leave the scene. Angela and Caledonia were not headed to their evening's rest, nor would they have admitted they were tired. Angela was virtually dancing with excitement as they left the sewing room.

"We're going to help out! We've actually been given a real honest-to-goodness job to do! Isn't that wonderful? Where should we start? Do you think we should make a list from . . . yes! That's good. We'll get out our residents' directories and split them in half. Then each of us can interview half the residents . . . talk to them and get a general impression of—"

"Angela, are you sure he expects us to ask questions directly of . . . Well, these people might be suspects, after all."

"Of course he does! How else could we form a reasonable guess about their involvement? I mean, that's what he wanted, isn't it? But I was thinking—there are two hundred of us living here. Give or take a couple. It would take forever if we talked to all the residents, so we'll concentrate on talking to those living close to Birdy. Or no, maybe I should do those and let you—"

"Oh no, you don't!" Caledonia might not exactly dance with excitement, but in her own way she was as pleased as Angela was with their assignment. "I want half the significant names to be mine to interview. I can do as good a job as you. You needn't think you're going to have all the fun, my girl."

"Well, all right, then. Come on, come on . . ."

Because they headed down the hall to the elevator, they missed seeing young Stevens bounding up the main stairway on his way to see Martinez, and by the time Martinez and Swanson left for the day, Angela and Caledonia were back in Angela's room, already doing what passed with them for serious work.

It took Caledonia a lot of argument to get as many names for her working list as Angela wanted to take, but Angela finally conceded—with reluctance—that perhaps the fairest thing would be to divide their listing half and half. "I'll take the ones right around Birdy's apartment," Angela said. "On either side of her and across the hall for two doors left and right of hers. That'll be five in all. You take the ones on the ground floor."

Caledonia nodded. "Suits me fine. Sounds fair enough."

"Good, good, good," Angela nodded in apparent agreement. Privately she was elated at her own cleverness. It was more likely, she thought, that Birdy had made enemies of people next door to her than of those living a floor away. "I'll be doing the most important work after all," she gloated to herself. But of course she said no such thing aloud—just smiled amiably at Caledonia and chatted a few more minutes before, with both women yawning, they wished each other a happy good night.

Chapter 4

FOR THE next couple of days, Martinez and Swanson were kept too busy to think much about the death of Birdy Benton. They had been called into consultation on a case of attempted murder near Escondido. A salesman of power tools had returned from two weeks on the road to find his wife entertaining a fast-food restaurant manager, a circumstance the salesman addressed with one of his heavier electric drills; happily, the drill's motor was not running at the time and the enraged salesman chose to use it as a club rather than as a dagger, so that the injuries it inflicted, while considerable, were not fatal.

The salesman agreed to plead guilty to the lesser charge of aggravated assault, and Martinez and Swanson were freed up to move on to a break-in at a mom-and-pop diner on the road to the San Diego Wild Animal Park. Thieves had come in—apparently just before the place closed for the night—and bound and gagged the elderly proprietor and locked him into his own freezer, then robbed the till of $51.92 and the refrigerator of ten pounds of hot dogs, and finally left a mocking thank-you note printed on a paper napkin which they stuck to the grease on the grill. But the old man had smothered to death before his morning help reported to work the next day, and the case had become one of murder. Martinez was pleased that one of the thieves had left a large, greasy thumbprint on the note. A rookie was sent back to activate the office computers and check the files, then to bring in for questioning whomever the fingerprint might identify.

Then the two policemen joined the search for a missing three-year-old up near Palomar Airport. Nearly every officer on the San Diego County force had become involved, whatever their usual specialties; the police felt strongly about crimes involving children. This child had been playing with his two brothers in the backyard sandbox, and neither of the older children, ages five and seven, had noticed the toddler wander away. At least that was what everyone hoped had happened. On the second day of an intensive search through the neighborhood, the child turned up sitting in a vacant lot several blocks away—dirty and disheveled, weeping bitterly, desperately hungry, and unable to account for the time he was gone.

"I went over that vacant lot myself, sir," Swanson said angrily. "The first day. Three of us did together. That little kid wasn't there then. He was kidnapped."

"Well, we can't prove that, can we? And he can't seem to tell us. Looks like there's nothing more you and I can do," Martinez said sadly. "Come on. The others will take over, and we've got a list as long as my arm of cases still pending."

The officers went on to Leucadia to look into a death in a carnation grower's fields. Someone, apparently intent on vandalism, had gone among the rows beheading the flowers, swinging a scythe first left, then right, then left again. . . . In fact the scythe was found discarded beside the field, but its wooden handles had retained no fingerprints. But Martinez and Swanson were not called in over the ruined flowers. The body of a man had been found between the fourth and fifth rows; apparently the scythe had caught him amidships, effectively disemboweling him. "Wow!" Swanson said. "What a way to go!"

Martinez shook his head. "At least it was reasonably quick. Looks to me like he was lying down when the blow caught him. And the mowing of the flowers stops right here. I'd guess this poor old fellow is one of the homeless people who haunt the beach cities. Look at those worn-out shoes. That unshaven beard. That bundle he was carrying. What I'm guessing is that he came in here to sleep—maybe so drunk that this was as far

as he got. Autopsy will tell us that much. And I'm guessing his
death was an accident and probably surprised the man with the
scythe almost as much as it did the victim."

"Somebody was trying to tear up the flowers and got this
guy without knowing he was in there? That what you're
thinking?"

Martinez nodded. "What's the address of that driver they
fired here last week? And get the name of the other grower
here . . . the one with the bad temper. Remember we had a
complaint about him socking a customer after an argument?
Well, let's find out where the two of them were last night.
Either one of them's a good place to start."

If Martinez thought about Angela and Caledonia at all
during those busy days, it is probable that he pictured them
earnestly at work writing paragraph after paragraph of personal
description about their fellow residents, editing their reports,
typing their reports, and perhaps organizing the reports into
a looseleaf notebook for his inspection. He certainly never
visualized them as they really were: busily calling on their
neighbors to conduct what they modestly called "semiofficial
interviews" with each resident about his or her relationship
with and impressions of Birdy Benton, then getting together
each evening just before dinner to compare notes while they
shared a little glass of sherry, usually down at Caledonia's
garden apartment where, Caledonia claimed, the furniture was
more comfortable for a woman of her size and where the
sherry was infinitely superior to the sweet kind that Angela
kept in stock.

"Nothing today, Cal," Angela said sadly at the end of their
first day on the job. "I talked to Carla Wiley and to Dr. Colquin
today. They lived one on each side of Birdy, you know, with
their apartments right next to hers. I thought they'd have a lot
to say, but about the only thing I was able to figure out from all
that was that Birdy must have been going deaf. Carla complained that Birdy used to play her TV so loud that Carla could
hear the program herself, right through the wall. I tried to con-
firm that when I talked to Dr. Colquin in the afternoon but . . ."

She shrugged. "Incidentally, one of the reasons all this kept me busy the whole morning was that these people really want to talk! You get started, they won't let you go."

"Ain't it the truth!" Caledonia sighed and poured out a second taste of the sherry before she sank back into the out-sized easy chair she'd had built just to accommodate her bulk. "Boy oh boy! I've suffered today in the hardest, most painful seats! I decided people do that on purpose. I mean, I think the chairs people set out for guests are deliberately designed to hurt. To make for shorter visits, you see? All the same, people will keep you there talking and aching, talking and aching . . . Even Tom Brighton. I went to see him first thing this morning, and I didn't get away till lunchtime. You didn't come to the dining room, so I just went ahead and ate. I knew you'd under-stand. Did you get anything to eat, by the way?"

"Oh, certainly. But I was late because Carla started talking about that loud TV and how she and Birdy wrangled because Birdy wouldn't turn it down. I figured that might be valuable information, so I didn't want to leave. But then she went on to talk about everything else that came into her head and I still couldn't break away—at least not without being rude. I found out about her brother's gallbladder operation and about the prizes she used to win for her roses back in Illinois . . . did you know that she developed a new rose that was accepted by the Whatever-it-is Association? She got to name it and every-thing! Well, I listened to how she gathered the pollen from one rose and transferred it to another . . . with a brush, I think she said . . ."

"I thought," Caledonia said, lazily holding her little glass of liquid amber up to catch the evening light that spilled gold through her venetian blinds. "I thought you just let bees polli-nate the plants."

"So did I," Angela said. "But I learned better today. Appar-ently that would be like letting your prize poodle wander through the dog pound instead of taking her to a selected stud. Who knows what kind of rose you'd get if just any old bee could come and bring pollen from heaven knows what other flower, and . . ."

The conversation ran on right into the dinner hour and until Mrs. Schmitt's latest creation was served, broiled lamb chops with a light glaze that hinted at the piquant flavors of garlic, rosemary, Dijon mustard . . . "Perfect," Caledonia sighed. "Wonderful! But I told you we'd have lamb again, didn't I? I really do believe this was one of Torgeson's special bargain purchases."

After they had paid due homage to the main course and while they waited for a slice of the black walnut cake that was dessert, they returned to discussion of their day's activities. "So did you find out anything useful at all from the Wiley woman? Or from Doc Colquin?" Caledonia asked.

"Not much. Mainly she talked about her own family and her own hobby. Well, except for when she took off about the birds—"

"The birds?"

"The noise they made. You mentioned that they woke you up some mornings."

"That's right. It might have been because there were so many. I mean, if there'd been three of four—or even a half dozen—I probably wouldn't have noticed. But there were literally dozens of birds at feeding times. In the trees, on her window ledge . . ."

"That's what Carla said," Angela nodded. "At six A.M. the noise was enough to wake her up from a sound sleep. All that chirping and cheeping and chattering and cawing and twittering and squawking and peeping and whistling and calling . . . if it wasn't jays screeching, it was doves mooing."

"That isn't called mooing, Angela," Caledonia said. "It's called cooing."

"Mooing or cooing, it's that sorrowful, fluttery, moaning noise, and Carla said she could hear it in her sleep right through a closed window. She asked Birdy to set the seed out a little later every day—after everybody was up—but Birdy just stared at her and said something about how the birds wouldn't like it and went right on with the early feeding. She even found a way to attract more birds. She paid some workmen to build her a wooden ledge—an extension of her windowsill that the birds could use as a feeding platform. Carla was fit to be tied about that!"

"I'll bet," Caledonia nodded. "There's something to be said about old age after all, isn't there?"

"About what?"

"The dulling of our senses has its advantages. You and I and Carla and maybe Tom Brighton are the only four people I know in this whole building who can hear the way we used to. And sometimes I'm not so sure about you. At least, you didn't seem to react very fast when I asked you to pass the salt five minutes ago!"

"Really? I'm sorry. I suppose I was thinking about Carla and about Doc Colquin. He's pretty hard of hearing himself, you know. He didn't mention the birds, and he didn't pick up on the overly loud TV. Of course it sat against the wall between Birdy's place and Carla's, so it was closer to Carla. But I'm sure the sound carried into his apartment all the same."

"Well, then, why did you take all afternoon for his interview? What did you talk about?"

"Overbites and gum-line cavities! Doc was a dentist, you know, and apparently he loved his work. Well, to be fair, I think he loves to talk about anything. His wife passed away three years ago, you see, and he moved here just a couple of months ago, so he hasn't made friends yet. And he's very lonely."

"Kind of hard to strike up a conversation about bicuspids around here, I suppose. I mean, there aren't any other dentists living here now, and the rest of us don't know much about the fine points of tooth decay."

Angela sighed. "A wasted day for me, I'm afraid. How about you?"

"Well," Caledonia talked easily between bites of her cake, "Tom Brighton showed me how to play Super Mines . . ."

"What on earth is that?"

"His newest computer game. That man has a whole new lease on life, now that he has discovered the computer. Amazing! And after he made me play it awhile, with him backseat driving over my shoulder, he showed me the accounting program he's bought and how it keeps track of his checkbook and his savings . . ."

"But about Birdy! What about Birdy?"

"Well, between the computer zapping me with a loud *kaaPOWWWW* when I made a wrong move and Tom talking about debits and credits, I did find out that Tom objected to the birds as much as Carla Wiley did. But for a more urgent reason."

"More urgent than the noise?"

"Oh, much more. You see, Tom's room is one floor down and off to one side of what was Birdy's place, so his windows were constantly getting streaked and nasty with bird mess. But you know Tom. He tried to tell Birdy—politely. Then when she ignored him, and even got that extra ledge built to attract more birds, he just went out and got himself a squeegee and he'd clean his own windows every now and then. I'd have collared Birdy and frog-marched her down to my room and made *her* clean the windows of all that—Tom calls it bird lime. But Tom just sponged and squeegeed away by himself. He couldn't even bring himself to ask the maids to come in and do it. That would have seemed like making a fuss."

"Isn't that typical? He's such a sweet man . . ."

"Anyhow, talking to him took all morning, what with the computer and all."

"And in the afternoon? What about the afternoon?" Angela signaled the waitress for coffee. "Decaf, please, Lisa. I'll be awake all night if I even smell regular coffee."

"It's all we have here at night, Mrs. Benbow," Lisa grinned. "Some people ask for regular, but we know better than to give it to them. Mrs. Wingate? You want some?"

Caledonia nodded and was served. As soon as Lisa moved off to the next table, Caledonia went on. "I guess you found the same thing. Some people just aren't home when we want them to be. I tried three different places, with no results. So I called on the Jackson twins next. Their place is across the hall, as well as down one floor from Benton's, but you never know . . . they are sharp-eyed little women, those two, so maybe they saw or heard something. But calling on them is such a chore! Angela, I swear you gave me the downstairs on purpose so you wouldn't have to talk to Donna Dee and Dora Lee . . . or is that Donna Lee and Dora Dee? Who can remember?"

"Caledonia," the Jackson twins had giggled, "you never remember which of us is which."

"Oh, I can tell you apart," Caledonia said grimly. "I just can't get your names straight!"

"Well, come in, come in . . . we're so glad you dropped by!" The twins shared a single large studio apartment and had decorated it in an excess of their favorite color, pink. The carpet was cream-colored and the walls were a neutral ivory, but these were the only items in the room over which the twins had no control. There were pink cushions on the pink-flowered chintz that covered their two daybeds. Their windows were obscured in cloudy pink sheers bordered with dark rose drapes. Their walls were hung with paintings and prints of pink azaleas, of roses, of little girls in frilly pink frocks . . . and centrally hung on one wall, a painting on black velvet of a kitten with a pink ribbon tied in a huge bow around its neck.

"Made me bilious to sit there and gaze at all that pink," Caledonia complained. "So I tried to make the interview short and sweet. But the twins wouldn't let me go. Served me chamomile tea and Girl Scout cookies, ran on for an hour about the old days in Anniston, Alabama, and what good did it do?"

"Well, I believe chamomile tea is supposed to be good for the digestion. Though some herbal teas make me a bit queasy, and . . ."

"That isn't what I meant and you know it. I meant that the interview wasn't at all helpful. Oh, they told me they didn't like Birdy and she didn't like them, but that led to their staying as far away from her as possible, not to their murdering her. I'd rule the Jackson twins out as suspects."

"And as sources of information?"

"Yup, that too. Well, unless you count their tattling on everybody they could think of. Doke Wicker, for instance."

"Who?"

"Doke. The guy they've hired to drive our van. Haven't you been downtown shopping since we got a regular driver? Well, according to the Jacksons, Doke had a violent run-in with our Birdy his first day at work, and he's been muttering about her ever since."

"I see. Sounds worth looking into, to me."

Caledonia nodded. "And Clara. They had all kinds of things to say about Clara and how she disliked Birdy."

"Oh, that's just silly. Clara loves to share the news, all right, and she plays favorites, I'll admit." Angela's tone was smug. She was well aware that she was one of those favorites. "And she gets mad at some of us, now and then. But—"

"Like Mrs. Gibson," Caledonia agreed. "Clara's so tired of Mrs. G's coming by to ask for mail at all hours. I mean, the woman's new, that's true—only been here two weeks. But you'd think it would sink in that the mail doesn't get into our boxes till just after lunchtime. I don't blame Clara for—"

"The point I'm trying to make is that Clara gets annoyed, but she wouldn't really do anything about it—let alone kill somebody."

"Well, I'm only telling you what the Jacksons said," Caledonia shrugged. "But they spent most of their time talking about Trinita Stainsbury."

"Trinita?"

"Sure. She lives right across the hall from them, and I suspect they spend half their day with their ears pressed against their door, trying to hear everything out in the hall. They loved telling me how day after day Trinita would rant and rave about Birdy being inconsiderate, Birdy being stubborn . . . Trinita's directly under Birdy's place, you know. If Tom next door got it bad from the birds perching overhead, Trinita got it twice as bad, and being as how she's so fastidious and nice-nelly, you can imagine what *she* said about having bird-poo streaked all over her window! I'll make it a special point to talk to Trinita, you can bet."

"I don't know." Angela was skeptical. "Trinita's a self-centered, silly woman. But if all she had against Birdy was the streaks on her window ... I mean, is bird-poo a good enough reason for murder?"

"Of course not. There had to be something else as well. But Trinita is a gossip herself."

"So is nearly everybody here," Angela said.

"Granted. And that's lucky. But even gossips have a specialty, and I'm betting Trinita's areas of special interest include our Birdy. Trinita will have some choice comments. If I can ever catch her at home, that is. She gallivants around all morning and most of the afternoon, with her committees and her bridge parties and . . ."

On the second day of their quest, the ladies began their interviewing of fellow residents immediately after breakfast. It was unusual for Caledonia even to appear at that early hour, but with something specific to do, she made the effort—yawning hugely and complaining bitterly. After a giant breakfast ("Got to keep my strength up, if I'm going to rise with the rooster!") Caledonia spent the morning listening to Janice Felton hold forth. Janice lived on the far side of Trinita Stainsbury's apartment, making her windows as vulnerable to bird-bombs as were the windows of Tom Brighton's place. But Janice had other things she would rather talk about.

"Caledonia, honestly, Birdy Benton made the Entertainment Committee meetings a real trial to attend. It didn't matter what program we wanted to arrange, she had some objection. But when we told her to come up with some better ideas, she suggested the dumbest things! An hour of meditation? I mean, really! Who's going to come downstairs from the solitude of their apartment, looking for company and for amusement, if when they get down to the lobby they're greeted with total silence, everybody sitting around with their eyes closed and humming some chant or something?"

"Oh, I can see that would be—"

"And there was the time she wanted us to hire a silhouette-maker. You know, those people who do your portrait in profile by snipping black paper with a tiny scissors?"

"Oh sure. Schneeren-something, they're called. I think. They used to have one every year at the Minnesota State Fair, when I was a girl."

"Can you imagine how dull that would be for our people? I mean, it might be interesting to watch the artist do *one*. But then there'd be a second, and a third, and pretty soon you'd be bored silly. And sitting there waiting all afternoon for your own turn to get a portrait ... I tell you, Caledonia, it was a relief when that Benton woman got angry at the rest of the committee for never accepting her program ideas and quit to join the Chapel Committee instead. I hear they had the same problem with her later that we'd had, but at least she wasn't our cross to bear any longer. Ask Trinita Stainsbury. She's on both committees herself."

Angela, meanwhile, spent the morning with Mr. and Mrs. Dover on the second floor and heard about a different source of irritation with the late Mrs. Benton. It seemed, she was told, that Mr. and Mrs. Dover were health fanatics and nature enthusiasts. Their own windows stayed wide open, summer and winter; they walked a mile each morning after breakfast—down to the seawall and back, though not, to be sure, as briskly as they might have walked a few years ago; they extolled the virtues of beans and broccoli whenever anyone would listen and touted the wonders of antioxidants. And they believed in airing out their hallway and taking advantage of the ocean breeze, as they told Angela.

As they related it, they would prop open the door that led from the hallway's end onto the iron fire escape—from which there was a beautiful view over the roofs of the garden apartments out to the open sea. They wanted, they told Angela, to let the fresh breeze whistle through the length of the hall and clear out dust and stale scents. "Particulates in the air," Mr. Dover lectured Angela, "lead to asthmatic-type swelling of the nasal passages. But let a fresh sea breeze in and people stop sneezing and wheezing. It's wonderful how much sea air can do, not to mention how good it smells."

But no sooner would the Dovers get the door neatly tied open with a length of clothesline they'd bought for just that purpose than Birdy Benton would pop out of her apartment, and with loud comments about her inconsiderate neighbors who wanted to freeze everybody to death with that west wind howling through the corridor, she would untie the door again and let it slam shut, closing off the breeze and the fresh air—and simultaneously infuriating the Dovers. The last straw, the Dovers told Angela, was when Birdy stole (as they put it) their clothesline door tie.

"She stole it? Good heavens . . ."

"It had to be her doing. The next morning when we went into the hall to pick up our paper, there was a large brown manila envelope—unmarked—propped against our door. And inside was our door tie, cut into six-inch lengths! Now, who else would do a thing like that? The paper boy? It was that Benton woman, you mark our words!"

"All very interesting," Caledonia said as she and Angela compared preliminary results at lunch. "But we haven't really learned a whole lot, have we? Except that Emma Grant's description of her as sweet was not really appropriate for Birdy Benton. She seems to have made enemies left and right, doesn't she? Well, I know what I'm going to do this afternoon. I'll talk to Trinita Stainsbury. I put her off, you know, because I dislike the woman so much. I mean, I haven't pushed it, after finding her out the one time I stopped by. But the twins mentioned Trinita's complaints and Janice Felton said that Stainsbury was on two committees with Benton, and I know I should get moving."

"Oh, Cal. I know how unhappy it would make you to have to talk to Trinita. So why don't I just do that interview myself? You can take . . ." Angela glanced at her tiny notebook where she'd listed the names she'd assigned to each of them. "Oh, here's one. Elmer Johanson up in two twenty-four. He's—" She broke off as the dining room's intercom crackled into electronic life and Trinita Stainsbury's voice, with metallic over-tones, came floating across the dining room.

"Today's program, dear friends, is one you shouldn't miss. Oh, it's so interesting. Bavarian folk dancers. So—so *fun!*"

Caledonia grimaced and whispered to Angela, "I'm no English major, but didn't she skip a word in there? Isn't it 'so *much* fun'?"

Angela leaned closer across the table. "That's the latest slang, Cal. Trust Trinita to be up on the jargon."

Caledonia just grinned and shook her head, and Trinita's voice clanged on: ". . . the kind of dancing, you know, where they slap their knees and their hips and their shoe soles. In time with the music, of course . . ." The announcement of the program went on and on until the diners no longer listened and went back to whatever they'd been talking about when it began.

Caledonia picked up their conversation where they had left it. "I'm wise to you, you know, Angela. You're trying to take the most interesting work for yourself, and you're fobbing me off with an interview that would be incredibly dull and no doubt totally useless. Elmer Johanson is on your list and you take him."

"But Cal! Elmer Johanson's room is right across the hall from the Benton apartment. Don't you think he's likely to have seen or heard—"

"—absolutely nothing, Angela. Elmer is a hundred and two years old and spends almost all day sleeping. When he does wake up, he mostly just watches TV, or so they tell me. He doesn't even come down for meals anymore; he has round-the-clock nurses, and one of them brings him a tray three times a day. Besides, he'd never see or hear anything suspicious. His glasses are nearly an inch thick, and that TV chattering away in his place all day must mask any sound from outside. He may not even know Benton is dead. Why, he may not even know she was his neighbor. No, no, no, you don't take the most fascinating interview and leave me with a man who has all three of the monkey virtues."

"Monkey virtues?"

"See no evil, hear no evil, speak no evil."

"Oh!" Angela clapped her hands delightedly. "I remember those little monkeys. When I was a little girl, Mother used to take us into the Japanese importer's shop to pick out one gift for ourselves each time we were very good on a shopping trip downtown. And I must have picked a set of those little figurines three or four times, at least. I thought they were so cute, how they sat there with their hands—"

"Angela! Hush. You're trying to change the subject, aren't you? Well, it's okay with me, provided you go on and interview Elmer as originally planned. I'm going to be talking to Trinita Stainsbury myself and that's final! But not before two o'clock! I always take my nap between lunch and two."

"Well, just because you take a nap doesn't mean I have to," Angela said huffily. "I can work on our project."

"Of course you don't have to take a nap, except that almost everybody else does. You're the only one I know who never snoozes after lunch. It's no wonder you can never stay awake for *The Late, Late Show*. You certainly miss some good movies. But that's beside the point. The point is that you might as well go straight to your place and write letters or read a magazine if you're not going to sleep, because whoever you want to talk to today, you're not going to get much out of them till they've had a little nap themselves."

Caledonia was right, of course, and Angela knew it. So Angela returned to her apartment and read the latest *New Yorker*, balanced her checkbook, and sewed a button back on a blouse cuff. But when she checked her watch, only a half hour had passed. "Only one-thirty! Time passes so slowly when you're waiting for anything." As she wandered restlessly around the tiny apartment, she glanced at her little bed, neatly made up for the day with a bright afghan across its foot. "I could lie down and close my eyes for just a second, I suppose. And then in a couple of minutes . . ."

She stretched her tiny frame out full-length on the bed and pulled the afghan up over herself. "Cozy," she said lazily. "I guess I was a bit tired after all. It feels so good . . ." She said nothing else for a full forty-five minutes, because within a second or so she had fallen into a sound sleep, taking full advantage of the very nap she had so scorned.

Chapter 5

ANGELA WOKE with a start. The realization that she had been asleep after all was nearly as bewildering as the persistent ringing that . . . had she set the alarm? But in the same second that thought crossed her mind and was rejected, she recognized the bell of her telephone as it rang yet again. "Hello? Hello?"

"Angela, it's me. Caledonia. Were you asleep?"

"Of course not. I never take a nap," Angela said, wondering, even while she told her little lie, why on earth she had bothered. Surely nobody would care if she had arrived at the age when a nap was nearly essential if she were to go full steam until suppertime—even though, she told herself, she really hadn't reached that age yet.

"I called to warn you," Caledonia said, "that you're on your own this afternoon, girl. It's my back."

"Your back? Wh-what do you mean, your back?"

"You know what a bad back I have. Well, I did something to it and it hurts so bad I can hardly walk."

"You did something to it?" Angela was still warm from the nest of her bed and her mind simply wasn't functioning yet.

"Angela, are you sure you didn't take a nap? You're talking like you're still half asleep. Now listen carefully. I wrenched my back getting up out of bed. I think. At least, that's when I first felt it. Maybe I hurt it earlier when I moved the bed."

"Why on earth . . ."

"Oh, I dropped my pencil behind the bed next to the wall, and I couldn't reach it unless I moved the bed."

52

"What did you want a pencil for?"

"You know I always put myself to sleep working acrostics. It's such a habit, I'm not sure I could nod off without it. Anyhow, to reach the pencil I moved the bed, and my back's about to kill me. So I've phoned the chiropractor and he'll take me right away. Doke's bringing our van around to the side street so I won't have so far to walk, and he'll wait and bring me back here. Maybe if I feel well enough after a treatment I'll ask Doke about what the Jacksons said—that he hated Birdy too.

"Come to my place about four and . . . or no, phone me first. If I'm not much better than this, I'll probably skip dinner and I won't have talked to Doke about the murder anyhow, believe you me, so I won't have anything to report. My point is, phone before you come, okay? Now, carry on and tell me everything you find out." And Caledonia hung up.

Angela went to the bathroom and let the cold-water tap run a minute. Her mind was already racing, but her physical movements were only gradually getting back up to speed. Perhaps a dash of water on her face might help rouse her.

Cal's being out of action was really disappointing, she was thinking to herself. (*Splash*—water hit her face and she tipped low over the sink to let the drips fall safely.) Their most important interview this afternoon was going to be Trinita Stainsbury, and that was Cal's job for today. Her job, she was musing, poor old Elmer Johanson, that's less than nothing. (*Splash*—the water hit her again and her eyes opened a tiny bit further.) She supposed she'd be that dull when she got to be 102. (*Splash—Splash*) If she lasted that long. She hated that she had to talk to him and that Cal had the (*Splash*) most interesting (*Splash*) and most worthwhile (*Splash—Splash*) . . .

"Hey, wait a minute!" Angela straightened up sharply, talking aloud in her moment of enlightenment. Water ran off the tip of her nose onto her chin, and the water from her chin ran off in a rivulet that plopped great wet patches on the bosom of her cardigan. She brushed at the droplets impatiently, her eyes at last wide open. "Nothing says I have to interview Elmer today! I'm sure Cal would approve if I just went and did the interview with Trinita myself, since Cal's busy!"

Five minutes later, toweled off and wearing a fresh cardigan, Angela presented herself at Trinita Stainsbury's apartment. With her sense of purpose so thoroughly engaged, it never occurred to her that Trinita might be attending one of her numerous committee meetings or greeting the folk dancers scheduled for that day's entertainment in the lobby or supervising the setup of chairs for the audience. And perhaps the force of Angela's determination sent vibrations that influenced Trinita, all unknowingly. Whatever the cause, Trinita was still in her own quarters and answered Angela's knock immediately.

"Why, Angela! What on earth . . . are you here about the pageant? There's no rehearsal for you for . . . it must be three more days. I can get my rehearsal calendar and—"

"No, no, no . . . it's something else entirely!" Not waiting for an invitation, Angela came straight in. She was only slightly taken aback by the mention of the pageant, which she had mercifully forgotten for four weeks, ever since Trinita had asked her to take part. In a weak moment, more to get rid of Trinita than anything else, she had agreed to portray a lamb in the Nativity scene. Now she put the thought of the pageant aside once again. "This is a semiofficial visit, Trinita. Caledonia and I are asking questions on behalf of Lieutenant Martinez. About Birdy Benton, you know. What people might have seen or heard . . ."

"Oh dear! Well, all right . . . if it's official, I'd better answer whatever . . . not that I have anything to tell, you understand."

Angela smiled happily and chose a small velvet-covered chair, plunking herself down, ignoring what Emily Post or Amy Vanderbilt might have suggested about a guest's standing until being asked to sit. "Sit down, Trinita dear," she said to her reluctant hostess. "We may be talking awhile."

Trinita Stainsbury's choice of clothing for that afternoon— a bright pumpkin suede jacket with gold nailhead trim topping a gold-colored knit dress with gold metallic threads interwoven throughout—had been chosen to complement her latest hairdo, the coppery dye job Angela had noted two days earlier. Trinita caught Angela's glance of evaluation and patted her auburn coiffure. "I'm not sure this shade is the most flattering to me. I like the softer, more pastel . . ."

"I remember the green you had last spring around St. Patrick's Day," Angela said with distaste. "And I remember when you went through your purple period . . . you had just bought lilac-framed glasses and you had your hair done in lavender to match those. You may not like this new color—I don't either—but it certainly beats those other dye jobs. I mean, at least it's one of the colors nature really gives to people." Angela was quite capable of saying even more, ignoring Trinita's open mouth and stunned expression. Her purpose, however, was not to blast Trinita's sense of style but to gather information. She pulled a small notebook and a pencil stub from the pocket of her cardigan. "Shall we get on with it?" she said in a businesslike voice.

Perhaps Trinita was too thick-skinned to let Angela's criticism really upset her. Or perhaps such bluntness was merely what people had come to expect of Angela over the years. In any case, Trinita moved right ahead with the change of subject without objection. "I don't know what I can tell you. I knew her, of course. Benton, I mean. But I didn't know a thing about her private life, because the only things we ever talked about were . . ."

Trinita's recitation was long and detailed. She began with the revelation that she and the late Mrs. Benton had quarreled about the birds, just as Angela and Caledonia had imagined was the case. Trinita went over to her windows and pulled the venetian blind up to show Angela the glass, befouled and streaked still. "They said they'd clean it for me once a week," Trinita grated between clenched teeth. Her anger had not abated one iota with Birdy's death. "Oh, they do come on Fridays, but you'd think, with Birdy gone now and the feeding over with, that they'd clean it up right away. But no. It's on the list for Friday tasks, so I'll have to wait till the end of the week. Look at that window! I can't even see the garden!"

"Surely you spoke to Birdy about it."

"Not at first. I did what everybody else does around here, trying to avoid face-to-face confrontations and arguments. I complained to the front desk. But that Torgeson . . . I don't know what he said to Benton, if anything, but the feeding went right on. Even got worse. More birds than ever. After the third time when Torgeson said he'd take care of it and did no good whatsoever, that's when I finally went upstairs to talk to her myself."

As Angela reported to Caledonia later, the conversation started politely enough, with Trinita explaining her problem. "The birds . . . the windows . . . and lately there's been some kind of berry in season that gives the birds an even greater output, if you catch my meaning."

But Birdy just smiled and said that was really too bad, but she didn't see what she could do about the birds' bowels and their personal hygiene.

"You can stop feeding the nasty things," Trinita had suggested sharply.

"But if they didn't have my seed to eat, they'd go and eat even more of the berries you're complaining about."

"But that's not the point!" Trinita was getting more and more exasperated. "It isn't what they're eating. It's that you're attracting huge numbers of them—absolute *herds* of birds— and that sill thing you've had built lets dozens and dozens of them at a time perch right above my windows! And the windows are getting so streaked and . . . and . . . *icky!*" Trinita's explosion of feeling was bringing her close to tears, which made her even angrier.

"Well, I still don't see the problem. Why don't you just wash the windows?" Birdy had asked.

At that point, Trinita explained to Angela, she'd lost her head completely, and her voice had risen in pitch and volume. Birdy, ordinarily soft-spoken, had raised her own voice to match and the argument became bitter.

"You're being totally unreasonable! You don't care about anybody but yourself!"

"I care about the birds! And if you don't love God's little feathered creatures, you're an unnatural monster. A monster!"

"You're the monster, you-you-you . . . you selfish, selfish, *selfish* woman!"

Trinita's arguments degenerated into shouting and name-calling that made no point at all except to heighten her anger, and her fury only increased when Birdy finally slammed the door in her face. "Open that door! I'm not finished with you, Beatrice Benton!" Trinita had shouted futilely. But the door stayed closed.

"So," Angela scribbled another line in her notebook, "you were angry about the birds."

"Well, about the windows, at any rate."

"Anything else?" she prodded. It really didn't seem to Angela that windows, even heavily streaked with bird leavings, could possibly account for Trinita's obvious bitterness.

"Anything more? Oh my goodness, yes! If the woman was that thoughtless, that inconsiderate, you don't suppose it stopped at defending her bird-feeding, do you? I can't tell you the number of times we argued over other things."

"Like?" Angela's tone was eager, her expression bright, but Trinita needed no urging to launch into another story about an argument she and Birdy Benton had on the Chapel Committee. Cutting out Trinita's emotional and highly colored descriptive passages, the story went like this: Birdy had been named the Chapel Committee's chairman ("Or rather, chair*person*, of course. I like to think I'm up to date," Trinita said with a simper), and as such it had been Birdy's duty to post a schedule of who would do the altar flowers each week. "We took turns, you see," Trinita explained. "Each of us did two weeks in a row, then someone else took over."

All very orderly, but when Birdy posted her first schedule on the chapel's bulletin board, Trinita's name appeared next to the first two Sundays in July. "I'd already told her I'd be out of town from the end of June till the middle of July," Trinita said in a sour voice. "But I guess she forgot."

"So? We all forget things. Nobody minds; that is, we all understand when it happens."

"Oh, it's not the forgetting that made me so mad. It was that she wouldn't change it. I went to her and explained the problem, of course, and she said that was too bad, but the schedule was already up. I said why not do it over. She said the others on the list had already made plans based on the schedule and it wouldn't be fair to change it around. I asked why not let me find someone who'd change with me. She said she didn't want to have the office type out a new schedule because they'd complained so much about typing up that first version. I said I'd just get a pencil and cross my name out and write in the new name, and she said nobody was going to mess up her neat schedule that way and make people think that *she* was indecisive or that *she* made mistakes and didn't correct them neatly. It didn't matter what I suggested, she just said no and wouldn't budge. I tried everything I could think of. Finally I got so angry, I went to the Residents' Council meeting and resigned from Chapel Committee altogether. I have plenty of other committee jobs of course, so it wasn't as though I wasn't going to pull my weight around here."

"Of course not, dear," Angela soothed, making another note. "Wasn't she a member of your Entertainment Comm—"

"And that's another thing!" Trinita launched into a recitation of all Birdy's suggestions for programs, each—as she put it—sillier than the last (though in Angela's opinion no sillier than the ones Trinita found acceptable). Birdy had wanted them to book a chicken that played the piano. "Sort of. What it really did was bang its beak down on the keys of a toy piano. It didn't play a tune, did it? And any animal can bang on a piano key! My dear little cat used to run up and down the keyboard, but you don't see me trying to book a cat running on a piano as an afternoon's entertainment for our residents."

Birdy had suggested a program presented by a man who made maps. "What was he going to do as an act? Draw an outline of the United States?" Then Birdy had suggested an appearance by a prize-winning knitter whose imaginative sweaters had taken a blue ribbon at the Orange County Fair. "I suppose she could have purled a few stitches for the audience. Thrilling as that might have been," Trinita said acidly, "I was forced to veto the idea." Finally Birdy had insisted they consider a program in which an animal imitator roared like a lion, cawed like a crow, snarled like a panther, gibbered like a monkey. "The dumbest collection of noises . . . we could all make the same clicks and grunts and whistles ourselves. In fact, some of the committee did, right while she was talking, and did that make her furious!"

Birdy had resigned from the Entertainment Committee in a huff. "That was just two weeks before I got into that argument with her about the Chapel Committee."

"Is it possible," Angela said, making another entry into her notebook, "that her stubbornness about that flower-arranging schedule was a kind of revenge for what she saw as your unjustified attitude toward her program ideas on the Entertainment Committee?"

"I never thought of that!" Trinita said. "I suppose—but no, she was stubborn about everything. It was just her nature. Once she made up her mind how things would be, she refused to change."

"Perhaps she *couldn't* change," Angela suggested. "All the magazine articles say we get more and more set in our ways as we get older. I've never noticed it in myself, but still . . ."

"Well, maybe, but I'd bet anything she was born stubborn! I remember once when her niece Babette—that's her niece by marriage, her nephew's wife, you know—said she was coming to visit. It was on a Friday, as I remember, and Birdy made all the arrangements for Babette to sit with her at the guest table on the garden side of the dining room—that's a table for two."

"I know, I know," Angela said quickly, biting her tongue to keep from adding *and get on with it, will you*?

"Well, the niece showed up, all right," Trinita went on, oblivious to Angela's impatience. "But she had her husband in tow. That's the nephew, Daniel Benton. Birdy's blood kin. Babette is a niece by marriage. Well, anyhow, let me tell you, Birdy simply acted like he wasn't there. I mean, she went to the little table and waved the niece to the place opposite her and sat herself in the other chair—and poor Daniel sort of stood there. I was so embarrassed for him, but the niece didn't say anything, and of course Birdy couldn't have cared less. He'd upset her precious arrangements and she was going to let him sweat for it."

"Did he stand there the whole lunch hour?"

"Oh no. Eventually one of the waitresses offered to set up the large guest table on the other side of the room, but of course Birdy wouldn't hear of it. She'd had her heart set on being close to the garden window, because of the lovely weather, so she insisted they crowd a plate onto the edge of the table and pull an extra chair up to that narrow edge, and the three of them tried to eat on a tiny table that's so little they couldn't have water glasses on it at the same time with the three plates. And that extra chair sticking out into the aisle threatening to trip everybody who passed. Poor Daniel had to stretch his arms way out even to touch the table. And that niece just sat there and said not a word. The truth was, of course, that it was just another case of Birdy's refusing to change once she had things the way she wanted. She was a selfish, opinionated, unreasonable woman, as I said, and stubborn to a fault. Furthermore . . . good heavens, Angela! Look at the time!"

Trinita had glanced at her watch and suddenly jumped to her feet. "It's nearly two-thirty and my Gardening Committee meeting was called for two-fifteen. So we'd be out in time for this afternoon's program, you know. Bavarian dancing is so jolly. I thought a cheerful program as we got close to Christmas would be—oh dear, I'm going to be *so* late . . . Well, they'll just have to wait till I get upstairs to the sewing room," Trinita concluded smugly, with one more pat at her coppery hair. "After all, I'm chairma—chair*person*, so if there's nothing else you wanted . . ."

Angela got to her feet as well. "No, no, I don't want to keep you. Unless, of course, you know anything about enemies Birdy might have had. I mean, someone who'd hate her enough to kill her."

"Oh, that could be anybody here," Trinita said brightly, pulling the door to the hallway open and standing beside it in a posture that said clearly, *Here's the way out ... take it!* And Angela did, without reluctance. She'd had about all she could take of Trinita's litany of holier-than-thou complaints. Not that Angela hadn't asked for the recitation. And perhaps Angela should have been grateful to glean a few more tidbits about the late Birdy Benton, but it had cost a lot of wear and tear on her patience. Thus, rather than walk with Trinita toward the lobby where Trinita would take the elevator to the second floor and the meeting in the sewing room, Angela muttered a quick good-bye and thanks and turned in the opposite direction, down the length of the hall toward the back door and the garden. Once at the door she hesitated. Go for a walk? Go to the library and read the paper? Or ... well, why not do the interview with Elmer Johanson?

"It won't take long. He won't have much to contribute," Angela told herself. "But he is on our list, so we'll have to do it sometime. Nothing says I can't do two interviews in one afternoon. There's plenty of time before I have to call Cal and report."

She stepped outside and eyed the fire escape. The door of its top landing was open—no doubt Mr. and Mrs. Dover taking advantage of the fine weather to air out the upper hallway again—and Angela knew the staff used the stairway often enough as a shortcut to the second floor. The steps were wide and there was a stout iron railing. All the same, the steps gleamed wet with accumulated moisture blown in from the sea and condensed on their metal treads, and they looked slippery to Angela's eye. She thought better of it, retraced the length of the hall, and took the elevator to the second floor.

Halfway down that hallway on the right she paused again, but this time because she had reached a door that stood ajar—Elmer Johanson's apartment, directly across from the door that had belonged to Birdy Benton. When Angela knocked, a crackly voice rasped out "Come in, come in," and she entered a darkened room that could have been a hospital ward.

Directly opposite the doorway and facing her across the low foot of an adjustable bed with the head portion cranked partway up was Elmer himself, a tiny, heavily wrinkled figure with only a few strands of thinning white hair on the head that rested among a mound of snowy pillows. Behind the bed Elmer's windows had the shades pulled and drapes drawn. Beside his bed stood a tray table on a rolling stand, pushed to one side, and an IV tree from which hung a half-emptied bottle of some clear solution, a wreath of tubing and clamps not connected to anything or anybody and draped around the metal stand. Beside the bed and back in a corner, two tanks of oxygen lurked, their tubes and nosepiece coiled together around them in storage position. There was also an oversized bedside table with a cabinet base; goodness knows what lay concealed behind its door, but on its top there were the usual odds and ends that invalids so often accumulate within easy reach—pill bottles, nose drops, a box of tissues, a tablet and pencil, two half-filled juice glasses, an ointment jar or two, a china mug and a small teapot on an iron trivet, an alarm clock, a flashlight, two nine-volt batteries, a spectacle case, and a stand to hold the TV's remote control.

"Well, come in. Don't just stand there." The raspy voice from the bed was nearly a whisper, but perfectly clear. "You're blocking *Gilligan's Island*. The one where Zsa Zsa drops in on the castaways. That's a funny one." Elmer wheezed out a laugh. "You're that Benbow woman, ain'tcha? The one everybody's scared of. Say exactly what you think any time you want to. Got 'em all buffaloed." He wheezed his amusement. "I like that. Come on in. Move it!"

The last two words were a bark of command, issuing from the dry, crackling throat with surprising force, and Angela obeyed with speed.

"I suppose you wanna talk to me about something. Right?" With a resigned sigh the little man on the bed moved a papery hand to pick up the TV's remote control and, with a sharp gesture, snapped off the set, which stood behind Angela and to her right, leaving the room with even less light than it had before.

"See how dark the world is without TV? I hear critics say how them talk shows only give us freaks, and the stories only give us violence . . ." The voice paused for a wheeze. Long sentences required breath control now beyond Elmer's enfeebled muscles. "Ain't so!"

His bony chest heaved with the effort of making his point, and he took a moment of rest before he went on. Then, his voice back to operating strength again, he said, "Well, maybe it is so. But at least TV's lively, ain't it? Real life is slow and dull. At least it was back in my day. Took me three years before I figured out I was probably in love and another year before I got up the nerve to propose to the missus. And we didn't fool around till after we was married, neither. Ain't that way on TV. On TV a man sees a woman and five minutes later they're in bed. Snappy work! And interesting to watch. Not like real life—slow and dull." He panted scratchily for a moment. "I like the way things go on TV. 'Specially at my age. At my age, all the action I can expect is on TV anyhow. Just as well though," he added, and the dry crackle in his throat was, Angela thought, a chuckle. "Bein'—you know—cozy with a real woman would probably kill me!"

"Mr. Johanson!" This was not the way Angela had planned the conversation to go, and it had just taken an embarrassing turn. "Please! I'm not here to discuss your . . . your love life!"

"Course not. Ain't got one to discuss, have I? You want to talk about that little woman across the hall, don'tcha? One who got herself killed? Don't look so surprised. I keep up on things. Nurses tell me. Those women love to talk. And they tell me you and that fat friend of yours do a lot of detecting. Well, you come to the right man. I got things to tell you about, all right."

The dry cackle came again. "People think I don't know what's going on. But I can still see, provided I have on my glasses, and I can hear with this little gadget . . ." He pointed to his ear where Angela could detect the pinkish plastic of a hearing aid. "I could hear 'em out in the hall by Birdy's door, all right. I could hear the man arguing, ya know . . ."

"You saw a man . . ."

"Didn't say that. Never really saw either of 'em very good. Just saw a little bit of 'em. Door wasn't open very wide. Mostly I heard 'em, like I said. And what jawin'! Young people got no respect for each other these days. Nor for anything else, do they? And talkin' that way to a woman! My mother woulda washed my mouth out with soap, even after I was growed up, if I'da jawed at a woman like that."

"Was it Torgeson? Talking to Birdy about the complaints?"

"Naw, not Torgeson. I'da known him, even through the crack in the door. Fat fellow with a red face, ain't he? Well, this was a thin man with glasses. I saw him pretty good. Better'n I saw the woman. Saw just a glimpse of her. But I recognized her right enough. Seen her go by in the hall every once in a while, and I notice women." He grinned wickedly. "But him . . . anyhow, he wasn't talking about birds. No, sir. He was jawin' about how she'd embarrassed him at lunch and how he wasn't gonna stand for it. Said he'd give her a fat lip."

"Oh! That was probably Daniel. The nephew. I just heard about that lunch. You say he was arguing with a *young* woman?"

"That's right."

"Was her name Babette? The niece? Did you hear him call her Babette?"

"That her name? No, I didn't hear him say it. Nice name. So he's the girl's husband, huh? Well, I guess that explains it, then. Husband and wife fight worse'n anybody else, don't they? Mrs. Johanson's been gone twenty years now, but I ain't gonna forget . . . her and me was like cat and dog." The dry cackle scraped out of his throat again. "I never threatened to beat her up, though, like this fellow did. Besides, I never woulda dared. The missus woulda knocked me into the middle of next week!"

"And the fight was all about Daniel being embarrassed at lunch?"

"Oh no. Not just that. He was mad about money, too. Money is the root of all evil. Don't you know that? Money got me into most of the trouble I've had my whole life. Wantin' it, not havin' it, if you get me. The missus and me used to argue about money all the time."

"Could you hear any details of the argument between Babette and her husband? What was the problem?"

"Well, I dunno . . ." He stopped and sighed, passing a thin hand over his forehead, and Angela thought perhaps he was tiring and she should delay further questions till later. But apparently he was just thinking, for he started talking again. "There was something about trying to borrow from his aunt. Said the old girl was always handing out a penny here an' a penny there, but he needed a lot, an' all at once, if it was to do any good. But the young woman said if anybody got money it should be her. She said she was the one who visited his aunt, fetched and carried for the old lady, listened to her stories about the old days . . . I heard that part plain enough."

"So you heard a young married couple arguing out in the hall. But I don't see what it has to do with Birdy's being killed." Angela was disappointed.

"Mmmmph . . ." Elmer's grunt expressed equal disappointment. "Neither do I. Course, it shows he ain't a nice man, if he'd threaten to beat his wife up."

"Wait. He didn't make that same threat against his aunt, did he?"

The white hair quivered as the head wagged slowly back and forth. "Nuh-uh. At least, not that I could hear. Remember what I told you though." He paused again to wheeze a couple of times. "I could only hear the loud bits. But say! The nurse mighta heard more. You wanna wait till my afternoon nurse gets back? She'd be the one who was on duty that day. I think she went down to the shop to buy herself some lemonade."

"She left you all alone?"

He grinned widely. "Sure. They only need to sit right here when I'm doing bad. I'm doing fine today. In fact, I'll maybe get up for a while. Walk down the hall maybe. Maybe go to the bathroom instead of using a bedpan. Say, that sounds like a great idea!"

Angela jumped to her feet and headed for the door. She had no intention of discussing Elmer Johanson's bathroom needs. "Listen," he said, with the most vigor he'd manifested so far, "is that all you wanted? Because there's maybe ten minutes of *Gilligan* left—the best part of the show. Want to watch it with me?"

"Oh no, thank you, Mr. Johanson. I've seen every episode myself a half dozen times."

"All right." The TV set snapped back on and light flooded from its corner. *Skipper, oh Skipper . . . What's the first thing you're going to do when we're rescued?* Bob Denver's pseudo-adolescent whine came from the speaker. Angela headed for the door.

"Come back to see me again sometime," the whispery voice sounded from among the pillows. "Pretty young woman like you brightens up my day!"

Angela was so surprised she could only giggle and say, "Oh, I will. Thank you, Mr. Johanson!" as she left. But she smiled as she walked down the hall, and she was thinking she could hardly wait till she reported to Caledonia—not that she'd learned much in her interviews that day, but that she'd been called a pretty young woman for the first time in forty years, and that alone was worth a little gloating.

Chapter 6

LATE THAT afternoon, Angela phoned Caledonia hoping to hear that her friend was fully recovered, only to be told to hurry on down to Caledonia's garden apartment, ". . . because I'm not sure how long I'm going to be able to stay upright. But I have a sort of halfway report, and I do want to hear everything you did."

Caledonia was half sitting, half lying on the loveseat that served her as a favorite easy chair, a position made more awkward by the fact that she was leaning against what appeared to be a large wad of toweling. "It's a homemade ice pack," she explained. "I made Doke get me a bag of crushed ice and a carton of plastic roasting bags on the way home from the chiropractor's. I seal a supply of ice into a bag, wrap the bag in towels to sop up the condensation, and lean my weight against it to get the cold through the layers of cloth."

"Whatever for?"

"The chiropractor says it'll make the pain in my back go away faster if I ice it."

"Sounds crazy to me. Everybody knows heat is more soothing. Whenever I fell roller-skating and got a sore knee, Mother used to put warm cloths on it. Whenever I had a tummyache she filled me a hot water bottle. It never would have occurred to us to put something cold against it!"

"Me either. But that's what he said. And I'm going to be a good girl and do what the doctor ordered. Matter of fact, I do feel a little better. But I'm not going to sit up straight till I feel a *lot* better. They're going to bring me a tray from the dining room, and then I'm going to bed early. But in the meantime, to business. Pour yourself a sherry and give me your report. You say you did two interviews this afternoon?"

It took Angela nearly an hour to finish telling all about her interview with Trinita, what with her insisting on reciting even the smallest details and what with Caledonia's objecting to Angela's stealing her thunder.

"I knew you wanted that interview with Trinita for yourself! You've been trying to do more of the interviews than I, and get the more interesting ones, ever since we started this project!"

Caledonia continued to be grumpy all the way through Angela's faithful recital of all that Elmer Johanson told her. "Serves you right if the old man had nothing important to say. I mean, who cares if that niece and nephew argue? But it's really disappointing. You steal my job as well as doing your own assignment, and all you have to report is stuff like piano-playing chickens and guest stars on *Gilligan's Island*? Didn't you get anything else out of the afternoon?"

"Well, I got a compliment. Elmer called me a pretty young woman!"

"Don't simper. It doesn't become you," Caledonia snapped. "All that shows is that his eyesight isn't as good through those thick glasses as he claims it is!"

Angela's sense of accomplishment was rapidly evaporating, and it seemed to her that the best solution to coping with Caledonia's obviously foul mood was to leave. But when she suggested it, Caledonia bit her head off. "Angela, stay! I mean, sit right where you are! Don't you want to hear what I unearthed? Don't you care that I managed to do a little snooping myself, in spite of my being in such . . ." She managed to assume a woebegone expression designed to draw sympathy, ". . . in such pain?"

Angela settled herself again in the little rose velvet chair, the only one in Caledonia's whole apartment that was small enough to let her feet touch the ground while her spine rested against the upholstered cushion of the back. Everything else in the room was scaled to Caledonia's magnificent proportions. "Oh, I'm sorry, Cal. I certainly didn't mean to . . . what did you find out?"

Caledonia's discomfort level was still high enough that she didn't draw the tale out for dramatic effect as she might have if she were feeling completely well. Still, it was an interesting story. Doke Wicker was, as she reported, almost the caricature of an ex-marine. His sandy hair was clipped short, his terse speech was delivered with reluctance, his square jaw was perpetually clenched as though he were with difficulty keeping himself under tight control. In his late forties, he was still in excellent physical shape, which he made evident by wearing tight jeans and a work shirt from which the sleeves had been cut away.

"I'm not sure he could have got long sleeves on over those bulging biceps," Caledonia said, and despite her pain she grinned. "And he had so many tattoos on his arms, I wondered if he hadn't cultivated those muscles just to stretch out his skin, so the artist would have more space for the eagles and anchors and snakes and all the printing . . . *Semper Fidelis* and Death Before Dishonor and Devil Dogs and several things I couldn't read. Probably just as well I couldn't, come to think of it. He seemed a fairly earthy kind of guy."

"Well? Never mind how he looked. What'd he *say*?"

"That he hated Birdy's guts. She was on his case from the minute he arrived here, apparently. Criticizing his driving, for instance, and since that was his job, he felt as though she was out to get him fired."

"Well, how was his driving? You can report on that firsthand. Since Doke took over as driver, I haven't had to go anywhere in the van. Besides, I never use the van if I can help it, any more than you do. How'd he do?"

Caledonia shrugged. "*Comme ci, comme ça.* I used to be a better driver. But he's better than that volunteer who used to drive for us and not near as bad as somebody like Emma Grant, for instance. So I finally asked him what in blazes Birdy complained about. He got so mad telling me, he darn near piled us up against an eighteen-wheeler delivering potato chips to a Von's market. Had to jam on the brakes, and that gave my back a fit, and he apologized all over the place, and . . ."

"Cal, that's all very well, but will you please get to the point? What did Doke say Birdy complained about?"

"I can sum it up by saying nothing he did was right to her. He drove too fast, he followed other cars too close, he braked too suddenly, he crowded the center line, he swung his turns too wide, he leaned on the horn too often . . ."

"Okay, I get it. Was his driving all she complained about?"

"Oh, by no means. She didn't like the informality of his dress, she didn't like that his breath smelled of tobacco, she didn't like that he wore such casual working clothes, she didn't like it that when she asked him a question, he gave her one-word answers without even a *ma'am* behind the *yup* or *nope*— and she never shut up about it once. And unfortunately she rode in the van at least twice a week, so Doke has had full measure of her complaints. And Angela . . ."

"Yes?"

"That's about it for tonight. I still ache and I've taken a lot of some over-the-counter painkillers. Doke and his temper will have to wait for investigation till . . ."

"His temper? You didn't say."

"Didn't have to. Did you ever meet an ex-marine who didn't remind you of a coiled spring just waiting to be released? They've all got that dangerous . . . Hey! I said I was through for the night. Don't get me talking about the Marine Corps. Remember, Herman was regular navy, and that's . . . don't get me started on the difference. Just go away, girl, and let me rest! I'll probably feel better tomorrow. I'm sorry if I bit your head off. But a backache is one of those things . . . everybody has 'em, but you get no sympathy, even when they're so bad you can't move without pain."

"Can I get you a sherry before I leave?"

"*No!* I told you I'm full to my earlobes with painkillers, and I've read all those warnings about not mixing alcohol with analgesics. So have you! What're you trying to do to me? Put me out of action permanently so you can take over our project and hog all the fun? And while we're on that subject, I want you to promise you won't go back to our interview list till I'm ready to work, too."

"Oh, Cal!" Angela hesitated by the door. "We have maybe four others to do before we transcribe our notes, and Lieutenant Martinez will probably want to see our observations written up by—oh, by Monday at the latest. Can we afford to take time off? Shouldn't I—"

"Angela, half a day won't matter. Why are you always in such a rush? I'm positive I'll be back in shape by tomorrow afternoon. For one thing, this ice seems to be working. At least I'm feeling a whole lot better. And I have my second chiropractor's appointment in the morning. At the very latest, I'd judge, we could get back to work day after tomorrow. So I want your promise that you'll wait for me, okay?"

"Well, all right. I guess it's only fair," Angela conceded.

Even though she wasn't fond of dining by herself, Angela enjoyed her meal. The main course was a dish Mrs. Schmitt had learned from a Greek friend, an authentic and delicious moussaka—made, of course, with ground lamb. For dessert there was a light custard over fresh fruit that almost convinced Angela—who never ate large amounts—to ask for a second helping. After dinner, she went to her apartment to watch television for the evening, happy in the knowledge that she had done a fine day's work and looking forward to whatever the following day might bring. "We haven't found out much that's valuable yet, but tomorrow will be different."

She couldn't have guessed how different it would be. For starters, of course, for the first time in three days there were none of the interviews that had occupied her time. She spent the morning after breakfast going for a walk to the edge of the sea, watching the dolphin feed in the kelp beds offshore, watching the canny pelicans follow the rolling dolphin for clues as to where to dive for food most profitably. A little like detective work, she was thinking: keeping one's eyes peeled for suspicious activity and then diving in where there's likely to be the most to show for one's effort.

Back in her own apartment she watched some television and not for the first time sighed with regret at the dearth of the quiz shows she had always enjoyed so much. Nothing but talk shows—talk-talk-talk-talk shows! And a lot of the talk was clumsy and ungrammatical, and most of it was stuff she'd heard before in one form or another. Nobody ever had any original ideas. Like today, Oprah featured fat women who wanted to get thin, Sally Jesse Raphael featured thin women who wanted to get fat, and Maury Povich featured thin men who loved fat women.

Angela had stopped at Caledonia's apartment early in the evening to share a small taste of sherry and a large taste of the latest news. Caledonia chuckled when Angela aired her complaint about daytime television's endless array of freak shows masquerading as discussions. "At least they didn't feature fat men who loved thin *men*!" Caledonia snorted.

"No, that was on *Geraldo* an hour later," Angela said sadly. "Personally, I could use a whole lot more of Bob Barker and Alex Trebek, myself. Where is Pat Sajak when you need him? I was so relieved when it was lunchtime. And of course that is really what I wanted to tell you about . . ."

The second new element in the day showed up at lunch: Birdy's relatives arrived in a contingent of five. Torgeson hosted them at the large guest table that stood almost in the dining room's center, where they were the object of every other table's unwinking attention. "A sad occasion," Torgeson's voice rumbled out loud enough for all the other diners to hear even if they hadn't been straining to do so. "Would that you were our guests for some reason other than the settling of your aunt's affairs—and your grandmother's, of course," he nodded to the three younger members of the group. "But the time comes to us all . . ."

He shook his head solemnly and one of the younger women, a wispy blonde who (as Angela reported later to Caledonia) was probably anorexic, sniffled softly into her handkerchief.

The remainder of the Benton party appeared unmoved either by Torgeson's comment on the universality of death or by Birdy's recent passing.

"I've seen that niece several times before, when she came in the afternoons to visit Birdy," Angela went on to Caledonia, "though I've seen the nephew Daniel only a couple of times. But I did recognize both of them. I'm positive you'd know them too, Cal. Both fortyish, kind of undistinguished, with brownish hair and glasses and little mouths all pinched up like they just said *prunes*. They sit there and look disapproving about everybody and everything all the time. Talk about people who've sucked lemons! The other three certainly look pleasanter. But anybody would. Those other three are all Birdy's grandchildren, Torgeson said."

"Oh? You stopped by the table to meet them?"

"After lunch. But he introduced them to us over the intercom before lunch. Nearly gave Trinita Stainsbury a stroke, his doing that. She seems to think that microphone is just about her personal property. She glared at him so hard I'm sure he could feel it. Anyhow, he said he wanted everybody to know who these people were and to stop by the guest table to offer their sympathies. As if we needed to be told that. Honestly! Torgeson instructing us on manners! What a nerve!"

"Torgeson's boorishness isn't news, Angela. What I want to hear about is those relatives. Tell me everything." Angela accepted the invitation eagerly. Save for good health, there is no commodity so precious to the elderly as a willing and attentive audience.

"The skinny blonde with the transparent skin—about college age, I'd say—is named Catherine Snelgrove. Birdy's daughter married a Cecil Snelgrove and Catherine is their girl, but both her mother and father have 'passed,' as they used to say in Charleston. The other two grandchildren seemed to be a little bit older, in their twenties, I'd guess, and they're children of Birdy's late son, so they're both named Benton, too. One of each. I mean, a boy and a girl. Well, a young man and a young woman, actually. The two of them look . . ."

"Wait! Wait a sec. Let's go back over this. First of all, Birdy's children—a son and daughter—are both deceased. Right?" Caledonia said.

"That's right. Not unusual for those of us living here, of course. Well, of course we're not all here because our families are dead and gone. Some of us never had children at all. You didn't, I didn't . . . Mary Moffett's son couldn't invite her to move in with him because he has a job that makes him travel all the time. Anna Olson's daughter lives in a tiny, tiny apartment in New York, so there's no room for Anna. And I suppose some kids don't want their parents with them. And sometimes the parents don't want to live with the kids, either! Like Emma Grant, who prefers—"

"Okay, okay, okay . . . it isn't important. I was just trying to get it all straight."

"When you think of it, Cal, it's a little unusual. Birdy shouldn't have been surprised to be murdered."

"Meaning what?"

"I mean, it's been a hard-luck family for years. Birdy's husband died after he fell off a ladder when he was putting up a TV antenna years and years ago. The daughter—that Mrs. Snelgrove—was hit on the head by a gallon of Dutch Boy that fell off a scaffolding Mr. Snelgrove was using to repaint the living room. Then Birdy's son, the father of the boy and girl—he was kicked by a horse. I mean, he wasn't even riding the horse; he was just admiring it in its stall, for goodness' sake! Not only that, but when the family sued the riding stables for negligence, they lost because Birdy's son wasn't supposed to be back in the stalls at all. There were signs, and the owner had just finished warning him to stay out. Bad-luck family? I should say so!"

"Angela, where on earth did you get all that information? Torgeson didn't tell you all that at lunch, did he?"

"Oh, no. It comes from Clara. Believe me, she knows everything Torgeson knows and a lot he doesn't."

"And she can't wait to tell us, right? Well, go on, spill the rest. What were they like? What did they say? What did they do?"

The thin blonde, Catherine Snelgrove, said very little during lunch and barely acknowledged the sympathy offered by the residents and staff in response to Torgeson's electronic invitation. She seemed languorous—or terribly tired. "Or maybe she was just sad," Angela suggested. "She seemed to have tears in her eyes, at any rate. The others certainly didn't."

The niece and nephew, Daniel and Babette, sat in glum silence, barely talking to the others, nodding only to those who stopped by the table, and not talking at all to each other. In response to Caledonia's urging, Angela described them again—the straight brownish hair, the pale skin, the huge, black-rimmed glasses that seemed to hide their eyes, making them look remote or secretive. "They're really the kind of people you'd never notice in a crowd. Except they seemed to be so angry. Maybe the argument Elmer Johanson overheard between them is the way they always behave! Maybe they stay perpetually mad at each other."

"Oh, it was probably just having to sit through lunch with Torgeson at their table," Caledonia said comfortably. "He'd upset anybody's digestion. What about the other two? The other grandchildren." They were in their early twenties and alike enough with their wildly curled red hair and bright blue eyes to be twins rather than just brother and sister. The utterances by Warren and Wilma Benton were short and emphatic and they were waving their hands a lot as they talked. The other diners could hear only snatches of conversation, but it was enough to rivet their attention.

"I came to the table and offered my sympathy, as I told you," Angela went on. "But I almost hated to. What I'd been able to overhear from my own table was a lot more interesting than what they said while I was standing close by. It wasn't as though they cared if people overheard, but . . . well, what it was, the twins started to argue with Torgeson about—"

"I thought you said they *weren't* twins!"

"That's right. Two full years apart. She's older than he is, or so Clara says. But I think of them as twins and you will, too, when you see them. Anyhow, Warren acted like the spokesman for the family. He said they'd gone to his grand-mother's room right after they arrived that morning and started sorting through her things, and she'd apparently been robbed. Torgeson was horrified, but Warren went on to explain that there hadn't been a dime of money or any expensive jewelry anywhere in the place. He said there were some high-priced knickknacks she'd had that he couldn't locate. And he worked himself up to be really angry. The longer he talked, the madder he got. He ended up accusing the staff here of robbing her."

"That isn't possible!" Torgeson had squealed his protest. "The only time your aunt's apartment was open was while the police were there. Your aunt had locked her hall door when she left the room. I know because we had to get a passkey to open it for the police, and the police found her own key in her pocket when . . . well, you know, when they went through her things after . . . after she was found." He hastened along. "Anyway, the door was locked again when the police left. And we don't just rely on the ordinary lock when a tenant has passed on. You saw. We put on a big padlock and secure the hasp in place with wood screws, and that padlock was undisturbed. Nobody took anything from there. Nobody."

"Then somebody robbed her while she was still alive," Warren insisted with irritation. "Grandma was, like, real wealthy, you know? Dad always told us so. And we were counting on . . . I mean, who's going to pay for her funeral?"

Torgeson's red face grew even redder, and Angela wondered, from her vantage point across the room, if he was about to break a blood vessel. "Surely you know that was all taken care of. All our residents make arrangements when they first move in. I've checked Mrs. Benton's folder, and everything was arranged and paid for already."

"Well, even if we don't have to pay to, like, bury Grandma, her money is still missing. I don't mean her trust fund. They only let her have so much a month out of that. She told us so every time she doled out some. She couldn't, like, you know, give us a gift without telling us about that stupid trust fund and how it limited her. What I'm talking about is cash, you know?" Warren's tone was reasonable, but Torgeson still looked apoplectic. "We're gonna get her estate, I'm positive. But that takes time, you know? We were sure there'd be, like . . . well, we talked about it in the car all the way here, you know? Like, about how we'd use the cash we found and—"

He twitched noticeably, and Angela surmised that someone had kicked him sharply under the table. He glared around him, uncertain of who had administered the correction, but lapsed into a silence as glum as that of Daniel and Babette, who had stared at him without speaking during his tirade. A period without conversation followed while everyone at the guest table paid attention to the business at hand, eating Mrs. Schmitt's excellent lunch, a rich ragout of lamb seasoned with fresh herbs. Then between the ragout and the lemon tart, when there was a natural pause in the meal, Warren's sister Wilma spoke up, and the temporary relaxation Torgeson had enjoyed as he ate vanished.

"Babette says Grandma slipped on your lobby floor and fell. That's how she got killed. She hit her head and—"

"Good heavens no, Miss Benton. I assure you—" Torgeson turned red in the face and sweat popped out on his brow, as he hurried to contradict her.

"That's what you told us, Babette," Warren chimed in. He ran a hand through his red curls. "You said Grandma fell!"

Babette shook her head. "I didn't. I said she was found lying in the lobby and she *might* have fallen." She shrugged and half turned away, and to Torgeson's discomfiture, she did not continue or defend him and Camden-sur-Mer.

It was Torgeson's job to wriggle out of responsibility, even if the worst happened and he was taken into court, and wriggle he did. "I assure you, Miss Benton . . ." Angela watched with interest from across the room, listening to whatever she could pick up, and interpreting each gesture, each expression, to fill the story out so she could pass the details on to Caledonia later, as she was doing now.

"He was trying frantically to imply that it was anybody's fault but ours."

"Ours?"

"Well, you know . . . CSM's. Camden-sur-Mer's. First he suggested that it was probably Birdy's own fault. He implied—not directly enough to be insulting, mind you—really rather delicately, for Torgeson—that Birdy was so clumsy she tripped over her own feet. When they didn't buy that explanation, he hinted that perhaps she was attacked by an old enemy out of her past—in other words by someone who was neither a resident nor a staff member here. He was really trying hard, but in the end he went too far. When the family denied that she had any murderous enemies, he hinted she might have been zapped by aliens in some sort of supernatural attack or something! I nearly laughed out loud when I overheard that. The man would have embraced any idea, no matter how silly, so long as it obviously had nothing to do with Camden-sur-Mer's indulging in excessive floor polishing or something. He was absolutely terrified of our being sued for negligence."

"Did he convince the family?"

"Hard to tell. Daniel and Babette never changed expression—just glowered most of the time. The Snelgrove girl sighed and looked terribly bored—which she probably was. It was the two redheaded grandchildren, Wilma and Warren, who asked the questions and argued."

"Regarding the burglary or a suit for negligence?"

"Either one. Or both. Whatever might gain them some financial advantage. Frankly, I thought that excessive concern for money was most unattractive."

"Do you suppose she actually was robbed? The kids are right about one thing. It is a little strange not to have any money at all in the apartment. Most of us do have some spare change on hand. To buy a soft drink, to pay the paper boy at the end of the week, to tip the delivery man from the drugstore, to get things at the shop like a box of Kleenex or a new lipstick . . ."

"Maybe she'd temporarily run out. It may have been time to go to the bank, mightn't it?"

They talked a few more minutes without reaching any conclusions, and then Angela wished her friend a pleasant good night and headed for her own apartment. Caledonia groaned as she rose from her loveseat, but this evening it was mostly stiffness rather than real pain, and a hot bath helped loosen the knots. "This is one time," she muttered as she sponged, "heat is doing the job better than cold. Maybe I'll take a second hot soak tomorrow morning before Angela and I get back to work."

The next morning, Caledonia huffed and puffed her way to a late breakfast just before the dining room closed at 9:00 and found Angela waiting impatiently for her. "Hurry up, hurry up . . . the family has just eaten and gone up to Birdy's room, and if you want to take a good look at them—"

"Angela, looking will have to wait. My eyes won't quite open yet and until I've had my coffee I'd be trying to peek at them through closed lids. Sit with me while I have a cup or two . . ."

Angela, fidgeting while Caledonia sipped, tried to interest her friend in conversation, but Caledonia's replies were monosyllabic. In response to each direct question, she would point at her drooping eyes and say, "Not quite ready yet," and take another mouthful of coffee.

"Ladies, good morning."

Angela and Caledonia looked up to see Shorty Swanson standing beside their table.

"Oh, Officer Swanson." Angela showed her pleasure in the warmth of her smile and the lilt of her voice. "How wonderful. But we're nowhere near done with the lieutenant's report yet!"

"What report? Oh! Oh, sure. I almost forgot. I mean, I didn't come for that. The lieutenant is here to see the Benton family, and I came in here to . . . to . . ." He blushed and looked shyly around. "Is Chita here this morning?"

"Your pretty fiancée is out in the kitchen, Officer Swanson," Angela said. "Chita will be glad to see you. She's almost done

for the morning. The dining room closes in a couple of minutes. You say the lieutenant is here? Maybe I'd better find him
and explain why our report isn't finished. I was thinking that
maybe by Monday . . ."

"Oh, gosh, Mrs. Benbow. I know the lieutenant will be
telling you this himself anyhow, so he won't mind if I . . . well,
I hope you won't be mad about having done a lot of work
already for nothing."

"For nothing? What do you mean?"

"I mean there might not be any murder. No case for us to
look into. And of course you were taking notes about who we
were going to talk to about a murder. But it isn't. If you see
what I mean."

"No, young man." Caledonia's eyes were now wide open
and her voice at full strength, rumbling like approaching
thunder. "I don't see what you mean. No murder? The woman
hasn't come back to life, has she?"

"Oh, no, ma'am. No. Of course not. It's just . . . right now,
from what our medical examiner is saying, we may end up
writing this one off as just another accident."

Chapter 7

LIEUTENANT MARTINEZ met Angela and Caledonia at Caledonia's garden apartment later in the morning. He had only a few minutes, he told them, before he went on to other duties. But he had a little time for old friends, having for the moment finished his scheduled business. "I apologize that you were not my primary focus on this visit," he said. "I really had to see Mrs. Benton's family about arrangements for the eventual delivery of the body. The medical examiner isn't finished, but . . ." He hesitated. "I suppose I'm a bit old-fashioned about family. But those people shocked me, and I've seen so much I'm almost shockproof."

"What shocked you, Lieutenant?" Caledonia asked.

"The family itself. At least they call themselves a family. Not a word of regret about Mrs. Benton's death. No sharing of sentimental memories of time spent with their aunt and grandmother. No! Their chief concern seems to be finding money in her effects. I went to her apartment to see them, and even while we talked, that pale young woman—Catherine, I think is her name—was pawing through the desk drawers looking for spare change. The redheaded girl had all her grandmother's purses laid out on the couch beside her and was going through every compartment, every fold of the lining, when I arrived. Odd. They didn't look especially hard up." He shook his head. "So sad."

"I'm sad, too." Angela's tone was mournful. "But for a different reason. I'm sad because our case is gone. Disappeared."

81

"Oh, I wouldn't say that, Mrs. Benbow. At the moment, the medical examiner is still working. We certainly haven't reached a conclusion as to whether this was a murder or an accident or—"

"But that's wonderful! I thought from what Shorty told us ... Oh, I can't tell you how glad I am to hear that, Lieutenant. We've done so much work already, and we've begun to feel as though we're getting somewhere . . ."

"You are?" Martinez was unable to hide his surprise completely. "I can't imagine—"

"We've been talking to maybe eight different people already, and while I grant you none of them seemed to be likely suspects, they certainly made us understand how universally disliked Birdy was. Between those birds she fed and the rigid way she ran committees—or tried to run them—and the loud TV and her abrasive manner and her antagonizing residents and staff alike . . . well, there is a whole long list of possible suspects."

"I see," Martinez said. He looked slightly dazed, but he was game. "You are telling me you actually interviewed some of the . . ." He hesitated again, choosing his noun with care, ". . . some of the suspects?"

"Exactly!" Angela said. "Just as you wanted us to."

"Oh, no," Martinez said. "Oh, no! That's exactly what I did *not* want you to do. If this is indeed a case of murder, you've been putting yourself in harm's way."

"But you told us to find out about—"

"No, no, no, not to find out. Just to think through. I wanted you to rely on your knowledge of your fellow residents. And the staff. I never imagined that you'd talk directly to—well, never mind. I'm sure you did a good job, even though, if this was just an accident, we might not need your information."

"I just don't believe that, Lieutenant." Angela had made up her mind, and her determination showed in her voice. "This is not an accident, it's murder. It *has* to be a murder!"

"Angela," Caledonia started one of her great, rumbling laughs that rose from her sandals right to her shoulder pads.

"Angela, I can't believe you're telling the lieutenant his business. I apologize for her, Lieutenant."

Martinez wasn't laughing, but a small smile lit his face. "No apologies necessary. I understand your feelings, Mrs. Benbow. And yours too, Mrs. Wingate." Caledonia nodded her agreement. "But you should be prepared for this to be a natural death. I mean, so far the preliminary examination has shown up no bruises or cuts, no evidence of a struggle or even of a little push. And without something of the sort, we have a woman who fell and subsequently died, and that's all. No assailant, with or without murderous intent."

"But what made her fall? I mean, if she wasn't pushed . . ."

"Well, that remains to be determined," Martinez said. "That's why the body won't be released for a couple more days, so that our medical examiner can finish his work, and specifically he can look for evidence of a heart attack or a stroke—some condition that might have caused even a temporary loss of balance. It wouldn't be unusual in a woman her age. Surely you can see that."

"Oh, surely," Angela said rather testily. "People keel over here all the time. Every other day somebody hits the floor from one cause or another. At our age we practically play Musical Chairs as we walk through the lobby, because if we should collapse, it's a lot more comfortable to crumple onto a chair or sofa than all the way to the marble floor. And it hurts a lot less."

"She's being sarcastic, of course," Caledonia explained. "She's annoyed. But she's right. We don't see well and we trip. We have little attacks of vertigo. Not Angela and me particularly, you understand, but all of us here. We totter a lot, for a bunch of reasons, and since nobody else is strong enough to steady us, we fall. Fortunately, it seldom does any permanent damage. Though with Birdy, it seems to have done *very* permanent damage. So much as I hate to say it, I'm betting there'll be evidence of a minor stroke or some kind of problem with the inner ear or something . . . it wouldn't be a big surprise, would it?"

The lieutenant smiled fondly at her and rose from his chair

to leave them. But he took each lady's hand in turn and offered it a continental kiss in farewell, which made Angela sigh with delight and Caledonia beam her pleasure. "Come and see us again before Christmas, Lieutenant," she said. "I hate eggnog almost as much as I hate cardboard Santa Clauses and plastic candy canes, but if it'll please you, I'll arrange for eggnog."

"Thank you, dear lady, but your excellent sherry will do fine for me. And I'll surely try to be here again very soon. But you know I can't promise." And he took his leave.

The two women sat in silence for a moment, each with her own thoughts. But those thoughts were widely different, for Caledonia continued to smile contentedly, while Angela's smile of pleasure at the kiss on the hand evaporated, replaced by a tiny frown that grew and grew. "You know, Cal," she said. "We ought to take this chance to talk to Birdy's family. Who knows whether they'll all stay here after they get the body? They might hold the funeral somewhere else, you know. I mean, this may be the only time they'll all be here together, and if we're to interview them—"

"Whaddya mean, interview them? Weren't you listening to the lieutenant, Angela? He didn't expect us to do actual live interviews. Didn't want us to. For our own safety, he said."

"Oh, don't be so silly. How else can we get really useful information for him? And even though you're betting Birdy's death was an accident, I'm still betting on murder! I mean . . . well, that sounds awful. But you know what I mean."

"Of course I do. You're indulging in wishful thinking, and I don't want any part of it!" But in spite of that denial, Caledonia found herself trailing behind the firm, eager steps of her tiny friend as they sailed along the second floor hallway to Birdy Benton's apartment. The door stood wide open and they heard a man's thin, complaining voice from within: "Not a thin dime! This is the most frustrating . . . hey! Don't you walk out on me when I'm talking to you. Babs . . . Babs! You're in this as much as I am, you know . . ." Angela and Caledonia moved cautiously toward the apartment door and Angela knocked diffidently.

Directly across the hallway was another open door, and from that darkened room came the faint sounds of a tinny Latin voice: *Lucy, chu an' Ethel can't be een da show*, followed by a woman's high-pitched wail, *Ricky-y-y-yyyy . . . plea-ea-ease* . . . Angela waved a greeting toward that dark room, and Caledonia thought that, deep in the gloom, she saw a pale hand wave in return. Then they both turned their attention toward the Benton apartment. After a moment's silence they heard a man's voice offering a rather pinched "Yes? Who is it? Come in," and they accepted the grudging invitation.

The apartment was in a frightful mess. The handbags that Lieutenant Martinez mentioned were still lying on the sofa every which way, some linings pulled out and torn, and all the ordinary contents of a woman's purse lay everywhere around them, obviously dumped helter-skelter as the bags were searched—lipsticks, combs, nail files, paper clips, sticks of chewing gum, pencils and pens, and folded handkerchiefs. To the right of the entry was a secretary desk—fake Chippendale—with the bookcase doors above hanging open and books half out or lying on their sides; the writing surface lay open, stacked deep with bills, receipts, canceled checks, and stationery pulled from the pigeonholes, while the drawers below all stood ajar with snapshots, used picture postcards, playing cards and scorepads, small scrapbooks, and what appeared to be account books spilling over each other and onto the floor. In another corner, newspapers and magazines lay in an untidy pile, and it seemed to Angela, entering ahead of Caledonia, that these had already been sorted through, if rather rapidly.

"Though whatever they thought she might have hidden between sheets of old newspapers, goodness knows," Angela said to Caledonia later while they talked over their day. "An awfully unsafe place to hide things, I'd have thought, because somebody would be sure to throw the trash out—including the old newspapers—without checking. I'd probably forget I'd put something in there, and I bet Birdy would have forgotten, too."

"Well, maybe they didn't think of that," Caledonia had

retorted. "They don't exactly seem like a bunch of rocket scientists."

But now, on the scene, neither woman expressed her opinion aloud. Instead, Angela took a slightly social approach. "You remember me from yesterday's lunch?" she began to the bespectacled man who stood up from a hunched position before the bookcase on the far wall. He had been going through the contents of the bookcase, one book at a time, riffling the pages, shaking the books upside down, then stacking each book on the floor in apparent token that its examination was complete. He continued to work, slowly and carefully, but his eyes were on the two women, his brows raised in inquiry, waiting for them to explain their visit.

"I'm Angela Benbow, Mr. Benton. I stopped by your table at lunch yesterday to offer my condolences."

"Well, yes, I do remember, and I've seen you around before, you know—usually in the dining room—when I've been visiting Aunt Bea."

"Aunt Bea? Aunt Bea?" Angela was momentarily confused. ("I thought he was talking about Andy Griffith and Mayberry there for a minute," she told Caledonia later.)

"That's what we called my aunt, Mrs. Benbow. You called her Birdy, I understand, but nobody in the family called her that. Anyhow, what I started to say, I work for a living, so my wife did the visiting for both of us. But I've come sometimes. Like on weekends or holidays. So yes, I've seen you when I was here. Is there . . . I mean, is there something I can do for you?"

"Well, we were thinking . . . this is Mrs. Wingate, by the way. My associate."

"Associate?"

"In investigation. We often help out the police, you see, and in this particular case, we'd been asked to interview some of the residents—"

"Case? I don't understand. What do you mean, *case*?"

"I called this a case, because Mrs. Wingate and I believe Bird—uh, Beatrice was pushed. Or that someone struck her.

Which makes it murder, or at the very least manslaughter. And since we've been told to ask a few questions, we thought we'd talk to you and the rest of the family . . . ask if she'd told you anything about arguments with people here at Camden-sur-Mer . . . ask if she'd told you about any problems or fears or . . ."

"Oh. Oh, I see," Daniel said rather vaguely. "Well, maybe we'd better call my wife in. She's in the other room. Sorting through Aunt Bea's things, you know. She'd answer your questions much better than I would. After all, as I told you, she's visited Aunt Bea more often than I have." He moved to the bedroom door and called "Babs! Babs!" and Babette, his wife, came out clutching a pink crepe slip in one hand, an empty satin lingerie case in the other, both of which she dumped on the already cluttered couch when Daniel told her what the visitors wanted.

"Look at this place!" Babette's voice sounded a knell of despair. "Just look! Not even a chair you can sit down in! Just push those papers off the end of the couch and clear that chair over there, won't you? Those kids . . . how on earth do they think we're going to get this all packed up, when they've dumped it every which way? No sense at all, kids these days. Now, how can I help you?"

Angela explained quickly, and Babette listened, her mouth slightly open. "You believe Aunt Bea was murdered? But I thought—"

"Mrs. Wingate and I are convinced of it. Of course," Angela went on rather apologetically, "your young relatives felt that it was probably an accident caused by negligence."

"Oh, that's just the twins!" Babette said with scorn. "You don't want to listen to them. They were just playing an angle—looking for some way to get money out of this whole thing by suing someone. But that's a lot of nonsense."

"But how lovely!" Angela clasped her hands in delight. "You call them the twins! I do it, too—because they look so much alike."

"Sure. And they even think alike," Babette said scathingly. "Mercenary little twerps."

"Babs!" her husband spoke warningly. "They're family, after all. And you'll give the wrong impression to our guests, who—"

"I'll give 'em exactly the right impression," Babette retorted. "Being family doesn't make the kids any nicer or smarter, does it? I know they invented that business about Aunt Bea slipping on the lobby floor to see if they couldn't gouge a little money out of this place."

"We, on the other hand," Angela dragged the conversation back to her own point, "believe your aunt was killed by someone else. But whether deliberately or . . . well, that's why we came to ask if you had heard her talking about an argument with her neighbors here or—"

"She fought with absolutely everybody," Babette said impatiently. "Every time I came she was complaining about somebody different she'd had a run-in with . . . oh, for instance, your desk clerk. What's her name, with the red hair?"

"Clara? Oh, but—"

"She told me several times that the reason she didn't get much mail was that Clara was stealing it. It was nonsense, of course. Aunt Bea didn't have many friends to begin with, and a lot of those were dying off, you know? She'd reached that age. Well, you know for yourselves. I don't need to explain to older folks like you." She seemed unaware that Angela and Caledonia were both glaring at her. "Well, anyhow, Aunt Bea argued with Clara about it, over and over, and I wouldn't be surprised if that redheaded clerk hated Aunt Bea with a passion."

"We were hoping for something a bit more realistic," Angela said coldly. "Clara's hardly the type to anger easily. So many people here get paranoid and take it out on the help that the old-timers like Clara have learned to ignore accusations of that kind and keep smiling. You'll have to do better than that."

Babette shrugged her narrow shoulders. "Well, then, I don't

know what to suggest. Except, you know, it has occurred to me . . . I wondered if the twins might not have killed her."

"Babs!" her husband said with alarm. "I really don't think it's too good an idea to—"

"No, I mean it," Babette said defiantly. "I wouldn't put it past those two to have been looking to get their inheritance early. It would be just like them."

"Inheritance?" Caledonia's ears had pricked up at the discussion of motive. "They're going to get a lot of money?"

"Well, that's what they think. Tell you the truth, Daniel and I expect to inherit. Well, not her entire trust fund, of course, but probably some little remembrance." You could tell by her smirk that the word *little* was a belated concession to good manners. "After all," she went on, "we were the ones who visited Aunt Bea all the time and ran her errands for her . . . went out to get those sacks of birdseed . . . you should see the bedroom closet! Most women have shoes all over the closet floor, right? Aunt Bea has sacks and cannisters of seed: wild bird seed, sunflower seed, thistle seed . . . all premium quality, too."

"Yes, yes, yes," Caledonia said impatiently. She'd heard quite enough about those birds in the past few days, and she didn't intend to be sidetracked into talking about them again. "Tell me about your suspicions, my dear. Do you really believe that your young . . . what would those kids be? Grandniece and nephew? Second cousins? I never could sort that out. You know what I mean . . . the twins. Do you really believe they killed your aunt?"

"Well . . ." Babette hesitated, but her husband, who had been frowning mightily at her from across the room, took over the conversation.

"Of course she doesn't believe that. She's just talking. Because neither of us likes the kids very much. Our cousins' children. They seem to us to be bad-mannered and self-centered. But I'm sure my wife wasn't serious when—"

"I was too!" Babette had the bit in her teeth. "Maybe not on purpose, but if they gave her a shove and she fell and hit her head, they wouldn't have gone into mourning. And they'd never admit it, either. They'd let her just lie there before they'd run for help and maybe get into trouble. They're spoiled kids, and Dan's right, their manners are simply awful! Look around you at this place. Dan and I are here to sort things into boxes and get them labeled. But the kids seem to be interested in just one thing—finding some cash around the place. They keep saying she has to have been robbed. And maybe they've got a point, because I tell you one thing, I just can't understand what's happened to her jewelry. For instance, Dan's uncle Ben gave Aunt Bea a gorgeous diamond for their fiftieth anniversary, and I don't see it around here anywhere."

"I don't remember ever seeing her wearing a diamond ring," Angela said cautiously. "But then we didn't play bridge in the same group. That's when your hands show the best and when women usually wear their fanciest rings and bracelets . . . when people will notice them. But since we didn't sit across the table from each other, I can't be sure . . ."

"I played bridge as a substitute in her group once," Caledonia volunteered. "And what I remember is that she didn't wear a ring of any kind. Now around here that's really unusual because it's like Angela said . . . we show off our stuff for each other whenever we think it will be noticed. All the gals had on their diamonds and whatnot. And I remember that her hands were bare."

"Well, there you are, you see?" Daniel said. "Not only the jewelry. She owned some lovely ornamental things, expensive things like a Steuben piece, a Lalique vase, a Staffordshire dog, a bisque shepherdess of old Dresden . . . I don't remember what-all. The kids have a point. Something's happened to most of the jewelry and things that she owned."

"But she didn't complain to the management, did she?" Angela said. "I mean, we'd have heard about it, if she did. Granted most of the time when somebody complains that they've been robbed, they really haven't. Generally it's just that they slipped a bracelet into a jacket pocket or laid a ring down on the bedside table instead of putting them away properly, and then the next time they look they can't find the piece.

But when someone comes to help them search, what's lost is found right away. We get a lot of that around here. But we always hear about it. There's so little real news," she explained apologetically, "that perhaps we make too much of such things. But we're interested in each other here. If you see what I mean."

"Be that as it may," Babette said, "the jewelry's missing. At least, so far it is. Maybe it'll still turn up in a pocket of something. I'm working on the closets right now."

"Don't neglect the shoes," Angela said.

"The shoes?"

"Of course. When I want to hide something, I always slide it way down into the toe of a pair of pumps. Nobody would think of looking there!"

Caledonia snorted. "Any second-rate sneak thief would! I've told you a dozen times, Angela—"

"You mark my words." Angela loftily ignored her friend, talking directly to Babette. "You run a finger into every shoe in the closet. Don't be satisfied with shaking them. When I put a diamond ring into the toe of a shoe, I pack it in good with tissue paper . . ."

"Angela, I don't think anyone's the least interested in how you hide things. Only in how Birdy—Beatrice, I mean—how she might have hidden things. Anyway, that's not important. Not to you and me, anyway. I'm concerned about . . ." She stood up again from the chair on which she'd been perching and towered commandingly over Babette, seated on the arm of the sofa. "You said Wilma and Warren are selfish and you wouldn't be surprised if they'd killed your aunt?"

"I'll say it again, she didn't mean a word of that," Daniel put in hastily, ignoring his wife's muttered, "I did too! I meant it!"

"What about that Catherine child?" Caledonia went on. "Is she the same as they are? Do you think she's greedy enough to—"

"Oh sure!" Babette stood up and gathered in the lingerie case and the slip she'd tossed on the couch. "She's combing the place for hidden cash, too. And grousing about Aunt Bea's being so inconsiderate as to die without a ton of money left lying around. Cathy's not usually very vocal about her selfishness—she doesn't talk much about anything, not even herself. But she's selfish, all right, and she adores the twins. Whatever they do, she does—whatever they believe, she believes . . . she's the original tag-along kid, that one!"

"But she wouldn't murder her grandmother," Daniel insisted. "Any more than Wilma and Warren would. I've got enough sense not to accuse—" He bit the rest of the comment off as his wife glared at him. "I guess I'd better get back to work. We don't really have anything to tell you, you know. We're as much in the dark about this as everybody else is. All I know is that I'm going to try to be back at my office on Monday, and I want to have all this sorting and packing done before the weekend's over. So if you'll excuse us . . ."

"We really do need to talk to the youngsters," Angela said, rising and moving toward the hall door. "Do you know where they went?"

"Sure," Babette said, heading back toward the bedroom to resume her own tasks. "They went to the Sundays Shop down in the lobby somewhere, or that's what they said. To buy a lemonade, they said. What on earth is a Sundays Shop?"

"The pink ladies run it. Our volunteers, you know. Profits go to help their work in our health facility," Caledonia explained as she moved ponderously across the room to join Angela in a graceful exit. "They sell lots of little things we run out of all the time and don't want to walk all the way downtown to get. It's three blocks to the drugstore, and I know I'd bite off a broken nail and just get on with my day before I'd walk that far to get a nail file! Anyhow, we have a tiny soda fountain in the shop, and even in winter our pink ladies make fresh-squeezed lemonade to sell there. If the youngsters have gone down there for lemonades, they've made a good choice."

But nobody seemed to be listening as she finished her explanation. Babette had turned and gone back to the piles of clothing she was sorting on the bed and on the dressertops, as Angela and Caledonia could see through the open bedroom door. Daniel had returned to his bookshelves. After a moment's pause, as though waiting for somebody—anybody—to bid them good-bye, Angela and Caledonia, with a glance at each other and a shrug apiece, headed out the door and down the hallway.

"That was downright rude," Angela complained. "You were just answering the question she asked. She didn't need to walk out in the middle of the answer!"

"Yup," Caledonia rumbled out the monosyllable, then glanced over her shoulder to be sure they were far enough from the Benton apartment that her lowest tones would not penetrate the now-closed door. "I almost said something, but I figured it didn't need saying—that Babette and her husband are in no position to complain about the kids' manners. They seem to be obsessed with money themselves."

Angela nodded her agreement. "What's that Daniel fellow doing looking through every book, every magazine, if he's not looking for something hidden in the pages? And what could that be except money? I mean, Birdy wasn't a spy hiding secret plans, was she? It has to be money he's searching for."

"Agreed. It's greed," Caledonia said smugly. "Get the pun? A-greed, it's—"

"Oh, for pete's sake, Cal! I got it the first time! You don't need to explain the joke! Not that it was much of a joke . . ."

And arguing as usual, the two made their way down the hall and into the elevator, then out across the lobby, out the front door and down the breezeway, past the nurses' station and to the Sundays Shop, intent on what they both knew by unspoken consent was their next objective, a little talk with the third generation of the Benton family.

Chapter 8

THE *SUNDAYS* of the Sundays Shop was actually neither *Sundays* nor *Sundaes*. It had originally been called by the unimaginative but accurate name of the Sundries Shop. But in the way most people have, the residents slurred *sundries* into *Sundays*, and at last Torgeson, tired of fighting the inevitable, had a new sign painted to hang beside the wrought-iron gate that locked the inquisitive and the light-fingered out when the shop was unattended. The new sign showed a gooey chocolate sundae but said in bold letters, *The Sundays Shop*, so you could take your best guess as to what the name really meant.

The shop occupied the endmost of three areas partitioned out in a little ground-floor ell just past the dining room, an area that had once housed the old hotel's gift shop and magazine stand but that now accommodated the nurses' station and a small office for the new staff member who bore the title of Manager of Marketing, which only meant that she guided prospective residents around on a sightseeing tour and watched while they signed their contracts, should they decide to move in.

One entered the shop to find one's way blocked by a pair of wire-frame pillars hung with a selection of greeting cards. "Though why our pink ladies seem to think we'd like nothing but cutesy-wootsy cards with soppy messages and pictures of kittens and babies in rompers . . . " Caledonia complained, every time she went into the shop. "What's wrong with a few

94

comic cards? I don't know about you, but my tastes didn't change one bit just because I passed sixty."

On the wall behind the entering shopper hung a pegboard displaying the kind of items one used to call notions, including packs of needles, spools of thread, a variety of scissors; personal grooming items like combs, toothbrushes, orangewood sticks, curlers, hair nets, and shower caps; a small selection of toiletries like soaps, toothpaste, and deodorants; and a limited selection of cosmetics that included pressed powder compacts, mascara, and lipsticks. A stock of newspapers and a few popular magazines lay on a wooden rack near the door. Further into the shop and beyond the greeting cards stood two small tables, their tops cluttered with a selection of the same kind of little gift items one finds for sale in a hospital's shop — miniature teddy bears clutching cardboard signs with cheerful messages like *Get Well Soon* and *Love Is a Fuzzy Bear*; faux-leather coin purses; purse-sized Kleenex holders; key rings with fobs of crudely stamped metal filigree; a couple of coffee mugs with hearts and flowers stenciled onto their sides; plastic picture frames containing pictures of rock stars; and silky pincushions in the shape of giant strawberries.

Across the furthest end of the Sundays Shop ran a small soda fountain fronted by a four-seat counter. A bored pink lady in full uniform—a chubby middle-aged matron—sat behind the counter ignoring her customers and reading a copy of *Soap Opera Digest*. "A grown-up candy striper," Caledonia muttered to Angela as they eased between the racks of greeting cards. "Except her stripes have grown together."

As Babette Benton had said would be the case, Catherine Snelgrove and her redhaired cousins sat at the counter. Their backs were toward the door, so they did not see Angela and Caledonia enter behind them. The girls were fidgety, Catherine folding and refolding her napkin, Wilma fiddling with her straw, bending and knotting it, and drawing a finger around the rim of her emptied glass as though to see if it would make music. It did not. Between them sat Warren, taller than either but with his head bent toward the counter, and from time to time he drew hard on his straw, and the half-bubbling, half-rasping sound of low-level liquid being siphoned rattled through the room. Each time he inhaled a few last drops of his lemonade, his sister scolded and Catherine uttered some small sound of revulsion, which made him snicker with apparent pleasure and repeat his noisy efforts.

"I interrupted," Angela told Caledonia later, "because I couldn't stand the sound effects myself, not because I was sympathetic with those girls. What a rude young man! Didn't his parents teach him anything at all?"

"I beg your pardon," was what she said. "Young people . . . I wonder if we could speak with you for a few minutes."

The three turned simultaneously and registered Angela's presence for the first time, but it was Caledonia who obviously struck them with awe, towering over them as she did, her royal blue satin caftan shimmering in the diffused light from the shop's chandelier, an ornate crystal remnant of the old hotel's glory days, now dusty and hung here and there with small spiderwebs. The chandelier glistened and Caledonia glistened right back . . . satin and pearls and diamonds . . . a commanding figure, and she took advantage of the fact to reinforce her friend's request.

"How about if you stop slurping and annoying your sister and your cousin, young fella?"

"Oh, thank you!" Wilma breathed the words out so softly Caledonia could scarcely hear them, and she chose to pretend the girl hadn't spoken.

"You three come out to the lobby with us where we can talk a minute. We need to ask you a few things." For a wonder, the three young people rose and marched meekly out of the shop as though they were children being commanded to action by their grade-school principal. Caledonia sometimes had that effect on people.

In the lobby Caledonia led the way to one of the many furniture groups, choosing one with a long couch that would easily hold the three cousins and where two smaller and more manageable chairs were available to draw up facing the couch so that Angela and Caledonia could present a somewhat united front. "And set up an adversarial position," Caledonia said smugly later. "I figured the more official the aspect of our questions, the more likely the kids were to be a little intimidated and maybe answer us honestly." They were just a bit over halfway down the length of the cavernous room, so that they were nearer the big Christmas tree—from which the yellow plastic Crime Scene tape had finally been removed—than they were to the front desk, and Caledonia noted with satisfaction the distance from Clara's inquisitive eyes and ears.

"Now, youngsters," she began when they were seated, having assumed command for the moment. "My friend here and I want to discuss your grandmother's death with you. There are a number of things—"

"Mrs. Wingate and I . . . I'm Angela Benbow, by the way, in case you don't remember that I introduced myself to you yesterday at lunch." Angela was not at all content to let Caledonia take over the question-and-answer session. This had been her idea to begin with, as she reminded Caledonia several times later, and it was her prerogative, therefore, to take charge of the inquiries. "In any event, Mrs. Wingate and I are undertaking a series of interviews on behalf of Lieutenant Martinez, because we feel very strongly that your grandmother did not die of natural causes."

"I told you!" Wilma's response was a yodel of triumph. "I told you! Grandma fell because that floor is so slippery, or she tripped over some of those dumb decorations under the tree. Anyhow, it's somebody's fault, and we ought to see a lawyer, because—"

"No, no, no, young lady," Caledonia intervened again. The girl was clearly getting out of Angela's control and needed to be whipped back into line. "You've misunderstood Mrs. Benbow's explanation. In her view—"

"In *our* view," Angela hastily took over, "it wasn't purely accidental either. We think it likely that someone hit or pushed your grandmother. We believe—"

"You think someone killed Grandma on purpose?"

Catherine Snelgrove spoke for the first time, and she had a little girl's tiny voice, breathy and so high pitched that it nearly squeaked—though whether because she was shocked or because her voice was rusty from lack of use was hard to tell.

"You don't really mean that, do you?" Wilma's voice was far more practically pitched, closer to middle C. "I mean, what kind of evidence do you have?"

"What we want from you . . ." Angela simply ignored Wilma's inconvenient question. "What we want from you is anything your grandmother might have told you about a quarrel with someone here. Was there someone who was particularly angry with her? Or did she ever express something like fear? Had anyone threatened her, for instance?"

"Grandma was, like, real feisty," Warren offered. "Or so my folks used to tell me. She, like, you know, fought with a lot of people back when she lived near us in Anaheim, so I guess she fought with a lot of folks here. She might have got a lot of 'em mad at her. But I don't know if they were, like, mad enough to kill her. That's getting awfully mad, isn't it?"

"Oh, most assuredly," Angela agreed. "I'd say that was awfully mad."

There was a moment's pause in the conversation while the young people apparently tried very hard to consider the possibilities, though whether they were thinking of much of anything was doubtful from their blank expressions. At last Warren spoke up. "Isn't it usually relatives who kill someone?" His eyes had narrowed shrewdly, and to Angela he suddenly looked like a redhaired ferret. "I read that somewhere."

"That's probably true, young man," Caledonia said. "Family or friends, Lieutenant Martinez says. Or acquaintances. But more often family. What's your point?"

"I was thinking that possibly Babs and Dan might of . . . like, you know . . ."

"You mean that you suspect your second cousins of murder?"

"Not our second cousins," Wilma said. "They'd be our aunt and uncle once removed."

"Oh no, not our aunt and uncle at all," Catherine whispered. "We've been over this so many times. Didn't we decide they're our grand-cousins?"

"Cousins once removed, I think," Angela said. "Or even second cousins once removed. Or is that plain cousins, but twice removed? Oh dear, it's so confusing . . . Let me see . . . my children's relation to my uncle's children would be . . . well, maybe it's second cousins, because my uncle's children would be my own cousins, so my children would be—"

"What does all this matter?" Caledonia cut the discussion off with annoyance. "You seem to have something to say about the two Bentons upstairs, young man. So go ahead."

"Well," Warren said slyly, "my point was that those two are the only people I know who might of, like, killed Grandma on purpose." He became aware that his sister and his cousin were staring at him. "Well, think about it, you know? We're going to inherit Grandma's estate, Wilma and me. And Catherine, of course," he went on to Angela and Caledonia. "Grandma always told us so, you know? But now Dan and Babs, they're all bent out of shape about it and they keep, like, insisting that when the will's read, they're going to be getting something, too. Not that it's true, of course, but they keep insisting it is. They keep pushing at us about it, and one time Babs got, like, real mad and said that if we three got all Grandma's money, it wouldn't be fair. And she said she and Dan, they'd take it, like, to court. See, what I've heard is they have real serious money problems, and they really need a windfall to, like, maybe bail them out. It was in the paper last week that his company might go under. It was right on the business page. So what I was thinking, maybe Dan decided to, like, you know, cut corners and get Grandma out of the way before her time so he could get her money right now when he really needs it, see? By killing her, you know what I mean?"

"Warren," his sister's tone was one of rebuke, "they're family. How can you say such a thing?"

"Well, family kills family . . .," Warren said. "At least that's what their . . ." he nodded, indicating Angela and Caledonia,

". . . what their policeman says. But you just think about it a minute. Suppose Babs and Dan did really kill Grandma. Then it wouldn't matter whether she'd put them in the will or not. Hey, don't you see it? I mean, like, isn't there a law?" He appealed directly to Caledonia, whose authority had obviously impressed him. "A law that you can't kill somebody and keep money you make out of it?"

"I think that's right, young man," Caledonia said. "A law obviously designed for the protection of the elderly from their greedy young relatives. I read about—"

"That's what I thought," Warren crowed, ignoring her further explanation. "You just take a look at those two, then! Listen, they had a big motive, that's for sure. And I just bet they did it!"

"What about you two?" Angela gestured first to Wilma and then to Catherine. "I mean, do you share Warren's opinion of your cousins? Well, not your first cousins, of course. That would be the three of you right here. Your second cousins. Or is that cousins twice removed?"

"Angela!" Caledonia's rebuke was more a bark than a word.

"All right, all right," Angela went on hastily. "I'm talking about Daniel and Babette. Those two. Do you honestly think they killed your grandmother?"

Catherine shrugged, but Wilma nodded. "Warren's got a point," she said. "They're up there right now going through everything, looking for money she might have hidden, and I think that's really disgusting."

"That's why we left and came down here for a while," Catherine whispered. "We agreed we hated to see them tearing things apart that way for a few dollars. It seems so . . . so uncouth, somehow."

Warren snickered. "Catherine didn't think it was uncouth when *we* were doing it. Of course we didn't find a thing." His voice turned petulant. "I wonder why Grandma didn't have any cash around the apartment? She had a lot of money, I'm positive of that. But I guess we'll have to wait till they, like, do that thing with the will before we can get hold of it."

"You're talking about putting the will through probate," Angela said. "Yes, I suppose you'll have to wait."

"Do you have any other suggestion? Besides Daniel and Babette, I mean," Caledonia said.

"Not really. I mean, we didn't come down here very often," Wilma said, "so how would we know anything about other suspects?" She hesitated as she registered the disapproval on Angela's face. "Listen, it isn't as though we didn't love Grandma. Of course we did. But you've got to admit it's not much fun, just sitting around and talking. And there's sure not much else to do here."

"Of course there isn't! You don't come here for the night life," Angela snapped. "You'd be coming to visit your grandmother."

"Well, we did that. Naturally. Just not very often. And when we did we talked about . . . well, mostly we talked about us, I guess. I mean, she'd ask us about our college classes and what parties we'd been to and how my tap-dance lessons were going . . . And she'd ask Warren about his band . . . he and four other guys have a rock group called 'The Pierced Nipples' ."

"Good heavens!" Caledonia winced visibly.

"Oh, it's a really good group. Real hot. But they're having trouble getting bookings."

"Maybe it's that name," Caledonia rumbled. "Have they ever thought of changing it to something less repulsive?"

Wilma didn't seem to understand the point. She just went on. "That's why Warren wants money. To promote the group, you see."

"And do you have ambitions to be a professional dancer? You said you're taking lessons . . ."

"Oh, no. I don't want to be a dancer. I want to get married to some neat guy and have a house at the beach and . . . well, of course that's all way off in the future, I suppose. When I get Grandma's money, I'll just get a better car. I saw a red Eldorado the other day. . . ." Wilma's voice was dreamy. "And maybe I'll get a few really great clothes. Go shopping on Rodeo Drive, maybe, or in the Paladion, instead of at the

Broadway. Cathy, well, she might want to have a year abroad studying art. She's a painter, you know."

"No. No, we didn't."

"Oh, sure. She's got a few paintings in some local shows, haven't you, Cathy? And . . . well, anyhow, that's mostly what we talked about with Grandma. What we were doing. Because she asked us. And the thing is, I don't remember her telling us much about her own life here."

"You probably didn't ask," Angela said tartly. "Mrs. Wingate and I seem to know a lot more about your grandmother than you kids do." And to all intents and purposes, the interviews were at an end. Neither Angela nor Caledonia objected when the three cousins excused themselves vaguely and wandered off, presumably back upstairs to resume the fruitless search for treasure.

Lunch was a quiet affair. Angela and Caledonia ate Mrs. Schmitt's lamb-and-onion hash with great pleasure, but each was wrapped in her own thoughts till the main course was over and a tiny caramel pudding was served for dessert. "I could stand two or three of these," Caledonia sighed over the first spoonful.

"No you couldn't, Cal," Angela said. "You'd be sick at once. It's far too rich. Especially after a full meal. Don't be so greedy."

"I didn't say I was going to order two or three. I just said I could . . . oh, never mind," Caledonia sighed. "I don't feel all that hungry anyhow. Those kids just about take my appetite away. At that age I was married and trying to make a home while my husband was at sea. I held a job and kept my house and wrote to Herman every day. Those three are still . . . well, they're still kids!"

"Twenty-year-old adolescents. They're so tiresome," Angela said. "I wanted to shake them all. Vigorously. But even though the kids may be rude and selfish, that doesn't mean they aren't good observers. They say Daniel and Babette are greedy, and I believe 'em. They say Daniel needs money, and I believe 'em."

"That whole family's a bunch of . . . a bunch of whatcha-macallits . . . of . . . what's the word I'm looking for?"

"I can't guess from so little information. Egotists?"

"No. Not that."

"Hedonists?"

"Oh, I expect they're that, but that wasn't what I had in mind."

"Well, whatever it is, you're probably right about them. And we haven't learned much we didn't know before, have we?"

"Sure we have. We found out that family will turn on each other in a New York minute. Another thing," Caledonia said, "is that each of them needs money. Or thinks he does. Well, at least we have something to pass on to the lieutenant when he comes back here."

"I know something we shouldn't pass on to the lieutenant though," Angela said, with a sly look.

"Oh? What's that?"

"Cal, haven't you wondered why nobody saw or heard Birdy getting killed? I mean, she was right there at the end of the lobby when somebody beaned her, right? And she staggered and fell dead under the tree, right? And somebody tucked her in further so she wouldn't be found right away, right?"

"Well," Caledonia said, "that seems to be about right. That's the presumption we're working on. So what's your point?"

"Don't be so dense, Cal. You know how far down the lobby we moved with the youngsters to keep Clara from overhearing us. And we still kept our voices down. Because from her vantage point behind the desk, she could have leaned over the desk and seen us, and she would have, too, if she'd heard us carrying on about the murder. You know how curious she is about everything. My point is, the murderer caught up with Birdy there in front of the Christmas tree. But if they had struggled, there was bound to be enough noise to reach Clara's ears. If they had argued, Clara would have heard the angry voices."

"So," Caledonia said, "that means the murder was actually

committed when Clara was on a break or off duty, is that your point?"

"No, no, no! The other desk clerks aren't as sharp as Clara, perhaps, or as inquisitive, but any of them would have heard an argument and a crash. And yet nobody heard a thing. So what does that mean?"

"It means," Caledonia said, after she considered a minute, "that one of our desk clerks is the killer, and that's why they didn't report—"

"No! Of course not. Clara wouldn't harm a fly, and none of the other clerks would either. Dear old Mr. Chisholm who's on at night? Be serious! Or that sobersided young fellow who's studying for exams at the college while he works here? I'm a more likely suspect myself! We know those people pretty well, and they're not murderers. No way."

"I guess," Caledonia said after another moment's thought, "what you're getting at is that the murder must have been done silently. There was no argument, no struggle. The murderer maybe stalked Birdy and certainly took advantage of a moment the lobby was completely empty— except for a desk clerk way down at the other end and out of sight."

"I agree. And that means it was deliberate murder, not something that happened by accident in the middle of a heated argument. But we can't tell that to Martinez."

"Oh? Why not?"

"Because he'd argue that the silence meant that there was nobody else there with Birdy at all. He'd say she was by herself and just had that heart attack they're looking for evidence of, or that she tripped over something . . . I truly don't know what's the matter with the man, but we don't need to give him ammunition for his wrongheaded idea that her death was not murder. It was murder, Cal. It really was!"

Martinez came back to Camden-sur-Mer that same afternoon. He spent some time on the second floor talking to the Benton family, and whether he'd have stopped to see Angela and Caledonia as well he wouldn't say and they couldn't guess.

But as it happened, Angela ran into him as he came down the main staircase to the lobby. She had gone to the front desk to get some of Camden-sur-Mer's fancy notecards.

"Years ago," she babbled to him as they walked down from the main building through the garden toward Caledonia's cottage, "the old luxury hotel had tons of notepaper printed with an artist's sketch of the building up in one corner. Then when this was turned into a retirement home, somebody found this huge supply of the stationery hidden away in the basement. So they give it to us free because the management thinks it's good advertising. I like to keep a supply on hand, and . . . Cal! Oh, Cal . . . yoo-hoo . . ."

They had reached Caledonia's place and Angela called out, both because it was in her nature to be excited and because she wanted to warn Caledonia they were coming to call, just in case her friend had taken a nap or perhaps slipped her shoes off and needed a moment to gather herself and to get those shoes back on. But Caledonia was at the door letting them in almost at once, and the warning had been, it seemed, unnecessary.

"So," Martinez began. "You say you have something you want to tell me?"

"Can't you tell us your news first? I know you must have some, because Clara at the desk told me you'd asked after the Benton family and had gone upstairs especially to see them."

"Good detective work," he smiled at Angela. "Yes, I came by to tell them the body of their aunt . . . their grandmother . . . would be released in just another day or so, and they can go ahead and arrange the memorial or funeral or whatever. There's nothing more medical examination can determine about Mrs. Benton, Doc Miller says."

"Well, what did your Doc Miller find?" Caledonia asked, moving to the bar and the sherry. "I assume," she went on, "that you'll have a tiny—"

"No, I'm afraid not. I'm still working today, and there are rules about that. Another two hours at least before I'll be my own man. But that doesn't mean," he said quickly, "that I can't take a minute to tell you about the case. You've asked what we found out with our medical exam, and the answer is—nothing. Absolutely nothing, I'm afraid."

"Uh-oh ... no heart attack? No stroke? No inner-ear problem? No stomach upset? No—"

"No nothing. She was as healthy as I am. At least considering her age."

"Then what killed her?" Angela asked.

"A subarachnoid bleed, Doc says. You'd call it a brain hemorrhage. Furthermore, she certainly fell and hit the floor, and most likely she hit pretty hard. But hitting the floor probably isn't what killed her. Doc Miller says something in the blunt instrument category would have to make the kind of injury she had. You don't want to hear the grim details of that wound, and not being a medical man myself, I'm not even sure I'd explain them accurately. Just believe me, something hit her on the head, or she hit her head on something. Besides the floor."

"Then it is murder!" Angela cried out. "We were right all along!"

"Well," Martinez said carefully, "it could still have been an accident. There were things under the Christmas tree she could have hit on her way down. The force of her fall against—oh, say the side of that crèche in the Nativity scene—would have created a serious injury."

"Well, so what? It's still a crime to push somebody and have them die as a result, isn't it?"

"Oh, most assuredly, dear lady. But we have no proof that is what happened. No proof at all. We determined earlier there were no bruises or cuts—no sign of a struggle. I told you that. At least for the moment, we've pretty much come to a dead end, even though we haven't found a physical reason for her to fall without being pushed."

"Well, now, we have something to contribute," Angela said. And she recited faithfully from first to last their conversations with the Benton family, the cross-accusations and the unflattering characterizations.

To her disappointment, Martinez sighed and shook his head. "Dear lady," he got to his feet, "if I arrested every unpleasant, greedy member of a family where there'd been a sudden, unexplained death, the jail would be full of nasty people innocent of any crime but their own nastiness. When I said there was no evidence, I meant there's nothing—including what you've told me—that's enough to get a warrant on."

"But you have to look into Daniel Benton's company and whether it's really going bankrupt. And check Mrs. Benton's will to see who really inherits. Oh, and look into that awful rock group to see if Warren really needs money. And the girls . . . well, you must see if Wilma has any debts and check on how much Catherine's art training would run, and . . ."

"Oh, Mrs. Benbow, I intend to do all of that. You don't need to explain my business to me. But it'll have to be delayed for a while. The problem is that the holiday season seems to arouse the blood lust in a number of our citizens. I'm on my way right now to just one of at least ten cases—in this one I'm going to question a man who was caught with his neighbor's body, riddled with bullets, in the trunk of his car right after they'd been quarreling bitterly, a quarrel that was seen and heard by at least ten other neighbors. Now that's what the courts call evidence! Motive, opportunity, bullet holes, witnesses . . . it couldn't be a better case if we'd been standing right there watching. I know you're disappointed, but I can't spend a lot of time right now on a death caused by a wound that might or might not have been inflicted on the deceased by a second party, a case that presents us with no known motive and not a single witness. And in the absence of such evidence, we're treating this death as though it were accidental. Well, temporarily. Till I can take it off the back burner and spend a little more time on it."

After the lieutenant left them, Angela and Caledonia agreed disconsolately that there was time for one small sherry before dinner. "Just for medicinal purposes," Caledonia said. "For the relief of melancholia."

"We started the day with the blues and we've ended with the blues," Angela said. "I was so sure we were getting somewhere, you know. All the enemies we discovered for the lieutenant, all the money-grubbing by the relatives, all that accusing of each other . . ."

"Aaaaaaah," Caledonia sighed, sipping her sherry. "I must admit this helps. Especially when Christmas is approaching so fast. Don't look so glum, Angela. Christmas cheers you up—you adore everything about it. I, on the other hand, really need this sherry to face up to the jolly season."

"You know," Angela confessed, sipping her own golden wine, "perhaps it's as well this case seems to have come to a standstill. I could use the time. I mean, there's so much left to do. I still have to write my cards. And I haven't wrapped any of my gifts."

"Colored papers and ribbons are such a nuisance," Caledonia said lazily. "Why not buy some of those fancy foil bags they sell in the gift-wrap section of the drugstore? Drop the gift in, tie the handles shut, and you've got it!"

"But that's part of the fun—picking an appropriate paper, finding a matching bow, deciding whether to use a single ribbon or possibly twine matching ribbons with each other to make . . . well, you know how nice I make packages look."

"And I know how hard you work. But if you say it's fun . . ."

"It is! I don't understand why you can't appreciate . . ." And in the squabble over gift wrapping and the flush produced by the sherry, part of their disappointment disappeared. They forgot the dead end their case had reached, and they went to dinner feeling quite pleased with themselves and with each other.

Chapter 9

IT MUST have been maybe 11:30, or nearly midnight, when Angela woke from a sound sleep with a start. Was it, she wondered, that there had been an earthquake? They hadn't been shaken awake by a temblor for quite a few years, but like most California residents, she was aware that it certainly could happen, and at any time. Perhaps, she thought, it had been gunfire or an explosion. When the marines up in Camp Pendleton were holding night maneuvers, they sometimes let off a blast that rattled windows and jolted sleepers awake for several miles around. No, she thought, they'd promised in a news release just a couple of weeks ago that they wouldn't make a lot of noise at night any more. The commandant of something-or-other had assured the public they'd practice shooting at each other and blowing things up only during the daylight hours. She waited, thinking the noise or the jolt or the whatever it was would happen again and then she'd know.

It didn't take long. There was a distant shout, a man's voice calling out in apparent distress, "Help. Somebody. Help me!" It was probably a terribly loud shout close up, Angela thought. But it was barely audible to her, for it came from what seemed a long, long way.

"It's that bar across the street," she told herself. Residents with apartments on the front of Camden-sur-Mer alternated between complaining about noise from the Lighthouse, as it was called, and watching as though mesmerized the comings and goings of the bar's patrons, a mixed bag that included

109

unshaven men in torn jeans and sandals; surfers up from the beach and still in their damp swimsuits, with sport shirts—worn because the management insisted—carelessly open to show an expanse of toasted skin beneath; and a few men and women in tailored pinstripes who clutched their briefcases as though they were carrying state secrets. Watching the Lighthouse was more fun than going to the movies, the residents said, provided one didn't leave the safety of one's room to actually cross the street, because there was almost always trouble over there; a fistfight right at the front door, a mugging in the parking lot—the police seemed to stop by at least once every night. A siren would alert Camden-sur-Mer residents that there was to be a show, and the second floor across the front of the old hotel would pop into life. If you looked carefully as the flashing blue light reflected in the front of Camden-sur-Mer, you could see eyes gleaming in the darkness behind every window, where drapes had been yanked hastily aside to afford an unobstructed view. It was well worth being wakened in the night now and then, second-floor-front residents often said. "Beats them reality shows on TV," Mr. Tolliver assured the residents of other parts of the building, whom he considered to be less fortunate in their choice of apartment. "The real thing beats pictures of the real thing every day of the week!"

"That's it, I expect," Angela told herself. "Somebody got himself beat up in the parking lot over there, and the police will be on their way. But I can't remember how long it's been since noise from the Lighthouse got loud enough to wake me up when . . ."

"Help! Can't anybody hear me? Help me!" The man's voice, hoarse with fear or pain, came again, and Angela, now more fully awake, realized the sound was coming not from the front where Camden-sur-Mer faced Old San Diego Highway and the bar across the street, but from the back of the building in the direction of the sea—from the back and from above.

"That's somebody up on the second floor of this very building!" Angela said. "What on earth—" She stumbled from her bed, pulled on a robe, kicked her feet into her fuzzy pink slippers, and headed for the hall.

"Help!" The voice came clearer and Angela was sure now that it was up on the building's second floor, at the far end from her own apartment. "Help!"

There were other people standing around in the hall. The Jackson twins were fussing and fluttering up and down, asking everybody what the problem was and getting no real answers. "I declare, nothing like this used to happen back in Anniston!" one said, and the other assured anyone who would listen that ". . . my daddy always warned us that there would be crime wherever there were more Yankees than Southerners." Trinita Stainsbury, her hair bound in a lime green turban, her body swathed in several layers of lime green organza, was halfway down the hall talking to Tom Brighton. "Of course I heard it," she was saying. "How could I not hear? Who do you suppose it is?"

Angela was not going to waste her time asking any of them what the noise was, since obviously none of them knew. She turned away and, not wanting to wait for the lazy old elevator, climbed the nearby utility staircase, much smaller than the grand staircase at the other end of the lobby but serviceable and possessed of an additional bonus—two landings on which she could pause to catch her breath. Even with the little rests she took, she reached the second floor in less than half the time it would have taken using that aging elevator.

The unknown man was still shouting as she came out of the stairs and into the second-floor hallway, but he was just making sounds now, not using specific words. "Oh! Oh! Oh!" he called. "Oh!" A pause. "Oh!" Another pause. "Oh!"

There were even more people out in the second-floor hallway than had heard and responded on the first floor. Among the others, Angela spotted Mrs. Dover talking worriedly to Carla Wiley. Tootsie Armstrong was just emerging from her own rooms, her hair so perfectly arranged that Angela was certain Tootsie had stopped to brush and comb before venturing outside to investigate the noise. Even old Elmer

Johanson had tottered out of his bed and was leaning in the doorway of his room.

"Should you be up, Mr. Johanson?" Angela asked, pausing in her headlong plunge down the hall toward where the others had gathered. It wasn't that her curiosity had abated. Just that her mother hen instincts were so strong. "Where is your private nurse?"

"Downstairs, I suppose," the old man wheezed. "She generally sits with the regular nurses and gossips the night away when I'm not having a bad spell. Gets pretty lonesome, I s'pose, with me sleepin' most of the time, and she figures I won't miss her. Not too bright that woman, but she's right. Don't need her tonight. I feel pretty good. For me."

"Do you want me to help you back into your bed?"

"Naah. I want to see what's going on just like everybody else does," he said cheerfully. "I ain't ready to go to any dance, but I'm all right. See?" As though to demonstrate his point, he pushed away from the doorjamb against which he was leaning and his body trembled markedly. "Well, I'm wobbly, I grant you. But I ain't goin' back to bed till I find out—"

Just at that moment, the back door of the hallway—the door that led to the steel fire escape and the outdoors—was jerked open, and a man stumbled through, falling to his knees just inside. Behind him came one of the nurses and another, older man, whom Angela recognized as Mr. Dover, the health fanatic who kept opening that back door for the fresh air. Both Mr. Dover and the nurse were flushed with exertion, and Mr. Dover was panting painfully and leaned against the wall to keep himself upright. The hallway onlookers surged forward, babbling questions and exclamations, Angela right with the others. "What's going on?" "What happened?" "Who's the fellow on the floor?"

Angela, as curious as everyone else, didn't need to ask that last question, for even with his thinning hair plastered to his head with sweat and his glasses askew on his nose, Daniel Benton was recognizable to her. Shamelessly she elbowed and wriggled her way into the front rank of spectators so she could see and hear everything.

"Pushed me over the edge. Right over the edge. If I hadn't been lucky enough to catch hold of the railing . . ." That was Daniel, gasping out a tearful litany of shock and outrage. "Tried to kill me. Nearly killed me!"

The nurse was talking at the same time and saying, "If you'd all just back up and give him room . . . The man's had an awful shock. An awful strain. Let him breathe, for Pete's sake, people. Back up here. Back up."

And Mr. Dover was trying to make himself heard above both of them. "Nearly yanked our arms out of the sockets, dragging him back onto the fire escape! He may look small, but he's worse than a deadweight because he kept wiggling and fighting, trying to pull himself back up at the same time we were hauling him in. You ever been deep-sea fishing and hooked a big one? It was kind of like that. We fought him the whole way. Course, he meant to scramble up, not to get away. But he was pulling and we were pulling. . . . Nearly lost him once, but I managed . . ."

"Has anybody called the police yet?" That was Mrs. Dover, getting in her two cents' worth. "Why doesn't somebody call the police? I mean, obviously somebody tried to kill this man . . ."

In the end, the show lasted less than five minutes, with the nurse fussing, Daniel Benton expressing shock and outrage, and Mr. Dover explaining how heroic he'd been. Then the nurse, one arm around Daniel, who leaned against her heavily, lugged the exhausted man down the hallway. "Everybody just go on back to bed," she said as she manhandled her burden into the Benton apartment. "There's nothing else to see. Excitement's over with, and you folks need your rest. Anything there is to find out you'll find out just as good in the morning as tonight. Better, probably, because they'll sort things out by then. I'll take care of notifying the police. Don't you worry." And then she closed the door firmly behind them.

One by one the residents retreated into their rooms, and

Angela retraced her steps toward the stairway. Halfway down the hall, she stopped where Elmer Johanson still stood leaning against his door, a smile of pleasure on his withered lips as he watched the drama wind down.

"Great show, wasn't it?" he wheezed. "Ain't had that much excitement since that Armstrong woman set fire to her wastebasket a couple years ago and the fire department come."

"Was that nurse your private nurse, Mr. Johanson? The nurse who helped rescue the young Benton fellow? She's obviously going to be busy with him awhile, so if you like, I'll help you back into bed."

"Naaw, that wasn't her. My night nurse is a practical. More a baby-sitter than a nurse, you ask me. Don't even wear a uniform. That there's some new woman. I seen her before, though, bringing the medicine tray through the halls at night. You take nighttime medicine?"

"No, I don't have . . ."

"Then you might of never seen her. She's only on nights, best I can tell. I wake up a lot at night, so I know 'em all. All the night nurses. Two at a time on each shift. This one's only been here a couple-a weeks."

"Perhaps I should send for your own nurse. If you want to get back to bed . . ."

"You keep tellin' me often enough that I need to get back to bed, I'm gonna believe you," the old man rasped. "I was watchin' *The Late, Late Show* on TV, but it'll be over by now. Somethin' about a doctor that gets himself hanged for murder and revived by his assistant, only his neck was broke so he walks real funny, with his head held on one side. And he goes around getting revenge on everybody and their brother . . ."

"Oh! I know that one. The doctor was Boris Karloff, wasn't he? And he gets the judge and the prosecutor and the foreman of the jury and all those people up to his house together and locks them in . . . Oh, that was a good one."

"Sure was," the old man agreed. "But I seen it three times already. Maybe more. Don't really need to get back to bed on that account. All the same . . ." He hesitated. "Well, maybe I should. My knees seem to be giving out and I'm a mite shaky. If you'd be a good lady and help me like you offered, I'd be obliged."

"Here, lean on me." Angela put one arm around the fragile waist and Elmer Johanson, with his arm across her shoulder, leaned much of his bony weight on her tiny frame.

"But it was no burden, really," Angela was telling Caledonia the next morning. "I doubt if the old chap weighs a hundred pounds these days, even counting his pajamas and robe."

"Do you suppose," Caledonia said, reaching across the breakfast table for the coffeepot, "that as I age I'll lose weight, too? I can hardly wait!"

Angela had phoned Caledonia just before seven o'clock, inviting her to breakfast to get the latest news and risking the blast of bad temper that might well have greeted her for violating Caledonia's strict rule—never to breakfast before nine o'clock. "In fact," Caledonia had once told her, "I don't intend even to rise from my bed before eight-thirty, unless I get a personal announcement that it's going to be Judgment Day."

All the same, when Angela said there had been an exciting development in the Benton case, Caledonia agreed to meet her in the dining room as soon as possible and managed to arrive in just over twenty minutes. Her face had been washed, but she had neglected to put on any makeup, not even lipstick, and there was a tiny speck of toothpaste on her lower lip. Her hair had been combed, but she had missed one spot in back that still protruded in a frill of tangled curls. She had donned a handsome flowered caftan of polished cotton, but she seemed to have it on backwards—not that most people would have noticed and not that anyone would have dared to comment.

"The only thing I ask," she told Angela as they sat down at their dining table, "is that you don't try to explain your news, whatever it may be, until I've taken in at least one carafe of coffee and maybe one of those big sweet rolls with a lot of butter. Okay?"

After about another twenty minutes, Caledonia had her eyes well open and had ordered up a full breakfast for herself.

"Now, my girl," she said, relaxing back into her chair, "what was it you wanted to tell me that was so important it couldn't wait till a decent hour?"

Angela knew her friend far too well to bother with a comment on Caledonia's sense of time and propriety. She simply launched into a description of all that had happened in the night—the shouting, the rescue of Daniel Benton, his accusation that someone had tried to kill him . . .

"So that's what all that noise was about," Caledonia said. "Here, pass the cream, will you? I've got to take in one more cup of coffee before the scrambled eggs arrive. I heard something . . ."

"Well, you should have. Your apartment is much closer to the action than mine, and I certainly heard that man yelling. I'm surprised you didn't get out of bed and come to see—"

"Well, I tried—I really tried. And pass the sugar bowl. Thanks." Caledonia spooned sugar into her cup. "You know how slow I am getting awake enough to get up, let alone to do anything useful. By the time I staggered up and put on a robe, the yelling had stopped and everything was quiet again. Obviously I wasn't needed. But naturally I hoped you'd tell me all about it today. I just didn't realize it was something that would get me out of bed at—" She raised her arm to peer at her watch. "Oh, glory, it's only just eight now. I haven't been up this early since . . ."

They talked on through Caledonia's scrambled eggs and sausage and an order of toast for Angela, but neither could come to any conclusion about the attack on Daniel Benton. "I think," Angela concluded with her last slice of toast, "that Lieutenant Martinez will have to work out what this means. But now surely he'll believe that this is really a murder case!"

"I couldn't really believe that Aunt Bea was murdered," Daniel Benton was saying to Martinez at just about the same moment. "But this attack has convinced me there really is a murderer loose around here." The night nurse had tucked Benton into bed in his late aunt's apartment, and it was there that Martinez had come to talk to him. But though Benton had snored in exhausted slumber the rest of the night till the very moment Martinez arrived to wake him, his temper was as short as though he were sleep-deprived. "Incidentally, where were you last night? It sure took you long enough to get moving on this. How come you waited till morning? What if he'd come back to kill me during the night?"

"We had men here last night. They looked over the scene of the crime and talked to the night staff. And we had a guard posted at the hall door of this apartment to watch over you. We kept you safe. The guard wouldn't even let your wife in to see you when she came around to check on you." Benton looked startled but said nothing. "We notified her of the accident, of course. Called your hotel," Martinez explained. "I suppose we could have waked you for an interview last night, but that nurse told us you were emotionally exhausted by the ordeal. She recommended we let you sleep. So we did. I hope, Mr. Benton, that this answers your concerns."

"Well . . ." Daniel was still rather obviously grumpy, but he controlled his annoyance grudgingly. "My point was that I wasn't sure Aunt Bea hadn't died accidentally. And I think you felt the same. But the attack on me proves otherwise."

Martinez shrugged. "Now, Mr. Benton, if you'll just start at the beginning and tell me everything you remember from the time you arrived here . . ."

"I'm in full agreement with Daniel Benton," Angela told Martinez later that morning when he stopped by her apartment. "Don't you just *know* that this attack proves Birdy was murdered? I told Caledonia so this morning over breakfast. This should settle anybody's doubts."

Martinez grinned widely. "Quite possibly, my dear lady. And I was certain *you'd* think so. That's why I came by on my way to my next duties. It's going to be a full day for me, but I wanted to satisfy your curiosity and urge you to go slow. I was sure you would have heard about the attack, and—"

"Heard about it! I practically saw it! Well, no, not exactly," she corrected quickly, having seen Martinez' look of amusement change to one of intense interest. "But I woke up the first time Daniel yelled, I'm certain of that. And I was upstairs before they got him hauled back to safety on the fire escape."

"I should have known you'd get right into the middle of things. Well, I'm going to tell you what that Benton man had to say. And in exchange, you can tell me any information you've picked up. Fair enough?" Angela nodded eagerly and didn't trouble Martinez with the knowledge that she had nothing for that exchange, that she had, in her opinion, picked up absolutely no useful data during her midnight foray into the hallways.

Benton, Martinez went on to tell her, had been with his wife in their hotel room down the beach, but he'd found himself unable to sleep. "He wanted to finish the search of his aunt's rooms, because they were still worried about her missing jewelry," Martinez said. So Daniel had tiptoed from his sleeping wife's side and walked the three short blocks to the retirement home. He saw nobody at all on his way upstairs. So as far as he knew, nobody was aware that he was in the building.

"He didn't see anybody! How did he get in?" Angela wondered. "At night all the doors are supposed to be locked except the big front entrance under the canopy. You know that. You probably had to come in that way yourself."

"Absolutely. And I asked about that. He claims he came into the lobby through the garden door. He found it standing ajar."

"The nurses left it that way, I suppose," Angela said. "They make the rounds during the night. Some people need medication and sometimes there'll be somebody taken ill who needs attention, and those nurses leave the door open so they don't have to ring to be admitted every time they come back from the cottage apartments, if you see what I mean. It's dangerous, I think, and the management keeps telling us they've warned the night staff repeatedly, but they do it all the same. But even if the door was open, where was the desk man? The garden door is perfectly visible from the desk. So surely the night man would have seen Daniel as he came in. There's someone on duty all night. Or there's supposed to be."

"Whatever the regulations," Martinez said, "Benton found the front desk empty when he entered."

"Bathroom break, I guess," Angela said with disgust. "They're supposed to get someone to sit at the switchboard for them if they have to go. But they don't always do that, any more than they always lock all the doors."

"I think I'll talk to your management about that," Martinez said. "Carelessness about security could lead to a tragedy. In fact, it nearly did last night."

Daniel Benton had walked straight in through the garden door, seeing nobody at the desk or in the lobby. He'd climbed the main staircase and traversed the hall to his aunt's apartment, unlocked the door with the keys he'd held onto, and worked away at his search for more than an hour without interruption and without any positive results. "If Babs is right about Aunt Bea's big diamond," he told Martinez, "my aunt really has been robbed. We can't find it anywhere in her place."

A lot of Dan Benton's search had been at floor level in the bottom drawers and shelves around the room that had been left till the last by mutual consent and still needed to be examined. His knees were aching and his back throbbed after only half an hour, he told Martinez, and after an hour or so, he could do no more.

"It's not a popular thing to admit these days, I guess, but I smoke," Benton told Martinez. "So I went out the back door onto the top landing of the fire escape. I suppose I could have stayed where I was, but Aunt Bea never let me smoke in her apartment, and it didn't seem right to do it just because she wasn't around to scold me. So I went outside."

But as he stood there, letting his tired muscles unknot and pulling the nicotine deep into his lungs, he heard a small noise behind him. Just a whisper of sound. And before he could react, before he could turn around to see who was there, standing at his shoulder, he was hit hard in the middle of the back. "Two hands, I guess. But who can say?"

"That's nonsense," Angela said scornfully as Martinez

reported the words accurately. "Why isn't he telling you what he felt?"

"Oh, he is, dear lady. As well as he can. Didn't you know? Your back is the least sensitive area on your body, and if somebody were to poke you in the back with one finger or with two fingers or even three fingers, and if they didn't tell you how many fingers they'd used, you couldn't tell the difference. Try it yourself. Say you put on a blindfold. And don't peek. Well, first ask someone to touch you on the back and not tell you how many fingers they're using. You won't be able to guess accurately unless the contact points are many inches apart."

"Good heavens, I didn't know that. Why ever do you suppose that is?"

"Nature's simply protecting you against feeling every wrinkle in your bed sheets, that's all. You'd never get to sleep if your back were as sensitive as, say, your face."

"I never thought about that," Angela said. "Isn't that interesting!"

Martinez glanced at his watch. "I must hurry along. This visit with you is not time I budgeted for this morning, but I really feel I have to tell you what little I know."

"How kind of you," Angela said, obviously pleased. "Because we're part of your team, and . . ."

"Yes, but more because if I don't, you're as likely as not to go off on some half—" He stopped midword and rephrased. "On some alternative theory."

"Well, go on with what you were telling me. You say Daniel couldn't report much about the push itself, is that right?"

"Absolutely right. It could as easily have been two people as one. It could have been one hand, two hands, or even a foot that administered the push."

"That would be an awfully high kick," Angela said doubtfully.

"For you, certainly. But he's not a very big man, so I could have reached his back with one foot myself. By the way, if you ever decide to push someone off a balcony, you should consider doing it with your feet. Your legs are much stronger than your arms, and if you're well-braced, a kick will certainly knock your enemy off his perch faster than a blow delivered with one hand. Or even two."

"So someone hit him in the back—or kicked him in the back—and he went off the edge of the fire escape. And then what?"

"And then, dear lady, he was so busy struggling to save himself, he didn't take note of anything at all. His arm caught in the bottom rail, and he grabbed on with both hands and tried to haul himself back up onto the fire escape. He says he thought he registered a flash of white or pale blue—maybe the clothing of the person who pushed him—but he was squirming and yelling and thrashing about and holding on for dear life, and he didn't even register his rescuers, let alone his attacker. It was much later that he realized the nurse who was helping him to bed was one of the people who'd responded to his cries, and that there'd been someone with her, hauling him back to safety. I'm afraid he's going to be of almost no help at all. And though we'll do what we can, I'd say that unless someone is heavily influenced by reruns of *Perry Mason* and simply shouts out a confession, we probably won't be able to find his attacker."

"Hmph!" Angela's snort was scornful. "Sounds to me like you've given up before you start. Exactly as you've given up on finding out who killed Birdy."

"Now, Mrs. Benbow. I didn't say I'd given up. Just that the investigation is on a weak trail and now rather a cold one, and therefore that I have more urgent things to do at the moment. Naturally if anything new were to develop . . . and new information . . ."

"I bet Caledonia and I could find out more than we have, if we try."

"No. Please don't, Mrs. Benbow. You never believe me when I try to warn you, but your activities might well be dangerous for you. You've already alerted the murderer that you're nosing around."

"Murderer!" Angela chose to ignore the phrase *nosing around* in favor of reacting to the important noun in Martinez' utterance. "Does that mean you have a clue who—"

"No, no, not at all," Martinez said hastily. "But whatever the case in Mrs. Benton's death, accident or murder, there is certainly among the residents and staff here or in the Benton family itself someone who *wants* to be a murderer. And contrary to what I had in mind for you and Mrs. Wingate, you've been letting everybody within earshot know that you're investigating matters. That puts you in a very dangerous position, and I'd be obliged if you stay out of the matter from here on in."

"And of course I had to agree. But I had my fingers crossed," Angela told Caledonia when they met at lunch.

"You should have called me. I was just down in my apartment," Caledonia said. "I'd like to have heard what Martinez said firsthand."

"I just told you!"

"That's not the same. It's always better to hear a report in person, if you can't see the event yourself. I wish you'd phoned me up and—"

"There wasn't time. He only stopped by as an afterthought, he said, on his way to work on something else. Something not related to our cases here. Oh, he'll be back. He'll check people's alibis and so on—the kinds of things policemen always do. But not today. And that means that we can go to work ourselves, without his fussing and worrying . . ."

"He does worry about us, doesn't he?" Caledonia said cheerfully. "Well, it's true you might be at some risk, but me? I'd like to see someone try to shove *me* off a balcony! Say, talking about shoving someone in the back, I want to try that thing about poking you in the back and you trying to guess how many fingers I'm using!"

And to the amusement of the other diners, who had—as Angela and Caledonia had—just finished their excellent ground lamb croquettes with asparagus on the side, the two passed the time till dessert was served trying the touch experiment, giggling like high school girls as they proved over and over Lieutenant Martinez' observation about the relative insensitivity of the human back from the sterno-cleido-mastoid to the coccyx.

Chapter 10

DURING THE next three days, policemen came and went. Lieutenant Martinez appeared in person from time to time and presumably interviewed possible witnesses and suspects, if there were any. But though he smiled at them and lifted a hand in greeting as he passed, he couldn't—or at least he didn't—take the time to talk with Angela and Caledonia. Doc Carter, the house physician for Camden-sur-Mer's nursing home facility, bustled in and out again, and Clara told the residents that Carter had declared Daniel Benton undamaged by his ordeal. In fact Daniel had moved back to his hotel room, returning to his aunt's apartment only during normal daylight hours to work on the job of sorting and packing or discarding. The rest of the Benton clan worked with him, and one after another the family members appeared carrying or dragging cardboard boxes to a large rental van until the apartment was emptied of its smaller contents. The larger pieces of furniture were donated to Camden-sur-Mer to use in guest quarters or to sell—"We couldn't get much for 'em, and it'll make a good tax write-off," Daniel told Clara when she expressed surprise at the gesture—and by the end of that week, the apartment stood empty, ready for workmen to repaint the walls and replace carpeting and drapes to the specifications of a new tenant.

"I'm not going to miss that bunch," Clara told the residents who stopped by the desk to chat. "They couldn't just pack and go. Reminded me of Birdy, always accusing and finger-pointing. Not to speak ill of the dead, of course."

"Accusing?" Angela said with obvious interest. "They accused you of . . ."

"No, not me particularly—just an unspecified somebody. They sent that kid down, that redheaded boy, over and over again to ask about some piece of jewelry or some ornament they thought she should have had that they couldn't find."

Warren asked about the diamond, of course, and one or the other of the family mentioned it to Clara—and to everybody else they spoke to—at every opportunity. But there were other things, they insisted. For instance, the large Steuben piece they'd asked about before. "Cost Grandpa over five thousand dollars for that chunk of glass," Warren told Clara. "He thought it was, like, beautiful. Are you absolutely positive nobody reported, like, maybe breaking it?"

"Are you sure she actually had it with her when she moved here?" Clara asked rather tartly. "People clear out their pos-sessions before they move in. Have to. Coming from a four-bedroom house into a two-room apartment means a lot of garage sales and giveaways."

"She wouldn't get rid of that. She and Grandpa loved it. She always used to show that off on top of the mantel back in Ana-heim. Here she put it on top of the TV—we've all seen it there. And now . . . well, now it's missing. Maybe we could get the whole $5,000 back, if we sold it. Maybe even more. I mean, like, don't those things go up in value if you hang onto 'em for a while?"

Clara assured the Benton clan that nobody had reported breaking a glass sculpture. "And our maids would have told us immediately. Because of our liability, you see."

Warren wasn't satisfied with the answer, but it was all he could get, and he had gone back to work with the rest of the family until the job was done and the cardboard cartons of goods were lugged out to their rented van. "You won't leave Camden just yet, will you?" Lieutenant Martinez asked them. It was a brief conversation but one that was overheard by most of the residents, since it took place in the lobby just before lunch when the residents had gathered to chat while they waited to enter the dining room. The family, all five of them, had been headed for the side door for what appeared to be their final exit when Martinez caught up with them.

"I have a job, Lieutenant," Daniel said. "Up in Oceanside. Surely I can return to work. After all, it's not very far, and . . ."

"Give us another couple of days," Martinez said soothingly. "I'll discuss it with your superiors if you like, and I'm sure they'll agree to—"

"No, no, no," Dan said hastily. "I'm self-employed. I guess . . . I guess it'll be okay."

"But, like, we got things to do," Warren whined. "I mean, it's my Christmas vacation. I don't have classes again for four more weeks, and all my friends are home from college too, so there's lots of parties and I got, like, a date for tonight . . . girl from way out in Pasadena, and I can't drive all the way up there just for a few hours to see a movie and get a beer or . . . well, you know what I mean. I thought we could get on home and . . ."

"I suppose," Babette conceded grudgingly, "that we could have a small memorial service for Aunt Bea in the chapel here. For the benefit of her friends here." Eavesdropping residents looked at each other with obvious dismay. It was difficult enough to go to a memorial service for someone they liked— and it happened often enough here. But to attend just for the sake of the family, and to try to look sympathetic as the virtues of the departed were extolled . . . "Oh, I hope they decide against that," Mrs. Dover whispered to her husband.

"I could use the vacation from housework anyway," Babette was saying, and Martinez soothed her with, "Well, in any event, it won't be for long. And I'm sure you're as anxious as we are to find out who attacked your husband. Your uncle," he amended with a nod toward the young people.

"Second cousin," Catherine breathed.

"Cousin once removed," Wilma corrected.

Still arguing the nature of the relationship, the group moved outside the door onto the sidewalk near their van, Lieutenant Martinez with them—unwilling to let them go, even for the moment, until he'd extracted a promise from all five of them not to leave the area—and further discussion was out of the hearing of even the residents whose ears were in perfect working order.

All during those three days after the attack on Dan Benton, Angela and Caledonia had talked long and earnestly to each other and to their particular friends about what they called "our case," but they could come up with no reason for the attack or with a likely suspect. They could think of no one else to interview besides the people to whom they had already spoken, although Angela did think of one more thing they could do to be (as she put it) helpful to the investigation. That same afternoon that the Bentons left with the last of their cardboard boxes, Angela insisted on dragging Caledonia up to the emptied apartment. Reluctantly Caledonia agreed to go over the living room carpeting on her hands and knees, while Angela crawled around the empty bedroom.

"We're looking for that diamond, Cal," Angela said. "So run your hands over the pile of the carpeting. It could have worked its way down through the fibers so you can't see it just by standing and looking. And run your hand all around the edge of the carpeting, near the baseboards."

Grumbling and complaining, Caledonia did what she was told. But no ring was found. The only things of interest that happened were the interruptions. For instance, old Elmer Johanson across the hall tottered out of his bed again and came over to see what they were doing.

"Spotted you on your hands and knees, and I figured you wouldn't of come here to pray," he wheezed. "You lose somethin'?"

Caledonia explained they were looking for clues.

"On the floor of that woman's livin' room? I thought my nurse said she got herself killed downstairs. By the Christmas tree."

Caledonia explained about the ring.

"Oh. Well, good luck," Elmer rasped. "I'd help you, but I can't lean over that far any more without fallin', and I can't bend my knees enough to get all the way down and crawl like you're doin'. And my eyes probably aren't good enough, even if I could get down on my hands and knees." He paused and caught his breath, which had been exhausted by talking without interruption. "Listen, young lady, you gonna keep that ring if you find it?"

"Of course not!" Angela was indignant. "We'll give it back to the family."

Elmer shook his head. "That's stupid," he wheezed. "Keep it yourself! They don't deserve it. They ain't the Waltons, that bunch. Rude and selfish. Don't deserve nothin'," he said again.

"But we couldn't keep it," Caledonia said. "That wouldn't be right."

"Right? What's that mean? Thing is, you get to a certain age, you can do and say anything you want to. Look at me. People never mind a thing I do. They just say, 'Well, he's old' and don't think nothin' of it. You're still young, compared to me, but you're gettin' on. Just do what I do—pay no attention to all those rules you learned when you was growin' up. We deserve some reward just for stayin' alive so long." His voice shook and he leaned against the doorjamb. Obviously the work of delivering a lecture had tired him, and perhaps even the effort of standing upright was getting to be too much.

"Would you like to come in and sit down?" Caledonia said worriedly.

Elmer's staccato wheeze of a chuckle sounded again. "You got nothin' for me to sit on. I'm on my way back to bed anyhow," he added.

"You need some help? Shall I go get your nurse?"

"You sound just like that little bitty friend of yours, always askin' if I need help. Don't you trouble yourself," he went on, turning carefully and starting a slow shuffle out of the room and back across the hall. "My nurse's downstairs gettin' lunch," he said. "But I can get in and outa bed by myself. It's another good day. I been having a run of good days lately. Shoot, on a bad day, I can't even *fall* outa bed, let alone stand up and walk. But today's another good day. All the same, I need to get back. Got a rerun of *The Partridge Family* at two. Kinda stupid, but a whole lot better'n some they got now. What do you s'pose a 'Fresh Prince' is supposed to be anyhow? Give me *The Brady Bunch* any day." He disappeared inside his own door, from which very soon Caledonia could hear a woman's melodic voice complaining, *But kids, how can we get to our next booking if the bus won't run?*

The work went on for a while. Trinita Stainsbury came in once. "To see if that wretched bird-feeding station has been dismantled yet," she said apologetically. It hadn't. She left quickly. Doke Wicker came in as well, seeming as surprised to see them as they were to see him there. "Measuring for new carpet," he muttered, waving a yardstick. "Folks at the desk asked me. Got nothin' else to do right this minute . . ." He glowered and then left. "I'll come back when you're finished with . . . whatever you're doin'," he said, and beat a retreat. Shortly after that, Caledonia gave up the search. At her weight, it was really hard to spend much time crawling, and her knees were scraped by the carpet, while her back was giving off the warning signals that meant *Get me some support—preferably a reclining chair or a bed—and* NOW! If she felt guilty about abandoning her work, the guilt evaporated when Angela came out of the bedroom at almost the same time panting, "I really can't do much more of this. Once around the room is all I can do, bent nearly double. How about you?"

It was a pleasant afternoon for December, and by mutual consent the women took the elevator down to the ground floor, crossed the lobby, and went out into the garden. "The gazebo?" Angela asked. And Caledonia nodded. It took the two several minutes of sitting and breathing deeply to begin to feel like themselves. And it took several minutes of talk before they dispiritedly agreed that they were getting absolutely nowhere.

"If I could think of anything else to do," Caledonia said, "I'd do it. But we may have a puzzle here that has absolutely no solution at all. At least, not one we can find. And if that's the case, I guess our work as deputy policemen is finished for the time being."

"Perhaps it's as well," Angela said mournfully. "I was thinking while I was crawling around up there that I really don't have the time to spare for helping the police investigation. I mean, this happened at the worst possible time of year for me. I've got my Christmas to prepare, and time is getting shorter and shorter."

Caledonia's snort made Angela flinch. "I know, I know," she said defensively. "You think I'm demented to make such a big deal of Christmas, but Cal, you have presents to wrap yourself. I'm positive you do. I mean . . . you do, don't you?"

"Don't be so coy," Caledonia said. "If you want to know whether I bought you a gift this year, just say so. And before you ask, yes, I did. But as for wrapping, well, I thought I'd wrap all my gifts in old newspaper this year. I hate all this tomfoolery so much, I don't want to waste a thin dime on red and green foil and ribbon. And have you seen how much they charge you to make the bows for you? Even the little ones you buy in sacks of two dozen at the drugstore. They cost maybe twenty cents each! Folks are spending more to wrap the gift than they did to buy it in the first place! Well, not me, I can tell you. I want the good stuff to be on the inside of the box. If I give a present at all, mind you." She looked at Angela's face and laughed. "Don't pucker up to cry. I already told you I've bought you a surprise. A nice one, too. You'll have something to unwrap . . ."

Caledonia sighed and stretched. Her legs seemed to have unknotted and her back had finally stopped aching. "All the same," she told Angela, "I'm afraid I'm going to stiffen up overnight, and I bet I won't feel so chipper tomorrow morning." And Caledonia creaked to her feet. "Maybe a nice hot soak in the tub will help. Come on down tonight at sherry time."

"You ought to go to those exercise classes with me, Cal. I

keep telling you . . ." And each went on her way to her own apartment.

When Angela opened her door and walked into her living room, she glanced at the two large tote bags standing on the floor near her secretary desk. She had prevailed on one of the handymen to search through her basement storage bin to find the wrapping materials she'd put away there last year, and the bags had been in her living room now for nearly forty-eight hours, rebuking her for her inattention. It was surely time to get to work on Christmas, she told herself. She sighed and set up one of her card tables, then went to her closet shelf and brought out shopping bags full of various brown paper bags containing the gifts she'd bought for her friends. Then she dragged over the wrappings and a straight chair and set to work.

It went slowly, at first, because her mind was still half occupied with the Benton Case, as she called it to herself, the capital letters quite clear in her mind's eye. But gradually as she worked, she became more and more absorbed in the colors and the tinsel and the little gift boxes—choosing, planning, measuring, cutting, folding, tugging, taping shut. One trinket could go into a satin gift box to be held together with a stretchy binding made bright with gold metallic thread. Here was a larger, cube-shaped box that would be perfect wrapped in the modernistic Christmas tree print of red, green, and ice white. And how about this bright blue foil paper to go around a long, rectangular carton? If it were trimmed in a silver foil ribbon knotted to hold a blown-glass ball of the same blue and silver, wouldn't that be handsome? Her clever fingers pulled and twisted and shaped . . . she used up what remained on a roll of Scotch tape and dug another out of her desk to load into the dispenser.

An hour passed, and Angela had lost all lingering sense of frustration at her temporary standstill in the business of playing detective, completely absorbed now in her task, while a pile of wrapped gifts on her coffee table mounted into a satisfying heap of eye-catching glitter and color. She was humming to herself, and at first she didn't hear the sound of knocking on her apartment door. But gradually the sound came through to her. "Oh dear," she said, dragging her consciousness back to the present. "Oh dear . . . I haven't got this bow secured yet and if I let it go, it'll all spring apart. Just a minute, just a minute! I'll be there in a . . . drat, it's slipping and I . . . just a minute!"

Annoyed and fussing, dragging a length of silvery ribbon, several loops of which were still wound around the fingers of her right hand, Angela skittered across the room and yanked open the door.

"Oh, thank the good Lord you're here. I was beginning to think you and Caledonia might have gone on a jaunt." A weeping, slightly disheveled woman launched herself into the room and threw herself into Angela's arms. Or she tried to. Angela stepped quickly aside and threw her free left hand up to forestall the move.

"Trinita," she gasped. "What on earth . . ." For she had recognized, behind the pink, swollen face and the squinched eyes that squirted tears, beneath the hair now dyed a kind of gentle fuchsia that very nearly matched the flushed features of the face, one of her least favorite people in all of Camden-sur-Mer, Trinita Stainsbury.

"All right, come on in," Angela said, guiding her distraught visitor toward an easy chair, then returning quickly to close the hall door against potential eavesdroppers—a list of which would have included every single one of her fellow residents, whose curiosity was almost as keen as Angela's when it came to an emotional situation involving one of their own.

"Here. Wipe your eyes." Angela offered Trinita a carved wooden Kleenex box, a tissue peeping from its top. "And the rest of your face," she added, noting that Trinita was suffering that indignity common to most people when they weep with vigor—a runny nose. While Trinita mopped and sniffled and mopped again, Angela divested her hand of the loops of silvery ribbon with no regret. She could get the loops back any time. A good crisis was well worth delaying everything else.

"Now . . ."

"Oh, Angela, I'm going to be charged with murder! That lieutenant of yours, the handsome one with the wonderful black eyes . . ." Trinita, Angela noted sourly to herself, was never too upset to register a *man*. "That lieutenant is going to accuse me of killing Birdy! I just know he is."

"Oh, surely not. Trinita, you must be imagining things. Why on earth would Lieutenant Martinez—"

"Because he found her Steuben glass sculpture in my apartment! Oh dear, oh dear, oh dear . . ." She was wringing her hands, and the tears squirted out again. "He thinks I stole it. But I didn't. I didn't! You've seen it there, Angela . . . standing all by itself right on the top shelf of my bookcase . . ."

Angela shook her head and bit her tongue so that she wouldn't say what had popped into her head: that since she went into Trinita's apartment as infrequently as possible and then only when she had business, and that since she concentrated on getting in and out as quickly as she could once she was there, she had never allowed herself the leisure to examine Trinita's apartment or its decorations very closely. Instead she said rather vaguely, "I guess I've seen it. I just didn't . . . It didn't register."

"Well, it's a lovely piece, of course. You really ought to examine it closely. It reminds me of Rodin's *The Kiss*, you know, except it's kind of abstract. Flowing lines all blended together, vague shapes . . . but it seems to be a man and woman embracing, except it blends off into a rock and a wave. Oh, you'll have to look at it for yourself. I've got a special light under it and when I turn it on, you'll see how . . ."

"Trinita, get back to the point! I'll see the thing for myself, whenever you like. But I really don't understand. How do you happen to have it?"

"I bought it," she said simply. "I paid Birdy twenty-five hundred dollars for it. It's worth twice that, Birdy told me. I had to talk her down to that, but it was a real bargain. I know that sounds funny to say about twenty-five hundred dollars. But I can afford it, you know. I mean, I have enough money to do what I want and go where I please, except that at my age there's very little left I want to do and nowhere I want to go. I'd rather be here than gallivanting around Egypt on a camel or riding in a howdah on a safari to India's tiger country or freezing myself in Switzerland or . . ."

"Trinita, don't recite the entire itinerary of the latest travel agency brochures. I know you're well off. Otherwise you couldn't afford the fancy clothes you buy for yourself. Or the . . ." she waved a hand at Trinita's head ". . . dye jobs you're always having done. Incidentally, what is this raspberry shade you've got?"

"Well, you said that coppery color I had before didn't suit me. And I've just bought a brand-new suit in magenta crepe. So I thought I'd have my hair changed. Do you like it?"

"I suppose it's an improvement," Angela said. "But that's a side issue. The point is, we've always realized you had money. But you don't need to apologize for buying something you like. I do it myself," she said, waving a hand at a little display case in which stood an array of tiny antique boxes. "But why would that suggest to the lieutenant that you killed Birdy? If *she'd* killed *you*, after you talked her into selling you the statue for half price, that would make sense. But not the other way around."

"But he doesn't believe I bought it!" Trinita wailed. "He thinks I stole it. It was that dreadful family of hers. Those vultures! One of them came past my apartment when the door was open and saw the Steuben. Well, I didn't try to hide it, did I? I mean, why should I? I bought it. But when the lieutenant came to ask me about it . . . well, I can't show him a sales slip or anything. I never thought to ask Birdy for one. Well, I mean, who would? And the Benton family told him that if she really had sold it, she'd have let them know. Especially because it involved such a large sum of money. I showed him my check stub, but when the lieutenant went through Birdy's bankbooks, there's no deposit of twenty-five hundred dollars listed, he says. So the long and short of it is, he doesn't believe me! I'm sure he doesn't! Because he told me not to . . ." She began to weep again. "He told me not to leave town! Just like they always say in the movies!"

"Oh, Trinita, surely not. I mean, he'd never put it that way."

"Well, maybe not, but that's what he meant! And he's trying to find out if I pushed that wretched little man, Birdy's nephew, you know . . . Somebody told him I was up and fully dressed that night! I wasn't! You saw me in the hall, Angela, didn't you?"

"I saw you, but you looked awfully dressed up to me. Some lime green creation . . ."

"It was a negligee!" Trinita protested.

"With a hat?"

"That's just a kind of wrap made of a cheesecloth sort of material that's been dyed to match the robe—much prettier than using a hair net, that's all! I have them in a lot of colors! I wear one to bed every night. To keep my hair tidy." Trinita preened a bit, then remembered where she was trying to go with her entreaty. "Oh, please, Angela. You've got to help me! You and Caledonia have a lot of influence with the police, and I was thinking you could explain to them . . . make them understand that I didn't do anything wrong!"

Angela felt a pang of genuine pity for the woman who sat before her, wriggling and gulping and sobbing and protesting. It was probably the first time she'd ever had anything even approaching a kind thought for Trinita Stainsbury, and she was mildly surprised that she felt regret as she shook her head. "Oh, Trinita, you're mistaken! We can't influence them! Even if we wanted to, Lieutenant Martinez wouldn't listen to us. He'll keep right on working on the case. He's got to investigate every lead, every—"

"I didn't mean you should talk him into quitting. I want them to find out who did this, just like you do. I only meant, couldn't you explain to him how I am? You remember the time I bought Tootsie Armstrong's gold sequin shoes right off her feet because they matched the outfit I wanted to wear? You remember when Janice Felton got a new bedside table delivered and I bought it from her right in the hallway? She never even got it into her apartment. The delivery man just turned around and brought it over to my place."

"Well, yes, I remember . . ."

"So buying that Steuben was exactly the kind of thing I always do. You tell him that! And as for my being fully dressed the night that Benton man was attacked, well, you can explain to the lieutenant my . . ." she preened again, in spite of herself ". . . my sense of style. Tell him, Angela. Tell him I would never just put on a terrycloth robe and tie my hair up with a strip of toweling or something."

"Well," Angela said, "I could do that, I suppose. I'm not sure how much good it would do, but I'll be glad to try."

"Oh, do, Angela! Please do! I don't want to go to jail just because I have good taste in art and an eye for a bargain! You can find the lieutenant another suspect, can't you? Please . . . if you'll do that for me, I'll . . . I'll even let you duck out on us one more time."

"Duck out? What—"

"On the third-from-last rehearsal for our little Christmas pageant. It's getting close now, Angela, and rehearsals are in a crucial stage. I mean the performance is next week and we have only three rehearsals left," Trinita said. "And you haven't been to a single one yet. But if you'll help me with the lieutenant . . ."

"Oh, I really can't. I'm telling you the truth when I say I have no influence with—"

"Angela, please!" Trinita wailed. "I'll tell you what. Besides you only coming to two rehearsals altogether, I promise not to use the public-address system in the dining room for a week!"

"What do you mean?"

"Well, I know how much you hate the sound of it. I've seen your face when the speakers snap on." She looked carefully at Angela's face and saw that Angela continued to hesitate. "For two weeks, then. Two full weeks," Trinita coaxed. "No public-address system for two weeks. Please, Angela . . . please . . ."

"Well, what could I do?" Angela said to Caledonia as they sat together in Caledonia's apartment before dinner that evening. "I mean, when someone you know asks for a favor—not to mention that she threw in what I consider a very handsome offer in exchange. So it very much looks as though we're back on the case, and Christmas wrapping will just have to wait."

Chapter 11

"BUT THE question is," Angela said to Caledonia at lunch the next day. "The question is, where do we start? We interviewed practically everybody in the place the first time around, when we were working on the project for the lieutenant."

"Oh, don't be silly. We didn't do any such thing. There must be easily two hundred people that we haven't talked to. Not that there'd be any point in interviewing most of them. Say, pass the catsup, will you? These lamburgers are a little bland. When in heaven's name is Mrs. Schmitt going to run out of . . . say, Chita . . ." The pretty waitress was hurrying past their table on her way to the kitchen, and Caledonia made a long arm to bar her way.

"Won't keep you long. Just want to know what's the deal with this lamb? Ordinarily I love lamb, but we've had it every supper for more than a week, and most lunches. I know Mrs. Schmitt wouldn't do that on purpose, so . . ."

"Don't say I told you," Chita said in a confidential tone, "but Von's market over on Catalpa Street told Torgeson they had a mix-up on deliveries and got triple their usual order of lamb from their wholesaler. Instead of sending it back, they offered half of it to Torgeson for a discount. You know he couldn't resist. Mrs. Schmitt is fit to be tied! You think you're tired of it? She says she's run completely out of ways to cook lamb, and if she doesn't get some beef or chicken to work with, she's going to quit. I don't dare tell her the residents are starting to complain. She's trying so hard . . . but don't worry. The lamb

138

won't last much longer. We're down to just a few dozen pounds." And Chita went on her way with a wide grin.

Caledonia laughed. "I dreamed last night of beef Stroganoff, myself. I find myself thinking about going off to Colonel Sanders' place and buying a whole bucket of . . ."

"Cal, you're off the subject. If we're going to help Trinita, we have to make plans."

"Okay, okay . . . what I think is, we'd better look over our notes and talk through our ideas. See if there isn't anything we've missed. If not, well, maybe we'll end up talking to all two hundred residents and staff after all."

It wasn't much of an idea, but it was all they could think of between them, so they met in Angela's apartment at about two-thirty—after Caledonia had taken her obligatory nap. But the business of the afternoon was delayed momentarily while Caledonia expressed her awe at the pile of Christmas presents heaped in bright array on the coffee table, the gifts Angela had already wrapped. Awe turned to amusement, however, as Angela began to burble apologies for the card table that was still set up in the middle of the room, its surface covered with bags and boxes bearing the logos of department stores and catalog order houses, side by side with the reels of ribbon and rolls of wrapping paper as yet unused.

"It's such a mess," Angela began, pushing the card table and its burden off to one side of the room. "But I thought I'd be getting back to it, you know, and what's the use of putting it all away?"

Caledonia shook her head and chuckled. "Forget it. I wouldn't even have noticed if you hadn't said something." And it was true. Her own housekeeping had always been nonchalant (to use the kindest word), and if it hadn't been for the tolerant attentions of Camden-sur-Mer's maids, Caledonia would live in a state of comfortable clutter. Now she just laughed and found herself a place on Angela's loveseat. From a little pocket cunningly fitted into one of the capacious sleeves of her caftan, she brought forth her reading glasses. With the flourish of a magician pulling a rabbit from his hat, she reached into the other sleeve, rummaged through its hidden pocket, and withdrew her tiny spiral-bound notebook—the notebook Angela had insisted she use, "so that we don't forget a single thing. And don't get things muddled."

Angela pulled out her own notebook and cleared her throat importantly, as though she intended to lead off, but what she said was, "You begin, Cal, if you'd be so kind. Because we can get our discussion of your interviews out of the way faster than we can mine. Because I have more of them. Just by accident, of course, whatever you think. Completely by accident. I didn't mean to hog the—"

"All right," Caledonia said briskly. "We've been all over that. I've forgiven you. So let's get on with the notes. And okay, I'll go first. My first interview . . ." She flipped open the cover of her notebook. "My first interview was with Tom Brighton." And as she read through the notes to herself she muttered a series of key words like *computer games* and *bird lime* and *window washing*. She flipped one page, then another, and at last she looked up from her scribbles. "Nothing here that I can see. He told me about the bird problems, of course. But Brighton wouldn't hurt a flea, as you know."

"I agree. No point in even talking about him." Angela wrote his name down on a fresh page in the notebook and put a big *no* beside it. "Go on."

"Well, that afternoon you'll remember that I talked to the Jackson twins." Angela wrote *The Jacksons* in her book and looked up, pencil poised and waiting. "Now there was a chore," Caledonia went on. "All the same, I remember everything those two said, and believe me, they had nothing to contribute that I'd call a lead."

"I thought they told you about Doke Whatsis—"

"Wicker."

"Whatever. And aren't they the ones who said Clara should be regarded as a potential suspect? And they put you onto Trinita as a suspect."

"They sure did. She made no secret of her dislike of Birdy. But 'suspect'? I thought we were on her side in this thing."

"We are on," Angela said with self-righteous hauteur, "the side of truth and justice."

"And the American way! I know. I know. Okay. Just thought I'd make that point." Angela wrote *Ask more questions* beside the name of Doke Wicker.

"Write that same note by Clara's name," Caledonia said. "We haven't asked her anything at all yet."

"But that's so futile," Angela protested. "It's not going to be a member of the staff, you mark my words. It's going to be . . . well, not one of us, either. Not one of us residents."

"You may not think so," Caledonia said. "But look at . . . well, for instance, look at Janice Felton." Caledonia turned her notebook to the last page she'd written before her back began to give her trouble. "It's my opinion," Caledonia said after looking over the notes, "that Janice disliked our Birdy as intensely as anybody else on your list did and maybe a degree or two more. But even though she thought Birdy was full of prunes—and I'd say Birdy felt the same way about her— Janice's complaints were pretty much nullified when Birdy walked out on the Entertainment Committee. All Janice had to complain about after that were those birds, the same as everybody else. So I'd cross her off the list, wouldn't you?" Angela didn't answer. Instead she sighed and wrote a big *no* beside Janice Felton's name on her list.

"And that's it for me, so let's go over your list now," Caledonia went on. "Maybe there's something there."

First Angela wrote down *Mr. and Mrs. Dover*, but no matter how often she and Caledonia went over Birdy's active interference with the Dovers' attempts to bring fresh air sweeping through the second floor, it seemed to the two women that they'd mined the Dovers for all they were worth, and Angela entered another big *no* beside their names. Then Angela added to the list the names of Carla Wiley, who had hated her neighbor's noisy TV, and of Dr. Colquin, the former dentist who lived on the other side of Birdy's apartment.

"I wonder . . . is he really as deaf as he pretends?" Caledonia asked. "That's the only thing I can think of. That somehow maybe he's faking it. I can't imagine why. But you said he never even mentioned those wretched birds that everyone else complained of, and he couldn't hear a problem with the TV . . ."

"Oh, he's deaf, all right. He's so deaf Birdy could have fired off a machine gun in her place without disturbing him, and nothing she said could offend him because he simply wouldn't have heard it. I ended up having to write out most of what I wanted to ask, didn't I tell you that? He was having so much trouble understanding my questions, I had to scribble notes. Actually, he's rather a sweet old chap, you know? Well, except for wanting to talk about the virtues of amalgam fillings versus porcelain and plastic. But all the information I got from him was that as far as he was concerned, Birdy was a good neighbor, and if she ever came out of her apartment except at mealtimes, he didn't know about it."

"Well, obviously that's not true." Caledonia squinted her eyes to indicate that she was trying hard to think things through. "So doesn't his telling us that she kept to her own place kind of make you suspicious? It's so obviously opposite from the way things were. I always get suspicious when somebody tells me something that just plain isn't true."

"But you see, he wouldn't know the difference," Angela said. "I mean, *he* never comes out of his own apartment except at mealtimes. He never goes into the lobby in the afternoon because he can't hear the programs. He doesn't do any committee work, he doesn't join in the sing-along. . . . He pretty much just stays in his own place all day. Being profoundly deaf can be a pretty lonely condition, I'm afraid."

"Okay, so scratch him off the list. But we're running out of suspects, you know. Because Carla complained about Birdy too openly to be a murderer. I mean, people who complain and carry on to anybody who'll listen aren't the type to lurk in dark corners with blunt instruments. Agreed?"

"I suppose so. And Carla Wiley certainly was vocal about her feelings. Anyways, she was much madder at Torgeson than she was at Birdy. I mean, she tried to get the office to do something about the noise—the birds, the TV—and Torgeson kept promising, but the noise kept right on, didn't it? If Carla was the vengeful type, she might have it in for Torgeson. But nobody has tried to kill the Wart Hog, have they?"

"Not lately." Caledonia laughed. "But at one time or other, nearly every resident here has threatened our administrator. He does have a talent for infuriating people, doesn't he? Anyhow, Carla's probably not a likely suspect either. Agreed? Now . . . is there anybody else in your notebook that we should think about?"

"Well, just Elmer Johanson," Angela said, as she wrote *no* beside the names of Wiley and Colquin on her list. "Of course I don't see that Elmer's a legitimate suspect at all, because he's so old and feeble he sleeps all day and . . ."

"No he doesn't. He told you he was feeling so well he was going for a walk down the hall, didn't he?"

Angela looked startled and glanced through her notes. "That's right, he did. How did you remember that? But you know, if he went down the hall, it wouldn't exactly be like taking a brisk walk—more like a brisk totter. I really doubt if he gets out of that bed for more than maybe to go to the bathroom, if that. I mean, he did mention using a bedpan."

"Now wait a minute, Angela. You saw him out of bed yourself one time."

"Oh sure, but he was so weak he was leaning against the door. He would never have got as far as the downstairs so he could argue with Birdy in front of the Christmas tree, even if he wanted to assault her. But he didn't say anything that would lead me to believe he would have. Wanted to assault her, I mean. In fact, he really didn't say much of anything about her, though he was pretty scathing about that argument he overheard between the nephew and his wife out in the hall."

"You know," Caledonia said, "something about that argument struck me as odd, when you first told me. And now that you mention it again . . . Wouldn't you think those two would have better sense than to stand in the hall, right out there, and argue so they could be overheard?"

"Well, to be fair, I don't believe it occurred to them that they might wake Elmer from his nap. After all, his door stands open all day long, and when you have your door standing open, folks generally assume you're wide awake. And he was, as it happens."

"I wasn't thinking of Elmer so much as of Birdy. Isn't it funny they would risk her overhearing them quarreling? She was Daniel's aunt, after all. Family. Wouldn't you think they'd be more careful? I mean, Herman and I never let the family know when we had a dust-up. And we had some bonny fights, I can tell you. Naturally we tried to avoid yelling at each other out in public. But when we just had to talk things over . . . well, I'm sure strangers did manage to overhear us sometimes. But we never let the family know when we argued."

"Why, Cal? I mean, surely family would understand . . ."

"The problem is, family thinks they have to get involved. They always insist on your explaining the whole thing when it's just plain none of their business. And they take sides. They give advice you don't want. At least strangers don't feel free to interfere! And family even give out ultimatums."

"Ultimatums?"

"Sure. You know, like telling you that if you argue and fuss, they'll cut you out of the will. Or like you won't be invited to the family Thanksgiving dinner again. Things like that. So we never ever argued in front of family, Herman and I. And I bet most people try not to. And that's why I thought it was odd that Daniel and his wife would stand right outside his aunt's door to have an argument."

"All right," Angela nodded. "Suppose you're right. What does it mean?"

Caledonia shrugged. "Darned if I know. I just thought it was strange, that's all. I guess we'll have to ignore it, won't we?"

"I guess so—and I don't see that it matters. I mean, I think you're right about family trying to get in on things and taking sides. But so what?"

Caledonia sighed. "You're right. Well, let's get on and finish the list. Something still might occur to us, although all we've got so far is a whole lot of so what. Let's see. You went to see Trinita next, didn't you?"

"And we've agreed not to suspect her, because she's our client." Angela caught sight of Caledonia's amused expression. "Well, what I mean is, we've agreed to help her, haven't we?"

"And we're not one inch further along in doing that, are we? Here it is . . ." Caledonia pulled at a tiny gold watch pinned to her caftan shoulder, and the watch reeled out on a fine golden chain till it was far enough from her for her eyes to focus on it. "It's nearly a quarter to four. We've been talking for more than an hour. And we've accomplished diddly-squat, haven't we?"

"At least we know the murderer isn't likely to be one of us. One of the residents, I mean. And I just don't feel as though it's one of our staff."

"You don't feel . . ."

"It's instinct. What they like to call 'a gut feeling' these days. Such an unpleasant expression. I'll just call it instinct, and you can laugh if you like, but instinct tells me it's just got to be one of the family . . . that dreadful family of Birdy's."

"Angela, I'm not defending them, and I didn't like them one bit better than you did, but surely you're jumping to conclusions on no evidence at all."

"Well, the lieutenant says most murders are committed by family or at least by someone close. And she really didn't have any close friends, so who is there that was close except the family?"

"Well, in a place like this, I should think 'close' could be taken to mean people physically close. At least, that's the way we've been thinking, isn't it? Interviewing everybody who lived near her. We've done all that, but I still feel as though—"

"Cal, that's it! You're right!" Angela jumped to her feet and began to skitter around the room, almost dancing in her excitement. "Close to her! People close to her *physically*! We did miss somebody!"

"What do you mean? We got the people living on either side

and across the hall, and not just on her floor but on the floor underneath. We finished all of them, and—"

"But we didn't! We didn't! We missed the most obvious. Cal, who is there that we haven't even seen, let alone talked to? A group of able-bodied people who are physically capable of beaning Birdy, or of trying to push Daniel off the fire escape. Think!" And when Caledonia simply stared blankly at her, Angela crowed, "The nurses, that's who! The private duty nurses who tend Elmer Johanson! You see, I forgot about them, because every time I've gone to his apartment, the nurse on duty's been out somewhere—downstairs having coffee, or talking to the regular nurses that work here."

"How'd you know where they were, if you didn't see them or talk to them?"

"Elmer said so. He said that's where they usually go when he doesn't need them on hand every minute. And he said something else . . . something about how his nurses see everything that goes on at Camden-sur-Mer. I don't remember exactly because it didn't seem important at the time. But what it means is that even if they turn out not to be suspects, those nurses are worth our talking to. Because who knows what they've seen and overheard? Unless Elmer were in some kind of crisis, his nurse would be sitting around wide awake but kind of bored, see what I mean? And that means she'd be paying attention to . . . well, to whatever was going on around her. So come on! What are we waiting for?" And Angela plunged toward the hall door.

Caledonia stumbled to her feet and lumbered after her tiny friend. "Hey, wait! Wait up! You've got a point. I grant you. But what's the hurry?"

"It's nearly four o'clock. Don't they change shifts at four?"

"I don't know." Caledonia was wheezing with the effort to keep up as Angela raced down the four steps to the lobby, turned a sharp left to the elevator, pushed the call button, and shuffled her feet impatiently as she waited for the antiquated mechanism to grind into life and bring the car to her level, sliding its carved oak door slowly open to let the two inside for the trip to the second floor. "Look, Angela, I know our own nurses go off duty at four, but Elmer's private staff are practical nurses, not even RNs. Their schedules might be different."

"They won't be. You wait and see . . ."

Caledonia was a bit annoyed to find that Angela was perfectly correct. A plump woman wearing a white lab jacket over dark slacks and blouse was just settling into a large armchair beside Elmer Johanson's bed, or so it seemed. At any rate she was adjusting the cushions behind her as Angela and Caledonia entered the room. Then she set her tote bag down on the floor, pulled a half-knit sweater from it, and started counting stitches to find her place. She had glossy black hair done in a thick French braid—her most attractive feature, Angela thought, for she wore her years badly. She may have been younger, but she looked every day of fifty. It's a good thing she's starting to turn gray, Angela thought, because Nature should be kind enough to bleach out that faint black mustache for her.

"Sssshhhh," the nurse cautioned, raising a finger to that tiny mustache. "He's sleeping. He doesn't rest good most nights. Just catches a few minutes sleep, then he's wide awake again. So I like to let him nap as long as he can when he does drift off. Can I help you?" She had carefully put down her knitting, risen to her feet, and tiptoed forward to herd them to the door and out into the hall, staying close enough that she could see and hear if her patient stirred. "The old man's hearing aid is out of his ear, lying on the beside table," she explained, "but we still might wake him. Let's talk out here."

Angela introduced herself and Caledonia and got a pleasant "I'm Betty Goodwin" from the nurse, who pointed to an incised plastic name tag on her own lapel. "Pleased to meetcha. So? What do you need?"

"We're on a semiofficial mission—helping out the police in the matter of Mrs. Benton's death. We're trying to find out what you may have seen or heard that would have a bearing on the crime," Angela began.

"Her that was across the hall? I thought that was death from natural causes."

"Well, some may think so. But officially the position is a bit different," Angela said, hoping the nurse would not notice the odd wording, and apparently she didn't for she merely nodded.

"Okay, so why'd you come to me?"

"Well, I was up here—during my investigations, you see—talking to Elmer. Just the other day. And he said he keeps up on what's going on around here by talking to his nurses. He said you girls hardly miss a thing. So I thought . . ."

"I do notice things, all right." Betty Goodwin was pleased at what she obviously took to be a compliment. "But I'm the night nurse and nothing much goes on around here at night. Well, except of course for Dan Benton being pushed off the fire escape. But things like that don't happen very often, do they? I mean, if you was to talk to Jennie, now . . ."

"Who's Jennie?"

"Jennie Pilgrim. The afternoon nurse. The one that just left here. Didn't you see her on the stairs?"

"We took the elevator," Caledonia said. "Listen, I wonder . . . if I were to hurry to the lobby, is there a chance I might catch this Jennie person before she leaves here? It would be wonderful to get two interviews out of the way at the same time."

"Could be," Betty Goodwin said indifferently. "Lots of times she don't go straight home. She stops to talk to the regulars. Nurses on private duty like us get around to a lot of different jobs in a lot of different places, and we make a lot of friends in the profession, you know—in different hospitals and places like this here. It's nice to see some of the other girls we've met and catch up on old friends and such. I'll go downstairs to the nurses' station myself later on, supposing the old fellow is feeling pretty good."

"Yes, yes, yes," Caledonia said impatiently. "My point was, do you think Jennie might be stopping down there tonight before she leaves? So I'd have time to get to talk to her."

Betty shrugged, making her crisp white jacket rustle stiffly.

"Could be. Hard to say. But you'll never find out standing here asking me." She seemed very pleased with her pert response, and Caledonia was tempted to issue a verbal rebuke but thought better of it and headed back down the hall, disappearing around the corner toward the elevator in a swirl of silk brocade.

"Now," Betty turned her attention to Angela, "what exactly are you trying to find out? Because I'm not sure I know anything that would help. I only got this here job about six months ago, and I didn't see that woman across the hall maybe once or twice that whole time. I saw her nephew more often. He was down here maybe eight, ten, a dozen times. Maybe more, counting the last few weeks just before his aunt died." She hesitated. "I thought he was real nice, you know? Some people act like us special nurses don't have no business being here. But he always stopped to talk."

She hesitated, and Angela, sensing that the nurse was on the edge of saying something more, let her tone ooze and coo, suggesting—she hoped—that she was a potential confidant. "Yes, my dear? Go on and tell me. You realize I need to know everything, but I assure you, I won't tell a soul. Go on."

"Well . . ." Betty took a deep breath, and her double chin quivered slightly. "He's a little . . . well, he's kind of a flirt, you know? In fact, I was awful surprised to find out he was married." She frowned deeply. "Awful surprised!"

"My poor dear," Angela let her voice drip with the syrup of sympathetic understanding. "Don't tell me he led you on!"

"I never did know exactly what that meant, but maybe you could call it that. What it was, I got to looking forward to the times he come to visit his aunt, you know? And I looked forward to standing out here in the hall with him and him talking to me. He treated me pretty nice, and—and—" She hesitated. "I guess I shouldn't tell you about this, really, but sometimes I think I'll just bust apart if I don't talk about it. You see, I'd got to thinking that maybe he and me . . . him and I . . . that we could maybe . . . Well, never mind, because just a couple-a weeks ago I found out about his wife. I guess she must of come here daytimes when I wasn't on shift, because I never seen her before. He used to come here nights—after work, I guess, and before he went home. Anyhow, always by himself, you see? Well, till this one time a couple-a weeks back, they come together. I heard his voice in the hall and I started out to see him as usual, and here he was with this woman. So I says hello to him, and he says hello back, but kind of funny. I guess he was embarrassed, but I didn't catch on right away and I just stood there. Well, finally he had to introduce her to me, and didn't he just stammer and stumble when he did!"

"Oh, you poor thing!" Privately Angela was thinking the woman had to be a complete moron. Any fool could have reasoned that a man of Benton's middle years and henpecked look was a married man. But what Angela said aloud was, "Poor thing! Of course, perhaps he didn't realize—"

"Oh, he knew I thought he was single. And he let me think so on purpose, you know?" Betty's round eyes filled with tears. "It was a real lousy thing to do to me!" She pulled a Kleenex from her jacket pocket and snuffled into it.

"There, there, there . . ." Angela awkwardly patted the woman's chubby arm. "There, there, there . . . perhaps he thought you two were just friends and it wouldn't matter."

"Huh-*uh*!" Betty insisted. "He just figured that if I didn't find out different, he could flirt all he wanted. Have all the fun he wanted. And I could tell he was getting . . . you know . . . he was getting . . ." She hesitated, perhaps out of deference to her audience. "He was getting more friendly," she finally said lamely. "I mean, he'd put an arm around my waist, he'd give a little pat here, a little squeeze there . . . Believe me, I know all the signs, and I bet it wouldn't of been long before . . ." She sighed deeply. "And I'd of said yes, too. That's what makes me so mad I want to . . . I just want to beat on him!"

Angela was uncertain how to approach the obvious connection she saw, but there really was no way to be both tactful and unequivocal in her questioning. So she chose the latter path. "Did you push him off the fire escape?" You couldn't be more direct than that, she told herself. If the Goodwin woman took offense, she took offense.

In fact, the Goodwin woman did no such thing. She mopped away at her eyes and nose with the now-soggy Kleenex and took another deep, steadying breath. "That rotten guy! I wish I had. But I wasn't even here. I mean, I was here in the building right enough, but I was downstairs. Old Elmer was wide awake and feeling chipper that night, so I figured there was plenty of time to go down for coffee with the girls and have a little gossip. I didn't hear the yelling or anything."

"He woke *me* out of a sound sleep. How could you miss all that noise?"

"Well, the nurses' station is in the front of the building and all the way kitty-corner from the fire escape. We sit around there with everybody talking at once and having a good laugh over some of the things patients say and do . . . wasn't a one of us knew anything at all happened. I didn't find out till I got back up here and old Elmer told me about the excitement. So no, I didn't push the scuzzball! I should of, but I didn't." She snuffled again and moaned in self-pity. "You tell me. Why do all my men end up bein' dirtbags like that?"

From inside the open door behind Betty Goodwin there came a noise halfway between a groan and a gurgle. "Uh-oh," Betty said, "he's waking up. I wanna be there in case . . ." She spun around to enter the gloom of Elmer's apartment. "You got anything else to ask," she tossed over her shoulder, "you come back another time, I'm s'posed to be on duty." Angela waved a good-bye, but she wasn't certain Betty even saw.

Chapter 12

CALEDONIA, ON her way to the nurses' station looking for Jennie Pilgrim, found her quarry almost by accident. As Caledonia entered the hall off which lay both the station and the Sundays Shop, Miss Pilgrim was coming from the shop door, a lemonade clutched in one hand. Either Jennie Pilgrim had grown up to match the implications of her name, or she had changed her birth name in later life to match her looks and personality. Her thin face was stern, her lips perpetually drawn tight together, and Caledonia thought she had never seen any person starched quite as stiff as Jennie Pilgrim seemed to be. "She almost creaked when she bent to sit down," Caledonia marveled later to Angela as she reviewed her interview with Elmer's day nurse.

"I was just going into the nurses' station to speak with friends," Miss Pilgrim said primly when Caledonia introduced herself and explained her mission, "but I will be glad to postpone that until tomorrow to speak with you now and answer your questions. Shall we sit down in the lobby?"

Not surprisingly, Miss Pilgrim chose a straight chair and perched on its edge, her ankles in their white stockings crossed demurely, her hands busily smoothing the tiniest of wrinkles from her unblemished white uniform skirt. She became aware that Caledonia was staring at her, and she pinched her mouth even more tightly, on the defensive. "I know a lot of practicals don't wear full nurse's uniform. You'll see some practicals in street clothes, some with bits and pieces of uniforms, like that

Goodwin girl. Very unwise, in my opinion. There are some people who think we shouldn't wear uniforms at all. A genuine pity so many don't. A nurse needs to have authority with her patients. A nurse needs to set herself apart from, say, a housekeeper or a nanny. A full uniform reminds people that we have special training. I once tried wearing a uniform in a soft blue, thinking a colored uniform might be a reasonable alternative. It was not. I looked—I looked like a waitress. And my patient's family treated me like one as well. But I learned from the experience. Never again." And the hands smoothed an invisible fold in the stiff, crackly fabric before they came to rest, folded together in Miss Pilgrim's lap. "And now?" she said brightly to Caledonia. "You wanted to talk to me?"

"I think you understand what we're looking for," Caledonia said. "Anything you've seen or heard that might have a bearing on the death of Mrs. Benton. And before you ask, no, we don't believe it was death due to natural causes."

"I see. It could have been an accident, or . . ."

"Well," Caledonia said, "if it were an accident, someone would have tried to help her or called for help, don't you think?"

Miss Pilgrim appeared actually to try to think about the possibilities. "That isn't necessarily true," she finally said. "Someone might have panicked and left her where she fell. And then, after she died, they'd be ashamed as well as afraid to admit what happened."

"Well, at any rate, that's not our job. Our job is to find who was involved."

"I wish I could be of use to you in your inquiries, but I don't know how I can. I'd just finished my shift. Of course I'd been on duty all that day, but I saw nothing in the least suspicious. I can't recall even seeing her down in the lobby, though I came downstairs myself at least twice during my shift that day, once to stretch and chat with friends, once for lunch."

"Well, you may have seen nothing in particular, but you're a woman of science . . ." Caledonia said, choosing her words carefully. Flattery, she believed, would be the ticket here.

". . . a woman of science," she went on, "who would be a keen observer. And you are certainly more likely than a casual bystander to spot either unusual animus toward Mrs. Benton or a personality type that might lend itself to violence. People who might wish Mrs. Benton ill, if you see what I mean." Caledonia was thinking that Miss Pilgrim was probably the kind of woman nobody ever complimented, and she might respond to pure butter. And in that supposition Caledonia appeared to be correct. Miss Pilgrim fairly basked in the warmth of Caledonia's words.

"Yes, it's true," she said. "I do see things that a lot of people miss. For instance, I can certainly tell you about that family of hers! I've seen them come and go as they visited her and heard them talk in the halls, and—this will shock you, I know—there isn't a one of them that really cared a thing about her. Except for the gifts she could give them."

Miss Pilgrim's eyes narrowed in disapproval, and her thin lips grew even thinner. "The grandchildren are self-centered and out for all they can get. They consider themselves first in all things and their grandmother only as an afterthought. The nephew is just as bad. He came down here far more frequently than the younger people, but he was attentive only because he needs money for some business venture. I'm told he sells insurance or something but wants to have a bigger office in a more prestigious location. So he worked on the old lady, pretending to be so affectionate, pretending to be concerned about her, when all he cared about was her money. And his wife isn't one iota better. She used to fuss over her aunt—or rather, her aunt-in-law—like a loving daughter. But away from her she said unpleasant things, you know. Out in the hall. I overheard her talking to her husband. I wasn't eavesdropping, mind you. She just wasn't careful about what she said and where she said it. Between those two and the grandchildren you have a highly dysfunctional family group and a thoroughly unpleasant lot, as I said before."

"I'm afraid that isn't particularly helpful," Caledonia said.

"We've met the family, and if it's any comfort to you, your assessment of them is an understatement."

"Nastiness ran in the family, of course. I can't say Mrs. Benton was a good neighbor. Not in the least. People living up and down the hall from her were complaining about those birds, though naturally they didn't bother us, being on the other side of the hall. But I can tell you that she played that television loud enough to wake the dead. We certainly took exception to that."

"So you could hear that TV too?" Caledonia said. "Interesting. Mrs. Wiley told us about the noisy TV. But we wondered if she weren't exaggerating a bit. Because nobody else mentioned it."

"Oh no," Miss Pilgrim said importantly. "No exaggeration there. Mrs. Wiley—a very nice woman, by the way—certainly had cause for complaint. It must have been as annoying to her, living right next to Mrs. Benton, as it was to us across the hall. We could pick up the sound even with Mrs. Benton's door closed—which she usually didn't bother to do. I offered to close our door, but Mr. Johanson objected. We like to lie in bed and look at people passing in the hall. We have so little else to entertain us at such an advanced age."

"Why is it," Caledonia said curiously, "that you nurses always say *we* when you refer to your patient? As though singular pronouns were naughty words. 'How are *we* feeling?' Or 'It's time for *our* pills.'"

"Do all nurses do that? Do I? I really wasn't aware . . ."

"Well, it isn't important," Caledonia said hastily. She certainly didn't want to antagonize Miss Pilgrim at this point. "What I want to know is anything else you might have seen or heard. My colleague . . ." She thought that was a nice touch. "My colleague is upstairs right now talking to Mr. Johanson's night nurse, but we both think it likely there was more to observe and overhear during the day than there would be at night. I mean, by nine o'clock people here are all in their own apartments writing letters, reading, and watching TV till bedtime. Miss Goodwin—I think that's her name?" Jennie Pilgrim nodded. "Miss Goodwin won't have nearly as much to talk about as you might."

"That really won't matter," Miss Pilgrim said. Her mouth had drawn down again into tight, disapproving lines, and her eyes were cold. "Betty Goodwin will manage to find something to say, and what she didn't actually see, she'll invent. Your colleague should watch his step. He shouldn't believe too much Betty tells him."

"Really! And it's 'she,' not 'he.' "

"She who?"

"My colleague. Not male. Female."

"Ah. Very good." Miss Pilgrim nodded approvingly. "Women are far better observers and reporters than men are. I'm not sure why that is, but it's true. Perhaps men have more faith in their own powers of deduction and skip ahead of the facts in forming their conclusions. Perhaps men are too arrogant to listen well. But I find that women usually do a better job of—"

"Yes, well, I happen to agree with you, but that's a side issue. What did you mean about Miss Goodwin? You said she had a tendency to . . . to lie about things?"

"Well, not exactly to lie." Jenny Pilgrim's mouth was drawn down into lines of strong disapproval. "But she's not—she's not a reliable witness. Don't take her too seriously."

"Okay. I'll try to remember that. Now, back to you. If you didn't actually see anything suspicious, what about your impressions of Mrs. Benton's neighbors? You said you don't like her family. But what about the people living close by her?"

"I've already told you they didn't like her." Miss Pilgrim rose to her feet in a single motion that should have looked graceful but just looked angular and tense. "But if you're asking me if any of them said they'd attacked her or even admitted they wanted to attack her—well, they did not. Nor did they give me any reason to suspect that they had done so. I'm sorry I can't be more helpful."

"You're on your way home, of course," Caledonia said, heaving herself to her feet. "And I don't want to keep you. But we would like to talk to the third nurse, Mr. Johanson's midnight-to-eight A.M. nurse. Do you by any chance know her name and how to get in touch with her?"

"Her name is Harriet Walsh—Mrs. Walsh—and she lives up in Oceanside," Miss Pilgrim said. "I know her phone number, of course, but I won't give it to you."

"I'm sure it's in the book," Caledonia said. "So why—"

"Because I hope you won't phone her—at least, not just now. She's probably still asleep. That's a hard shift because you have to adjust your whole sleeping and eating schedule, but even if everybody knows you're working nights, there's always something that interrupts you during the day. Salesmen phone, delivery and repair people come to the house, neighbors and friends even forget and call or come by . . . you never get enough sleep. I know because I used to work the late shift myself. The graveyard shift. And that's not so much of a joke, you know. Did you know that most patients who die do so around three-thirty in the morning? There are reasons for that—depressed respiration, low metabolism added to whatever ailment they have—but it's a bit eerie. I couldn't work that shift any longer. Not just because it's so sad to lose a patient, but because of losing sleep myself every night. Or rather, every day. So please don't call her. Try to see her here when she's on duty. She'll appreciate that."

"I'm not quite sure how I'm going to do that," Caledonia told Angela as they compared notes later. "I stay up late every night, but not till midnight. Oh, now and then, if there's a really good show on the late movie . . . but usually I'm in bed by that hour. And as for getting up in time to see her before she goes off duty . . ."

"I can do it, Cal," Angela said eagerly. "I'm always up and finished with breakfast well before eight when Mrs. Walsh is through with her shift. Let me!"

And thus it was that the next morning at about seven-thirty, replete with pancakes and bacon and wide awake after generous helpings of coffee, Angela took the elevator up to the second floor and walked briskly down the hall to Elmer Johanson's door. The gloom inside the apartment seemed forbidding, but just as she stood hesitantly at the door, wondering whether to speak or just to walk in, a bright bluish light sprang to life from somewhere to her right and a mellow male voice sounded: *Radar! Get us more sponges from the supply tent! Trapper, get over here . . . I can't do triage all by myself!* Elmer Johanson was awake and joining the 4077th M*A*S*H unit for another day of meatball surgery near Ouijongbu, Korea.

"Come on in and watch with me," the ancient voice quavered from across the room. "Good episode, this one. Good show altogether, ain't it? Never shoulda gone off the air. Thanks be for reruns, right?"

"Is Mrs. Walsh in there?" Even with the TV going strong and shedding light out into the room, Angela's eyes had not adjusted enough to let her see into the far corner.

"I'm here, ma'am." There was a rustle of movement and Angela could see a heavy, vaguely menacing shape advancing toward her.

"She wants to talk to you about the murder. I'm right, ain't I?" Elmer Johanson cackled, apparently pleased with himself to anticipate Angela's self-introduction. "Listen, you two," he went on sternly. "Mind you do your talking outside. I got my program here and I don't want interference—no female gibble-gabble. You just go stand out in the hall there. Go on. Shoo!"

Mrs. Walsh was now visible to Angela, and forbidding as she might have loomed through the darkness, her shape and size melted into comfortable, motherly proportions as she got near. She wore a navy blue cotton dress with tiny flowers printed on it, the kind of dress another generation of women habitually used for everyday around their homes, the kind of dress Harriet Nelson or June Cleaver would have recognized at once. But two things kept Mrs. Walsh from looking cute and fashionable, like those archetypal television housewives: her roly-poly outlines, far more womanly than girlish, and a full-length apron that covered her from shoulder to hemline and whose huge pockets bulged with all her personal and professional paraphernalia: a stethoscope, a thermometer in a plastic case, a notebook and pen, a collection of pill bottles that clanked together as she moved, and a small pliers and a screw-driver—though the need for the last two Angela could only guess at. Was an LPN expected to repair the mechanism that raised and lowered the bed or something? In addition Angela could see the corner of a newspaper folded open to the cross-word puzzle, the top of a copy of *Newsweek*, the edges of a wax-paper-wrapped sandwich, and the outlines of several quarters (perhaps for the drink machine) and a bunch of keys (probably car keys, Angela thought, which would mean that somewhere in those pockets there'd also be a wallet with a driver's license). Obviously the apron served as a medical bag, purse, tool kit, and briefcase. Therefore, even had Mrs. Walsh been young and slim, she would have seemed stout and stodgy with that laden apron. As it was, the apron and its contents merely accentuated Mrs. Walsh's age, profession, and accu-mulated adipose tissue.

"I'm not sure that I can tell you anything at all," Harriet Walsh said easily, in response to Angela's explanation of her mission. "I don't recall seeing Mrs. Benton but a very few times, and then she was on her way to or from breakfast. She wasn't one of those who can't sleep and prowls the hall."

"Oh? Some of the people up here do?"

"Of course. The older people get, the less they can sleep through the whole night. But I needn't tell you that. Anyhow, I'm almost never lonely all through my shift. Somebody or other will be strolling around, trying to walk off insomnia, and they'll see our light on and our door open and they'll stop by to talk. That deaf old fellow down that way, Dr. Colquin, the dentist. Or Mrs. Dover. She tiptoes out so her husband won't wake up, because he's one who does sleep sound. Of course, we don't sleep well, either." She nodded toward her charge, now laughing jerkily at the antics of the *M*A*S*H* crew. "We wake up and go back to sleep and wake up and fall back asleep all night long. And some nights we can't sleep at all. We've been doing pretty good lately, though, sleeping sound most of the night through, for a change. I've worked a lot of crossword puzzles this last couple weeks while Elmer's been snoozing."

"Anybody in particular seem nervous these last two weeks? Anyone with more insomnia than usual? It occurs to me that if I'd committed a murder, I couldn't sleep well afterward. I'd keep having nightmares."

Mrs. Walsh shook her head. "No unusual patterns. I'm sure I'd have noticed anyone up and about more often than usual."

"How about Mrs. Benton's family?"

"Oh, I don't remember ever seeing a one of them. Well, not till the night when that nephew of Mrs. Benton's fell off the balcony out there. I saw his wife come around—I guess somebody notified her what happened. But I also saw her leave again right away because the police wouldn't even let her in to talk to him. The police told her he was going to be all right by morning and she could see him then. Said he was sleeping and of course he was safe there inside his aunt's apartment. So she just turned around and left."

"She told you all this?" Angela said curiously.

"No, but I could hear her talking to the guard at the door. I missed all the excitement, coming in as late as I do. It was all over by the time I came on duty. I just got in on that little tag end." Her voice was so sad that it was obvious she'd rather have seen things firsthand than hear about them much later.

Angela felt disheartened. Nothing so far seemed worth the effort of the interview. But there was one more thing. "We've had a few ideas given us by your colleagues," she said, being as vague as she dared and hoping Mrs. Walsh didn't challenge her for specifics. "And I'd appreciate it if you'd help me with a general assessment of both of them. How responsible their opinions and observations might be."

"By colleagues I guess you mean the other two girls on private duty for Elmer, don't you? Well, let me think . . . it's hard to tell about other people, of course. But I'd say Jennie Pilgrim would probably give you a fairly accurate report. She's smart as a whip. Trouble is, she's very . . . oh, what's the word nowadays—I hear it on all these talk shows . . . very judgmental.

That's it. Too critical, we'd have said in my day. What I mean is that for Jennie, nobody ever quite measures up. She wants perfection from everybody. She says I'm too fat and too easy-going. She says Elmer is a meddling old fool who's trying to boss everybody else, trying to make the world into a perfect place, like one of his precious TV programs. As if she wasn't trying to do the same thing! But of course she can't see it. She's meanest about Betty Goodwin—calls her a romantic, self-important idiot. Jennie just doesn't approve of anybody at all. Except herself, I guess."

"My associate, Mrs. Wingate, would probably agree with you. But Miss Pilgrim didn't have a lot to contribute that we'd call helpful. We got the most interesting suggestion from things Betty Goodwin said. About a romantic connection with . . . well, with somebody else involved in the case. I don't want to say too much, but . . ."

"You're talking about Betty and that big crush she had on Mrs. Benton's nephew, aren't you? Well, I wouldn't place a lot of reliance on that story, if I were you."

"Miss Pilgrim did tell us Betty Goodwin wasn't completely reliable. She wasn't specific."

"Well, I don't want to be too critical, especially after I just accused Jennie of the same thing. After all, I get along with Betty just fine, because I just let her talk and tell her stories and I don't pay much attention. But the truth is . . ." Harriet Walsh sighed. "Oh dear, I'm going to have to say unpleasant things. The truth is, she makes things up. She's not stupid and she's not a liar. She just . . . she remembers things differently than they happened. Not right away. At first she tells the story like it really happened. Or almost like it happened. But she loves to go over and over things, and every time she tells the story, she makes herself more important in it till she seems to be right in the middle of everything that happens. Like . . . well, let me tell you about one I remember. Do you recall the time food kept being missing from the kitchen?"

Angela nodded. "Mr. Torgeson thought it was certainly one of the kitchen workers, but Mrs. Schmitt swore that all of them were honest and completely trustworthy, and he finally listened to her. They questioned the kitchen people, all right, but they questioned everybody on the staff as well."

"That's right," Harriet Walsh said. "The maids were all upset about it. They say they're suspected all the time and they're sick of it!"

"Look, people around here are always losing some piece of jewelry or getting money from the bank and hiding it away and then forgetting where it's hidden. And the easiest thing, when you can't find your earrings or your billfold, is to blame the maid! But I can only remember once in all the years I've been here that a maid actually did steal something. We have a wonderful staff. And all the more wonderful because they don't get angry when some old darling accuses them of grand theft."

"Well, this time they were really insulted," Harriet insisted. "It's one thing to be accused of theft by someone who's nearly senile. It's quite another thing to have your boss accuse you. Eventually, of course, he went on to question everybody. Us too. The private nurses. You know, there are three of us working for Elmer and three more were working for the late Mrs. Ada Stone, down in the garden apartments, and at the time they had two more working nights in the assisted-living wing. That Mr. Torgeson and his secretary, they questioned us all."

"Didn't you object to being suspected?"

"Of course not. It was only sensible. Besides, it wasn't just maids and nurses they questioned. They called in the whole office staff and the gardeners and the handymen. They talked to the boy who delivers for the drugstore and the paperboy and the soft-drink delivery man. Even the pink ladies and the plumber and his staff who were redoing the bathroom in the guest suite. But you could tell they didn't really think it was any of us."

"Yes, I remember. It turned out to be Mrs. Pender from the garden apartments, didn't it? I seem to recall that people said she thought she was running out of money and was worried about paying her bills here. So she was trying to save money by taking supplies and food for her own kitchenette from the pantries and supply closets here in the main building. It didn't seem like stealing, she said, if she wasn't taking from any one person . . . just from Torgeson and the corporation."

Mrs. Walsh shook her head sadly. "Poor soul. She ended up over in the nursing home section, really not able to care for herself reliably anymore."

"We call it the health facility. It doesn't sound as frightening as calling it a nursing home. Not that it matters what we call it. We'll all end up over there, I suppose."

"Well, anyway," Mrs. Walsh went on, "Betty Goodwin thought it was absolutely fascinating and kept rehashing the story and rehashing it, and every time she told it she got more and more central to it until, about the fifth telling, she was saying that she was right there when old Mrs. Pender tiptoed in with her shopping bag and tried to pick up a bottle of detergent and a big can of V-8 for her own use. Of course, we knew that wasn't true. Betty was right here on duty that night. Our patient was having a real bad time that week, and I don't suppose she left his side for a minute. Anyhow, finally, whenever Betty told the story, the trap was all her idea and she was hidden there, watching, all by herself and jumped out and overpowered Mrs. Pender and called the police . . . all on her own."

"And none of this was true?"

"Of course not." Mrs. Walsh laughed comfortably. "Your Mr. Torgeson may not be any genius, but he's not that silly either. I mean, would you put Betty Goodwin in charge of catching your thief? Especially with her being an outsider around here as she is? All of us LPNs are outsiders in a sense, whenever we work temporary duty, you know. I think that's what bothers her more than anything else. Being an outsider. And you know what else I think? I think she finally comes to believe her own invented version of things." Mrs. Walsh shook her head with maternal concern. "Such a nice girl otherwise. They both are, really, Jennie and Betty. But you see, my point is, you have to be careful of what either of them tells you."

"Revisionists," Angela said disgustedly when she finally

caught up with Caledonia in midmorning to make her report. "And we thought we had a couple of interesting leads!"

"Well, they *are* interesting. Weren't you convinced Pilgrim knew what she was talking about when she said Birdy's family didn't love her at all? And if they didn't love Birdy, then they're more likely than ever as suspects."

"I suppose you're right," Angela said glumly. And then her face brightened. "Yes, I suppose you're right. And the attack on her nephew might be . . ." She hesitated. "Well, I'm not sure, but maybe connected to his little flirtation with Betty Goodwin. Listen! Do you suppose Emma Grant would take us in her car, and . . ."

"Now wait. Remember that Mrs. Walsh said we shouldn't believe what Miss Pilgrim said any more than we should believe Betty Goodwin's tale of being Dan Benton's light-o'-love."

"Light-o'-love?" Angela giggled. "Wherever did you dredge that up?"

"I dunno. In some old play I studied back in school, I seem to remember. How do I know? Isn't it better than calling her a love object?"

Angela's giggle turned to a snort. "Cal, nobody has ever been called a love object! Sex object, maybe. I've heard of that. But love object? You made that up to get me off the track. Don't you want to help Trinita? Don't you think we should interview the Benton family again?"

"Well, it would be okay if they were still here in town, maybe. But they've scattered off to their various . . . the kids are back at home in Anaheim, Clara says. The family home. Or homes. And we certainly don't want to go way up there."

"But we could find Daniel. He and his wife are just up in Oceanside. In fact, he has an office somewhere. We'll just have to look in the phone book to find him."

"Why zero in on Daniel?" Caledonia said. "Why not his wife as well?"

"Because he's the one who was anxious for money—who wanted to promote a loan from his aunt. Besides, I want to ask him about Betty Goodwin. His . . . you know, his flirtation. So I propose we ask Emma Grant at lunchtime if she'll drive us up there."

"Emma? Why . . ."

"You don't want to take the bus up to Oceanside, do you? Emma will be glad to drive us over, provided we pay for the gas."

Chapter 13

Emma Grant's driving had not improved with the years. She had always been cautious in the sense that she refused to exceed thirty-five miles per hour. The problem was that she held to that speed inflexibly on highways and freeways as well as on city surface streets. Furthermore, when she chose a freeway lane she stuck with it, even if somehow she'd got edged into the fast lane, and there she rolled along, hunched tensely over the steering wheel, looking neither left nor right as irate drivers pulled around her, leaning on their horns. Once safely back on the surface streets, she relaxed happily and sat back, but she still kept to her thirty-five-mph rule. Unfortunately, she took thirty-five as the bottom of her speed range as well as the top, regardless of traffic conditions, the presence of pedestrians, or her approach to red lights. Thus the smoothness of her passage was punctuated by sudden stops that bounced the occupants around mercilessly, and because she didn't slow even to corner, she cornered wide, swinging partly into the wrong lane at every turn.

Angela did not seem to mind the violent stops, the racing starts, the corners taken wide, the glares of other drivers, even the frightened looks on pedestrians' faces. She gabbled happily all the way to Oceanside and chattered incessantly as they drove back and forth on the streets of the long, narrow downtown area, searching for the address of Daniel Benton's insurance office.

It had been no trick at all to find his agency in the phone

book, for it was called Benton's Acme Insurance. "Well, that should tell us something," Angela said. "Nobody names a legitimate enterprise Acme anything. Not since Wile E. Coyote started buying those weird devices to help him catch the Road Runner. Don't you remember that every time he buys one of those awful machines that doesn't work, it comes from the Acme Company?"

Their problem in finding the Benton agency was twofold: first, they didn't really know the town and had a hard time locating the street, Milton Eisenhower Avenue; and second, the number they sought—203B—didn't seem to exist. The numbers appeared to jump from the one hundreds to the three hundreds. But at last they spotted a single doorway between two shops with a small sign that said *201–209 Upstairs*.

"I don't know why we didn't see it the first two times we passed this way," Emma Grant complained. "Of course that was your job. I have to watch the traffic. You're looking for the address."

"The Christmas decorations got in my way," Angela complained. "I have trouble with all the wreaths and plastic candy canes on the light poles. I don't know how people concentrate with all the colors and the twinkling lights and the greenery and ribbons flopping around in the breeze. They catch your eye and you can't look past them."

There was another short delay while Emma Grant struggled to find a parking place she could manage. "I don't park parallel," she told them. "It has to be one of those places where cars park slanty-wise to the curb or we'll have to find a parking lot." Neither one seemed to be available in the immediate area, but for a wonder someone pulled out of a place next to an alley, so all Emma had to do was head in and back up again a few feet. And when the time came to leave, she had only to drive forward and turn a little bit to get out into a driving lane. So Emma was happy and Angela and Caledonia could pry themselves out of their seats in the huge old Buick and head toward the door to the 200-level numbers.

Emma refused to join them. "Even with my hearing aid

mended," she said, pushing aside her iron gray hair so they could see that she was once again wearing the device, "I don't pick up on some things, and if I can't follow what's going on, it's very frustrating. I don't want to be a nuisance with my 'What?' and 'Beg pardon?' all the time." She smiled in self-deprecation. "I can do that to you in the car going home when you tell me all about everything that happened. Don't worry about me. I'll be fine. I brought my new issue of *Reader's Digest* along, and I'll just sit and read till you get back."

Angela, leading the way up the stairs, had no trouble locating a door marked *203* followed by *203A Coburg and Sons* on one line, *203B Benton Acme Insurance* on another. That hall door led into a cramped reception area just large enough for a tiny desk and secretary's chair, a typewriter on a rickety metal stand, and one visitor's chair. Four doors led off of the reception area, each with someone's name on it in black paint, but the letters were too tiny for Angela to read at a distance. A pretty young redhead sat at the desk that boasted only one telephone, a Rolodex, and a copy of *People* lying open to an article on a shaggy-maned rock star. The girl was wearing a bright green blazer and a matching skirt so small that it disappeared completely under the hem of her jacket as she sat. As the ladies entered, the receptionist looked up eagerly, but when she saw two aging women she appeared to lose interest.

Caledonia was still puffing hard from climbing the stairs, so Angela took over. "Is Mr. Benton in?" The receptionist examined her own inch-long, plum-colored fingernails with a frown and nodded. There was a pause before Angela realized the girl was not going to speak. "Well, may we see him?" Angela persevered.

"Sure," the girl said, pulling a nail file from her center drawer to saw away at some invisible rough edge on one of those perfectly shaped fingertips. "Door to your far left there." She waved one of her wonderfully clawed hands to indicate which direction she meant by *left*.

"Aren't you going to announce us?" Angela persisted, with increasing irritation.

The receptionist completed her nail maintenance and put the file carefully back into the drawer before she answered. "You want me to get up and walk over there and stick my head into his door and tell him you're here?"

"You don't have an intercom? Or a paging system?" The receptionist shook her head. "In that case, my dear, you just sit right where you are. Don't you trouble yourself one little bit. You might rumple your suit when you sat back down again. Or you might get a run in one of those stockings if you were to brush against your desk. It would be such a pity to disturb you and run that risk."

"Well, thanks. Thanks much. That's real nice of you." The girl smiled radiantly, and it was obvious that Angela's sarcasm had passed several feet over her head.

"Hopeless," Angela muttered. The girl didn't seem to hear, and Angela pulled herself up as straight and as tall as she could manage, given her diminutive size, and stalked toward the indicated door. The receptionist was already engrossed in her *People* article, and Caledonia, who had finally caught her breath, glided majestically along in Angela's wake.

At the last door to the left, clearly marked *Daniel Benton*—as Angela could read for herself, once she got close enough to bring the painted name into focus—Angela hesitated a moment, then knocked. "Come in," Benton's voice sounded in response. "Please come in . . . oh. Oh, it's Mrs. . . . . Beanboy? Mrs. . . . Mrs. Bombay?"

"Benbow," Angela corrected him. She was already annoyed, and he wasn't improving her temper one bit, but there was no point in making an issue of his forgetting her name. "He might have genuinely forgotten," she explained to Emma Grant on the drive back to Camden, "and if he didn't just intend to get my goat, what would be the point in my showing that it made me mad? Give him the benefit of the doubt, I figured. It would start things out on a better footing."

"And you remember Mrs. Wingate, I'm sure," Angela went on. Benton nodded and indicated the two visitors' chairs. Angela and Caledonia seated themselves—Angela quickly,

Caledonia gingerly—and Angela started right out without lengthy introduction. "We do need to talk to you. A few questions have come up. I hope you have a few minutes . . ."

Benton checked his desk calendar and ran a finger down the page, pausing here and there as though checking times. Unfortunately for the credibility of the pretense, however, Angela was at an angle to see that the page had only a single entry, far down the page—indicating that whatever that appointment was, it was scheduled for late in the working day. Angela supposed the little act was Benton's attempt to bolster his own ego by making himself important in the eyes of his visitors, like those businessmen who deliberately keep people waiting even if they have a firm appointment. She'd always hated that. But she was careful to keep silent and merely to look attentive.

"Well, as it happens, I do have a few minutes," Benton said at last, pushing the calendar aside and leaning forward with his elbows on his desk. "But I hope you'll make this short and sweet. You've already talked to me and the others. All the kids, I mean, and Babs. You asked us all sorts of questions, and so did the police. They talked to us two, three times about my aunt, and when I was attacked I must have answered questions over and over. I can't imagine what else we'd have to talk about, Mrs. . . . Mrs. Bonbeau."

"Oh, this is something brand-new," Angela assured him. "New information, I mean, that we thought . . . well, it's only fair to check it out with you before . . . before we draw any false conclusions. You see?"

Benton ran impatient fingers through his straight, thinning hair and sighed. "Very well. Fire away, then. And I hope this will be enough for you. It would be nice to think I didn't have to answer a bunch of useless questions again and again and again."

"Okay. We'll try to get it all in on this visit, then. First of all, what about your new office?"

"What new office?"

"Well, we heard you wanted to open one."

"Oh, of course. You can't blame me, can you? I mean, this

is pretty cramped and the help is ... nonexistent. I need a secretary-receptionist of my own. Someone who has my business interests in mind, not someone who thinks she works exclusively for Coburg and Sons just because they have the most space in the office. If I had a first-floor office in a better location, I'd get more business. But that's kind of like Catch-22, isn't it?"

"Pardon?"

"Catch-22. I mean, I can't make more money till I have a bigger office in a better spot and a better staff. But I can't have that new office and hire a staff till I'm making more money. It goes around in a big circle and there doesn't seem to be a way out."

"Unless you have an unexpected windfall, of course."

"Seems unlikely now," he said unhappily. "When my aunt was alive, she sometimes gave us little gifts of money. She could be generous with her family, when the spirit moved her. So I had hopes of promoting a sizable loan. Now I have to wait to see if I'm in her will. And even if I am, there's going to be a delay getting my funds till the will goes through probate, you know? I'd be lucky if I got out of here and into my own place any time before *next* Christmas."

"I see," Angela said, and pretended to write in her little spiral-bound notebook. ("But you know," she told Emma in the car going home, "what he said made a lot of sense to me. His aunt was worth more to him alive than dead, I think. Even if he inherits a lot of money, he'll have a long wait till he can make use of it. So I wanted to cross him off my list of suspects right then and there. But of course we had another topic to ask about.")

"There's one more matter," she said to him, ostentatiously turning a notebook page and licking the tip of her pencil, to indicate that she was ready to note down his responses. "It's a bit delicate ..."

"No point in tiptoeing," Caledonia boomed. "Are you cheating on your wife?"

Benton blinked rapidly, and his mouth quite literally

dropped open. Angela nearly giggled aloud. ("Authors are always saying someone's jaw dropped with surprise," she said to Emma Grant later. "I always wondered whether that was just a literary device. But you know, it's true. His mouth was actually hanging slightly ajar.")

"What did you say? Am I doing what?"

"You heard me, young fella." Caledonia had assumed her best quarterdeck manner. One couldn't help but understand why, though the late Admiral Herman Wingate had commanded whole battleships with ease, he was in turn commanded by his wife when he came ashore. "No evasions now. We have information that you have been . . . canoodling. Canoodling behind your wife's back."

"Can . . . canoodling? I don't understand—"

"Yes you do!" Caledonia said. "I mean flirting. Carrying on. Playing around. Indulging in what the English call 'having a little slap and tickle.' Lovely phrase, I always thought. In short, having an affair."

Benton had caught his breath and put on an air of dignity. "I can't imagine who would have said a thing like that—"

"Who said it isn't important," Angela said grandly, not to be left out. "But since an affair might have a bearing . . ."

"Why would my having an affair," Benton said cautiously, "have any bearing on my aunt's death? I don't see—"

"Well, perhaps so and perhaps not," Angela said. "But it might well have a bearing on the attack against you, mightn't it?"

"Oh, surely you can't believe that. You can't even imagine my wife being jealous of me, let alone slinking through the hallways of the retirement home to push me off the fire escape. It's ludicrous."

"So is the picture of your affair, at least to me," Caledonia said. "I've learned not to be put off by the most unlikely possibilities. I mean, you want to talk about unlikely . . . how about the woman you chose?"

Benton bristled. "There's nothing wrong with her. At least, not to look at her. She's an attractive woman who—"

"Aha!" Angela was jubilant. "So you do admit you've been having an affair!"

Benton's face fell. "Well, I didn't mean . . . that is . . ." He went momentarily silent, then went on reluctantly, apparently aware that denial was now not an option. "Oh, all right. Since I slipped. I hope your work as investigators means you're honor-bound to keep what I say confidential. What I'm trying to say is that I hope you won't feel you have to discuss my . . . my unfortunate misstep with my wife. Or with anyone else, for that matter, except your superiors. That detective who's in charge. Do I have your word on that?"

"Oh, certainly," Angela said. "Only our investigative team needs to know." That, she thought, was clever wording. *Investigative team* would include not just Lieutenant Martinez, but Emma Grant, who had, after all, been promised a review of their meeting. "Our investigative team," Angela said firmly. "Go on . . ." She held her pencil poised.

"Well, the truth is, my wife and I haven't been getting along so well lately," he began. "She really doesn't understand me." Angela caught Caledonia's eye, and they both sighed. It was going to be an old, familiar story.

"So when this young lady came into my life . . ." Benton went on, "It hasn't been all that long ago. Maybe eight or ten weeks, I suppose. I thought she was good-looking, of course. But more important to me is that she obviously enjoys my company. You see, Babette and I have been married fifteen years. That's a long time. I shouldn't be surprised if my wife thinks I'm boring and dull after all these years. But this young lady laughs at my jokes and really seems to listen when I talk. My wife and I haven't had a good laugh together in I don't know how long. And Babs doesn't want to hear about what goes on here at the office. She just wants to talk about what happened to her during the day. It makes me feel . . . well, as though I really am dull. But this young woman—she actually seems to enjoy my talking about my work. She makes me feel . . . important. And smart. And . . . well, witty." He sighed and fell silent.

"Go on," Caledonia prodded. "Go on. I'm sure you two didn't just talk."

"No, we didn't. All the same, our meetings were quite innocent. I don't know what you've heard, but what I did was, I just took her out to dinner a couple times. And that was it, I swear. We never left the restaurant."

"Out to dinner?" Angela was taken aback. "I didn't know . . . you two went out on a date?"

"I wouldn't call it a date," Benton protested. "Just a bite to eat and maybe a few drinks. Only three or four times. Twice I told Babs I was taking a client out to dinner. But I don't have enough clients here to account for many dinners. That's part of why I quit. Babs would have caught onto the lie pretty soon. Besides, it wasn't right. I mean, I felt . . . well, I felt guilty, even if nothing bad was going on."

"Let me get this straight," Angela said. "You'd go over to see your aunt and wait till your ladylove got off work to go out for a meal? That would be close to midnight, wouldn't it?"

"Midnight?" Benton was clearly confused. "No, closer to five o'clock. Maybe as late as five-thirty. And yes, I told Babs I'd gone to see my aunt, on a couple of those nights Kim and I were going out to dinner. But I never actually went down to Camden. I'm not sure . . ."

"Kim?" Angela asked. "Who's Kim?"

"Kim Clark. Didn't she have her nameplate on her desk as you came through the outer office? We've asked her to set it out every day, but she forgets things. And that's another reason I don't take her out any more. It dawned on me that the girl is not too intelligent, and it's not really very flattering to be thought clever and charming by someone like that. Now, my wife Babs is very bright, and a compliment from her would really mean something. I guess I just finally figured out that what I really wanted was for my wife to laugh at my jokes and compliment my good sense and listen to me—and having Kim do that just wasn't good enough." He paused and sighed deeply. "I've never done that kind of thing before, and I won't try it again. Oh, I don't deny I had ... you know, some romantic ideas about Kim. I don't deny I had ..."

"Designs?" Angela suggested. "You had hopes of turning your platonic little affair into something more?"

"I guess." Benton looked completely downcast. "Sure. What man wouldn't? But I didn't make any major moves, if you know what I mean. And what little I did scared the life out of me. I don't like searching for out-of-the-way places to eat and telling lies. No more. No more."

"Very sensible, young man," Caledonia said. "And I have a piece of advice for you. How long has it been since you asked your wife how *her* day was? How long has it been since *she* saw admiration on *your* face? How long has it been since you took *her* out for a romantic little dinner at some expensive restaurant? Try it. You may get a pleasant surprise. Yes sir, if you want to get, you have to give."

And Caledonia rose majestically, her taffeta caftan rustling around her, and nudged Angela to her feet as well. "Wait, Cal," Angela was protesting. "I haven't asked—"

"That's enough for today," Caledonia said, putting one great hand under Angela's tiny elbow. "Come along, Angela. We'll get back to you if we think of anything else, Mr. Benton."

"But . . ."

"Come on!" And Angela was propelled out of the tiny office ahead of Caledonia, through the reception room, and down the stairs.

"Not so fast, not so fast," she panted. "You're going to make me fall! Did you see, Cal? That girl in the front office had finally put her nameplate out onto the desk. I caught sight of it as you pushed me past. And that was her, all right. '*Kimberly Clark*,' it said. Kim! Why are all the empty-headed little girls with legs longer than their bodies named Kim these days? Or Heather? Or . . ."

"Never mind! My back is aching again—and it hurts too bad for me to stick around here one more minute! I need to get back home, and then we can sort this all out. Come on!"

As they'd promised, they reported to Emma Grant in the car

and swore her to secrecy. "I mean, if it slipped out about his flirting with his receptionist," Caledonia said, "he'd probably get pushed off the nearest balcony again. His wife would be glad to oblige. And this time, maybe, nobody would be around to haul him back."

"Do you think," Emma asked, "that the wife pushed him off the first time?"

"He says the idea is ludicrous," Angela said. "But in my opinion, it would be natural for a wife to lose her temper at a cheating husband . . ."

"But he says he didn't really cheat!" Emma protested.

"Well, she didn't know that, did she? It *looked* like he was cheating," Angela said. "Besides, he may think it's impossible to visualize, but my impression of his wife is that she's a strong, determined woman and she's quite capable of pushing him off the back stairs."

"What about the story you went over to look into? That he was having an affair with one of the nurses?" Emma said. "I didn't quite understand about that. And you haven't mentioned . . ."

"Of course Angela heard the story firsthand from the nurse herself," Caledonia said, "so she can say better than I. But we've been warned the nurse exaggerates."

"You know, have you thought . . . Oh dear!" Emma Grant said, glaring at a passing car as she rolled down I-5 at a steady thirty-five mph, her shoulders hunched and her arms tense. "Why is that man honking at me so loud? I'm in my lane! Anyhow, what I started to say . . . have you thought about that nurse as a suspect? A woman scorned and all that? I mean, if she thought they had a . . . well, what you call nowadays a relationship, and then if she discovered that he didn't think so at all, how mad would she be? You see what I mean?"

"You mean would Nurse Betty Goodwin have pushed Daniel off the fire escape? You know, that's a strong possibility," Caledonia said.

"But why would Betty Goodwin kill Dan's Aunt Birdy?" Angela asked.

"What makes you think the two things are hooked together?" That was Caledonia, skeptical as usual. "Try thinking about them as separate actions—somebody killing Birdy, and then later, and for a totally different reason, somebody pushing her nephew to his death. Or trying to."

"Well," Angela said, "maybe. But that makes it a lot harder to find the truth, doesn't it? So I'm going to keep right on trying to think of somebody who'd have it in for both the aunt and the nephew."

"You do it your way," Caledonia said, "and I'll do it mine. And we'll see. Oh, thank heavens!"

The last gasp of pure relief was occasioned by the fact that Emma Grant had at last taken the exit from I-5 without slowing in the slightest and was headed for Camden's city streets and home. "At least," Caledonia muttered, "we can't get hit quite as hard when both cars are going thirty-five as when one is going thirty-five and the other's going seventy-five! I swear that's the last time I go on a freeway with Emma!"

Chapter 14

"IT'S IMPERATIVE that we talk to you," Angela said, gripping the telephone tightly. "I mean here. Not on the phone." Angela hated talking at any length on the phone, having the illusion that she was generally more effective at explaining things, not to mention at persuading people, in person.

"I grew up," she had reminded Caledonia, while she reluctantly dialed the number, "in an era when the phone was used for business and for emergencies; nobody called up just to chat. So I don't feel as comfortable with the phone as young people do. I mean, I can't imagine phoning long distance unless I have really important news, like somebody died or somebody inherited a fortune. And then I'd make my announcement and get off the phone again. Quick."

"You phone me up just to chat once in a while," Caledonia said.

"Not really. Sometimes I phone to ask if I can come down to your place and chat. I don't chat on the phone. At least not for long."

Now Angela obviously had something she thought important enough to use the phone for, but she still felt as though she should just say what she had to say and hang up. And she still felt that she could make her points much better if she were talking to Lieutenant Martinez face-to-face.

"I wish I could do what you want, Mrs. Benbow," he said. "Come there to listen to what you have to say. But we have a list of things to do that will take us the rest of the week to finish. Can't you give me some idea what it is that you want to discuss?"

"Well, not discuss exactly. More to tell you than to discuss. Or rather, I want to tell you one thing and to ask you another. Or rather, not to ask you exactly. More to explain to you. One thing to tell, one thing to explain. Or perhaps not to explain. Perhaps more to—"

"Mrs. Benbow!" Martinez interrupted as gently as possible, but the need to get back to the point overwhelmed even his ordinarily impeccable manners. "Mrs. Benbow, please. I told you I have a long list of things on my agenda. You're lucky to have found me in the office at all. And I'm only here to pick up a warrant. Swanson's checking our calls at another desk, and in five more minutes, we're on the road to Temecula to arrest a possible serial killer. An onion grower's field hands have been disappearing, and we think—"

"Now who's delaying my getting to the point?" Angela said with satisfaction. "Apparently I'm not the only one who—"

"All right, Mrs. Benbow, all right. I accept my culpability. Now let's call a truce and get back to your announcement and your inquiry. How about the announcement first?"

"Well then, here's the news. Caledonia and I were talking to the special nurses who work for old Elmer Johanson. You know, the elderly gentleman right across the hall from where Birdy lived? Well, one of them claimed to be having a flirtation with Daniel Benton. We thought that sounded promising. Even if it isn't very helpful in discovering who killed Birdy, it might help us find Daniel's attacker. I mean, if he was being unfaithful to his wife, or if she thought he was—well, isn't cheating on a wife a good motive for that wife to do violence to the husband? And how about the lover tossed aside when he returned to his wife?"

"You know, I heard the same rumors you did. About Benton's being a bit overfriendly with Miss ... Miss ... that heavyset, dark-haired nurse. The one who's on duty from four in the afternoon till midnight."

"Betty Goodwin."

"Yes. That's right. Goodwin. Anyhow, what I started to say, Miss Goodwin didn't hesitate to tell me all about her romance. Or I should say, her imagined romance. The longer I talked to her, the less convincing her story became. I decided she had invented quite a lot of the gentleman's interest in her."

"Very perceptive of you. We had to talk to the other nurses and listen to them say how she lied a lot and invented starring roles for herself, before we began to doubt her word. All the same, Cal and I went over to Dan Benton's insurance office today to talk to the other half of the supposed romance, and—"

"You went to see him in person? Good heavens, Mrs. Benbow, I thought I told you not to get personally involved. At least, after you had misunderstood my first instructions to you, I thought it was clear that . . ." He sighed. "Never mind. I should have guessed you wouldn't be content to sit on the sidelines. And since the damage is done, you might as well tell me the results of your visit."

"Now that's the interesting thing," Angela said, and her satisfaction was clear to Martinez, even separated from her by nearly forty miles of fiber-optic phone cable. "Dan Benton was having an affair, all right, but not with Betty Goodwin. With the flibbertigibbet in his office. His receptionist. Kim Something-or-other. He claims it was only a brief fling and that it was already over and done with. And I believed him. I mean, the girl is so vacant, I don't think anybody could stay interested in her for long. My late husband, Douglas, used to laugh at me if I got annoyed when he rolled his eyes at one of those pretty, mindless young girls. He used to say, 'You don't have anything to worry about, in case you were thinking of being jealous. I don't want to trade in a high-quality, long-term investment for a quick profit.' So anyhow, the point is," she went on hastily, aware that Martinez had cleared his throat and was probably on the point of interrupting, "the point is, I'm inclined to believe Dan when he says he broke off his affair shortly after it began."

Martinez let his interest show. "Mrs. Benbow, that situation may be worth my asking a few more questions. And I certainly will look further into Mrs. Babette Benton in regard to the attack on her husband. Jealousy can be, as you say, a powerful motive. And now, I don't mean to rush you, but—"

"Wait, wait! There's my other thing. My inquiry. It's . . . well, Trinita Stainsbury asked me to talk to you about her being a suspect."

"She wants to be a suspect?"

"Good heavens no! Quite the opposite. She *hates* being a suspect and she wants me to convince you she couldn't possibly have killed Birdy."

"Mrs. Benbow, it's very noble of you to defend a friend, but there's really no need. Even if there were a murder, I told Mrs. Stainsbury when I spoke to her that she was not under suspicion. I simply wanted to know how she came into possession of the glass figurine, a Steuben sculpture, I believe, that stands on her bookshelf. I identified it—correctly, I understand—as being the piece Mrs. Benton's family thought had been stolen from her apartment."

"Mrs. Stainsbury says you think she stole it."

"Not at all, and I tried to make that clear. I'm aware there's a certain amount of pilfering around any facility of this sort. But we've found that it's usually done either by casual or part-time help—and you have very little of that, since most of your workers are longtime employees—or by elderly people who've lost track of who owns what. I really wanted to be sure Mrs. Stainsbury wasn't one of them. Well, I found Mrs. Stainsbury still has her memory intact, so I was satisfied. And if it will calm her fears, you can assure her of that. Oh, but there is one thing that puzzles me. Someday when we have a moment of leisure, I must ask you about the color of her hair. Am I wrong, or does it change each time I see her?"

Angela laughed out loud. "Cataloguing Trinita's changes of hair color will be the longest story I'll ever tell you, Lieutenant. So I'll save it till you have more time."

And on that pleasant note, they said their good-byes, Angela smug and self-congratulatory because she had at least given

Martinez one piece of information he thought worth looking into. She was also delighted that she had good news for Trinita. Not a bad day's work, she told herself.

For his part, Martinez also felt pleased with himself. Looking back on the conversation, he remembered it far differently from the way Angela did. For instance, he thought he had delivered yet another emphatic warning to Angela to keep away from active involvement in matters best left to the police. Of course, it was his second warning to her. Or was it his third? He grinned to himself. No matter. At least he'd done it. And he fairly ran from his office to get to his next obligation, without another thought for his Camden friends.

Angela, on the other hand, had time to bask in her satisfaction. She settled back in her chair and smiled across the room at Caledonia. "Thank you for the use of your phone. You were right—a phone call was all that was needed. Now I think we can have our little sherry," she said. "The lieutenant is up to date on all our investigations, he says Trinita is in the clear, and while we were talking, I realized the very next thing we need to look into, you and I."

Caledonia poured out the sherry and brought one of the tiny thimbles to Angela, then settled into her own huge, comfortable chair. "What exactly do you mean by 'the next thing we should look into'? I thought we'd gone about as far as . . . goodnight, Angela! You don't intend to go over to the Benton home and talk to Daniel's wife, do you? To ask her if she knew about her husband's philandering, and to try to find out if she pushed him off the fire escape because of it? That would be," she glared at her tiny friend, "most unwise. Most."

"Of course not, Cal," Angela laughed lightly, sipping her sherry. "I agree that would be stupid. In the first place she'd never tell us. In the second place, if she doesn't know about his womanizing, I'm not going to be the one to tell her."

"Good decision."

"What I thought was that we should see if we can't find more of Birdy's missing things. What did the family complain was missing? Besides that ring."

"I don't remember anything except the diamond. Were there other things?"

"Perhaps I forgot to tell you all that Clara's been filling me in on. Every time the Bentons complained something was missing, she'd tell me about it. Let me think . . . well, there was a ruby set in a pin, I recall that. And wasn't there a piece of Dresden? A bisque shepherdess about two feet high, they said. Not the sort of thing somebody could walk off with under their jacket, I'd say. Oh, and an antique Staffordshire dog."

"I hate those things," Caledonia said.

"Birdy's things?"

"No. Staffordshire dogs. Clunky-looking, with a sappy expression on their faces. And age doesn't improve the ugly things one little bit."

"Whether you would buy a Staffordshire dog or not is quite beside the point, Cal. Somebody did, or if they didn't, one was either broken or stolen. And we should try to find out what actually happened to it. We can start by asking the maids if they know anything about Birdy's odds and ends. They'd know if an ornament had been broken, or if something of Birdy's suddenly showed up in someone else's apartment. Then we can start asking questions about the jewelry—maybe starting with the apartments on the main floor today and fanning out for the next couple of . . . why, we should be able to cover all of the main building apartments by . . . well, perhaps by next Monday. Then we start asking questions up and down the garden apartments, and . . ."

"I have one idea you ought to consider before you start insulting the maids with your third degree or barging into our neighbors' apartments, annoying everybody with your questions. Why not look downtown? You remember John Singletary, your favorite jeweler, don't you? Well, assuming you were a resident here at CSM, and assuming you wanted to sell some jewelry, wouldn't you go see John?"

Angela beamed. "Indeed I would. What a good idea, Cal. Sometimes you surprise me. And if John can't help us, we can walk back one block further to Antique Row to continue the hunt."

It was already late in the day, and they had been on an expedition to Oceanside already. At their ages, one adventure a day was generally their limit. Thus it was the next day in midmorning when they set out, after their usual squabble about whether to walk (Angela's suggestion), to order a limousine and driver from the local service (Caledonia's choice), or to go with the retirement home's van. They compromised on the van, despite Caledonia's insistence that the seats were too crowded, the springing was so stiff that the ride jolted every bone in her body, and the access step into the van was too high. Angela's reminder that they could interview Doke Wicker "subtly, so he doesn't realize we're questioning him," as he drove them into town finally made Caledonia agree, despite her reluctance. And thus at ten in the morning, groaning and huffing, Caledonia hauled herself aboard behind Angela, glaring as Angela moved them into the three-quarter seat just behind the driver. "It's narrow for you, Cal, but Doke can hear what we say. If we sit in the broader back seat, we'll have to shout."

"Where to, ladies?" Doke pitched his half-finished cigarette out the window and looked at them over his shoulder as he put the van into gear.

"Do you know John Singletary's jewelry store?" Angela asked.

Doke nodded. "Oughtta. Bought my girl her engagement ring from him. A topaz. But it was pretty. Good guy, that Singletary fella. Couldn't have treated me nicer if I'd been a millionaire buying a diamond. Got your seat belts fastened?"

They drove a block in relative silence, though Caledonia, squeezed against the arm of the undersized seat, groaned when they cornered the first time. Finally she glared at Angela and whispered, "Well, get on with the questions. I didn't agree to sit in this steel vise just for the ride."

"I don't see anything wrong with your driving," Angela began.

"Huh? Somebody been complaining?"

"Oh, not to me," Angela explained hastily. "It was just that we heard that Mrs. Benton had said something."

"Her that just got herself killed? Yeah. She sure did. Every time I took her to her doctor's or the bank or downtown shopping. 'Watch out for that bicycle, Mr. Wicker,' " he whined in a falsetto, presumably imitating Birdy's voice. " 'Slow down—slow down—you're going entirely too fast!' I've been driver for a general's jeep, and in maneuvers I've drove a troop carrier and a Hum-Vee—and she's going to tell me how to handle a Toyota van? Hah!"

"Somebody said," Angela prodded, "that Mrs. Benton had suggested you be dismissed."

"Could be," he nodded. "Wouldn't of put it past her. Don't matter none to me. If I don't drive for this place, I'll drive a delivery truck or be a chauffeur for some rich guy out at La Costa. Always work for a top-notch driver. I could go there tomorrow . . . Here we are, ladies."

The van jerked to a stop in front of the jewelry store, where the windows twinkled with the seasonal reds and greens of rubies and emeralds, a display that made both women gasp with pleasure. "Be back for you . . . when? Half an hour? An hour? Good enough." Wicker slid the door shut behind his passengers, and the van swirled away.

"Well, that was as good as useless," Caledonia said. "We don't know one thing more than we did, and I've got a bruise on my side from the arm on that stupid seat."

"Oh, Cal, that's not quite true. We know Birdy was after his job, but he didn't really mind, and—"

"He *says* he didn't mind," Caledonia growled. "Don't forget that he gave me a whole different impression a couple of days ago. I don't think you can cross him out yet."

"Mrs. Wingate! Good morning!" John Singletary called out. He had spotted the two standing in awe before his window display and opened the shop door to greet them. "And Mrs. Benbow. How delightful. Admiring my little Christmas decoration? I get a lot of favorable comments. And is there something I can do for you today?"

Angela explained their mission briefly. "And we're actually sort of halfway, semiofficial now," she said with satisfaction. "Very different from last time."

"I should be delighted to help out, even were you completely without official backing," Singletary said, smiling warmly as he ushered the two ladies to the little parlor area created at the back of the store for the comfort of important customers. He saw each of his visitors seated in one of the thickly upholstered wing chairs, then took a smaller side chair for himself. "Exactly what information can I give you?"

"Mrs. Benton was said to have some jewelry that has gone missing, according to her relatives, and it occurred to us that perhaps . . ."

"Are you talking about a ruby pin and a nice little diamond solitaire?" the jeweler asked.

"I guess so. Though her family said it was a huge diamond," Angela said.

"Families often do. And perhaps they really remember the heirlooms that way—bigger and more expensive than they really are. But let me get my book and I can tell you exactly when she brought the pieces in."

"What do you mean, 'brought them in'?"

"I mean, brought them to me to buy and resell." He consulted a black log he pulled from under a counter near the cash register. "It was quite some time ago, as I recall. Yes, here's the first entry. Nearly a year ago for the ruby. Then July for the diamond ring."

"Six months ago! And her family didn't even miss it till now. Shows you how little attention they paid to her week by week, doesn't it?" Caledonia said. "Of course, they didn't report the stuff stolen till after she died and they could search the bureau drawers."

"Stolen! My word! Well, that would explain why your Lieutenant Martinez came by here a week ago to ask about the same pieces."

"The lieutenant already knows about the jewelry?" Angela was mildly dismayed. "Oh dear. And I thought he'd be so proud of us for figuring this out! Well, as long as he already knows, there's no reason for you not to tell us the rest of the story, is there?"

"The rest? What story do you mean?" Singletary put his logbook away and rejoined the women. "Look here. I was about to pour myself a cup of tea. The pot was freshly made just before you arrived. I hope you'll join me?"

"Now, John," Caledonia said, "we're not here to buy anything. You can't coax our pocketbooks open with sweet talk and a pot of tea."

"I shouldn't dream of it," he smiled. "Just a cup of tea with two friends, that's all."

Over a pleasantly steaming cup of Earl Grey, Angela pursued her inquiry. "What I meant, John, was that surely Mrs. Benton didn't just wander in and say 'Here, buy these.' I know you're far more careful than to buy under those circumstances. You'd make her identify herself and tell you the history of the pieces and . . . and . . . well, all kinds of things. And what I want to know is why she sold them."

Singletary sat back and sipped his tea. "Let me think and remember here. Well, she said that living up at Camden-sur-Mer was expensive, and though she had enough coming in each month to pay the rent there, thanks to a trust her husband set up for her, she never had anything left over after paying her basic expenses. She wanted cash to buy clothes, to stock her little kitchenette, to pay for some remodeling she was having done, and for things she called incidentals. I thought that would have to be a lot of incidentals. The ruby pin brought her five hundred dollars and the little diamond six hundred. But she told me that wouldn't last three months."

Caledonia laughed aloud and set her cup and saucer down onto the tiny table by her side before she spoke. "Mrs. Benton told people up at CSM that she was going broke buying birdseed. That must be her 'incidentals.' Pounds and pounds and pounds of premium birdseed!" and she went on to explain to

Singletary about the birds and the annoyance they had caused everybody within earshot—not to mention those living directly beneath Birdy's apartment.

Singletary swallowed a snort of laughter with some difficulty. "I'm sorry. I shouldn't laugh, of course. It must have been a terrible nuisance for you. Who would think that such controversy could be stirred up by a few innocent songbirds."

"Innocent but messy! And not just a few. That's the crux of the problem."

"John," Angela interrupted. "I'm curious about that diamond. The family was making such an awful fuss about it, I thought it had to be something special. Could we see it?"

"But it's already gone. And I made a small but entirely satisfactory profit, even though it had an outdated setting. It was a really nice little ring, you know, and I asked Mrs. Benton whether she wouldn't rather hang onto it so she could give it to someone in the family someday. But she said no. Most emphatically. She said she'd see them in hell—I beg your pardon, ladies, but I'm quoting her exactly—before those greedy young people got the ring her husband gave her so long ago. She'd rather turn the ring into money that she could spend on those birds of hers. Still, I could give the family the name of the buyer, with his permission of course, if they wanted to negotiate for the ring."

Angela put her teacup down and got to her feet. "They don't really want the ring any more than Birdy wanted them to have it. They only want the money it would bring. That crowd has very little room in their souls for sentiment. So don't worry about it."

"Oh, I won't. Still, if they want to talk to me . . ."

Angela and Caledonia took their leave and started down the street, moving briskly in the cool air of a December morning in California. It was in the third in the line of shops selling used, secondhand, and just plain junk furniture, clothing, china, glass, and jewelry—all calling themselves antique shops—that the two women found success. Ye Olde London Antiques and

Collectibles had a Staffordshire dog prominently set out in the very center of its window.

"That silly dog looks pretty good set up there with all the imitation antiques, doesn't it?" Caledonia said in a surprised voice. "In the midst of those mounds of fake tortoise shell and Avon perfume bottles—look, there's one in the shape of Mickey Mouse, and one's an Edsel sedan—among all that clutter that dog, ugly as it is, absolutely shrieks class! And gee whiz, it ought to—look at the price they've put on it!"

Angela gasped. "I didn't know Staffordshire cost so much!"

"It doesn't. It never did. This place obviously hopes somebody will come along who doesn't know diddly-squat about antiques."

The women moved further into the shop, picking their way between rust-covered andirons laid helter-skelter on the floor, avoiding a display of 1930s toasters (doubtless with 1930s crumbs inside them) that overflowed a Grand Rapids table, and edging past two display cases crammed with Little Orphan Annie Ovaltine mugs, Charlie McCarthy teaspoons, and glasses that had originally held pimento cheese spread or grape jelly.

The merchant who bustled forward to meet them didn't mind in the least discussing the provenance of what was undoubtedly his prize piece. The dog had come to him, he told them, from "a dear little old lady from the nursing home. Couple of blocks over toward the ocean there . . ."

Angela started to correct him, as she always did when someone confused their retirement home with a nursing home, but Caledonia nudged her firmly, and Angela decided against making an issue of it. "End of last August a year ago, as I remember," he went on, his smile never wavering. "You interested in looking at it closer? Genuine Staffordshire. Got that printed right across its bottom," he said proudly.

Caledonia propelled Angela out of the shop and onto the sidewalk beyond, calling "Later, perhaps" back over her shoulder. "I wonder if he knows he's being insulting?" she muttered. " 'Dear little old lady' indeed!"

"Don't be cross, Cal. Be flattered," Angela said smugly. "If he feels free to talk about dear little old ladies to us, it means he doesn't see us as being in the same category. And I do flatter myself I look a lot younger than . . ." She hesitated, as much out of habit as out of reluctance to say her age aloud to Caledonia, who after all knew it very well. "Younger than I really am," she finished lamely.

"Come on," Caledonia urged her. "Let's get this over with and get home. I'm hungry and it's almost time for lunch. Here's the next place," and she dived ahead of Angela into the cool, dark interior of the Thieves' Market next door. Inside its cool depths, locked cases held black velvet trays of mine-cut diamonds and Victorian mourning rings. Sterling silver pickle forks with mother-of-pearl handles gleamed next to engraved calling card trays and initialed napkin rings. Glass-fronted cabinets, lit from within, sparkled with a display of cut glass, and there was room to walk between the items of furniture, carefully set for display on Persian carpets. Caledonia relaxed, though she still tried to hold her caftan close against her to avoid brushing things off desks and tabletops—a sterling and crystal inkwell, a silver pen tray, a pair of very old Ben Franklin glasses with wire frames, a leather-bound pocket Bible with intricately carved brass edges fitted to the binding and a filigree brass lock. "Oh look. Look there!" Angela pointed at a large glass display case across the room. In a locked china closet stood a Dresden shepherdess, displayed by itself on its own shelf.

"That piece just came to us at the first of last month," a woman said smoothly, and Angela and Caledonia turned quickly to see that a clerk had come up quietly and was standing just behind them. "A very sad thing," she went on, "I read in the Camden newspaper that the woman who owned it has just passed away. But I can tell you quite a lot about its origins. It's in absolutely first-class condition—"

"Oh, we didn't want to buy it," Angela said hastily. "We're from Camden-sur-Mer ourselves, and we knew the woman who owned it. We were trying to find out . . . you know . . . how she happened to sell it in the first place."

"She said she had very little money for discretionary purposes and obligations to meet that required cash. I'm the owner here, and I waited on her myself. I was delighted to pick up the Dresden piece. It's a real find." The clerk laughed. "And she was so absolutely charming. About those obligations—she said she was feeding wild birds. Isn't that sweet?"

"Another fizzle!" Angela waited to express her disappointment till she and Caledonia were out on the street. "No theft involved at all. And in each case, the exact same story—that she needed cash, and she got it by selling off things she owned and didn't want anymore. There's absolutely nothing interesting to show for our whole morning's work!"

"I wouldn't say that," Caledonia responded. "When those awful grandchildren howled that she'd been robbed, I kind of wondered if it might not be so. But the truth seems to be she chose to sell her jewelry and ornaments to have spending money in preference to saving the things for her family to inherit someday. Tell you what I'll do. I'll agree to walk on up to CSM with you instead of waiting for the van—four whole blocks from here, and you know that's a real stretch for me— provided you join me at the Bakery Cafe for a cup of hot cocoa and a pastry before we leave downtown. Okay?"

"Oh, Cal, it's nearly lunchtime. And it'll only take a little while for us to get back home. Not enough time to digest a snack, and . . ."

"Well, *you* don't have to eat a pastry. But I'll never make it if I don't have some fuel for the old furnace. Come along . . . Bakery Cafe, then home."

And Caledonia strode forth along the sidewalk in a flurry of her silken caftan. Angela, pattering in the wake of her giant friend, could imagine that Caledonia was a sailboat, brightly colored canvas billowing out in the wind, bow pointed eagerly ahead, navigating straight on through wind and wave, heading for hot chocolate and a prune danish.

Chapter 15

AFTER LUNCH, despite Angela's pleadings that "We've hit a dead end, Cal, and we need to talk it out," Caledonia was adamant about taking her usual nap. "Besides, you're going to be busy, Angela. Didn't you tell me a long time ago that there's a rehearsal for Trinita Stainsbury's Christmas pageant today?"

Angela's hand flew up to cover her mouth. "Oh! I forgot! She forgave me for skipping the earlier ones, and I forgot to ask exactly when . . . oh, drat!"

"I'd like to be the mouse in the corner watching you and Trinita play theater, but since I certainly don't want to be roped into doing something with that pageant myself, I'm going to stay far, far away from the whole thing, and you can just tell me all about it later. For now, I'm off for that nap." And grinning widely, Caledonia headed for her own apartment.

Angela, as usual, was too restless to consider a nap, so she made her way to the library, but there seemed to be nothing on the shelves she hadn't read before. She hesitated next at the door of the billiards room. There was a selection of exercise equipment lined up against the far wall—three exercycles, some graduated weights in a rack, and two or three sturdy jumping ropes, seldom used, to be sure, but there if wanted.

Angela eyed both the baize-covered table and the exercise equipment with distaste. She had never learned billiards—she thought it was a silly game and had steadfastly refused to learn, even when her late husband had volunteered to teach her. And she genuinely despised exercise. Her doctor had taken her to task about it during her last checkup. It was, as she had told him, both the exertion she disliked and "All that repetition! It just goes on and on and on!" Despite his cavalier assurance that if she just tried it she'd love it, she knew herself better than he appeared to. "I'd hate it," she said to him, "and the longer I did it, the madder I'd get. It's a choice of getting exercise or getting an ulcer, for me."

"Your endorphins will take over—" he began, but she had cut him short.

"I've walked till my feet nearly fell off without getting the slightest lift to my spirits," she told him crossly. "I went to a gym at a spa and bounced around on a trampoline once not too long ago. It was novel, I grant you, and kind of fun at first, but it got boring in a hurry. I certainly didn't feel any pleasure from it after a few minutes. And I thought that was what endorphins were supposed to do—start up after you'd been exercising awhile. Well, they don't for me. I don't think I have any endorphins!"

The doctor shook his head in disbelief, which annoyed Angela considerably, and simply recommended exercise again. "You've got to do it, Mrs. Benbow. And I know you'll come to enjoy it."

"Have you ever noticed that doctors really don't listen to their patients?" Angela asked Caledonia later with considerable annoyance. "I wish that young doctor of mine would just once assume that I know what I'm talking about!"

All the same, now that she was actually thinking about exercise, she told herself that perhaps she really ought to try. "But I won't use those exercycle things. I mean, talk about spinning your wheels . . . those things would be exercise, yes, but an exercise in futility. Maybe I'll go walking." And she set off briskly from the library and started down the garden path. But she hadn't completed one round trip to the seacliff and back to the main building before she was thoroughly chilled. A fresh wind was blowing off the sea, and the usual California sunshine was dimmed by clouds; there was even a hint of moisture in the air. Angela headed indoors.

"If I went up the steps here," she said to herself as she reached the main staircase leading to the second floor, "I could go along the front hall and then do the length of the east hall, go down the fire escape, and come back in this door. And if I was to make that circle a couple of times, I bet that would be the same amount of exercise as using one of those stupid cycles."

So she started up the big staircase toward the second floor, pausing only three or four times to catch her breath.

"Climbing is a lot harder than walking on level ground, all right," she gasped at the second landing. But she persisted. At the head of the stairs, she turned right, then at the east hallway she turned right again. Down the hall she went, out the fire escape doorway, and down the fire escape.

Droplets of moisture in the damp air blowing in from the sea had coated the ridged metal of the steps, which glistened wetly, and Angela grabbed tight hold of the cold metal railing to steady herself. Her feet clanged against the metal treads, and as she neared the bottom she felt one foot slide a little, sufficient warning of the slippery surface. She grasped the railing even more tightly and with both hands as she inched cautiously down the last two steps to the garden level, where she started the circuit back to the main building, walked briskly through the sliding door into the lobby, and back to the main staircase once more. "Once around," she applauded herself. "Good for me! Now the second lap."

Panting heavily throughout the climb and taking more frequent rests on the way than she had the first time, she made it up the stairs. But at the head of the staircase she stopped, and making certain no one was around who could see her, she leaned against the wall while she caught her breath. "I'm not sure I can go one step further. Perhaps I should copy Cal's example and go back to my apartment for a nap." She pulled a handkerchief from her sleeve and dried off her brow. "It's warmer in here than I thought. Maybe I'll just take the elevator down and go to my apartment."

She walked slowly along the hallway, thinking perhaps she

wasn't going to make it, but by the time her lagging feet had brought her to the elevator door, she was feeling somewhat better. "Oh well, might as well go on," she muttered. "After all, the worst is over," and she turned her steps into the eastern hall. But she was moving slowly and when she was about halfway down, she stopped again and mopped her brow once more with the tiny handkerchief.

"Hey, you feelin' all right?" A scratchy voice sounded from inside the wide-open door of one of the apartments, and Angela realized she was panting and mopping within old Elmer Johanson's line of sight. "You sick or anything, young lady?"

Angela came across the hall and peered within. "No, no, I'm fine. Thank you for asking. How about you? Have they left you all alone again? Your nurse doesn't seem to be here."

"Sent her off to visit some of the other nurses. I'm happier when she's gone. Good woman but sour as last week's milk. Name's Pilgrim, but it oughta be Puritan. Has the tightest mouth of any woman I ever seen. She don't approve of me. But then, she don't approve of lotsa things. Come to think of it, I don't know nothin' she really likes. Now you . . . you're a lot better lookin' and more cheerful. Say, you wanna come in for a cuppa tea? She left me with a potful and I think I got a clean cup somewhere. . . ."

Angela hesitated, but in her view, she had more than fulfilled her obligation to exercise, and she certainly would feel better sitting down. She came into the darkened room. "Though I seem to be having more tea today than usual," she muttered. "Funny how things like that go in streaks. Tomorrow I suppose everybody will invite me for coffee." She seated herself in the easy chair beside the bed.

"Whatcha say?" Angela waved a "never mind" gesture and Elmer turned on his bedside lamp. "Gotta have a little light to pour the tea by," he explained. "Miss the cup otherwise. There we go. Want sugar?" She shook her head and he handed a brimming mug across to her. " 'Course, it ain't real tea. One-a them herbal kind, you know? Miss Pilgrim don't think real tea would be good for me. So I'm back to my childhood again. Your ma ever give you chamomile tea when you was little?"

"Of course," Angela said. "No conscientious mother would have given her children real tannin and caffeine. I grew up on chamomile and rose hips and tansy teas." She sipped quietly. "This is probably very soothing. Helps you sleep. If you need help. I take it you're feeling well or Miss Pilgrim wouldn't have left you, let alone to go for a social visit."

He cackled happily. "Every morning I wake up surprised to find out I'm still here. But the way things are goin', I may make it another week or so! Eatin' pretty good lately, and my legs ain't as wobbly as sometimes. Been goin' to the bathroom on my own and everythin'."

"A hundred and two, didn't someone say? My goodness, Mr. Johanson, that's a tremendous accomplishment."

He cackled again. "No accomplishment. Ain't nothin' *I* did. In fact, I don't think I got much to be proud of in my life. I always thought maybe I'd make a million dollars or write a book or discover a new continent or something. But time went on, and there was things to do, like makin' a living, or raisin' my kids . . . They're all dead and gone, did you know that?" He fell quiet, and his eyes closed.

Angela sipped her tea and waited, and sure enough, Elmer's eyes opened once more, lively with intelligence. "Wasn't asleep. Just restin'," he assured her. "Started to say I thought I'd do somethin' worth doin' and I never did. Wanted to leave the world better when I was gone than it was before. Make up for my sins, you could say. Besides, it'd be a shame if all people remembered me for was how long I could last before I died. You ever think about things like that?"

"We all do, Mr. Johanson," Angela assured him. "People die left and right in a retirement home. Because we've all reached that age, so we can't ignore it."

"There was a time when I didn't believe it, you know," the old man said. "Other people died. Old people. My grammaw and grampaw died when I was little. But they was old. Maybe fifty and sixty." He wheezed out a laugh. "Now I'm twice that age and still here. If I'm goin' to discover a new kind of penicillin or build a bridge or a skyscraper, I better get started, don'tcha think?" The wheezing laugh crackled out again.

"Were you thinking of ordering in some steel girders and a supply of nuts and bolts?" Angela said indulgently, sipping her tea.

"I was just talkin'. I ain't really goin' into the bridge-buildin' business." The eyes drooped closed, and the room fell silent.

After a while, Angela decided Elmer was not going to wake again for a while, and she set her half-emptied mug down, stood up, and tiptoed toward the door.

"Where ya goin'?" Elmer was not asleep after all. Or if he had drifted off, he was awake again. "Have another cuppa tea. Talk awhile. No good programs on TV today. They got all that Christmas stuff you know. A real pain. Except maybe Bing Crosby or Jimmy Stewart. I like them fine. But that Jimmy Stewart, he's in black and white. I got used to color. Ain't that funny? Used to think black and white was just great. Now the only thing worth watchin' that way is old Humphrey Bogart movies and the Dick Van Dyke show. Rest has gotta be in color."

Angela came back into the room and perched on the edge of the chair again as he talked, poised to leave at her first polite opportunity. She was feeling stronger than before her tea break, and she was also feeling guilty. She should, she thought, finish her exercise program—she should walk the rest of the hallway, go down the fire escape, and back to the building through the garden once more. Then, of course, she would go back to her own place to rest up before the rehearsal and having to face Trinita doing her Cecil B. de Mille imitation.

"Hey there! You daydreamin'? I been talkin' to you!" the old man rasped.

"Oh, I beg your pardon. I was . . . well, yes, my mind was a long way away," Angela confessed.

"Thinkin' about your detective work?" Elmer's eyes were

shrewd as a hawk's. "You got any ideas yet about who killed the old lady?"

"Actually, yes, we do. We're getting closer all the time," Angela told him. "In fact . . ." She hesitated for a moment, wondering if she should tell Elmer about Betty Goodwin's imaginary romance. There was no point in upsetting him. On the other hand, didn't he have a right to know if one of his nurses was a habitual liar? Or the next-door thing to it . . .

"I wonder—did you know that Betty Goodwin says she had a . . . a flirtation with Mrs. Benton's nephew? I mean, she told me at some length that they were almost . . . well, almost betrothed." That was not the word she had intended to use. But *betrothed* was as apropos as anything else, she supposed. Especially considering there was no truth in Betty's story anyway. And Angela went on to give Elmer Johanson a summary of their interrogation of Betty and her colleagues and about her own visit to Benton's office in Oceanside. She ended with the man's confession of his affair with his receptionist. Not really Elmer's business, she supposed, but it certainly tended to show up Betty Goodwin's story as just that—a story.

Elmer heard her out before he grunted his reaction. "That man! In my day, he'd-a been buggy-whipped right outa town. Did that to a feller once who'd been foolin' around with our hired girl. He was a married feller, too. Me and one of my neighbors went over to see him one night. Made sure he wouldn't fool around again no time soon. Felt sorry for his poor wife. Like I feel sorry for that Daniel feller's wife. He got no right to go behind her back that way. Teach him a lesson . . ."

"You mean someone ought to teach him a lesson? Oh, I think he's cured of his roving eyes. He doesn't want his wife to find out, and he's so afraid we'll tell her . . . well, in short, I think he'll be good. At least for a while. But my point was, his affair wasn't with your nurse, Betty Goodwin. She was just imagining—"

"Scared him good! Scared him good!" Elmer was chuckling with delight. " 'Course that Daniel fellow ain't no bargain to begin with. Argues with his wife, grubs around for money from his aunt . . ." Elmer's chuckle turned into a sharp cough. "Sorry . . . hard to take a deep breath . . . but I can't help . . . scared him . . ." The cough subsided into a wheeze again.

"Yes, I think we did scare him. But it's your nurse I really wanted to talk about . . ."

"Betty? Nice girl. Smiles a lot. Cheers me up."

"But the lies she tells . . ."

"Don't care if she tells stories. She makes me smile. Let her make things up. Don't matter none if they're true or not. Know what I mean?"

"No, I'm not quite sure . . ."

"I mean, leave her alone, Mrs. Benbow. I like her, and she ain't doin' no harm. Don't you bother her none. Don't you get her upset."

"Well, surely, Mr. Johanson, I understand how you might feel protective about her. But if she lies about that, what else might she be lying about? Do you see? So I can hardly ignore it. At the very least, I intend to look further into your Betty Goodwin and her background."

Elmer tried to speak, coughed two or three times, then fell completely silent. Angela thought the long conversation had probably taxed his strength. She stood up and moved toward the door, and this time the old man did not try to stop her.

"Well, thank you for the tea, Mr. Johanson," she said and hesitated, but he did not answer. So after a moment, she left the room and walked down the hall toward the fire escape. She had opened the door and was half outside when she heard a whisper of sound—not footsteps, but someone in the hall behind her—and turned to see Miss Pilgrim just entering Elmer's room. At least he would have company now, she thought to herself, and began her cautious climb down the metal stairs.

Angela had no time to nap when she got back to her room. The rehearsal for the Christmas pageant was scheduled for 3:00, and although Trinita had been forgiving about Angela's skipping the earlier run-throughs, Angela felt she'd better not push Trinita's patience. The woman took things like this pageant so seriously. So Angela went to the lobby exactly on time to join the other actors. "Although I don't know why," she told Trinita Stainsbury, "with so much else going on, I have to rehearse to be a camel."

"You're not a camel," Trinita reminded her sharply. "You're a lamb. The camels enter with the wise men. You're already in the manger when the scene begins. And although you have no lines, you do say *Baaa-baaa-baaa*—and you want to get it right, don't you? Incidentally, that should prove you're playing a lamb. Camels don't say *Baaa*."

"Really! What *do* camels say?" Trinita didn't answer and Angela went on defiantly. "You don't know any more than I do. For all we know, you and I, camels *do* go *Baaa*." She sat down behind the two chairs Trinita had designated as a manger stall and let her mind wander, unencumbered by any sense of involvement with the Nativity scene being played out before her. From time to time, as it occurred to her, she let out a loud *Baaa! Baaa!*—more of a bray than a bleat, really—that drew a sharp "Angela! Really!" from her director and a series of annoyed stares from Janice Felton—playing the Madonna—whenever one of the sheep sounds blasted into the middle of her lines.

But at least, if it had been up to the Virgin Mary and the sheep, the rehearsal would have moved right along at a smart pace. The problem was with Joseph, as played by Grogan, who had come to the rehearsal from approximately the midpoint of his personal cocktail hour. Although he was so mellow he did not in the least resent being interrupted by barnyard noises, neither did he remember a single line until prompted—more than once each time—by Mary Moffett acting as stage manager. So the rehearsal moved along very slowly, and by the time the three Wise Men (Mr. Brighton, Mr. Dover, and Mr. Springfield from the garden apartments) were due to enter, it was 4:30 and time to disperse the cast to their various apartments so they could get ready for dinner. Trinita Stainsbury was beside herself.

"How can we put our pageant on without a proper rehearsal? I mean, the first time Angela wasn't here and we had to skip the three shepherds because two of them—the Jackson twins—had hair appointments. The second time we started early in the afternoon and still had to quit before the Wise Men even entered, because the children were already arriving to give that afternoon's program and the staff had to set up the chairs for the audience. And of course that was the day they found Birdy's body, so rehearsals were called off for the rest of that week. We absolutely *must* rehearse all the way through at least once! I swear to you, this pageant is jinxed!" None of Trinita's actors paid the slightest attention, heading off in five different directions, chattering and laughing, and at last Trinita herself gave up her complaints and stalked off, rigid with indignation, to her own apartment.

Angela found little sympathy from Caledonia when they finally met for dinner. "You don't care that I suffered through an hour and a half as a sheep. You think it's funny that I walked my little feet off trying to follow my doctor's advice. You're just not very sympathetic! I like your hair, though," she told her huge friend. "So that's where you were this afternoon! At the hairdresser. I wondered, when I didn't see you after your nap."

"Well, I certainly wasn't going to sit in the lobby waiting for you to get done being Greta Garbo. So I had plenty of time. Incidentally, I do have to applaud you for your new resolve about exercise. That's really admirable. I hope you intend to keep it up."

"Keep it up? Oh, I don't know . . . perhaps next week . . ."

"Now what good will that do? You have to ride an exercycle or go for a walk or something every single day."

"I heard three time a week was sufficient. So I thought . . ."

"Now, Angela, if you tell yourself that, it's too easy to put it off till tomorrow. And put it off again the next day, and again the day after that. You should start a program of exercise every single day. In fact, you probably should exercise twice a day."

"What! Twice?"

"Sure. That one walk isn't enough. Twice the length of the

hall? Twice up the stairs? I'd say four times around the course every day would be a minimum to do the slightest bit of good."

"Oh, Cal, surely not!" Angela put the unpleasant notion to one side of her mind and spent the remainder of the dinner hour chatting about everything and nothing. Idle conversation was a pleasant diversion from thinking about the possible need for a more active lifestyle.

"I'm tired tonight," Caledonia said as they left the table. "And Ted Turner's showing the first part of *Gone With the Wind* at nine o'clock. I thought I'd just go to my place and watch some TV. You going to watch *Gone With the Wind*?"

"Again? I've probably seen it four times in the last three years. I used to think there'd never been a finer movie made. But after four reruns, I need a rest. Even from Clark Gable. No thank you, Cal. There must be something else on besides that."

But back in her own apartment, Angela realized that she was doomed in her TV viewing. *White Christmas* was in its sixth showing for that month—each on a different cable station. And she had tired some years ago of the children's cartoons—the Grinch stealing Christmas, Charlie Brown choosing a Christmas tree, and the little drummer boy pounding out *Ah-rum-pah pum-pum* over and over. Public TV featured its umpteenth performance of *The Nutcracker*, and even ESPN seemed to have forgotten about everything but figure skating for the duration of the season. Obviously there would be no TV for her tonight.

She went through her own small bookcase, but everything had been read at least once and there was nothing she wanted to reread. She glared at the small heap of unwrapped gifts, and her conscience made her sit down and start the work again, but after half an hour with only two packages completed, she still felt the need for something that would occupy her till bedtime.

She also realized with surprise that her arms and legs felt . . . well, strange. Was she stiffening up from her exertions of the afternoon? Oh, surely not! Not after just one day's exercise. Perhaps her muscles felt, not tired, but prickly with nervous energy. And if that was it . . . more exercise! Surely! Caledonia had said that twice a day was best. The question was, did Cal really know what she was talking about? Angela thought she had read somewhere that it was best to exercise just once. To do whatever you were going to do all at the same time, continuously. It was not as good to split the exercise into two or even three separate sessions. Or was it the other way around? Maybe whatever she'd read had said that just one session of exercise a day was the wrong way, and it was best in two or three separate sessions. Yes, that must be it, since Cal had given essentially the same advice.

Angela came out of her room, started to turn toward the lobby, and hesitated. The main staircase she had used this morning was the length of the lobby away, but almost directly across the hall from her was the door to the east service stair. Perhaps this evening she should spare herself the walk through the lobby and just start upstairs by the nearest way. Laziness won and she made her way up the service stairs—four steps and a rest, four steps and a rest, four more steps . . . Her arms and legs protested mildly, but her breath didn't seem to come as short as it had earlier in the day. Could the exercise be paying off already?

She tried to march down the hall at a brisk pace, swinging her arms as she had seen walkers do along the beach, but halfway along the hall, either the pace she was setting now or the stairs caught up with her, and she stopped to catch a deep breath, just as she had during her afternoon exercise session. And just as in the afternoon, she pulled out a little handkerchief and touched away the moisture from her brow.

"You okay, young woman?" The old man's voice from within the room was perhaps not as vigorous as it had been in midday, but it was strong enough for her to hear easily. Angela walked over to the open door and peered within.

Bob, a woman's throaty voice sounded, *your patients won't miss you if you go with Carol and me for one afternoon,* and a man's mild voice protested gently, *But, Emily, Howard and Jerry and I have tickets for a Cubs' game*—The voice cut off as Elmer Johanson waved the remote control in the direction of the TV set, clearly activating the mute.

Angela stepped into the room and glanced around, left and right. Except for the old man on the bed, the room was empty. "Isn't Betty Goodwin around tonight, Mr. Johanson?"

"Sure she is. She just went to the kitchen to get a snack," he said. "Be right back. You need a nurse?"

"No, no, it's just that ... well, as long as I'm up here anyway, maybe I should ask her a few more questions."

"Now, Mrs. Benbow, you don't want to be botherin' her. Didn't I tell you to leave her alone?"

"I wish I could. But you know that in a murder investigation there's no sparing anybody."

"Listen—you go upsettin' her, you're upsettin' me. She don't smile, I don't smile."

Angela sighed. "But if your nurse had anything to do with the murder or the attack on ..." She lifted her head and half turned toward the doorway. She thought she had caught a faint rustle of sound. She stepped to the hallway and glanced out, half expecting to see Betty Goodwin coming from the direction of the elevator, but there was no one in sight. The door at the opposite end of the hall, however, the one leading onto the fire escape, was standing wide open. Angela thought the door had been closed as she entered the hallway, but she couldn't be sure—she hadn't paid too much attention. Perhaps, she thought now, the sound she had just heard was the Dovers coming out to tie the door open as they were in the habit of doing.

"Betty didn't have nothin' to do with no killin'." The old man was still talking. "You want to find who done it, you just go talk to the family again."

"Oh, I'll do that, too, Mr. Johanson. I'm not done by any means. But I'm getting closer. Actually, I have a feeling I've already got the information I need to put it all together. I just have to think it through." She turned as though to leave.

"Well, you put it all together," Elmer said grumpily, "without botherin' Betty Goodwin." And he snapped the TV sound back on. *Emily,* the soft-spoken male voice was protesting, *you don't understand. It's kind of a guy thing. Like Mr. Carlin says . . .*

Angela turned away and walked slowly down the hall toward the open door and the chilly little wind that was freshening the air in the hallway. Was there something about Betty Goodwin yet to discover, she wondered? What could it be? Old Elmer was certainly protective of his nurse. Could it be that Elmer knew some secret about her? There was an old movie on TV the other day, Angela recalled, and the detective discovered that the old man's nurse was really his illegitimate daughter, whose existence was unsuspected by the other heirs until . . . Still mulling over the movie plot, Angela stepped outside onto the exterior landing and was dismayed to find her feet slipping on the metal tread. The surface of the fire escape had grown practically slimy with moisture, and she was thinking that she had better be extra careful on the steps this evening when she heard a faint swish of sound again.

It reminded her of the afternoon, when she had turned at the sound to see Miss Pilgrim just whisking into the Johanson apartment, and Angela really expected that when she turned this time she would see Miss Goodwin entering her patient's room. Instead, Angela was shocked to realize that someone was standing, not halfway down the hall, but immediately behind her. Out of the corner of her eye, as she started to turn, she registered that close presence, but there was time for no more observation, because Angela was suddenly hit hard in the middle of the back, and she pitched forward into the guardrail at the edge of the landing.

The metal caught her just above the waist and she grabbed at it with both hands. There was no way she could cry out even if she'd had time, for the force of that railing hitting her amidships knocked the breath out of her. A muffled "Ooooff" was all she could manage.

One minute she was upright, turning around to see who was behind her.

The next, she was bent over the damp rail, leaning out

toward the dark garden below, gasping for air. She tried to straighten up and look at whoever was behind her. She wanted to protest. To ask questions. To pour anger onto her assailant. But almost immediately, before she had struggled out of that bent position, she was pushed a second time, and with her weight already off balance and too far forward, she had almost no chance of recovering. Her shoes were slipping on the treads and her hands were sliding futilely as she clutched at wet metal.

Her thoughts raced frantically. Time seemed to slow down as she clawed at the railing. She had time to think, "I'm going to fall. Just like Dan Benton. But I can't hold on like he did! I can't support my weight with two hands! Oh, why didn't I diet when I had the chance!"

And then the blackness of the garden seemed to come up toward her. Or perhaps she was falling down to meet the darkness. In either case, she lost consciousness.

Chapter 16

ANGELA AWOKE slowly and painfully. The first thing of which she was aware—before her eyes opened and even before she tried to move—was that she was aching all over. Then gradually she became able to compare aching parts to realize that her abdomen was the sorest area, but since every inch of her seemed to throb and even a tiny movement was painful, it probably didn't matter which part hurt worst. She lay as quiet as possible, eyes closed, trying to collect her fuzzy thoughts. She was in a bed . . . probably her own—it felt familiar to her somehow. And she realized that Caledonia was in the room talking loudly and insistently to . . . Angela listened a moment more and placed the second speaker's voice—Doc Carter, the doctor on call for all residents at Camden-sur-Mer.

It also seemed to Angela, as her woolly thoughts began to focus, that something important had happened. Or was it that something important was going to happen? She tried to think what day it was. It felt like a holiday somehow. Could it be Christmas yet? Surely not—she had several presents yet to wrap. Was there a special program today? It would come to her, of course. She only had to find the key—the event, the activity, the plan—and today would slide into focus for her. It always worked that way. She would awake disoriented, uncertain. She would do a backwards countdown of the days of the week by whatever was planned that would make each special—Thursday she had a meeting, Wednesday a pageant rehearsal, Tuesday a bridge game—till one occurred to her that felt just right, and she knew she had found one that fit as *today*. Then everything else would fall into place and reality would take shape. But the routine didn't seem to work at the moment, perhaps because her aches and pains interfered with her thinking straight. She decided to concentrate on the conversation that flowed somewhat sporadically around her. Perhaps there would be a clue in what Cal was saying.

"I was only kidding about exercising twice in one day," Caledonia was saying. "She should have known I was only kidding! She knows how much I hate exercise myself! Exercise is absolutely the last thing I'd ever tell her to do. . . . If she's had a heart attack, I'll never forgive myself. It is a heart attack, isn't it?"

"Well, one can't be sure without testing, of course, but it seems to me she just fainted. Blacked out. Her heart is certainly strong enough right now. An EKG would show us more. But we'll work on that tomorrow. For now she should sleep. Rest. You say she did her exercises twice today?" Doc Carter's voice was soothing as he tried to calm the agitated Caledonia. "Is she accustomed to taking vigorous exercise?"

"Gosh, no! Just the opposite. She's like I am about it most of the time. All the same, for some reason she decided this afternoon she needed to start up a sort of routine. So she made up a walking course—up the stairs to the second floor, along the hall, and down the fire escape and back again. I thought it was ridiculous, and I got to teasing her about it at dinner. But I was only mocking her when I said she ought to do it all over again. I was sure she'd understand it was just a joke!"

As Caledonia rattled on, Angela had opened her eyes just a tiny slit and was able to see her huge friend was standing by the bedroom door wearing a worn red velour bathrobe. That in itself would have been a clue that something really important had happened. Caledonia belonged to the generation that, short of being driven out of their homes by some natural catastrophe like fire, flood, or earthquake, would not voluntarily have come into public view in their nightwear. Especially not that shaggy red robe, Angela thought.

"I suppose Mrs. Benbow may have fainted from the unaccustomed exertion," Doc Carter was saying. He was standing close beside the bed, with his black bag perched on Angela's nightstand, as she was also able to see through her nearly closed eyes. "Didn't her own doctor tell her to take it easy when she first started into an exercise routine? I suppose he's some young sprout who doesn't understand patients over sixty. I get so tired of—"

"I was pushed," Angela managed to whisper.

"She's awake!" Caledonia charged forward to the bedside. "Oh, Angela, you're awake!"

"You fainted, Mrs. Benbow," Dr. Carter said, following the unwritten medical rule that one must first state the obvious to one's patients.

"I didn't faint," Angela corrected him weakly. "No fainting, no heart attack. Somebody tried to kill me, and I fell off the balcony."

There followed a brief flurry of questions and orders, a series of contradictory attempts to rouse Angela and ask for explanations, alternated with attempts to soothe her and get her to lie back down—a time, in short, of solicitous confusion. At last Angela was able to growl at them to settle down so she could explain. "I was pushed off the fire escape. Just like Dan Benton," she said. "Except I couldn't hold on because I weigh so much. And I fell into the garden."

"You didn't fall," Caledonia contradicted her. "At least not to the ground. You were found unconscious, lying in a heap right outside the hall door."

"I didn't fall over the edge?"

"Uh-uh. You collapsed right on the top landing there. What you call the balcony. Are you serious that somebody tried to push you?"

"Of course!" Even with her voice so weak, Angela showed her irritation. "I wouldn't make up a thing like that." She tried to sit up to make her point more emphatically and gasped with pain. "Oh . . . I'm so sore . . ."

"Here," Dr. Carter said, sitting down beside her and gently

undoing her blouse and skirt. "Let me take a look. We just got you to your room here and listened to your heart, but I didn't have time yet to really look at . . . why, Mrs. Benbow, the soft tissue at your waist is badly bruised!" He probed her sides with his fingers. "I don't think you have a broken rib, but . . . what on earth did they hit you with?"

"Ouch! Ow! That hurts!"

"Sorry. I just want to be sure . . ."

"They didn't hit me with anything. It was me. I hit the railing when they pushed me. Hard. Then all of a sudden I felt like I couldn't breathe. And then I fell over the edge. Or at least I *thought* I fell."

"That could have been what made you faint, Mrs. Benbow. Lack of oxygen. Hitting that railing knocked the wind out of you, and you couldn't get your breath for a while. Though you were breathing on your own by the time you were found."

"Found. Who found me?"

"A nurse who works for the old man on the second floor. Nurse Goodwin. You know her? She was coming back from the kitchen, fetching a snack for her patient, she says, and she looked down the hall through the open door and saw someone lying outside on the fire escape. She thought somebody had been killed. She ran down there, found it was you and that you were definitely still alive."

"And she called another nurse—one of our regulars—and they lugged you down here. And then they called Doc Carter, who was already doing his rounds over at the nursing home, and then they called me," Caledonia said, unable to stay out of things any longer.

"And now you should sleep, Mrs. Benbow," Dr. Carter said. "You're not a youngster, you know, and this has been very hard on you." He was rummaging in his black bag as he talked, finally finding the little bottle that he was searching for. He struggled briefly with the childproof cap and finally managed to shake out a single capsule.

"That's sleeping medicine, isn't it?" Angela said. "I don't want it. I want to tell you all about . . ."

"Tomorrow will do nicely for that, girl," Caledonia said. "We'll leave now so you can rest. I'll want to hear all the details, naturally, but tomorrow morning will do just fine. So I tell you what—I'll get up early for once and join you at breakfast. Let's say eight, all right?"

"Let's say seven," Angela said. "That's when I usually get up and—"

"Not seven tomorrow," Dr. Carter assured her. "This is strong medicine and it won't wear off right away." He extended his hand with the capsule lying on his palm. "Trust me, after all you've been through and with this in your system, you'll be lucky if you're up by nine, let alone eight. Don't shake your head, Mrs. Benbow. This will ensure a good, relaxed rest. Just for once, behave yourself. Trust me." It was a mark of Angela's sore and weakened condition that she downed the capsule with little further argument, and within minutes she was deeply asleep.

Angela was surprisingly resilient for a woman of her years; even though her midsection still ached with every breath, and even though she woke later than she'd planned, feeling groggily that the sun was too high and the clock must be wrong, and even though she'd had to rush through her getting dressed, she was indeed at breakfast by 8:00. True, her thinking was muddy and slow, and even repeated cups of coffee didn't seem to wake her fully. But she was there and able to tell her story, with sufficient embellishment to satisfy her own thirst for drama, to Caledonia, who had joined her—only a few minutes late—and listened with flattering attention.

"And who was it who pushed you? That's the main point, isn't it?"

"Well, of course, but—"

"Mrs. Benbow!" The women looked up to see Lieutenant Martinez rapidly approaching their table. He took Angela's hand gently and solicitously, and she blushed with pleasure. "Dear lady. I'm so relieved to see you here. When Mrs. Wingate phoned this morning, she told me you'd been injured, and—"

"Not injured much, mind you. She's tough," Caledonia said with pride. "Sit down, Lieutenant. Have some coffee with us. Angela is just telling me all about the attack on her . . ."

Martinez pulled up a chair and there was a short pause while he was furnished with a cup, coffee, cream, and sugar. Then he turned again to Angela, who repeated her story with great pleasure. Caledonia listened without complaint to a second repetition of Angela's adventure, and Martinez was flatteringly attentive. At last the tale wound toward its end, with Angela crumpled on the fire escape landing. When she began to explain how she felt as she awoke later in her own room, however, Martinez at last interrupted. "Dear lady, that part of the story can wait. When I arrived, you were about to tell Mrs. Wingate who attacked you."

"No I wasn't!" Angela's voice was sharp with frustration. "Because I don't know! I looked at him—or her—and didn't get a chance to really see."

"You looked and didn't see?" Caledonia said. "She doesn't mean that, Lieutenant. She says things that don't make a lot of sense. You mean you didn't recognize the attacker. Right?"

"No, Cal. I mean I'd only started to turn around and my eyes weren't really on the person yet when I was hit the first time, and then of course my head snapped forward and I wasn't pointed in the right direction anymore."

"Surely you saw something," Caledonia urged.

"All I really saw was a shoulder. Sort of. But my eyes never stopped moving, so I couldn't really see. You know what I mean."

"No, I don't." Caledonia grunted. "Doesn't make sense."

"Well, I understand," Martinez said. "That's perfectly normal, Mrs. Benbow. We don't really see when our heads— and more important, our eyes—are moving. But we feel as though we do, because our brain supplies what's missing between where our eyes started and where they stopped, aimed at something new. In between is really a blur of color and shape, but thanks to the ability of the human brain to fill in the blanks, we *feel* as though we see things clearly the whole time."

"I don't believe that," Caledonia said skeptically. "I see things while I'm turning," and she did so, whipping her head from left to right and back again. "There! I could see the garden through the windows, and I could see what's on top of our table, and—"

"Nevertheless, Mrs. Wingate, you didn't really. You saw them *before* you turned, you saw them *after* you turned, but you didn't see them *while* you turned. Mrs. Benbow is absolutely right. If her head never stopped moving, she never focused on her attacker and she literally did not see who it was."

"Hmph!" Caledonia said, her grunt heavy with skepticism. "All I know is she had our only chance to identify the pusher-offer, and she blew it."

"I'm sorry," Angela said sulkily. "But all I can tell you is that whoever pushed me had one shoulder. And he—or she—was wearing something white."

"You caught sight of what they were wearing?"

"Well, I thought I did. Of course it could have been pale blue or pale yellow. How could I tell in that dim light? And it was so fast, and I was so surprised . . . I mean, I hadn't heard a thing and then there was somebody right there, right behind me. Close enough to touch. And they did, of course. Touch me, I mean. Hard. After that, I was too busy just hanging on to try to get a look at them."

"If you've quite finished with your breakfast, Mrs. Benbow . . . Mrs. Wingate? It would be to our advantage to continue this discussion in private," Martinez said gently. "There are a number of questions . . ."

And at Caledonia's insistence they went to Angela's apartment, where Caledonia tucked her tiny friend onto the couch with an afghan spread across her and a pillow from the bed brought for her head, in spite of Angela's annoyed protests. "Cal, I'm just fine. And I hate having something tightly wrapped around my legs. If you'd just take this coverlet away . . ."

But once they were finally settled, the afghan kicked loose so that it merely rested across Angela's legs, she was happy to take Martinez and Caledonia once again through every detail of her trip along the upper hallway and her memory of her conversation with Elmer Johanson. It really wasn't much.

"I told him I wanted to talk to his nurse again. That Betty Goodwin. And he told me to leave her alone because he liked her. Something like that. And that was about it," Angela said with regret. "Oh! I do remember something else. While we were talking, I heard someone in the hallway. I thought it might be somebody eavesdropping, and I went over to see. But the hall was empty."

"What kind of noise was it?" Martinez asked.

"What do you mean?"

"Well, you must have thought it was a suspicious noise or you wouldn't have gone to investigate. Was it a sharp sound like a door closing? Did someone cough? What sort of—"

"It was like a swoosh. Like a whisper. Like somebody moving down the hall and their foot scraping the carpeting. That's all. I really thought it was Miss Goodwin coming back. I expected her to walk through the door—but she didn't. Actually, I think what it might have been was the fire escape door being opened. The rush of the breeze starting through. Because it was standing open when I peeked out. But I don't remember its being open as I entered the hallway."

"You think somebody came into the building through the fire escape door?"

"Maybe. But what I thought at the time was that maybe the sound was the Dovers propping it open." And she went on to explain the Dovers' penchant for exercise and fresh air. And everything else that had happened. In fact, her descriptions were maddeningly meticulous—until it came to the crucial moments immediately before and during the attack, when she had very little to report, accurate or otherwise.

"The long and short of it," Caledonia said, "is that you haven't the faintest idea who got you."

"Right."

"Or why!" Martinez put in.

"Also true."

"Not much to go on here," Martinez said, getting to his feet. "But little as it is, I should get started. If you think of anything else, you'll let me know at once, won't you?"

"You mean you're going to investigate?" Angela asked.

"Well, it certainly looks as though you've stirred things up, and that somebody's getting very anxious. Though one can't be completely sure that this attack connects with Mrs. Benton's death or with the attack on her nephew . . ." He saw her about to protest and hurried on. "Mrs. Benbow, you'll stay put right here, I hope, now that you realize you're in danger."

"I'm in danger? Nonsense," Angela said, but her scorn was half hearted. The truth was she'd been genuinely frightened by the attack, though she'd never admit it, and she ached so acutely she really had little option but to rest, at least throughout the morning. In fact, after the lieutenant left and Caledonia returned to her own quarters, Angela fell asleep, waking only when Dr. Carter arrived to check her out and declare her in excellent shape ". . . considering."

"Considering?"

"The severity of your bruises. Your age. Don't you bristle at me, Mrs. Benbow. Your body simply does not recover as well at your age as it would have when you were a girl. Now I'm going to leave more medication with you . . ." He shook three tablets out of a small box he'd taken from his black bag. "These'll do you a world of good. One with lunch today, one after supper tonight, one again tomorrow night. All right?"

"What are they?" Angela eyed the medication with suspicion.

"Pills," said Dr. Carter, and laughed jovially.

"I think they give classes at med school," Angela said to Caledonia at lunch, "on how to avoid answering a direct question. I asked what the pills were, and he said they'd do me good. I asked what they'd do, and he said I'd feel much better two days from now if I took them. I said I was feeling dull. Dopey. Would they help with that? He said absolutely—I'd feel marvelous. Just take the pills and shut up, was what he meant. I bet he got an A-plus in Circumlocution 101!"

"Well, are you going to follow the doctor's orders?" Caledonia asked, reaching for the saltshaker. "This stew needs a little help," she explained, and then grinned. "By the way, it's beef stew, in case you didn't catch the flavor. We are apparently—thank heaven—done with that lamb at last!"

Angela smiled absently and took out her hanky, working loose its knotted corner to reveal that it served as a pill carrier. "I just wish I didn't have so much trouble swallowing pills," she said. "That's one reason I hate taking medicine. But considering that I feel just like I did the one time I had a bad hangover, I guess I better do what the doctor says." The pill was popped into her mouth, and she took a swallow of water. Then another. "Pills!" she said with distaste. "There. It's down. What's for dessert?"

After lunch, each woman headed for her own apartment. "I'm for a nap. As usual," Caledonia said. "You'd do well to rest, too, Angela."

Angela just waved. She thought she could hardly sleep, despite the fact that she still felt rocky. After all, she had dozed away most of the morning. Surely that was enough. But even thinking about sleep made her yawn. She pulled her door key from her jacket pocket and was about to enter the room. Probably, she was thinking, she should start up again with the job of Christmas wrapping. Then, before her door was even fully open, she heard her name called, and a woman in white uniform came up the four steps from the lobby to join her.

"Why, Miss Pilgrim!" Angela recognized Elmer Johanson's daytime nurse. "Can I . . . can I do something for you?"

"We were so sorry to hear about your accident, Mrs. Benbow. I trust you're recovered."

"Barely," Angela said stiffly. Miss Pilgrim brought out the worst in her.

"We were wondering if you might have time to stop upstairs to talk for a little while."

"We? You and . . ."

Miss Pilgrim's tight mouth pinched slightly. "Not me, you understand. My patient. Mr. Johanson. We thought perhaps you'd join us for a cup of tea."

"I just had lunch! I couldn't possibly—"

"Well, even if you don't want tea, perhaps a little visit—"

"I feel pretty awful, to tell you the truth. Weak and shaky . . . I don't really think I should. Perhaps another time."

"Listen, Mrs. Benbow," Miss Pilgrim said sharply. "My patient said he'd like to talk to you, and if you don't want tea and you don't want to stay long, that's all right with me. But if he gets upset, it's bad for his blood pressure, and at his age even the slightest spike in pressure could carry him off like that!" She snapped her fingers crisply. Angela, not used to being addressed brusquely by people in service professions, was silent, her mouth hanging slightly open with surprise—or perhaps with awe.

"Tell you the truth, I don't care about you very much, Mrs. Benbow," Miss Pilgrim went on. "It seems to me, to be honest, that you do a lot of nosing around in things that are none of your business. And you're not very tactful about it. Officious, that's what you are, to be perfectly frank. But I do care about my patient. And I suggest that you pull yourself together and go up to see him. You feel bad? Well, you'll get over it. But he won't ever get over what's ailing him, which is plain old age. Old age is terminal, Mrs. Benbow. Try to understand and indulge him a little."

Angela might feel groggy, but her mind was working all the same. She really did want to talk to the old fellow again anyway. Perhaps he'd seen something she hadn't. That sound in the hall, for instance. Was it really the outside door, or had one of the Benton family been sneaking back to Birdy's vacant apartment? If so, they'd have had to pass the old man's line of sight. Or had he seen Betty Goodwin tiptoe past on her way to push Angela off the fire escape? Yes, she'd better talk to him.

"You've got a point, Miss Pilgrim," she said. Miss Pilgrim relaxed slightly from her aggressive stance. "I'll be upstairs as soon as I have a chance to freshen up a bit. Say ten minutes at most."

"Very well, Mrs. Benbow," Miss Pilgrim said with tight-lipped satisfaction. "We'll be expecting you." And she turned smartly, her stiff uniform crackling with her movements, and strode toward the elevator.

Once inside the apartment, Angela hurried to her bedroom to get to her phone and tell Caledonia about her summons to Elmer Johanson's presence. "I hope you weren't in bed yet. Or that at least you weren't asleep . . . but I thought I'd better tell you where I was going. I mean, you might worry if you phoned or came by and I was gone. I don't suppose I'll stay up there very long, of course. Just ask a few questions and leave."

"You sure you wouldn't rather just rest? Are you up to playing detective right now?"

"Well, perhaps I do feel a bit better than I did. That new pill of Dr. Carter's may very well have been some sort of tonic. To help wake me up and make me feel stronger. Yes, I'm positive I feel better. Not a lot better, of course. But better."

"Don't you want me to come with you?"

"No, you just take your nap. I'll be fine, and I'll rest when I get back here. Okay?"

Angela stopped long enough to splash cold water on her face and was relieved that it really seemed to revive her yet a little more. Then she eased her way to the elevator, rose to the second floor, and tiptoed down the hall with tiny steps, walking as smoothly as she could so as not to make her sore muscles twinge. As Angela entered the Johanson apartment, Miss Pilgrim rose from the easy chair near the bed and lifted a finger to her lips. "Sssshhh . . . he's sleeping. He won't stay asleep long and you can just sit here and wait." She gestured Angela to take her place in the easy chair. "I'll take this little straight chair over here by the TV . . ."

"No you won't!" Elmer had roused and his voice was hoarse with sleep or with his irritation—or both. "This here's a private tea party, and you ain't invited. Git goin'!"

"Mr. Johanson, I shouldn't leave you alone when—"

"Don't be silly. You do it all the time."

"Not when you're so weak," Miss Pilgrim retorted. Then she turned to Angela. "We weren't feeling strong and well this morning, and we shouldn't be left on our own when we're having a bad day."

"Ain't havin' a bad day!" Elmer pounded a fist furiously on the bed. "That's your imagination. Go talk to some of the other old hens around here. Git, I say. Git!"

Miss Pilgrim bit her lips, turned on her heel, and left without another word. Angela, listening closely, could hear the rustle of the starched uniform, the sound fading as the nurse walked further down the hall. Finally the sound disappeared altogether, presumably as Miss Pilgrim rounded the corner into the front hall and perhaps went into the elevator. At any rate, Angela certainly could tell that Miss Pilgrim had gone. So it would seem, Angela told herself, that whoever had been sneaking around in the hall the night before wasn't a nurse in a starched skirt. Of course of Elmer's three LPN's, only Miss Pilgrim wore full uniform. So perhaps all one can say, Angela was thinking, is that it wasn't Miss Pilgrim. At least, not unless she was wearing something other than . . .

"You gonna talk to me or not?" Elmer's raspy voice interrupted Angela's rambling thoughts. "Okay, that's better. You got your eyes pointed straight at me now. But say—you don't look so pert to me. You feelin' okay? Listen, I'm right sorry about—I'm sorry you had an accident. And I wanted to say so. Here . . . pot's hot 'n everythin'. I got the rose hip tea today. Lots of other stuff in it, too. I disremember what all was on the label. But them herbs'll do you good. Let me pour you a cup . . ."

"Oh, I don't really think . . . I mean, I just had lunch, after all."

Elmer paid not the slightest attention to her but started dispensing his tea into a clean mug. "This here tastes a lot better with sugar." He waved a small sugar bowl at her and raised his eyebrows in query.

"No, thank you. These days I try to be careful of calories, of course, so I try to drink tea and coffee black, though I prefer both cream and sugar."

Elmer handed the mug across to her. "Well, then, here you go . . . drink slow. It's still blisterin' hot. Now. Want to ask you if you know what really went on out there." He jerked a thumb once toward the hallway and once to his left, indicating, Angela supposed, the fire escape. "Nurse Pilgrim says you just got dizzy and fell. Is that the straight of it? That how you remember it?"

"Not at all. Somebody pushed me," Angela said, taking a sip of her tea. "Oooh, you're right, this is hot. But not too hot to drink," she added politely, taking another sip. "Yes, I was pushed. I was standing out there minding my own business . . ." Elmer snorted but said nothing. "No, truly. I was minding my own business. Just thinking that I had to be careful because the steps were slippery. And somebody tried to push me over the edge."

"Who? Who done it?"

"I haven't the faintest idea." She sipped again. "But *you* might know."

"I might?" The old man glared ferociously. "Well, maybe I might, but I don't. You got some funny ideas, young woman. Say listen, don't you want some sugar in that after all? It's like I told you, all them herbal things taste better with a little sugar." He stuck one bony hand out commandingly.

Angela yielded to his unspoken request, passing the cup back to him. "You may be right. When I was little, Mother always used to put sugar into . . . but just one spoonful, now. Let's see, where were we? Oh, yes. I was saying that I thought you might have an idea about who pushed me. Because whoever came down the hall would probably pass your open doorway. You'd have to see him. Or her. For instance, if it was Miss Goodwin . . ."

Elmer was stirring the mixture in the mug, and his stirring became faster and harder so that the little drops of tea spun out onto the coverlet. "Dang! Dagnabit! Miss Dragon's gonna have a fit! Likes everythin' neat around here. Here . . . drink it up." He passed the tea back to her. "Now what was you sayin' about Miss Goodwin pushin' you?"

"Now, now—I didn't say that. You're jumping to conclusions," Angela said and took a taste of her drink. "Oh ... you're right about the tea. It's much better with sugar, thank you." She sipped in silence a moment while she tried to gather her thoughts. How could she explain this so she didn't antagonize the old man? She was certainly not operating on all cylinders this afternoon, she thought. She tried again. "Mr. Johanson, all I was trying to say was that anybody coming the length of the hall would have to pass your door. And you might have seen anyone who was, oh, say, tiptoeing down the hall in my direction. It could have been Mr. Benton or one of the grandchildren. Or a complete stranger. I didn't mean to accuse your Miss Goodwin. I only used her as an example. Did you see anybody?"

"No. Didn't see nobody. 'Course, I wasn't lookin'. I was watchin' TV, and—" The old man started to cough. "Blast. My lungs don't work right, my stomach don't work right, my bladder don't work right—and sometimes I think my brains don't work right neither. I thought you was tellin' me Miss Goodwin pushed you."

"Oh, no. At least, I don't really know. I never got turned around to get a good look before the push, and afterwards I was too busy grabbing the rail to try to see who it was. I couldn't even guess. That's why I asked you."

The old man coughed again, harder. "You gonna have to let me be awhile," he wheezed. "Can't catch my breath. Here . . ." He stretched out a skinny arm and grabbed her mug of tea away from her, set it over on the bedside table, and made shooing motions with both hands. "You go find the Warden. Tell her to get back here. She's got somethin' she does when my cough gets bad. You go tell her I need her. Git . . ."

Angela decided not to bother with a show of annoyance. He was being rude, of course, but he had a good reason. She eased herself out of the soft chair, moving toward the elevator and the first floor as fast as she could with her aches and pains. Miss

Pilgrim was not hard to find, as it turned out. Angela simply left the elevator and there the woman was, standing over by the big Christmas tree in the lobby, talking with one of the regular CSM nurses, and she responded quickly and without comment to Angela's summons, heading rapidly into the elevator and disappearing as its heavy door slid shut.

"Good to see you up and about, Mrs. Benbow," the CSM nurse was saying cheerfully. "We heard you'd fallen or fainted or something. Doc Carter was over to see you this morning, though, right?"

Angela nodded at her and hesitated. The nurse's face was familiar but a name escaped her. Angela racked her brains. Was this Mary Washington? Thelma Zumwalt? Or was this Jeanne Blanchard? Yes. Blanchard. That was her name. She's been here three years, Angela was scolding herself silently. How could I forget? Angela smiled at Nurse Blanchard and then shook her head slightly. "Sorry to be slow to answer. Yes, I'm up and about. But I'm not feeling . . . I thought I was much better, but . . ." She shook her head again. The heaviness, the grogginess, the fuzziness she'd felt earlier had all come back with a vengeance, and she was feeling faintly nauseated.

"Are you all right, Mrs. Benbow?" Miss Blanchard was saying. "You really don't look well."

"To tell you the truth . . ." Angela hated admitting to weakness, especially to someone she didn't know well, but she thought perhaps this was one instance in which she should make an exception. "To tell you the truth, this is probably a relapse. Just a small one, but perhaps I'll go to my apartment and rest, after all. Everybody says I should. I think . . . I think I will." She turned toward the four steps that led to her hallway and hesitated, swaying and feeling dizzy.

"Mrs. Benbow!" The nurse moved forward quickly to take her arm. "Let me help you."

"Oh yes, please. First door on the left, just at the head of the steps. Here are my keys . . ." She fished around in her pocket. "Here . . ." She held the keys out and then, to her own surprise, she dropped them. Her fingers just let go, and the keys fell to the floor with a jangle. "That's funny," she started to say, and then she looked up at Miss Blanchard and smiled, just a little. "Well, maybe not so funny. My fingers are just the first part of me to let go. I seem to be turning to jelly, one inch at a time!" And she slid slowly toward the floor, her eyes rolling back, the small smile still on her lips.

Chapter 17

FOR THE second time within twenty-four hours, Angela roused herself from a blackness that was not a natural sleep. Awareness returned first, far more quickly than the ability to control her body, and she realized that she was in the process of being sick to her stomach and that she could not apparently stop herself. And since she seemed to be too weak or too uncoordinated to walk on her own, she was, as she finally realized, being supported, steered, encouraged, soothed, fussed over, and finally cleaned up by Dr. Carter and a nurse. At last, with her heaving reflexes quiet, her ruined outer clothing removed and deposited in a hamper, her person gently sponged and toweled, Angela—wearing only her slip and underwear, no outer garments—was guided back to her bed. It was a mark of how drastically she had been weakened that her unclothed state distressed her not at all, and she registered only that she had become both more comfortable and more able to think.

Dr. Carter filled a hypodermic from a small vial, tapped the syringe judiciously, squirted the obligatory drops into the air, then plunged the needle into Angela's plump shoulder.

"Ow!" she croaked out. "What're you doing? I hate shots!"

"Ah, there she is," the doctor said cheerfully. "Wide awake and back with us. Feeling a lot better, too, I'd be willing to bet. Mrs. Benbow, why didn't you tell me you reacted so profoundly to some sleeping medications? I'd have been more careful of which one I gave you."

"A reaction to my medication?" Angela said blankly.

"Probably," Carter said. "Food poisoning could do it, of course, but you've eaten nothing that hasn't been served to everyone else here, have you? And none of them is sick. A virus is a possibility, but Nurse Blanchard here tells me there's nothing special going around the place, and I'd expect at least one or two other residents to have the same symptoms if some kind of flu was the problem. So my best guess is the Xanax I gave you. Most people tolerate it very well, but once in a great while . . . well, I'll be able to tell you more later today after the lab takes a look."

"A look? At what?"

"You don't want to know, Mrs. Benbow," Dr. Carter said, hastily tucking a screw-top container away in his black bag. "Don't think about it. Now, we've been working with you . . ." he checked his watch, ". . . maybe twenty minutes altogether. Nurse Blanchard tells me you collapsed at the door to your room and she phoned me as soon as she got you onto your bed. And since then the three of us have been pretty busy. So we haven't had time to phone your friend Mrs. Wingate for you, but we'll do it now because I think you should have someone with you for a while, though with the shot I've given you, you'll be wide awake and functioning within another half hour, I'd guess."

"I'm through woopsing?"

Carter grinned at the childish term. "Oh, I don't think you have to worry about that. In fact, I expect you to feel weak but eager for supper in another hour or so. Assuming I'm right about what ails you. We'll see, but I certainly expect you to revive."

It was true, Angela realized, that she felt more awake than she had since the night before. "What was in that shot?" she asked suspiciously.

"Call it a tonic. An antidote to the sleeping medicines I gave you before. Your reaction was so violent—"

"I told you this morning," Angela said crossly. "I told you I was feeling dull and my head was spinning a little bit. I thought those pills you gave me for today were supposed to wake me up from the pill you gave me last night."

"Goodness, no, Mrs. Benbow. Xanax is a sedative as well . . . though it's a totally different chemical from the barbiturate I gave you last night."

"You weren't giving me something to wake me up?"

"Certainly not. I wanted you to sleep today. A lot. It never dawned on me that you'd fight the effects—that you'd try to stay up and stay active."

"I had things to do," Angela said sulkily. "I can't afford to spend the afternoon lounging around—though I suppose now I'll have to." She repeated just about the same complaint to Caledonia when her friend arrived under full sail a few minutes later, in time to get a summary of Angela's troubles from Doc Carter and to bid him and Nurse Blanchard good-bye.

"Can't I leave you alone for five minutes without you getting into trouble?" Caledonia said cheerfully. "Of course I realize it's not your fault if you're allergic to Doc Carter's little pills."

"Not an allergy," Angela said. "Doc Carter says just a strong reaction. And maybe some side effects." But she sounded skeptical.

"All right, all right—but whatever you call it, surely now you'll take your doctor's advice and get some rest. And I'm here now to see that you do just that."

"Cal, I'm not going to take it easy. I still have things to do. If you want to help me, well and good. In fact, for what I have in mind, I really need your help. You see, I'm not at all sure this is just a reaction to Doc Carter's sedative, no matter what he says. Sit down for a bit while I clean up a little more and put on a dress. I can explain through the bathroom door. Okay?"

"You could use a little freshening up, all right," Caledonia said. "I've seldom seen you looking so bedraggled."

"Well, they had to keep cleaning me off," Angela said. "It was . . . it was embarrassing." She went to her closet and pushed hangers around impatiently, finally selecting an A-line dress of periwinkle blue that hid her girth satisfactorily. "This should do to go visiting." She hung the dress up beside the bathroom and ducked inside, leaving the door ajar so she could still be heard. "You see, I can take all sorts of medicines and never have a sign of a bad reaction. No side effects, no nothing. So I've been thinking—now, don't laugh, but I think I was poisoned."

Despite Angela's warning, Caledonia, perched on the edge of the bed as Angela worked at repairing her person, did laugh, a snort of surprise and amusement. "Oh, come on, girl. Who'd want to poison you?"

"Elmer Johanson, that's who." Angela's voice was slightly muffled under a damp washcloth. She had run hot water into the washbowl and was scrubbing vigorously.

"That dear little old man?" Caledonia's voice was raised to near-bellow to be sure Angela could hear over all the splashing and huffing. "Are we talking about the same fellow, Angela? Elmer, who's sixty years older than a goat and who can hardly walk? Elmer, who has IVs and oxygen tanks all over his apartment? Elmer, who spends his time in a hospital bed watching TV reruns? Listen, even if he could manage to get hold of poison, and even if he could coax you into taking it, why would he want to do it?"

"Oh, I have a theory about that. And don't be so sure he's so helpless. He's been out of that bed a lot recently, don't forget. I don't know where he'd get hold of poison, but he certainly got me to take it. Every time I go up there now, he's feeding me some of those herbal teas. He gave me some this afternoon, and I got sick within minutes."

The sloshing noises ceased and Angela was obviously toweling herself vigorously as she talked, so her words came out jerkily. Still, Caledonia could hear clearly, and heavy skepticism laced her response. "Now why would he do that? I mean, he wouldn't poison somebody just because they don't share his enthusiasm for *My Mother the Car*, and what else is he interested in these days?"

"In protecting Nurse Goodwin. Listen to me, Cal." Angela's voice was muffled again as she pulled clothing on over her head. "I think the whole reason he invited me to come upstairs today was to ask whether or not I saw who pushed me. I started to explain to him, and he got very upset. Something I said made him think I was accusing Betty Goodwin, and he got very defensive. And then was when he offered me the tea. The timing is highly suspicious, I'd say." She came out of the bathroom and turned for Caledonia's inspection. "Well, how do I look? Presentable?"

"Mmmmm, a little far-fetched, I think. Not the dress. The theory. You look fine, but you think all twisted."

"Well, how about this? Not only did he offer me tea as soon as I mentioned his nurse, but when I said I hadn't seen the person who attacked me—had no idea who it was—he took the tea back!"

"He took back the tea? That's . . . well, that *is* odd. But . . ."

"Of course it didn't seem strange at the time. He got to coughing, you see, and he said he wanted Miss Pilgrim to help him get comfortable again. He wanted me to go fetch her, and I thought at the time he was taking my tea back to hurry me on my way. But now I wonder if he wasn't taking it so I wouldn't get any more of the poison than I had gotten. I mean, when I said I wasn't after his precious Betty Goodwin, maybe he was sorry he poisoned me and tried to stop in mid-dosage, if you see what I mean." She motioned Caledonia to follow her out to the living room and join her where they could both sit in more comfort.

"Okay, I allow that you have cause to be paranoid," Caledonia said. "You were attacked, after all. But, Angela, you're really stretching it. That little old man can't possibly be suspected of—"

"See what Lieutenant Martinez says then. He'll believe me!"

But the lieutenant proved to be a hard sell for her theories when he showed up at her apartment fifteen minutes later. "Serendipity," Angela sighed, registering her pleasure at his arrival, though it was hard to tell whether her murmur was satisfaction that she could now fill him in on her afternoon's activities or a happy reaction to his mere presence.

He had been on his way to see her anyway, he said, but as he came past the front desk in the lobby, their enthusiastic clerk Clara had told him of Angela's illness. "It made me laugh," he said. "Oh, not your being sick. I'm really very sorry about that, dear lady. But about Clara's telling me the latest news as soon as I stepped through the front door. I can never get over the way everybody in this place knows everything about everybody else—and doesn't mind talking about it. It's what living in a small town must be like."

Caledonia laughed aloud. "Absolutely. And that's why Angela and I are so much help to you, Lieutenant. You're too young to know that strong urge to share that the elderly feel—almost as though if they talk about their experiences and exchange reactions, they're still part of the world. Do you know what I mean? Telling our stories and passing on the gossip is a way of feeling that we're not left out of things—that life hasn't passed us by. So sooner or later everybody around here talks about whatever it is they know that we don't know, and we're good listeners, Angela and I, which is why we always have information to pass on to you. Whatever would you do without us?"

"And speaking of sharing experiences, Lieutenant," Angela said, seizing the momentary pause to get back at the center of attention, "if you hadn't come, I'd have sent for you. Because I have something tremendously important to report. You see, I wasn't just sick! This," she said grandly, "was another attempt on my life!" And she plunged headlong into her theory about old Elmer Johanson defending his favorite nurse with poisoned tea.

"Mrs. Benbow, you're incorrigible. Elmer Johanson? I can hardly . . . well, I'll look into that, of course. Among other things. But I can hardly think of him as a suspect—except in the sense that everyone here is a suspect. Surely his physical condition makes him highly unlikely."

"It doesn't take much energy," Angela said sulkily, "to poison a mug of tea. No more energy than picking up a teaspoon and stirring. I'm telling you that the man tried to do away with me, and you won't take me seriously!"

"Oh, I take you seriously. So seriously that I don't want you talking to *any*body about this case from here on," Martinez went on earnestly. "Whether I believe you were poisoned today or not, you certainly were attacked last night. And the attack on Dan Benton was real. So was the attack on his aunt—and hers had fatal results. Incidentally, that's why I stopped in here—to tell you there's really not much doubt she was killed by some kind of attack. This morning the medical examiner and I had a moment, and I was able to get him to explain some of the things in his report on Mrs. Benton. I got a different slant on what happened to her. Remember I said accident was just as likely as murder? Well, she had a bruise that was probably caused when she fell, almost certainly already dying, under the Christmas tree. But she had an injury at the base of her skull, as though someone hit her with an upward stroke of something—something with no sharp edges but something heavy. Not an injury she could easily sustain by falling against anything that was near or under that tree."

"I told you so! I told you so!"

"I knew you'd be pleased," he said dryly. "But you can surely see why I don't want you getting in my way." The look on Angela's face—astonishment mingled with outrage—made Martinez hasten on. "I mean, you mustn't put yourself in further danger. You must stay out of things now, Mrs. Benbow." When she bristled, he said hastily, "Oh, you can do all the things you'd ordinarily do. Just don't go asking a lot of questions. And don't wander the halls alone at night."

"I can still talk to people?"

"Of course. As I say, lead your normal life. Just . . . just stay out of trouble. Please. For my part, I'm off to Oceanside to interview the niece and nephew again. Then it's back to the office for a full evening of paperwork." He moved to the door and gave a little half bow of farewell. "Mrs. Benbow . . . Mrs. Wingate . . . I am grateful to you both for all your help. But now behave yourselves, both of you." His dazzling smile took the sting out of the words, and both women smiled warmly in return as he waved his good-bye and closed the hall door behind him.

"I'll say it again," Angela beamed. "Just like Gilbert Roland at his best."

Caledonia nodded in agreement, then yawned, stretched, and checked her wristwatch. "Well, it's getting on toward dinnertime. It would be the sherry hour, but I'm sure you don't feel like coming down to my place for a tiny drink. You may not even feel like having dinner."

"Oh, but I do. Doc Carter was absolutely right. I'm much better and I'm even getting hungry, though I'm not at all sure I'd be up to a sherry. Besides, I have something else I want to accomplish between now and dinnertime."

"You're not going to ask more questions, are you? You heard the lieutenant."

"No questions. But the lieutenant didn't believe me when I said I was poisoned by the tea."

"Neither do I, girl. Neither do I."

"Well, I'd like to prove whether I was or not. So I have this idea—I propose we go upstairs to see Elmer Johanson."

"I thought you weren't going to ask any questions."

"I'm not. Not a one, believe me. I'm going to set a trap!" Angela's eyes were blazing with enthusiasm. "I'm going to get Elmer to give me another mug of tea, and then I'm going to tempt him into poisoning me again! Only this time I won't drink it . . . not a sip. I'll just get a sample to Lieutenant Martinez, we'll have him analyze it, and then he'll find the poison, and . . ."

"Oh, Angela, you can't just walk out of Elmer's place with a cup of hot tea in your hand. If he's innocent, he'll think you've gone crazy. If he's guilty . . ."

"Oh, he's guilty, all right!"

"I said *if* and I mean it. If he were guilty, you'd tip him off and he'd be able to flush the poison or throw it out his window or something and you'd never be able to prove—"

"No he won't. He'll never know, because I'll be very careful. I won't take the whole cup. I'll just sneak a little bit. I know exactly how to do it. I'll hold the cup out of sight, and you . . . you'll distract him! Now the first thing to do is find some sort of bottle or jar . . ." Angela went into her bedroom and began hunting around in the drawers where she kept cosmetics. Nothing.

"How about a medicine bottle?" Caledonia said. She had come into the room behind Angela and stood near the door watching with amusement as her friend pawed through one drawer after another. "One thing old people have plenty of is leftover prescriptions. And if you don't have some you've nearly emptied, I do. Look in the medicine chest, why don't you?"

"Good thinking!" Angela transferred her attention to the bathroom and the mirrored door behind which stood a bewildering array of over-the-counter curatives: cough syrups, painkillers, cortisone creams, antibiotics, sleeping medicines, antihistamines, antacids, laxatives, fungicides, iodine, foot powder, and a diuretic. These were jammed in between boxes of baking soda, tins of Band-Aids, a thermometer, a carton of Q-tips, two tubes of toothpaste and a brush, a jar of rich night cream, a roll-on deodorant, and a half-dozen little brown bottles with prescription labels. Angela, rummaging among the boxes and tins and bottles and jars, finally came up with a small prescription bottle containing just one pill. "Here's one I can use," she called out. "The label says May 1972. This should have been tossed out a long time ago anyhow."

Angela shook out the lonely pill and tossed it into the toilet. Then she scratched off the label, already curled up on two corners, "so it'll come out of my pocket here smoothly the minute I need it. It's really perfect," she went on. "The top is tight, so it won't leak, and there'll be enough of a sample for the lieutenant to analyze. Come on, here we go . . ."

Caledonia sighed and began the heavy task of rising to her feet. "Okay, okay—wait for me. I'm coming. I wouldn't for the world miss the sight of you trying to get yourself poisoned!

Besides, somebody has to protect you—if only from making a complete fool of yourself."

Elmer was suitably surprised to see his visitors. It was nearly four o'clock, and the changing of the guard was under way, with Miss Pilgrim giving over her charge to Miss Goodwin. Elmer acknowledged his introduction to Caledonia with interest—"You're a big-un, ain'tcha? Used to see you in the dinin' room, back when I first arrived and I was still comin' downstairs to meals. But I don't ever get downstairs no more. So we never really had a chance to talk face-to-face for long. Glad to meetcha formal like."

He waved a scrawny, blue-veined hand at his nurses, gesturing them to leave. "Go over the gossip down in the lobby, you two. Don't bother me and my guests here. Just bring out a extra chair for the big ol' gal, an' leave me a pot of my tea. Oh, and make sure I have three clean cups."

"Oh, none for me, thank you," Caledonia said hastily. "It's almost time for dinner. And we're not staying long."

"I'll have some," Angela said. "Thank you. You have the most interesting teas. What is it this time? More rose hip?"

"It's cranberry tea, actually, Mrs. Benbow," Miss Pilgrim said, pulling two clean mugs from the bottom of the nightstand and checking the temperature of the teapot that stood on the stand's top. "Mmmm . . . still warm enough. Freshly made only about fifteen minutes ago. Mr. Johanson keeps a glass of fruit juice and some tea beside him constantly. I think he sips more from boredom than anything else."

"He's got more fruit juice bottles in here than most people have Kleenex," Betty Goodwin said cheerfully as she pulled a small folding chair out of a closet and set it up beside the easy chair near the bed before she followed her starchy colleague out of the room. And it was true, as Angela could see—the closet shelf was lined with a variety of juice bottles. Three more—grape, cranberry, and apple—sat on the floor near the nightstand, ready for use.

Miss Goodwin's head popped back into the room around the doorjamb. "I'll just be downstairs in the lobby when you want me," she called to her patient, and the head disappeared again as quickly as it had appeared, as Miss Goodwin presumably followed her colleague down the hall.

"Well, sit down, sit down," Elmer said impatiently, turning his attention to the teapot while his guests moved toward the chairs. To Caledonia's dismay, Angela took the easy chair. It was natural, perhaps, since the easy chair was closest to the bed, but that left only the more precarious perch for Caledonia, and it was a chair of the lightweight, folding variety that institutions always use to make extra places at entertainments and meetings. Caledonia eased her bulk onto the tiny seat and glowered, but Angela and Elmer seemed oblivious to her discomfort, and that increased Caledonia's annoyance. She began a series of weight shifts and deep sighs designed to call attention to her plight, but she might as well have saved herself the trouble. Nobody noticed.

Moving very carefully, Elmer was pouring out two mugs of tea. "Don't want to spill none this time. Got hell from the Dragon about what I dripped onto the covers earlier. Say, we heard you was sick. Sorry about that, of course, but it ain't the flu, is it? I shouldn't be around nobody with a cold or nothin' like that. They say I might catch it and get carried off by it. I mean, I'm goin' soon anyhow, but I don't wanna hurry it up none. So if you got a cold . . ."

"No, Doc Carter says it was probably just a . . . . well, an allergy, you know. A side effect of the sleeping medicine. Anyhow, it's nothing you could catch." Angela took a deep breath and plunged headlong into her planned attack. "I notice Betty Goodwin still works for you."

"That's right," Elmer said. "Here's your tea."

"Oh. Aren't you going to put sugar into it?"

Elmer shrugged and set the tea back on his bedside table, rummaging through the jumble of odds and ends on its surface. Presumably, somewhere in the muddle, lay the sugar bowl and a spoon.

"About Betty Goodwin," Angela prodded. "I've been thinking that perhaps we ought to ask her more questions." She glanced ostentatiously away from the old man as he pushed the items on his nightstand first this way, then that. "In fact, I've been wondering about her more than ever," she went on insistently. "What do you know about her background? Has anything like a murder ever happened in a household where she was working before? I know you like her, but that can't stop us from considering her as a suspect."

She peeked through the corners of her eyes and was gratified to see Elmer was still fumbling among things on the tabletop. Surely if it were only sugar he was putting into her cup, he would have done it before now and passed the cup across to her. Now he was reaching into the drawer of the nightstand, and Angela felt certain he was going for the poison at last. She looked quickly away so he wouldn't catch her watching, and as she turned, she caught a glimpse of Caledonia gazing steadily at the old man as he worked.

"Sssssssst . . ." Angela whispered, behind a hand that masked her mouth. "Look down. Or look out into the hall. Or at the ceiling. He won't get out the poison if you look right at him."

Caledonia grinned, but turned her attention to her wristwatch, seeming to check it, set it, check it again, reset it . . .

"Here . . ." Elmer was holding forward the steaming cup. "Come over and get it, will you, Mrs. Benbow? I can't stretch no further'n I'm reachin' this minute." He fished a Kleenex from his bedside supply. "Got no napkins. This'll have to do."

Angela smiled sweetly. "Of course. Mmmm, this smells wonderful. I do enjoy your herbal teas, Mr. Johanson." She carried the cup and the makeshift napkin back toward her chair, and while her back was still toward the bed, she grimaced at Caledonia and jerked her head twice. She meant to indicate that Caledonia was to create the agreed-on diversion, but as Caledonia told her later, she looked instead as though she'd been afflicted by a nervous twitch.

"I couldn't figure out what on earth you were trying to tell me," Caledonia said later. "If we're going to execute a conspiracy, we're going to have to work out a set of signals. Making faces just won't cut it."

"Well, what else could I possibly have wanted?" Angela said crossly. "Besides, you did it, didn't you? Created the diversion, I mean."

In fact what happened was that just as Angela reached her chair with her mug of tea in one hand, the other hand in her pocket clutching at the little vial, ready to dip out a sample whenever Elmer turned his head away, Caledonia fell off the edge of her own chair and hit the carpet with a thump, followed by a loud "Ooof!"

"Too much twisting and wriggling," Caledonia explained ruefully later. "I should have known better, with that midget-sized seat. Not mine, you understand. The chair's seat. A three-X bottom just won't fit on a junior petite chair!"

At the time, however, Angela assumed that the fall was a fake, that her friend was following orders and deliberately creating the requested diversion. So Angela ducked down a little with her back to old Elmer, flicked her thumb to remove the cap from the little bottle, dipped the bottle into the mug, then set the mug quickly onto the floor while she recapped the bottle, wrapped it in the Kleenex, and returned it to her pocket. Then she turned to Caledonia with dramatic cries of dismay.

"Of course I wasn't hurt. Not permanently," Caledonia said later. "But you might have shown a little more concern."

"I thought I *was* showing concern!"

"Hah! Some concern. Standing there wringing your hands and pretending to sob and saying 'Oh, poor Caledonia' over and over!"

"I didn't know you'd really fallen," Angela said defensively. "Besides, you weren't hurt, were you?"

"Only my pride. As for my body, well, I'm bruised but not broken. I've got too much padding for a little fall like that to do any permanent damage."

"Well, the most important thing is that your falling gave us the excuse to get out of there quickly so we could get our sample analyzed while it was fresh."

"Does that make a difference?" Caledonia asked curiously.

"I don't know. But we couldn't take a chance, could we? So it was wonderful to be able to say we had to get you to the nurses' station to be checked out. Elmer didn't even suspect what we were up to! And Swanson has taken our sample to their lab, and . . ."

The women had hurried to the elevator, Caledonia limping slightly after the fall, intending to put in a call to Martinez from Angela's apartment. But as they stepped out at the lobby level, Angela spotted Martinez' young partner, Shorty Swanson, saying good-bye to his girl at the doorway. Now that he and Chita Cassidy, Camden-sur-Mer's prettiest waitress, were formally engaged, the sight of them holding hands and kissing as they met or as they parted no longer excited comment, favorable or otherwise. Originally some had been annoyed, others charmed by the open display of young love. Now, after six months, everyone took it in stride. This evening Chita had been helping to set the tables for dinner, and Swanson had been asking more questions among the late Mrs. Benton's neighbors. They had met at the dining room doors as he headed toward the front door and his car, and that's where Angela spotted them.

It really didn't take her long to explain what she wanted, and Swanson, nodding his agreement, took the little medicine bottle in its Kleenex wrapping and presumably headed straight for headquarters and the lab. "The lieutenant will be in touch," he promised.

And now, about a half hour after dinner, the women sat in Angela's apartment, Angela happily crowing over her own cleverness. But Angela could be tiresome when she was excessively pleased with herself. The third or fourth time she repeated the story of her Elmer-trap, Caledonia held up a hand to stop her. "Please!" she said. "Enough! You don't need to tell it to me. I was there. I saw it for myself." But Angela might have spent the rest of the evening in self-congratulation if a knock at the door had not interrupted her.

To the delight of both women, it was Lieutenant Martinez. He bowed to both ladies, refused the offer of a sherry—"Not while I'm on duty, thank you"—and pulled a notebook from his pocket. "I suppose I should scold you both for paying no attention at all to my warnings to stay safely out of matters. But somehow—as you often do—you've managed to be very useful indeed. It would be ungrateful of me not to acknowledge at least that much."

"You have the lab analysis of the tea! Already!"

"Yes, Mrs. Benbow, I do. Oh, we can really move when we have to. Of course we've had nearly three hours to work, and it turned out to be a fairly simple job. But . . . well, let me give you the results and then I'll tell you what I did about it."

"Oh, do, please!"

"All right." He flipped open his notebook. "There was a lot of tap water, of course, and sugar—various fruit sugars and plain old cane sugar. But you're interested in what I might call active ingredients. Well, there was oxalic acid—"

"Acid?"

"The kind of acid that occurs naturally in cranberries, Mrs. Benbow."

"Oh. I see. Well, Elmer said it was cranberry tea."

"Then there was tannic acid and caffeine . . ."

"Don't tell me," Caledonia said. "Those come from real tea leaves."

"I guess the herbal mix had honest-to-goodness tea in it then," Angela said. "I thought they didn't. I thought they were made of other things like jasmine blossoms and marigold leaves."

"Let the lieutenant go on, Angela," Caledonia shushed her. "He's not through."

"That's right. All of those were of no real importance. The significant ingredient we found . . ." He paused, and Caledonia suddenly realized that the lieutenant was not opposed to injecting a little drama into his report, ". . . was codeine."

"Codeine? I knew it! I knew it!" Angela was jubilant. "Well, have you arrested him?"

"Oh, I went directly upstairs as soon as I got back here."

"Aha!"

"It was possible that you might be onto something. But there were two problems . . ."

Angela, flushed with the pleasure of having her deductions verified, simply ignored the *but* clause. "So go on," she said. "What happened when you confronted Elmer? Did he confess?"

"No, dear lady, he did not. I questioned both Mr. Johanson and his nurse. Of course, it's that Goodwin woman on duty tonight, and she can be hard to pin down to reality, as I'm sure you're aware. But both of them—Elmer and the nurse—deny that Elmer has access to codeine in any form. And that's the first problem with your theory."

"But that can't be true!" Angela was indignant. "Surely you don't believe them?"

"Oh, but I do believe them. Because the old man challenged me to find any codeine, and his invitation was what I needed, since I lacked a warrant. He's got dozens of prescriptions, but none of them contains codeine. I didn't stop with that bedside pharmacy of his. I looked everywhere. Quickly but, trust me, I was thorough. Finally I had to agree that there's probably no codeine at all in the Johanson apartment."

"Oh dear!" Angela was truly dismayed. "I was so sure. . . . But there was codeine in the sample I gave you. You said so. So where could he have got hold of it?"

Martinez smiled. "You're asking the wrong question, Mrs. Benbow. You shouldn't ask. 'Where could he have got it?' but 'Where did it come from?' "

Caledonia gave an impatient noise. "You're stringing this out, Lieutenant. Get to the point!"

Martinez turned to Angela. "Where did you get that bottle, Mrs. Benbow?"

"My medicine chest," Angela said promptly. "There was one tablet left of an old prescription dated more than ten years ago, so I threw the pill away. I even destroyed the label. But I remember when I got it and what it was for. I was still living in

Washington, DC, with my husband and I broke my foot. Silly accident. I just stepped off a high curb and I must have put my foot down funny, because all of a sudden I couldn't walk on it at all! It hurt terribly. I wore a cast for eight weeks, and even after that it ached. My doctor tried two or three different prescriptions to help with the pain. And one of them . . ." Her face fell. "Oh no! Don't tell me . . ."

"Mrs. Benbow, I think it must have been *your* codeine we found traces of. Bits of tablets rub off over time and form a residue inside the bottle, and of course the powder would dissolve when you poured in the hot tea."

Angela was torn between embarrassment and anger. She decided on the latter reaction. "So you're just going to give up? Just like that? He could still have drugged me, you know. Don't ask me where he found codeine, but he could have . . ."

"He could have, perhaps. But he didn't. If he'd wanted to poison you," Martinez said, "if *any*one wanted to poison you, they'd have given you a massive dose. I said there were two problems with our theory, and that's the second one. With the tiny amount of codeine in your sample, the most someone could have done was to cure your headache!"

"But you investigated! Why'd you bother to come back here and question Elmer and search his place if the dose was so small it couldn't have killed me?" Angela's voice was sullen.

"Well, the old man's not a trained chemist, is he? It was just barely possible he did have lethal intentions and just guessed at how much codeine to give you. But I knew that was unlikely. People who don't know any better usually overshoot on the dosage when they mean to do someone harm. And incidentally, that saves a few potential victims, because sometimes an overdose makes them sick enough to throw up the poison before it takes full effect. If Elmer had overdosed you earlier and it didn't work, he'd have given you twice as much when he tried it a second time. We'd have found not the merest dusting but enough codeine in your sample to put the entire east wing of this place into a two-day sleep."

Angela looked up hopefully. "How about that first time? I was sick! You know that. I was sick, and I passed out—"

"Mrs. Benbow, I stopped by the nursing home across the street for a minute on my way here. To talk to your Dr. Carter. His lab has completed its analysis of your stomach contents—"

"Oh, yech!"

"—and there was no poison."

"No poison this morning, either? Then what . . ."

"Carter still thinks you were reacting to the medications he gave you. You didn't have the flu, that's certain. And there was no sign of food poisoning, unless you count a mysterious mixture of more than a dozen herbs that apparently came from old Elmer Johanson's teapot. You may very well have had a reaction to all that gunk, poured into a stomach made more sensitive by the sedatives. At least that's what Doc Carter thinks."

Caledonia burst out laughing. "She was full to the brim with sleeping potions that didn't sit well, she took aboard a full breakfast and followed it up with tea made from dandelion roots and lilac leaves, or some such, and when it makes her sick, she insists somebody poisoned her! Angela, you as good as poisoned yourself!"

"Mrs. Benbow," Martinez said, "let it go. The old man didn't poison you."

"But you said we had given you useful information. If it wasn't that Elmer is a poisoner, what—"

"It gave me a reason to start inquiries about his background, which I confess I hadn't bothered with before."

"But she's from right here in California and he's from the Midwest. And he's a good thirty years older than she, so they wouldn't be in the same—"

Martinez shrugged. "I didn't say checking would necessarily turn up anything incriminating. But in my view, eliminating a suspect is every bit as useful as adding one to the list. To prove—or at least to suggest—that one suspect was not involved after all allows me to concentrate on the other

suspects. It looks like that is exactly what you've done for
me: eliminate a suspect."

And to Angela's disappointment, that was the way matters
were left.

Chapter 18

THROUGHOUT THE following morning, Angela tried hard to be pleasant to people, but in spite of her best efforts she bit their heads off. She barked at Chita for slow breakfast service and at Caledonia for being so late for lunch that they had no time to talk about "our murder," as Angela called it. She found fault with Mrs. Schmitt's excellent wiener schnitzel: "First all that lamb, now veal—don't they do anything with fully grown, adult animals around here?" And when the dining room speakers suddenly erupted with Janice Felton's voice, reminding the diners that there was a dress rehearsal of Trinita's Christmas pageant in the lobby at 2:30, Angela slammed her fist on the table in frustration, making the silverware jingle in response.

"How can we be useful to the lieutenant if we just carry on with our everyday lives as though nothing unusual has happened? Am I the only one who cares who killed Birdy? I keep thinking we need to talk some more, you and I . . . to go over our notes, to reconsider the facts . . . If we could just analyze everything that's happened, everything we've learned and heard, if we could think things through together, I'm sure we could come up with something that would be helpful."

"Uh-huh. Sure. Well, you analyzed yourself right into being attacked night before last. Listen, your apartment is full of Christmas presents and wrapping materials, and I should think you'd want to get back to work on them instead of going in circles trying to solve a murder. Besides, the lieutenant told you to knock it off, didn't he? If you insist on worrying away at the murder, just sit down quietly and think things through by yourself. Your intuition is good—give yourself a chance to use it. And you don't need me for that. Anyhow, I have a bridge game this afternoon and there's that pageant rehearsal you're supposed to attend."

"Oh, that."

"Yes, that. Trinita really needs for everybody to be there. She phoned me just before I came up here for lunch to ask if you were well enough. She didn't want to disturb you, but she wanted to know if she could count on you today. I told her," Caledonia went on in a tone that was almost menacing, "I told her she could. You're not going to make a liar out of me, are you?"

"But they don't really need me. And I don't need the rehearsal. I mean, how much rehearsal does it take to stand absolutely still and say *Baaaa* every once in a while?"

"There are no small parts, just small actors," Caledonia quoted blithely. "Stop pouting and behave. And don't say you can't. I know you're capable of being charming and cooperative, if you'd just try. Even Trinita is being good, isn't she? I mean she promised you not to use the P.A. system, and she hasn't."

"That announcement . . ."

"She made Janice do it for her, didn't she? I could see her across the room while Janice was talking, and it was killing her, but she kept her promise. And if she can maintain decorum, so can you. Tell you what. If you'll behave yourself and go to the rehearsal, you can come to my place for a sherry before dinner tonight and we can talk then . . . provided you feel well enough, of course."

"Oh yes. I'm fine. Fine." Angela was still a little shaky but she'd never have admitted it, especially when she was in such a grumpy mood. "Sherry at four, then."

And after the wiener schnitzel was topped off by a slice of sour-cream-and-raisin pie, the women parted, Caledonia to her nap and then her bridge game, Angela to her own apartment.

No nap, of course—annoyed with the world as she was, even if she'd been aching for sleep, she'd have fought it. Besides, she felt wide awake. So she tried to watch television, but she had little success, despite an enhanced cable service; soap operas bored her, talk shows alternately shocked and disgusted her, there seemed to be no old movies on today's schedule that she hadn't seen at least three times, and even CNN appeared to be recycling the news, their announcers broadcasting, in voices that quivered with feigned excitement, the same items every half hour, over and over. Finally, reluctantly, Angela turned with a sigh to the as-yet-unwrapped Christmas gifts. Working rapidly, she bent the bright papers and twisted tinseled ribbon, and by just about two-thirty—when the dress rehearsal was scheduled—she had covered the last little box in red and green foil, frizzled the last length of ribbon into a curly bow, affixed the last tag, and put away scissors and sticky-tape, bundled the leftover rolls of paper and ribbon into their storage box ready to be taken back to the basement, and moved the pile of wrapped presents under her own Christmas tree.

Moving slowly because her fingers felt clumsy with fatigue and her arms shook slightly at the unaccustomed exertion, Angela folded up the table that had temporarily served as a work surface and slid it out of sight behind her armoire. The room looked suddenly bigger without the laden table set up in its center, and it certainly looked brighter and more festive with the little pile of wrapped gifts. Until she delivered them, the boxes would be a nice addition to her own holiday decorations, and gazing at them with satisfaction, she began to feel more reconciled with the world. She was positively gracious to the other actors when she arrived in the lobby just five minutes after the scheduled time for the rehearsal to begin.

The other actors were milling about at one side of the lobby, there being no wings in which to conceal themselves, wearing a confusion of makeshift costumes. To get to her place onstage—the open area of the lobby in front of the giant Christmas tree—Angela had to make her way through a forest of capes made of bedspreads, beach towels, shower curtains, and even a pair of flowered chintz drapes; robes that were in real life bathrobes, dressing gowns, or flannel nightshirts; and a bewildering melange of headdresses, most of which had been heavily influenced by Yassir Arafat, but which included a few bath-towel turbans and even one doughnut-shaped cushion (meant originally to relieve pressure on the coccyx) now painted gold, strung around with bright-colored necklaces and perched rakishly on the bald pate of one of the Kings of Orient.

"Oh, there you are," Janice Felton greeted Angela crossly. She was ordinarily a businesslike woman who wore clothing that looked as though she still worked in an office: sensible shoes with blouse-and-skirt outfits. Now, although she carried a clipboard with a cast list on it and importantly ticked off Angela's name, she wore a flowing light blue garment with a matching wimple that made her look rather like the illustration on a bottle of Liebfraumilch—obviously Janice's idea of what the Virgin Mary should be wearing for her lying-in.

"Not just late," Janice accused, "but you don't even have on your costume!"

"Nobody's ever given me a costume," Angela defended herself. "What kind of costume am I supposed to have anyway? I'm just a sheep."

"But I know Tootsie Armstrong was making a sheep suit out of an old white terry bathrobe. She brought it to me to ask what the ears should look like—she had made big floppy hound ears, and I had to tell her a sheep has little tiny ears like . . . like . . ." Janice tried desperately to find something to compare a sheep's ears to. "Well, you know. Little pointy things anyhow. Never mind. The thing is, she's remaking it, and I guess it's not ready. You'll have to do without today. We'll locate it before the show—that's a day and a half away, after all. Meantime, just take your place in your stall. You know your lines?"

"Of course," Angela started toward her place. "*Baaaaa.* That's it. Where's Trinita? Are we going to be late getting started? I don't want to be here all afternoon."

"She said to start without her," Janice said. "I've got the

script if anyone needs prompting. Now ... is everybody ready? Places, everybody. Places!" And she positioned herself center stage, Frenchy—their resident piano player—struck up "Silent Night," and Angela moved quickly over to her assigned place at Janice's right.

The maintenance men had done their work, and the manger setting, such as it was—a kind of threefold screen of grayish boards—was in place in front of the Christmas tree. Angela's "stall" was outlined by a short length of foot-high white pickets, propped up by bricks—the kind of temporary fencing gardeners buy in three-foot lengths to stand around flower beds to warn the mowing machine away from the petunias. In front of the makeshift manger hovered Mr. Grogan in a brown smoking jacket and a kind of burnoose made of old sheeting. And someone had furnished a very realistic baby doll to represent the Christ Child; the doll lay in a little cradle exactly center stage.

And there was an audience; three or four of the residents, presumably people who had nothing better to do, had dragged up chairs to watch. Angela caught sight of Elmer Johanson's evening nurse, the imaginative Betty Goodwin, sitting halfway down the room chatting to another nurse, one of Camden's regulars who appeared to be, at least for the moment, off duty. Angela stood inside her picket fence looking at Betty Goodwin with speculation, wondering if it would help to ask just a few more questions. It couldn't hurt, she told herself. If she did it judiciously, Lieutenant Martinez needn't know about it. She would just have to be careful how she told him anything she discovered.

"Angela," Janice warned sharply. "You must be on all fours!" Reluctantly, Angela sat stiffly down on the cold marble. To her dismay, she had discovered that getting all the way to the floor was not as easy as it had been as recently as four or five years ago. How long had it been since she'd even tried? And now that she was down, she wasn't sure she was ever going to be able to get up—not without help.

"Angela, sheep don't sit like that!" Janice was a stern shepherd. "Get on all fours, like I said!"

Angela glared, but levered herself into a position on hands and knees. "Oh! Ouch!" The marble was hard on unpadded patellae. She bit her lip, determined not to let the others know that her age was making the role of the sheep more difficult for her than she had anticipated. On-stage the rehearsal began, and Angela realized with surprise that she was hearing the lines for the first time—she had daydreamed through that other rehearsal and simply hadn't registered Trinita's version of the dialogue of the Nativity story. It was, to say the least, unusual. The Virgin Mary started things out with a lament that apparently concerned the perils of not phoning ahead for reservations. "Not a single room for rent! Not a one! And so this manger has had to serve us for the birth of our precious son."

"Mary, old girl, let's have a look at this baby here. . . . Aw, he's a cute one." Mr. Grogan's voice was blurred with his daily ration of spirits but all too understandable, and it was apparent that, perhaps having decided that his part was dull as written, he was ad-libbing. "You know, Mary, that's one good-lookin' kid we have."

"Child, Mr. Grogan! Child! Joseph would never refer to his son as a kid! And that's not how the script reads! I'd be obliged if you'd stick to your part!" The drill sergeant's voice belonged to Trinita, arriving late to her own rehearsal. Trinita was entering the lobby from the first-floor residence hallway that led to her apartment, and behind her Angela caught sight of Lieutenant Martinez, who strode the length of the lobby and disappeared out the front doors. Angela ached to know what had been going on.

She also ached literally along the whole length of her bent back. Add that to the pain in her knees, and she thought that perhaps she should just give up and do what she really longed to do—rise (to relieve her aching bones and muscles) and scurry after the lieutenant (to relieve her aching curiosity). She was restrained only by the thought of how humiliating it would be if she tried to rise and couldn't without asking someone to help her. That her rising would disrupt a dress rehearsal never entered her consideration.

"Child then," Grogan was saying sulkily. "Kid, child . . . same thing," he snarled. Then, blearily remembering that he had a job to do, he attempted to get back to the script. "Dost thou not think the baby is beautiful? And we ought to name him something . . ." He hesitated, apparently searching for his next line. From his bewildered expression, it was obvious that memory had failed him, and again he reached into his woolly subconscious for inspiration. "What dost thou think of Joseph Junior?"

The Virgin Mary was obviously stricken dumb by the suggestion. The director, however, was not. "Jesus!" hissed Trinita from the audience. "Jesus!"

"Don't you yell at me!" Mr. Grogan's defense was slurry with self-pity. "I'm sorry! I'm doing my best. I'll try to remember the line . . . whatever it is . . ."

"We will name him Jesus!" Trinita prompted again in a splutter of anger. Grogan stared vaguely at the baby doll in the cradle and said absolutely nothing. For a long minute there was silence on the stage.

"Oh! Oh! Someone cometh!" In desperation, Janice pushed on with the drama as scripted and jumped ahead to her own next line, delivered in a ringing, artificial voice. She gestured toward the milling group of bathrobes at the far side of the lobby. "I say, someone cometh!"

There was no response, the waiting actors being far too busy pushing and shoving and whispering to have heard a cue. "Oh, oh, someone cometh!" Janice intoned again. The other actors paid absolutely no attention. "Someone cometh!" Janice's voice had risen to a shout, and her arms waved desperately. It would appear that the Virgin Mary was approaching hysteria.

"Shepherds! Front and center!" Trinita's voice was enough to galvanize Emma Grant, Daisy Culpepper, and Minetta Holbrook, who leapt into the acting area, all three wearing men's outsized sweatshirts, belted over baggy leggings, and headdresses of checkered dinner napkins.

"We've been out in the fields every night since November," Emma Grant intoned.

"Doing our job, watching sheep by night," Daisy said, and sidled over to pat Angela on the head, presumably thereby identifying Angela's role, for any who had mistaken her for a fuzzy coffee table or an upholstered bench.

"Baaaa," Angela said unhappily, but correctly on cue. Trinita had presumably wanted the sheep to respond to stroking as a cat would purr at a touch, but Angela hated having anyone mess up her hair, and Daisy was patting with enthusiasm. *"Baaaaa."* Angela jerked her head aside.

"Angela! Stay still!" Daisy whispered and sidestepped to a position where she could give Angela's head one more pat.

"And this great big star came zooming in overhead," Minetta went on with her speech. "I mean, it was so *big . . .*" she went on, gesturing widely with both hands.

"Minetta! Everybody! Stop trying to pad your parts! Just say the lines as I wrote them!" Trinita's glare was ferocious and Minetta Holbrook pulled her arms down quickly.

"It was *real* big," she muttered defiantly. Trinita gave her a long, steady look, and Minetta beat a verbal retreat to Trinita's original script. "And then this angel appeared. All of a sudden . . ."

The rehearsal staggered on. It really didn't take more than fifteen minutes to finish with the shepherds, and for the Magi to enter with their lumpy camel (the Jackson twins wearing pillows strapped to their backs and bent over under a length of brown canvas). The three Kings of Orient presented their gifts to Joseph Junior, then a gaggle of miscellaneous "villagers" joined the group onstage and Joseph, tottering perilously as he bent to the cradle, succeeded with difficulty in lifting high the baby doll for the assemblage to admire. And finally an angel drifted in—Mrs. Dover sporting a queen-sized bedsheet, chicken-wire wings, and a blonde wig because Trinita insisted that all angels were blondes.

"Venite adoremus," Mrs. Dover intoned, spreading her

arms in blessing and waving her hands gracefully over the assembled cast members. *"Venite adoremus Dominum."*

The cast began to drift toward center stage for the finale, and Angela squirmed into an upright position, then pulled herself to her feet, finding to her relief that after all she could stand up without calling for some of the cast members to help her, so she was able to join the others as the cast sang "Oh Come All Ye Faithful" at the top of their lungs. The piano banged the melody out *fortissimo*, drowning the worst of the singers' weaknesses, and the rehearsal came to an end with a smattering of applause from the four residents in the audience.

"Thank you all. Good job. Good job," Trinita said, her voice cheerful in token of her unshakable optimism. "But do look at your scripts again—some of you are a bit shaky on your lines. Still, I believe there's a saying in the theater, 'Bad dress rehearsal, good opening night,' so don't worry about the little things that went wrong today. Now go change for dinner. We don't want people to see you in your costumes. It would spoil the surprise of our performance."

The cast scattered and Trinita began to gather up into a large basket the few props—the Wise Men's gifts, the cradle, and the Joseph Junior baby doll. Angela was the only actor still left on stage, mainly because she was watching Betty Goodwin down the way, deep in conversation with the Camden-sur-Mer nurse, and wondering if she really should approach Miss Goodwin with further inquiries. Was it wise? Hadn't Angela asked everything there was to ask? She should do something, but was it helpful to ask the same questions of the same people? . . . And as Angela stood there, Trinita walked over and took her arm. "Don't you worry, my dear," Trinita said. "We'll locate that costume of yours. I'm sorry it wasn't ready, but it will be here for the show."

"Oh, that wasn't what I was thinking about. It really isn't important." Angela caught sight of Trinita's expression—a mixture of surprise and annoyance—and backed down quickly. "Oh, I don't mean your pageant isn't important! I meant . . ." She relented and changed tack. "I meant that I'm

sure you will find the costume. I'm happy to rely on you."
Trinita relaxed and Angela pressed on. "What I really want to
know—what did the lieutenant want with you? I suppose that's
what delayed you joining us in the lobby, wasn't it?"

Trinita nodded happily. "He asked all the questions he's
asked before, and I answered them all over again. But he said
it was just to be sure. It was purely routine! So I didn't mind a
bit. Because, you see, he doesn't suspect me anymore. I really
must thank you for that, Angela. You were a good friend to talk
to him for me."

Angela wasn't against being thanked. Ordinarily she'd have
basked in the moment, but she had other things on her mind.
But she had zeroed in on a single aspect of what Trinita was
saying; the lieutenant was still asking questions of suspects,
including those he'd questioned before. And if that was true, it
had to be a perfectly sensible course of action for her to take
herself. So she merely nodded to Trinita and gave her a brief
half smile of farewell, then headed off down the lobby to inter-
cept Betty Goodwin before she went on duty. She had nearly
reached her goal when her attention was diverted. Daniel
Benton had come quickly in through the front door and headed
for the desk where the ever-present Clara rose from the switchboard to talk to the visitor.

What a happy coincidence! Angela changed direction so
immediately that an observer would have said she'd been
heading for the desk all along. Betty Goodwin might have to
leave the lobby for her duty station, but Angela could always
find her up there with the old man. Dan Benton was another
matter. The youngsters up in Anaheim might as well have been
in Timbuktu for all they were accessible to Angela. But Daniel
and his wife were within reach, although she hadn't yet faced
up to the problem of how to contact them. She didn't relish the
thought of another ride to Oceanside in the back seat of Emma
Grant's car, and yet she might have had to arrange one if she
were to have a chance to talk to any of Birdy's family at all.
But wonder of wonders, here was Daniel Benton now!

Angela was beaming with satisfaction as she arrived at the

desk just as Clara was leaving. "I'll fetch it for you right away," Clara said. "Mr. Torgeson left it somewhere on his desk. He's out for the afternoon, but I'll try to find it," and she disappeared into the inner office.

"Ah, Mr. Benton! How fortunate," Angela said. He had been looking the other way and hadn't seen Angela's approach, and he gave a nervous start at her voice. His head turned left and right, obviously hoping to find an escape, but Angela was there, and unless he wanted to be rude, there was little he could do but stand his ground. Angela extended a hand to be held, shaken, or kissed, depending on Daniel's idea of etiquette. He stared at the hand a moment, and then took it briefly in what was a cross between a shake and a squeeze.

"Of course. It's Mrs. Uh . . . Mrs. Uh . . . Mrs. Barbell," he muttered the name of which he was obviously so uncertain. "I'm here . . . ," he explained in that way people so often do, feeling the obligation to justify their actions to the world around them, "I'm here to pick up an inventory and receipt. We kept the nice pieces of Aunt Bea's furniture, of course. Split them up amongst us. But there were several things no one wanted, and I donated them to Mr. Torgeson. I thought he could sell them for the benefit of . . . you know, of this place. I don't suppose he got much . . ."

"Of course not. You took the good stuff for yourself," Angela snapped, and then was sorry because she should be soothing him, buttering him up, if she wanted him to answer questions. Fortunately, her cynical tone was lost on Daniel.

"Yes. True. But even if it's only a little, my lawyer says it'll be tax deductible. I'm not quite sure whether from our income or from the total of the estate . . . he's researching it right now."

"Well, every little bit helps, doesn't it?" Angela said, and thought to herself that this sounded more sympathetic.

Daniel apparently thought so, too. He even smiled a bit. "Absolutely. Every little bit. But of course I need receipts. The IRS is fussy about that these days, or so my lawyer says."

He fell silent and waited for her to say whatever it was she'd come over to say, and Angela was equally silent, uncertain how to approach her actual topic of interest. Daniel began to shift his weight from foot to foot and to drum his fingers impatiently on the countertop. If this was a stare-down, he was the first to blink.

"Have you—" Daniel finally cleared his throat and launched into a question of his own. "Have you and your friend discovered anything useful about my aunt's death? Lieutenant Martinez promised to keep me up to date about the investigation, but he told me nothing when he came over to my office. He had plenty of questions, but no information. Oh, by the way, I suppose I have you to thank for his visit. You told him about my little . . . my office romance, didn't you?"

Angela hesitated, uncertain quite how to answer him. This conversational turn might, she considered, ruin the effect of sympathy she'd been trying to achieve. The best defense being a good offense, however, she threw her head up and spoke haughtily.

"I certainly am not responsible for your problem with the police. I'm sure the lieutenant got his information from the same source Mrs. Wingate and I did—straight from Betty Goodwin." She looked across the room to where Betty Goodwin had been sitting, but the nurse was gone. There was, in fact, nobody else at all in the empty lobby now, which looked dark and shadowy with the Christmas tree blocking the light from the south side windows. They were completely alone. Angela cleared her throat, aware of a sense of dread. "Look, Mr. Benton," Angela said, pushing away any feeling of apprehension. "I need to ask you a few questions myself. Can't we sit down a moment?"

He shrugged and moved away from the lighted desk area, with Angela pattering behind him, and selected the nearest couch, an overly padded sofa with billowy seat cushions. His choice was, as Angela quickly discovered, a colossal mistake for her purposes. Daniel could sit in relative comfort, but she was so tiny she sank into the padded softness and it was difficult even to shift position enough to face him. She struggled into a half-turned position and then hesitated. "Uh—" The truth was, she simply didn't know how to approach her subject. The one question she wanted to ask was, "Did you or didn't you kill your aunt?" And that of course was the one question she could not ask directly. "But I bet if I did," she was thinking, "I could tell a lot from his reaction. Caledonia is right. My intuition is good, and I bet I'd know right away whether he was telling the truth."

"Well? I thought you said you had something to ask me," Benton was saying. He waited, looking at her curiously. She remained silent, still searching futilely for the right approach, the right question. . . .

"Mrs. Uh—Mrs. Birnbaum, I really don't have much time, and when your desk clerk locates the receipts I came to pick up, I'll have to—"

"Did you kill your aunt?" The last thing on earth she'd meant to do was to come out with those words, but now that they were out, Angela took full advantage of their shock value. And shocked he seemed to be. If the truth were known, so was she. She really hadn't meant to say any such thing. "It was just nervousness," she told Caledonia later. "I didn't know what to ask him, now that I had his attention, and it just sort of came out!"

"Mrs. Beanbach!" His voice vibrated with apparent sincerity. "I'm not surprised when that police lieutenant treats me like a suspect. It's a policeman's job to suspect everybody, I suppose. But I never thought other people could really—"

"Well, did you? Did you kill her?"

"No!" To Angela's surprise, he reached over and took her hand. "No, I didn't. She could be disagreeable sometimes. And she could be stubborn. But she was family." He hesitated and sighed. "I can tell you Babette didn't kill her either. My wife isn't capable of physical violence any more than I am. I mean, a few weeks ago we were driving out in the country and ran over this squirrel—I was nearly sick and Babs cried all the way home. Hurting a living creature is not something either of us could ever do on purpose. Do you believe me, Mrs. . . . uh, Mrs. Bernboat?" he insisted.

"Oddly enough, I did, Cal. My intuition said he was telling the truth," Angela reported to her friend later. "His hand was steady when he grabbed mine. Not sweaty, not fluttery and nervous. He was being honest with me, I believe. But the point is, that hand business—it gave me an idea."

Angela didn't wait to see if Clara found the receipt Dan Benton wanted. Acting on her inspiration, she bade him a hasty good-bye and headed for the other end of the lobby where the elevator door stood open and inviting, beckoning her to the second floor.

Chapter 19

A T THE time, Angela's inspiration seemed perfectly clear and quite wonderful to her. Later, it seemed anything but clear and a great deal short of wonderful to Caledonia. "You see, I decided," Angela tried to explain, over a tiny serving of pre-dinner sherry, "that if I simply asked people straight out if they killed Birdy, and if I held their hand while they answered, I would know whether or not the answer was the truth."

"What a wacko idea!" Caledonia said. "You've had some weird notions, my girl, but this probably could win some sort of prize for weirdness! Ask people straight out if they committed murder? And perform some sort of laying on of hands while you do it?"

"Well, it works. I mean, that's how the fortune-tellers do it, you know. They hold your hand slightly up in the air, not letting it rest on the table. As your arm tires, you can't control your reactions completely, even if you're trying to hold absolutely still, so you give indications of how you feel in spite of yourself, and the fortune-teller picks up those tiny, involuntary movements. It's called muscle reading. I used to do it very well. I was the best fortune-teller the college carnival ever had."

"Muscle reading?"

"I should have thought of it a long time ago. We learned about it in our psychology class in college. Everybody does it, you know, without knowing they're doing it. For instance, you always know when I'm mad about something, before I even say so."

"Oh, that's easy. Your mouth gets tight, your shoulders get tense and rise up almost to your ears, your hands start making short, choppy gestures . . ."

"Well, there you are! Even when I don't want you to know what I'm thinking, I give you clues in spite of myself."

"Well," Caledonia said with reluctant amusement, "*you* certainly do. You get so stiff with anger I could break a board across your back and you wouldn't know it! And when you're pleased, you walk differently. Kind of light and fast . . ."

"You see? You're muscle reading! And my point is that everybody gives themselves away, even if they can keep their faces straight and stand absolutely still. They can't stop themselves from involuntary movements that show up in—well, the hand, if it's held up in the air the way I told you. You don't want all the details, but the point is, this is surefire! I don't know why I didn't think of this before."

"It sounds absolutely crazy to me! You don't even like to touch people, let alone hold hands with them. You nearly had a fit when Tootsie Armstrong gave a bridge party and made all eight of us have a group hug before we left her apartment, all because of one of those New Age, self-help books she'd been reading about how people need to be touched. Old people in particular. As for holding hands with murder suspects . . ." Caledonia sighed. "Oh well, this is your story. You go on with it."

Aware that Elmer Johanson's nursing staff was changing shifts, Angela had decided to start her inquiries with Miss Pilgrim, if she could just catch her before she left, so she was pleased to run into the nurse standing right beside the elevator on the second floor, presumably on her way home for the day and chatting with—of all people—the van driver, Doke Wicker.

"So you'll stay around for a bit this evening, and if need be," the nurse was saying, "you'll drive over to Dr. Carter's place and fetch him here instead of his having to come on his own.

He's such a slow driver at night. Last year when Mr. Johanson had an emergency, it took nearly half an hour for Dr. Carter to arrive. I'd rather you picked him up if he's not doing his rounds across the street at the nursing home. Agreed?"

Wicker nodded his bristly head. "Okay. But you'll see I get standby pay for tonight."

"I said I would. Mr. Johanson's got excellent medical insurance and if it won't pay, I'm authorized to meet medical expenses from his account, and I'm sure—"

"Is Elmer worse?" Angela found herself genuinely concerned.

"We haven't been too well today." Miss Pilgrim turned to Angela. "We're having a bit of trouble with breathing. We've probably been out of bed too often lately, and we aren't strong to begin with."

"Oh dear. I was hoping to speak to him. Just for a moment, mind you. Do you think he'd be well enough . . ."

"Please leave him alone, Mrs. Benbow," Miss Pilgrim said, the hospital *we* deserting her. "I think he's really in terrible condition. Perhaps nearing the end."

"He's dying?"

"Well, no. Or rather, yes, though perhaps not at this exact moment. Obviously when one reaches a hundred and two, the end cannot be too far away. And today he's so much weaker than he's been. So I'm afraid that soon . . ." She shrugged and turned back toward Wicker, as though to continue with her instructions.

Angela plunged quickly ahead. She didn't want them to get away. She might never get an opportunity like this again, to kill two birds with one stone, so to speak. "The truth is, I really came to see you and Miss Goodwin first. I needn't disturb Mr. Johanson if . . . oh, and I'll talk to you, too, Mr. Wicker, as long as you're here."

"Me?" Wicker was monosyllabically startled. "Why me?"

"You see," Angela pressed on, "I'm making one final survey of everyone associated with the case. And I want to ask you both one more question." She reached forward and in keeping with her plan, she took Miss Pilgrim's hand in her left and Wicker's hand in her right. Their reaction was immediate and verged on violence. Both pulled strongly backward, and had Angela not seized the hands with a good grip to begin with, both would have disengaged at once. As it was, Angela merely tightened her grip, although she barely retained hold with her fingertips on Doke's calloused hand, as he continued to pull against her. So she rushed ahead with her question. The words blurted out on top of each other.

"What-I-need-to-ask-is-did-you-kill-Mrs. Benton?"

"Good heavens! Of course not!" Miss Pilgrim said with distaste.

"Me? Naaaa. What for? Why'd I want to kill the old cow?" That was Doke's response.

"And what did that tell you?" Caledonia asked, as Angela continued her report later. "You knew they'd only deny it."

"Of course. I didn't care what they said. I only cared what they did."

"And what'd they do?"

"Well, Miss Pilgrim jerked her hand again and actually did pull free. It was an even stronger reaction than when I first took hold of her. Doke Wicker, on the contrary, suddenly let his hand go slack in mine. He wasn't pulling against me any longer."

"I see." Caledonia was quietly amused. "And did that tell you anything?"

"Well, no. Or I don't think so," Angela said with disappointment. "Doke was so perfectly relaxed, he didn't seem to have any feeling at all about the murder. And I thought Miss Pilgrim was just showing distaste and discomfort about the whole thing, but especially about my holding her hand. So in my opinion, neither of them is guilty."

Caledonia allowed herself a grin. "You're something, you are. One is innocent because she pulls away, the other is innocent because he relaxes. Great lot of use your homemade lie detector is."

"Well, I had other things to go on, you know. I'd already

decided they were both innocent. In fact, I was just asking them because they were there . . ."

"Like that mountain the guy climbed because it was there. Well, what'd you do then?"

"I went off and made the rounds on that floor. I went to Carla Wiley's and to deaf old Doc Colquin on either side of Birdy's."

"Learn anything important?"

"No, I'm afraid not. No sweating, no pulling away, no trembling . . ."

"I thought you said pulling away didn't count. When Pilgrim did it . . ."

"That was deliberate pulling away. I'm talking about tiny, involuntary movements of the hand! And there weren't any. So then I went on down to the Dovers' apartment, but I could get hold only of him. To touch hands, I mean. He answered the door, and she stayed back inside their living room. But he answered for both of them."

"Well, What'd you decide about him?"

"I'm not sure. I mean, he had a funny reaction. He let me take his hand, but he started to shake when I asked him about the murder. He didn't pull away, mind you, but his hand started to tremble. He didn't sweat, but he did shake."

"So are you saying you think Mr. Dover might be your killer?"

"Well, no, not really. All the same, that slight shaking—"

"How about Mrs. Dover? Maybe she did it, and he's covering up for her."

"Oh, I don't think so. I mean, his reaction came when I asked him if *he* did it. Then when I asked about her, his hand got steadier, not shakier. So I certainly don't think she's guilty either."

"Maybe she did it, and he doesn't know."

"Now, Cal, how can a wife commit a murder and her husband not suspect something is wrong? Especially if they live in a two-room apartment like the Dovers do. I mean, they see each other all day, every day . . . she'd give it away sooner or later. Don't you agree?"

"Oh, I don't know, but for the moment I'll take your word for it. By the way, what'd she think of your standing there at her door holding her husband's hand?"

Angela grinned wickedly. "Not much, probably. But she'll forget about it, because I'm certainly not going to do it ever again."

"So that does it for your second-floor investigations?"

"Except for Nurse Goodwin, of course. And Elmer himself, naturally."

"Listen, I don't want to be rude, but is this going to be just another recital of 'no quivering, no sweating'—ending up with your telling me those two are innocent? Another story with no point?"

"No! Certainly not! I'm building up to a grand climax here!"

"Your sense of drama is going to be the death of me someday, but go ahead. Tell the story at your own pace. Just so you actually do thrill me when the point finally arrives."

Angela nodded with satisfaction and plunged on in her narrative. From the Dovers' apartment, she had retraced her steps along the second-floor hall to the Johanson apartment. The old man was awake again, lying back against his pillows, his eyes on the television set. The screen was hidden around the corner from Angela's view as she stood in his doorway, but she could clearly hear the sound of something being kicked, a man's *Ow! Laura, that hurts!* and in the confusion of the crash of breaking china, a woman's wail of *Oh, Rob!* Elmer grinned and waved, but weakly, Angela thought. He ignored her as she gestured Betty Goodwin to come out into the hall.

"We're making one final survey of everyone we've talked to, Nurse Goodwin," Angela began, and reached out to take the Goodwin hand in her now-routine performance. Betty Goodwin flinched in surprise but did not pull away. "We're asking everyone the same question. Did you kill Mrs. Benton?"

Nurse Goodwin's mouth went slightly slack, but she stared directly into Angela's eyes and her hand squeezed back in a grip as strong as Angela's. "Of course I didn't kill Mrs.

Benton," she said. "I had no reason to. Even if she was nasty to us and played her TV too loud. Even if she did overhear parts of my . . . my flirtation with her nephew." She leaned forward earnestly, and for a moment it was Angela who rocked backward on her heels as though to pull away. "I'm surprised you never asked me straight out before, and I appreciate the chance to tell you just as straight out that I didn't kill her." She squeezed Angela's hand again, and Angela, feeling an enormous sense of discomfort, was the one to disengage her hand.

"Well, thank you, Miss Goodwin. I think that's quite enough. We just wanted to ask. Merely for form's sake, of course."

"Ain'tcha gonna ask me?" Elmer's voice came weakly, and he raised the remote control to switch off the TV so he could be heard. "You gonna ignore me like I ain't here?"

"Certainly not, Mr. Johanson," Angela said. "I fully intend to ask you. I'll be happy to do it right now, if that suits you." She moved into the room close beside the bed.

"Betty, you go get us some hot water and make fresh tea," Elmer said. The force of his voice was reduced but the command in his tone was unmistakable.

Betty Goodwin took the teapot from its trivet on the bedside table and headed for the hallway. "I won't go all the way to the main kitchen," she said. "You might need me today."

"You think I'm dyin', like Pilgrim does? Pilgrim thinks I'm dyin'," he explained to Angela. "You think so too, Betty girl?"

"No, of course not," Nurse Goodwin said hastily. "But all the same, I could heat water in the microwave in the community lounge on this floor and just pour it over a couple of tea bags. That way I can be back here before you know I'm gone!"

"Don't want no lukewarm water poured over no tea bags!" Elmer said, hauling himself into more of a sitting position in the bed. "Want my herbal tea from the main kitchen. Real herbs steeped in real water boiled on a real stove. Microwave ain't no good. Does somethin' funny to the water. Leastways I think so. You agree, Mrs. Benbow?"

"Well," Angela said cautiously, "I never found any

difference in taste. I mean, things cooked in a microwave seemed to taste fine to me. And a lot of fancy restaurants use them these days, so they can't do too much to flavor. But about the tea . . . I don't really want any. It's almost dinnertime and . . ." But Miss Goodwin had disappeared at a trot, the teapot clutched firmly in both hands, and Angela supposed she might have to indulge Elmer to avoid insulting him.

"Why do you always send out for tea when I come, Mr. Johanson?"

"I've got so I kind of enjoy you comin' to visit, an' if I give you tea, it makes you stay awhile. Truth is, you're a lot more interestin' than the TV." He cackled until the dry laugh turned into a racking cough. "Whew! Gotta watch that. Can't get my breath when I'm coughin'. The lungs must be givin' out, for sure." He took a gasping breath, then another. "That's better. Now, where was I? Oh sure. I was tellin' you I got so I kinda like you. Didn't think I did before. Sorry, but you're kinda pushy. Never liked pushy women. Anyhow, that ain't important, 'cause I changed my mind about you."

"Actually, Mr. Johanson," Angela said, "it's a little embarrassing to admit, but at one time I suspected you of wanting to kill me."

"Now, that's funny, that is." He started a laugh and gasped out another rasp of breath. "Ooops . . . I better try to hang onto my funny bone—seems like laughin' is bad for me. But then, everything is, these days."

"There's nothing to laugh at," Angela said with dignity. "It's not amusing to be pushed off the fire escape . . ."

"No, no—I was sorry about that! I meant you was funny pretendin' you just suspected it was me. You've had that all figured out for a long time, haven'tcha?"

"What! Wait! Wait a minute! Are you . . . I mean, I thought . . . I mean, are you telling me that you're the one who pushed me?"

"Oh, you're a quick one, you are!" he said with heavy sarcasm. "Sure, it was me. Don't pretend you never suspected I done it."

"Well, of course I suspected you. But no more than I suspected anybody else."

"How so?" The old man was grinning wickedly. "How come you didn't catch on to me?"

Angela's mind didn't seem to be working as fast as usual. "Well, I—I—just couldn't believe you could manage it. I still don't. You spend most of your time in bed, and you're so weak that—"

"Aw, it don't take no real strength to push somebody off a fire escape. Back in Chicago, a couple-a people got done that way. 'Course, it takes more strength to push 'em out a window. Because of the high sill. With you, I just braced good against the wall, so I wouldn't fall myself, and I pushed." He panted heavily a moment and then went on. "Thought you'd go over easy like that Benton fella did. But you're tougher'n he is. You hung onto that railing for dear life and then just collapsed in a heap. I knew I wasn't gonna be able to lift you up to toss you over the edge. So I give it up and just let you lay there." He took another couple of deep breaths. "Then later, like I say, I was glad I didn't really hurt you. Because you're fun to have aroun'."

"But why? Why try to push me at all?"

"Because you was after Betty. Or I thought you was. You know, if you'd of gone after Pilgrim, I'd of let you do it. I could stand for her to get hauled off to jail. Did I tell you she's convinced I'm dyin'? She's got a oxygen tank standin' by over there in the corner, got the doctor on notice to run over here . . . 'Course I'm dyin', for Pete's sake! We all are! And when you get as old as me, I s'pose it gets more obvious." His breath rasped heavily and he sighed. "Point is, it ain't gonna happen right today. And maybe not tomorrow either. And if that woman would stop fussin' it might not even happen this week! But she's about to worry me into the grave and no mistake. So if you take Miss Pilgrim away, I might last till the end of this month! Or next month! But Betty's different."

"She's different, all right. She tells lies and she imagines romances and—"

"Ain't no harm in that. And she's good to me. Listen, at my age, pleasures get small and few, and we hang onto 'em the best way we can. I wasn't goin' to let you take Betty away from me!"

Angela shook her head. "But, Mr. Johanson, if Betty Goodwin pushed Dan Benton off the fire escape—probably out of a desire for revenge—you just can't protect her. The police should be told . . ."

"You ain't too swift on the uptake today, are ya? Didn't I just tell you that was me, too?"

"But—I thought—you're saying Betty Goodwin didn't . . ."

" 'Course she didn't."

"But why? Why would you push Daniel?"

"Because he hurt Betty. Broke her heart."

"That was just an imaginary romance!"

"You say so. She says different. Anyways, he wasn't a nice man. He deserved for somebody to teach him a lesson." He was silent a moment, catching his breath, which rasped deeply. "He was downright disrespectful to women, you know, an' that ain't right. Have I told you all this before? What I didn't hear for myself, I used to hear from the nurses. He never come to see his aunt, you know, unless he wanted money from her. No way to treat family! And his poor wife . . . he argued with her an' cheated on her . . ." He paused for breath. "I remember tellin' you there ain't no reason to stand for nasty people when you get to be my age, an' that goes double if they do you wrong personally. Just wipe 'em out, that's what I say. Why not?"

"Well, for one thing, because you'd go to prison! And at your age prison is likely to kill you!"

"At my age, anything is likely to kill me! Honest, Mrs. Benbow, I don't know why more old people don't try to get the world straightened out the way they'd like it to be. At least they oughtta do things they've wanted to do all their lives but held off 'cause they might get in trouble. Like, oh, say some smart-mouth kid starts in on you an' calls you Grampa—tells you get a move on. S'pose you just walk over and punch him in the gut! That'd teach 'im a lesson, wouldn't it? Think twice before he got lippy with some ol' geezer like me."

"I suppose he would at that," Angela conceded.

"Or how about—you ever been to a restaurant and the waiter was so slow you thought he'd gone on vacation? He gets your order mixed up an' don't much care, an' he don't refill your coffee cup, an' he don't see you run out of bread . . ."

"I certainly wouldn't leave him a tip."

"Sure. But a better idea . . . why not trip him, next time he walks past with a full tray?"

"Oh dear! Things would fly all over. Other people might get splattered with . . . you know, with falling food!"

"But it'd get him fired, wouldn't it? You never even wanted to do that? Or somethin' like it?"

"Well . . . I was in a store the other day looking at a pretty scarf and the salesgirl was too busy talking to a friend to wait on me. I wanted to just take the scarf and leave."

"Didja do it?"

"Of course not!"

"Why not?"

"Because . . . because that's shoplifting! It's against the law."

"You ain't got the idea yet. The point is, whadda you care about the law? Laws was made to keep people from runnin' over you at stop signs and let you get a divorce when you need one. But there's those of us can take care of ourselves by ourselves . . . watch out for our families . . . We don't need no help from no law. 'Course, you're prob'ly still too young. You're more likely'n I am to let other people tell you how to act. Maybe you got to get as old as me to do different. 'Cause they'll put you in jail for it, if they catch you at it. An' when you're young, a prison sentence looks like a big deal. When you get to be my age, even a life sentence ain't nothin'."

Angela shook her head. "I don't believe a word of all that. And neither do you."

"Maybe I do, maybe I don't. You can think I'm just talkin', if that makes you happy."

Angela shook her head. "Well, you did just confess to pushing me. And to attacking Dan. It's only . . . I can't seem to take it all in. Just to start with, you seem too nice to be . . . an outlaw!"

He grinned at her. "You didn't know me when I was young, back in Chicago. I was a mean one, I was. But I retired and got respectable."

Angela ignored him. "Furthermore, you're not . . . you're not well. It's hard to believe you have the strength. Oh, I know you said the pushing itself wasn't hard. But you had to walk half the length of the hall to get to the fire escape, and then you had to get yourself back here."

"You got a point. Don't know as I coulda done it today, and I couldn't of done it that night either, if that hall was much longer'n it is. I mean, it about wore me out. Hadda lie down an' catch my breath when I got back."

"Look. What really bothers me about this, the physical effort aside . . . there's such a thing as right and wrong. Morals . . . ethics . . . No matter how you try to deny it. There's right and there's wrong!"

"Maybe. But it sure ain't like it used to be, when everybody agreed on what was right. These days it's kinda mixed up. In my day, we didn't beat up strangers or shoot innocent bystanders. No sir, if I took somebody out, everybody knew why. It was because they done wrong. Wrong to me, or to my boss, or to my family. You see?"

His voice seemed to have grown stronger, and his eyes were bright. He was sitting bolt upright in bed. "I see it on TV all the time. These days, a couple-a boys shoot their folks and the jury says, 'But their parents was mean to 'em when they was little.' Makes me so dang mad . . . what happened to 'Honor your father and mother'? Hold that trial twenty, thirty years ago, those kids'd be in jail this minute! If they even got to trial. Somebody mighta kilt 'em before they got to the courtroom. Just because they done wrong, you see what I mean? But these days we sit back an' let the courts take care of these guys—except they don't even do it! Half the world don't even know how to act decent no more. And what's worse, the other half thinks that's okay! I swear, the world is goin' straight to hell in a handbasket."

"And that," Angela told Caledonia, "was when Betty Goodwin came back with the tea. She nearly had a fit, seeing him sitting bolt upright and waving his hands in the air while he talked, and she pushed me out of there in a hurry. But that was fine. At the moment, I couldn't think of anything else to ask him."

"You? You ran out of questions? After all that? I don't believe it!"

"Well, you have to admit he gave me a lot to mull over! Besides, I couldn't wait to tell you! Who'd have expected that?"

"You, for one. After you were sick, you were babbling about him having poisoned you, even if it turned out not to be true. He's been one of your prime suspects right along, hasn't he?"

"Of course not, Cal. I mean, even if he could drag himself down the hall to attack Dan and later to push me, it isn't reasonable to suppose he killed Birdy. He certainly couldn't make it downstairs and back without help. That was why I decided it wouldn't have been he who did the pushing, if you see what I mean. I had given up on him as a suspect."

"Well, you sure were wrong." Angela nodded agreement and they sipped at their miniscule glasses of amber sherry in silence for a moment. "I have to hand it to you," Caledonia went on. "You promised me a big ending to your story, and you gave it to me, all right." Angela said nothing at all.

"I guess all this detective work has given you an appetite, hasn't it?" Caledonia continued. "What do you suppose we're having for dinner tonight? At least it won't be more lamb. I mean, I love good lamb. But enough is enough!" Angela still said nothing and Caledonia shook her head. "Okay, let's have it. Something is bothering you."

"Well, isn't it bothering you? Doesn't it really get to you, that old Elmer is the one who pushed me off the fire escape?"

"It bothers me that *anybody* would push you off the fire escape."

"Oh, I'm over being upset about the attack itself. But his doing it . . . that's what really gets me. I don't think I'd feel this unhappy if it was one of the others, like the Dovers, or Nurse Goodwin, or Babette Benton, because I don't really know the Dovers, I think Nurse Goodwin is a little touched in the head, and I don't like Babette. So it would have seemed perfectly reasonable to me if one of them was guilty, you know? But it doesn't seem right it should be him. I . . . I was getting to like him!"

Caledonia sighed. "Poor Angela . . . well, like him or not, you're going to have to report all this to Lieutenant Martinez, aren't you? I admire Elmer's spunk myself, but the lieutenant needs to know this, for what it's worth."

"I suppose you're right," Angela said with reluctance. "But what will he do to Elmer?"

"Probably nothing. I mean, Elmer didn't succeed in bumping you off, after all. It wasn't even a very good try, when you get right down to it. And I suppose they'll take his age into account."

"You know what's most remarkable about it? He seems rather pleased with himself, trying to be a one-man, geriatric vigilante committee."

"Robin Hood in support hose? Batman with gray hair and wrinkles?"

"Absolutely. You know . . ." Angela put down her glass of sherry and got up abruptly from her chair. "Cal, I may be a little late to dinner. You go ahead without me, will you?"

"Hey! Wait a minute! If you're going out detecting, I'm going with you!" But Angela was already out the screen door and headed up toward the main building. Caledonia gazed thoughtfully after her and then went to the telephone.

Chapter 20

ELMER WAS watching TV, alternately dozing off and rousing to use his remote control and skip from the early news to *The People's Court* to a rerun of *I Dream of Jeannie*. Betty Goodwin sat quietly beside him reading a paperback with a bare-chested pirate on its cover; the pirate was leering suggestively at a cowering maiden who seemed about to topple forward from the weight of her remarkable bosom, all the more prominent because of being squeezed in and up by some ingeniously cantilevered bustier. Elmer and Betty both looked up as Angela entered.

"Say! This is a treat," Elmer said. "Twice in one day!"

"I changed my mind about having a cup of tea," Angela lied. "I know it's close to dinner, but your herbal teas are so tasty." Betty Goodwin glared, but Angela—intent on getting a few minutes of privacy with Elmer Johanson—ignored the nurse's disapproval. "You have so many different flavors . . ." Angela went on with false enthusiasm. "It's always such a pleasant surprise. How did you pick all those flavors out anyway?"

"Sampler my great-grandaughter sent me for my last birthday coupla months ago," Elmer said. "Sent a big, big box. So big we had to store it down in the main kitchen. I'm only halfway through it now." He seemed slyly amused, and Angela thought he probably saw through her subterfuge.

But if he was aware that the tea was merely an excuse, Betty Goodwin didn't seem to be. At Elmer's direction, she got the pot from its trivet beside him and, shaking her head in disapproval, started for the door. "It's nearly dinnertime," she said. "I won't be very welcome in the kitchen, getting in their way and all. This time I'm going to microwave your water and—"

"No, you won't!" Elmer's contradiction was a command. "You go get me real herb tea."

"But you're not feeling too—"

"Don't you worry about me, Betty. I'll be just fine with Mrs. Benbow here. She'll yell for help if we need it." Still frowning, the nurse disappeared around the corner, and Angela moved over to the vacated chair beside the bed, pushed aside the paperback with its Technicolor cover, and seated herself close by the object of her visit.

"We didn't finish our question-and-answer session today, Mr. Johanson," she began. "It took me so by surprise, everything else we were talking about, that I completely forgot to ask my biggest question."

"Yeah, I know. The one where you hold my hand to see if I'm lyin'. Saw you doin' that with Betty, there by the door this afternoon. I got the idea, all right. That's how I used to do it with girlfriends when I was sparkin'. I'd hold their hand an' ask could I kiss 'em goodnight, and you could always tell when they said, 'No,' whether it meant, 'No,' or whether it meant, 'Yes, but you gotta ask more'n once.' "

Angela laughed in spite of herself. "Well, since you know my system, it might not work so well."

He grinned back. "Don't let that stop you. You're the first person held my hand in years, an' I don't wanna miss this chance. Provided you forgive me for pushin' you. I did apologize for that, didn't I? Yeah, I remember I did. I sure wouldn't want you to get real close to me and then smack me one. So am I forgiven?"

"Well, I'm a little surprised at myself," she said, "but I really do forgive you. I'm sure you acted on impulse and you wouldn't do it again."

"Sure wouldn't. You got my word on it. Well, let's go, huh?" Elmer activated the remote, the TV set closed its giant eye and sank back to sleep, and Angela took his free hand in hers.

"Here's how we do it. I ask you, did you kill Birdy Benton?"

"Naaa," he said. "I didn't. I admit I tried to git you and young Benton both. But I didn't kill the ol' witch. That was one mean woman, you know. I ain't surprised somebody kilt 'er, but it wasn't me."

"You just have to say yes or no to my questions," Angela said. "It's supposed to work with a one-word answer."

"But I can say more if I want to, can't I?"

"I suppose that's all right. Let's see . . . oh yes, I should probably ask you next if you know if somebody else killed her."

"Sure I do."

"Oh. Oh really. Who?"

"Don't know *who*. That ain't what you asked. You asked did I know whether somebody else besides me kilt 'er, and sure I do. She's dead, ain't she?"

Angela looked sharply at him, suspecting that he was having fun at her expense. But he looked blandly back and she decided he hadn't meant to tease her. "All right, then. Let me ask again, another way. Do you know who killed her?"

"Nope."

"Did Betty Goodwin kill her?"

"Nope. Don't know who did, but Betty definitely didn't. I tol' you she's okay—tol' you maybe six, eight times already."

Angela sighed and let go of the old fellow's hand. "Oh dear, I had this all worked out. I was absolutely convinced that your Betty had done it, and that you knew it. But you don't show me any reaction at all to those questions."

"No guilty twitches and trembles, huh?"

"Not a one," she agreed. "And now I'm not sure what to ask next."

"Well, how about this, Mrs. Benbow . . ." A man's voice behind her made her turn, and there was Lieutenant Martinez framed in the doorway, his handsome face dark and serious. "How about asking if Elmer here had any kind of an argument with the late Mrs. Benton? Don't ask if he killed her. Ask if he hit her."

Elmer jerked his hand away from Angela, and his brows creased into a thunderous scowl. "You're that policeman, ain'tcha? I remember from earlier on. You asked all kinds of questions before. How come you're askin' more now? Who said you could come in here? Didn't they tell you I'm probably dyin'? You wanna put me in my grave? Where's my nurse? She'll tell you I can't be disturbed. I need my rest . . ."

"Lieutenant, you're on the wrong track," Angela protested. "I started out suspecting Elmer—because I suspected everybody. Everybody who knew her had reason to be angry with Birdy. But after I met him, I realized he could be ruled out as a suspect. Getting down into the lobby is impossible for him. Why, he nearly wore himself out going down the hall to the fire escape when—" She bit her tongue. The last thing she'd meant to do was tell Martinez about Elmer's pushing her. She had forgiven Elmer, it was true, but she could not trust Martinez to react with similar charity.

Martinez didn't seem to notice her slip. He had moved all the way into the room and stood on the far side of the bed from Angela, watching Elmer closely. "You're a lot tougher than you look, aren't you, old fellow?" he said.

"Maybe. But she's right, you know. I ain't been in the lobby for . . . must be a year and a half now." Elmer eyed Martinez as warily as Martinez looked steadily back, and Angela thought of a TV program she'd seen about sumo wrestlers. They had watched each other just that way as they circled at the start of a match and searched for an opening in their opponent's defenses.

"I didn't ask about your going to the lobby," Martinez said. "Let's start at the beginning. On the day she died, did you argue with Beatrice Benton?"

"Sure. Argued with her every time I run into her. Mostly just saw her goin' past my open door, but when I was out of bed, if we was in the hall at the same time, we argued. Mostly about her TV. I couldn't hear my own, hers was so loud."

"I'll ask again. How about the day she died?"

"Yes. Or anyhow, I s'pose it was that day," Elmer admitted grudgingly. "Days kind of run together for me, you know."

"You were out of your bed," Martinez prompted, "and you saw Mrs. Benton out in the hall."

"That's the way it happened, all right," Elmer conceded with a little cough. "Thought I might as well get on her again about the noise from her TV. She wasn't too pleased. Said I'd do better to mind my own business. 'Close your own door, if you don't like it,' she said. Said she'd play her TV in her own room any way she wanted to. An' then she said that while we was on the subject of things that riled people up, I should think about Betty makin' eyes at her nephew. That really got under her skin, she said. 'You tell that fat slut to stay away from Daniel,' was what she said. She was makin' me mad, an' I tol' her so." He coughed once or twice and fell silent.

"Go on," Martinez prompted. "You had a few words with Mrs. Benton . . . and then what?"

"And then I . . . wait a minute! Shouldn't you give me a warnin' or anythin' like they do on TV?"

Martinez smiled, but Angela thought his expression was less friendly than that of a cat who had just discovered an open tin of Chicken of the Sea temporarily abandoned on the kitchen counter while the lady of the house goes to answer the doorbell. "All right," Martinez said. "Anything you say can be used against you in court. If you want a lawyer present, you can have one. If you can't afford a lawyer—"

"That's enough. I can afford one but I don't want one," Elmer said sharply. "I don't trust you further'n I could throw you, but that's a lot more'n I trust any fool lawyer. You just go on an' ask your questions."

"All right, then, and remember, you've been warned. Now—you argued with Mrs. Benton," Martinez said. "You admit that much?"

"Sure. Everybody around here did."

"You got especially angry on that particular day, am I right?"

Elmer seemed to be thinking carefully. "Well, okay. I guess so. More even than other times. Because she said something real nasty. Said if I didn't get Betty Goodwin to leave her nephew alone, she'd get my granddaughter to fire Betty. It's my family hires these LPNs to baby sit for me, you know. I pay the bills, but the family does the hirin' and firin'. So that old witch says to me she'll get my granddaughter to fire Betty, and that really made me mad!"

"And you hit her!"

"An' I . . ." Angela thought Elmer had started to agree but stopped himself just in time. "Who says?"

"What did you hit her with, Mr. Johanson?" Martinez looked around the room. "Something heavy and hard, with a rounded bottom. Let's see . . . how about one of those IV bottles hanging from the tree? No, they've got a couple of yards of tubing hanging from them. Besides, why would you be carrying one of those around with you? How about . . ." His eyes turned toward the open closet door. "Aha! A bottle of fruit juice!" Martinez moved over and took a bottle of cranberry juice from a shelf. He hefted it once or twice, bounced it in his hands, grasped it by the neck and took a practice swing like a golfer getting ready for a shot . . . up from his side toward an imaginary woman's imaginary head about five feet above the floor.

"Not too difficult to imagine this as a weapon," Martinez said with satisfaction. Elmer continued to watch and to say nothing. Martinez hefted the bottle again and swung it upward from his side once more, toward his imaginary victim. Elmer seemed to wince. "It's about the right weight. The shape is right," Martinez went on. "What was it, Mr. Johanson? Your nurse was away for a moment and you wanted a fresh bottle? You'd gone to the shelf here and picked one up . . ." Martinez stepped into the closet, mimed picking up the bottle that he still carried, then turned as though to return to the bed. "From this angle," he said, peering toward the hall door, "you could see Mrs. Benton coming out of her apartment, and you decided to go out and talk to her about that loud TV. You walked out there into the hall, still carrying the bottle." He swung it casually as he walked a few steps back toward the hall door. Angela found her eyes would focus only on that heavy glass bottle, and Elmer watched as closely and as silently.

"You argue with her," Martinez went on. "She's sharp with you, she threatens your nurse, and finally you lose your temper—that vicious temper of yours that got you into so much trouble in the old days. So you bring that bottle up hard against her head. Crack! So what happened then?"

"It's your story," Elmer said. "You tell it."

"All right, I will." Martinez went on. "Mrs. Benton was stunned. I'm not sure whether she fell or not, but if she did, she got back up on her own. And then . . . well, I'm not sure. Maybe then she threatened to report your attack and have you arrested. Maybe she made a fist and started to take a swing at you . . ."

"Aw, nothin' like that. She staggered, all right. Went down on one knee. An' after a minute she sort of shook her head an' blinked an' rubbed at her forehead. . . . I think she said 'Ow' or somethin' like that, an' then she just stood up again an' turned around an' walked away from me. Real slow. Down the hall an' around the corner. I guess she went on downstairs. I dunno."

"And you went back into your room and forgot the whole thing. Am I right?"

Elmer shrugged. "Not forgot. Just didn't think no more about it. Then when I heard somebody'd kilt 'er, I was kinda sorry I lost my temper and hit her. A gentleman don't hit a woman. Not unless he gotta."

"Mr. Johanson, you don't seem to understand. Nobody else was involved at all. You killed her."

"Oh no, I didn't." Elmer was firm. "I know when I kilt somebody. I done it before, you know. A couple times. Back in Chicago. Mostly I just roughed people up when they owed Frank money. Frank was my boss, an' that was what I did for a living, you know. Went out an' got his money for him. But a couple times it got bad an' I lost my temper, an' . . . well, I done my time for that, so it don't do no harm if I tell you now. Besides, seems like you know it already. Point I wanna make is, I know about killin'. And I didn't kill nobody this time."

Angela, who had been watching, fascinated, could keep silent no longer. "He's right. She walked away under her own power."

"The walking dead, Mrs. Benbow," Martinez said gently. "Mrs. Benton was bleeding inside her head. It may have taken a while before she lost consciousness, but I have no doubt she was dazed and dying when she walked down this hallway. And now . . ." Martinez came around the bed to stand near Angela's chair.

"Mrs. Benbow, I think you'll understand why I want to talk to Mr. Johanson alone now. I promise you I'll come and talk to you and Mrs. Wingate about all this later and at length. But right now I need some time without your . . ." He paused, apparently searching for a more tactful way to put his point. Finding none, he settled for blaming himself.

"Mrs. Benbow, I can't concentrate if I have to keep answering your questions. So if you please . . ." And he pulled Angela's chair slightly back to allow her more room to stand, almost as though she were seated at a table. "It's your dinner-time anyway," he coaxed. "People were already gathering in the lobby when I came up here . . ."

"Very well," Angela said and stood. "Mr. Johanson, Betty will be back in a moment. And I won't be far away if you need me—just down in the dining room." Turning back to Martinez, she warned, "You be easy with him. Miss Pilgrim and Miss Goodwin both think he's not doing well . . . don't you put any pressure on him."

Martinez had a hand under her elbow and was propelling her gently but firmly toward the hallway. "Trust me, Mrs. Benbow. I'm well aware of Mr. Johanson's age and physical condition. Give me some credit . . ." And then she was outside the door, and he was closing it in her face.

"Not with a bang," she assured Caledonia as they tackled their dinner, an elegant chicken paprikash; Mrs. Schmitt was outdoing herself, apparently in an effort to help her diners forget about the recent glut of lamb recipes. "The lieutenant didn't slam the door. He just eased me out," Angela went on. "But he might as well have slammed it for all I was able to pick up after that."

"You mean you stayed and tried to listen?" Caledonia's serene happiness over the meal was tinged with amusement at the mental picture of Angela, excluded from Martinez' session with the old man but applying one ear to the keyhole.

"Well, I suppose I did hesitate there. Just to see if I could hear . . . but I couldn't and that was that. So I came down here. I just hated to leave the old fellow all alone like that . . ."

"He wasn't alone. Martinez was with him. What is all this protective attitude? You didn't feel that way when you thought he'd poisoned you. You were gleefully setting a trap to prove—"

"Well, I've gotten to know him better. He's really quite a delightful man. He has a good sense of humor, genuine wit."

"Angela, he told you he was some kind of hoodlum! And he went to prison for killing somebody."

"But that was fifty, maybe sixty years ago. He's paid his debt to society."

"Angela, 'I done time' is not the same thing as paying his debt to society. Besides, is murder a debt that he could really pay with a little time in prison? Remember, the leopard doesn't change his spots."

"Oh, he's what the lieutenant said. A tough old man. Surprisingly tough. But I'm not certain I believe all that about his being a crook and going to prison. I mean, don't you think he could have been making the whole thing up? Or he could be hallucinating."

"We'll know soon enough. You did say the lieutenant promised to tell us all about it, didn't you?"

"That's another thing I wonder about, Cal. The lieutenant. He arrived at Elmer's with the whole thing almost completely worked out. And what was he doing there at just that minute?"

"Oh, that. I sent for him. I told him you'd found out who

pushed you, though it was just a guess, and that you'd gone upstairs to confront old Elmer again. That was enough to bring him in a hurry."

"When did you tell him all that?"

"As soon as you left for Elmer's. Now, don't glare at me! For all I knew, you were going up for a cozy chat with a murderer—and you were! I got on the phone and, wonder of wonders, the lieutenant was still right here in the building."

"But I saw him heading out the front door!"

"Maybe he was on his way to the Sundays Shop to talk to the pink ladies. Or to the nurses' station. Anyhow the desk located him easily enough, and when I told him that you'd gone back up to Elmer's, he must have headed there himself. On the double. Well, as I say, we'll find out soon enough." But though the two women waited at Caledonia's apartment, lingering over decaf till nearly ten o'clock—well past Angela's accustomed bedtime—Lieutenant Martinez did not appear.

"He promised to come and tell us all about it," Angela complained.

"I'll bet he didn't say he'd come tonight, though, did he?"

"Well . . ."

Finally, reluctantly, Angela went back to the main building and her own quarters, where she was surprised to find herself drowsy and nodding off very quickly. And equally surprised to find herself waking to a sunny morning after a full night of nearly dreamless sleep. "Amazing," she told her reflection in the mirror as she brushed her teeth with her new electric toothbrush. "Amazing I could sleep at all, let alone so well."

She pushed on with her morning schedule—breakfast followed today by a lecture from a local florist, who obviously hoped to sell some of the tuberous begonias and cut-leaf philodendron he'd brought along as demonstrations. Then Angela returned to her apartment for another long period of waiting. About ten o'clock there was a knock at her door, and she gladly interrupted a talk show (*Homeless transvestites: our focus today on* Geraldo) to answer the summons. It was not, however, Lieutenant Martinez, but Trinita Stainsbury carrying an armload of what looked like crumpled bath towels. "It's your sheep costume, dear," Trinita said. "I know it will fit, since you gave us your measurements yourself. But it would be a good idea to try it on to be sure."

"Oh dear . . . it'll mess up my hair . . ."

"I'll just wait here in the living room and watch your TV while you change." Trinita simply couldn't hear opinions that contradicted her own, and with a sigh, Angela gave up and went into her bedroom.

The costume could have passed for long-sleeved pajamas with attached slippers—"Just like the Dr. Dentons I had as a child," Angela muttered, "except that it's got mitts and a hood, too. And it seems to have a whole lot of extra cloth in the sleeves!" Indeed, there was so much excess material built in between the sleeve and the garment that when Angela held her arms out, a great white terrycloth flap appeared on either side, stretched between her wrist and her waist. There was also a kind of false nose that was to be held in place by an elastic band, a plastic cone with a black button sewn on the end, apparently meant to be an approximation of a sheep's muzzle. Angela slipped the muzzle over her face, settled the hood into place, and edged disgustedly into the living room for presentation. Edging was all the walking she could do, since the seamstress had somehow made the body of the costume too long and the legs so stubby they were separated only as far as Angela's knees.

So in she came, sidling with foreshortened gait, to be greeted with ooohs and aaahs of appreciation by Trinita— "Wonderful! Remarkable likeness to a sheep!"—and with first a snort, then uncontrollable gales of laughter by Caledonia, who to Angela's dismay had joined Trinita in the living room while Angela was changing, and who now was trying to say something between spasms of laughter. "You look just like a *xzyxxxcb* . . . just like a *ccrllxb* . . ." was all Angela could make of what Caledonia was sputtering.

"You don't like it, I take it?" Angela said sulkily, her voice muffled by the false muzzle.

"You look like a great white condor," Caledonia finally managed. "That beak . . . those wings . . ."

"She's a sheep," Trinita said. "Look at the ears! Look at the tail!"

"Tail-shmail!" Caledonia laughed. "She looks more like a white bat!"

"It seems just fine to me," Trinita said stiffly. "And I'm not sure there's any time to make alterations. You haven't forgotten that we perform our pageant today, have you?"

"No, of course not," Angela lied. "Who could forget? I'll be there, bleating my heart out! And you can quit laughing any time now, Cal. I don't appreciate . . ."

"Dear heavens!" Lieutenant Martinez came through the apartment door, which Caledonia had left ajar behind her. "Are you feeling unwell to be in your pajamas at this hour? I certainly didn't mean . . ." He hesitated and looked closely a moment at the conical nose-mask and at the huge dolman sleeves Angela extended as she raised her arms in greeting. "Oh. I see. It's a costume. You're supposed to be . . ." He hesitated again, ". . . a white bat. Have I got it right?"

"Give me the costume, Angela," Trinita said with obvious annoyance. Angela gratefully retreated to the bedroom for a fast change. "I'll do something about the sleeves and about that nose piece," Trinita shouted after her. "Nice to see you, Lieutenant," she added in a more normal tone, "but I can't stay. We have the premier performance of our little Nativity play at two o'clock today. I wrote it myself, and I am directing, as well, and you just cannot believe how many last-minute details . . ." Her voice rose once more to the level of a shout. "Angela, Tootsie and I will work on your outfit, and we'll get it back to you in plenty of time for you to suit up before the show."

Angela came hastily back into the living room, her skirt and blouse askew, her hair standing on end, and the costume and mask bundled together in a heap that she shoved into the arms of the waiting Trinita. "Yes, do get this worked on," Angela said, ushering Trinita out with a none-too-subtle push toward the hall door. As soon as the door was closed, Angela turned quickly toward Martinez and Caledonia. "You've come to tell us what happened to Elmer, haven't you, Lieutenant?"

"Absolutely, dear ladies. You already know most of it, of course. The upshot is that your Mrs. Benton was killed by old Elmer Johanson, but it wasn't premeditated murder. I believe he just happened to go out there into the hall with that heavy glass bottle still in his hand, and it was a coincidence that he had the bottle with him when his temper flared up so violently."

"Odd," Caledonia said, "I never thought of fruit juice as a lethal weapon."

"Oh, a large glass bottle filled with liquid weighs almost as much as a baseball bat," Martinez assured her. "He'd have done a lot less damage if he'd hit her with his fist."

"I can't get over it," Caledonia said. "She was hit hard enough to kill her, but she got up and walked to the lobby!"

"A blow on the head can be like that," Martinez said. "Or so our medical examiner told me. It's not like in the movies where everybody drops like a stone when they're hit on the head. Sometimes the victims fall unconscious immediately after the blow and sometimes they don't. Sometimes it takes a day or more till the effects show up, sometimes there are no visible effects at all. Some people can die after a mere tap on the skull, some people survive terrible head injuries. Hard to say in advance what might happen. And Mrs. Benton—well, she didn't die immediately. She managed to get as far as the lobby, where she talked to Clara about the mail delivery for a minute or so, and she spoke to one of the nurses—I found all that out over the course of our interviews with the staff—and then she wandered down toward the big Christmas tree where, in a moment when nobody was nearby, she apparently collapsed and fell into the lower branches, and those branches closed in over her. That's where she died, but not where she was hit."

"So . . ." Angela, having smoothed her clothing and her hair, was ready to enter the conversation again. "So it's true. Old Elmer did kill her. What are you going to do about all this, Lieutenant?"

"I have only one duty. I'm not judge and jury. I don't decide whether the old fellow was justified, or what his intent was. I merely apprehend anyone who commits a crime and I bring that person to—"

"Oh, stop lecturing! I know what your police manual says," Angela said impatiently. "What do you actually intend to do?"

"I shall arrest Elmer Johanson and he will be brought to headquarters and charged with aggravated assault, at the very least. He will have to stand up in front of a judge. And there my responsibility to the citizens of San Diego County ends."

"You won't consider how old he is and that any sentence at all is as good as a death sentence?"

"That's not my job," Martinez said gently.

"The shock might be the end of him!" Angela said.

"I doubt it. He knows the routine. It's not going to come as a surprise. He's had any number of brushes with the law in the past. Granted that was over sixty years ago back in Chicago. And granted he's apparently been behaving himself since then. But when he worked for Frank Nitti as a minor league enforcer, he—"

"Frank Nitti?" Caledonia said. "The Al Capone guy?"

"That's right. Elmer—who was nicknamed 'the Swede' back then—worked part-time for Nitti. And thus for Capone, I suppose. He wouldn't admit it, but the Chicago police think so."

"The Chicago ... you've talked to them this morning?" Angela was incredulous. "How did you have time to—"

"Not this morning. I checked on his background just after you thought you'd been poisoned, remember? And a past like his made me think. He wasn't lying to us, Mrs. Benbow. He was a pretty unpleasant fellow before he went to jail. He did twenty years. As I say, he must have behaved himself after he got out because he has no record since that I can find. But I had to wonder whether or not he'd really changed. I asked myself, wasn't he still as ruthless at a hundred and two as he'd been at forty-two when—according to the Chicago police summary— he'd lost his temper and crushed a man's head? That's what I asked myself. And that's why I came upstairs last night in such a hurry after Mrs. Wingate told me it was Elmer who had pushed you."

"But . . . but he's such a bright, funny man. He's . . . he's . . . I like him!" Angela protested.

"I've heard," Martinez said, "that there were people who liked even Al Capone himself, if you can believe it. I understand he could be generous when it pleased him, and he cared deeply for his family and friends. That didn't make him any less a dangerous killer who might explode and kill again."

"But Elmer's reformed. He's not a killer anymore."

Martinez smiled. "Dear lady, it doesn't really matter if you say he's a killer or if you just say that he killed someone. Either way, a woman is dead by his hand, and I am duty-bound to arrest him. But . . ." He hesitated and both women waited. "I've talked with his three nurses and with his doctor, and they assure me that it will be remarkable if Elmer Johanson lasts through the end of this month."

"He said his lungs were giving him trouble . . ."

"Fluid," Martinez said. "His doctor expects congestive heart failure to take the old fellow away any time now."

"I know all about that stuff," Caledonia said wisely. "It's like a bilge pump that's failing. The pump has to work to clear the seawater out of the bottom of the boat, but if it's not working really well, the water leaking in gets ahead of the pump and the pump has to work continually, when it shouldn't be working but a few minutes at a time at most. So the pump is going to wear itself completely out."

"The analogy's a good one," Martinez nodded. "Same one his doctor used, as a matter of fact. And the doctor says the cycle is pretty far advanced with Elmer. Furthermore, Elmer has an NHM order on his chart by his own choice . . ."

"NHM?"

"No heroic measures," Caledonia nodded. "I've got the same order in with my own doctor."

"Oh. Oh, I see," Angela said. "I've got the same thing, but we said no CPR."

"Whatever." With a wave, Caledonia dismissed the argument as being unworthy of pursuit. "The point is, the old man really is dying now. Isn't that what you're saying, Lieutenant?"

He nodded slowly. "His doctor thinks so."

"Elmer denies it," Angela said.

"Oh, he understands what's happening, all right. He just doesn't admit it," Martinez said.

"So!" Angela cut back to the point she wanted to make. "Are you going to barge in there and arrest a dying man, Lieutenant?"

"Oh, I am indeed," Martinez said. Then he added deliberately, "Given time."

He paused, but the women said nothing, and he went on, "You see, I've weighed everything and I've decided for once to do exactly what I've been told to do. Our captain has issued a stern memo ordering us to be sensitive to how the public perceives the police during this Christmas season. We've been told not to let people see us as . . . well, as a bunch of Grinches. We're ordered not to make 'unnecessary' arrests. Violent criminals, yes, of course. Those who are a danger to the public. But we're to wait till after the first of the year for other arrests. So I think perhaps it would be wise—and I'm sure the captain would approve—if I delayed making this particular arrest till after Christmas. Elmer Johanson certainly couldn't be called a danger to the public at the moment—not in his weakened condition. If that were to change, of course, I'd have to reassess my position. But if things keep on the way they're going at the moment, I'll wait to make my arrest till the holiday season is over."

"But, Lieutenant," Angela began, "if he's doing as badly as you and the others seem to think, he's likely to die before—" She was abruptly interrupted by a sharp dig in the ribs from Caledonia's elbow.

Martinez ignored the disturbance. "Perhaps it will even be after New Year's before I can get around to making an arrest," he said thoughtfully. "Because there are still quite a few loose ends that need to be tied up, you know. Things the district attorney would need to make a strong case—things we should look into as soon as we can spare the time from our other cases. Oh, for instance, we should collect all of Elmer's fruit juice bottles and have our lab check them carefully for blood . . ."

"But she didn't have an open wound," Angela protested. "Besides, that particular bottle was surely thrown out long ago."

"Maybe it was," Martinez said, "and maybe not. But we need to check and recheck everything, just the same. And it will all take quite a while, if I'm really thorough. Of course, eventually I shall certainly have to come back here to arrest him for his crime."

Martinez checked his watch and rose gracefully to his feet. "And now I must really be on my way. There's a lot to do today, but if I have a moment this afternoon, I shall try to return and watch your Christmas pageant, Mrs. Benbow. The truth is, I'm most curious to know how a large white bat figures in the Nativity scene." And before Angela could explain, he was gone.

"Cal, he means to let Elmer go!"

"No, he means to let Elmer die in peace," Caledonia corrected. "Although if Elmer happens to survive too long, he'll be arrested after all, I suppose. That's a very nice man, our lieutenant. He's following the rules, but he's making them bend a little."

"I see—I see . . . the lieutenant isn't failing to do his duty at all. He's just . . . he's just doing it very, very slowly!" Angela said and smiled broadly. For once, she saw no point in further comment.

Chapter 21

Trinita RETURNED to Angela's apartment immediately after lunch with a costume that had been sliced and reseamed till the sleeves looked more like sleeves and less like wings. "Oh, and just leave off the false-nose thing and put brown mascara on the tip of your own nose," Trinita said before she hurried away to see to other last-minute details.

Angela donned the reworked costume unhappily and slunk out to the lobby. It was a bit early, but the truth was not only didn't she want anyone to see her costume and comment on it, she had been shedding tears over both Elmer's guilt and Martinez' compassionate, albeit slightly extralegal, gesture, and she didn't want to explain to anyone should the tears come again. She took her place quietly in her "stall" and sank to a sitting position on the floor, where she made herself as inconspicuous as possible while the rest of the cast assembled at the side of the stage area and the audience took their places throughout the chairs set up in rows across the lobby. In order to make herself less visible to them as she waited, Angela was practicing a technique she had read in a book—looking with unfocused eyes into the distance, moving not at all, and thinking unrelated, tranquil thoughts. Thinking of a meadow . . . a sunlit sea . . . poor old Elmer . . . Martinez' gentle humanity . . . But whenever she let her mind stray from rippling grasses or rolling waves, she found the audience looking at her, so she disciplined her wandering thoughts as much as she could . . . meadows, sunshine on the sea . . .

She was nearly asleep herself under the influence of a kind of auto-hypnosis when she realized with a start that the pageant had begun. "This is one mighty good-lookin' kid," Mr. Grogan's voice rang out. "Child. I meant child!" Angela, moving slowly so as not to attract attention and assuming a position on all fours—as was suitable for a barnyard animal—was thinking that Grogan appeared to be completely sober today. Trinita would be pleased.

The pageant wound its anachronistic way through the arrival of the shepherds, Angela drawing a round of applause and a ripple of laughter when, in response to the pat on the head, she let out with her first *Baaaa, Baaaa, Baaaa*; through the three Kings of Orient and their gifts of a tray of junk jewelry, a bottle of vanilla extract, and a box of potpourri—all the prop manager could find for gold, frankincense, and myrrh; and through the arrival of the miscellaneous villagers, with their expressions of awe and adoration—"Look at him, would you?" and "Mighty healthy youngster you have there, Mary" and "Wow, that's a real-looking doll, isn't it?"

Then came the angel, blonde wig shining in the lobby's dim lights, wings spread and hands waving. *"Venite adoremus . . ."* she intoned, and as the cast members gathered center stage to sing their praises to the infant Messiah, Mr. Grogan bent reverentially over the little wooden cradle and lifted the baby doll high into the air. "Behold your King," he chanted, ad-libbing again, dimly remembering one of the carols. "Before him lowly bend! Aw, gee! Aw, *gee!*"

Mr. Grogan's face became a study of shocked dismay and distaste, and the hand that had been beneath the infant bottom was yanked out into the clear. "Hey! This was supposed to be a doll, not a real baby! This kid just wet on me!"

After that the pageant was a shambles. Half the cast doubled up with ill-suppressed amusement and left the stage hurriedly, making a series of strangled noises; the other half bravely tried to sing at least one chorus of "Oh Come All Ye Faithful," as the script enjoined them to do. One half of the audience was roaring with laughter; the other half—quite unaware of what had happened to Grogan—was straining to hear the rest of the performance. And Trinita began fluttering back and forth, shouting directions, ignoring the audience, and totally bewildering those of her actors who remained. "Don't let the camel leave! Where do you villagers think you're going! Haven't any of you ever heard the show must go on? Keep singing! Stand up straight! Angel, flap your wings! Villagers, get closer together in the center of the stage! Mr. Grogan, put that baby doll down! I can't help it if somebody gave us a Betsy Wetsy to use!"

"That was some pageant," Caledonia said.

"You watched? I didn't think you were going to bother to attend," Angela said. The two were alone in the quiet of Caledonia's apartment in that lovely golden hour of the December sunset, just before dinner. Angela had put the sheep costume aside and now, comfortable in her usual clothing, joined Caledonia for their customary thimbleful of predinner sherry. "A little wine for thy stomach's sake," Angela quoted her Bible and lifted her glass in a toast, but if she were hoping to divert Caledonia from the subject of the pageant, it didn't work.

"Oh, I wouldn't have missed it. There were other things to amuse me, too. Like watching young Officer Swanson and his girlfriend."

"When are he and Chita getting married?" Angela asked.

"Oh, sometime after she graduates. Or so she says. By the way, Lieutenant Martinez was there, too. He laughed harder than I did at Grogan. And he applauded your sheep routine longer than anyone else did, too."

Angela smiled. Approval, even if only for her animal impersonation, always made her happy, especially if the approval came from her handsome policeman. "I'm glad he had time to come to the performance. He's been far too busy lately. Oh . . ." A thought struck her. "He didn't go upstairs to Elmer's place, did he?"

"Huh-uh. Just left by the front door and drove away when

the show was over with. And I have a hunch we won't see him around here till the day he goes up to make an arrest . . ."

". . . and finds to his dismay that Elmer passed away peacefully that same day. Is that what you mean?"

Caledonia nodded. "He's got all Elmer's nurses on his side, our lieutenant has. And they'll phone him the minute . . . ," she hesitated, ". . . the minute it's safe for him to come here."

"What about Birdy's family? Is this fair to them? Doesn't the family of the victim have some rights? I'm not sure I care about that bunch getting to see justice, mind you. Come to think of it, I'm not sure of what justice is in this situation. But there's such a thing as bringing matters to a close . . ."

"Won't hurt 'em to wait for a while to hear the end of the story," Caledonia said. "That lot doesn't deserve first consideration. Besides, arresting Elmer now wouldn't serve any of the interests of justice, would it? He's too sick and weak to be a danger to the public, and the arrest of a hundred-and-two-year-old is not going to serve as a lesson to other criminals, is it? On balance, at least in my opinion, the lieutenant is doing the best thing all around. Even if it isn't exactly according to the book." The two paused again and sipped in silence.

"You know, Cal, I'm starting to feel a little like Christmas! I mean, I felt all Christmasy when we were putting up decorations, and then it rather left me, what with everything else. But now, all of a sudden, I'm in the mood for presents. So I brought yours down here with me." Angela reached inside her large shopping bag and pulled out a handsomely wrapped box.

"Beautiful! Here—let me at it!"

"No! I'll tell you what it is if you insist, but just don't open it till Christmas Eve! It's a crystal sherry decanter. Really fine English cut glass. An antique."

"Not that piece I looked at about two months ago in the antique show on the main street down here?"

"The same." Angela sounded smug. "I hope you like it."

"Oh, you know I will! What a lovely thing to do! I can hardly wait." She made a move to slide her finger under a fold of the wrapping, and Angela shook her head sternly.

"Oh no! Don't peek till Christmas."

"Well, all right, if you insist." Caledonia hauled herself to her feet with difficulty. "But you better open your gift from me right now. It was hard to wrap, and I decided not even to try. And now, after all that's happened, I'm worried that you won't like it." She went into the bedroom and returned with a brown paper sack. "If you just hate it, I can return it, I suppose. It cost a lot more than you'd think. Premium quality . . . Go ahead. Open it."

Angela opened the sack and peered inside. "It's fur!" she said. "Something furry . . . with leather on the back . . ." She dragged out a tangled cream-colored mat and spread it on her lap. "What is it?"

"You won't believe it, but it's one of those little throws to put over the end of your bed—so you won't have to pile on heavy blankets to keep your feet warm on chilly winter evenings. You've always complained that the rest of you is comfortable but your feet are like chunks of ice. So I thought—"

"Oh. Oh, how very nice. I'll love it! Whatever made you think I wouldn't like it?"

"Well . . ." Caledonia shrugged. "Might as well level with you. This is sheepskin! Honestly, I bought it before the pageant. But now, considering how the pageant turned out—and considering all the lamb we've been eating here lately—maybe you'd as soon not be reminded . . ."

To Caledonia's relief, Angela's face creased into the lines of amusement. "My very own little sheepskin to remind me of my starring role! And to keep my toes warm at the same time. Thank you, Cal."

"Altogether not too bad, then?"

"Altogether," Angela said, "not too bad. And at our age, I guess there are a lot of things in our lives that ought to satisfy us if we can only say 'It could have been a lot worse.' " She smiled, folded her sheepskin back into its paper sack, and raised her little glass of sherry.

"So . . . here's to things that could have been worse."

"And to friendship." Caledonia raised her own glass.

"Oh yes," Angela agreed. "Friendship. Above all else." And in quiet contentment, they sipped their sherry as the sun slid downward to go to sleep behind the winter ocean.

Who can spot the murderer?

MURDER BY OWL LIGHT

For those spirited senior sleuths Angela Benbow and Caledonia Wingate the murder of the gardener at posh Camden-sur-Mer retirement complex is a delightful break in their dull routine.

They're off and running, bird-dogging a murderer as resourceful as they are—and as shadowy as the owl light of dusk that conceals his deadly work.

MURDER BY OWL LIGHT
by Corinne Holt Sawyer

Published by Fawcett Books.
Available wherever books are sold.

MURDER HAS NO CALORIES

MURDER HAS NO CALORIES

by Corinne Holt Sawyer

Published by Fawcett Books.
Available wherever books are sold.